THE MYTHICS

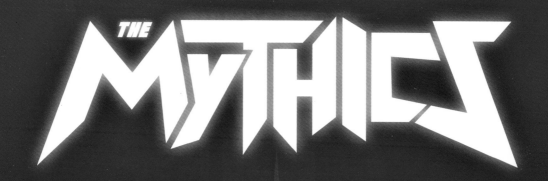

PAPERCUTZ™

MORE GREAT GRAPHIC NOVEL SERIES AVAILABLE FROM
PAPERCUTZ™

THE SMURFS #21

BRINA THE CAT #1

CAT & CAT #1

THE SISTERS #1

ATTACK OF THE STUFF

ASTERIX #1

SCHOOL FOR
EXTRATERRESTRIAL
GIRLS #1

GERONIMO STILTON
REPORTER #1

THE MYTHICS #1

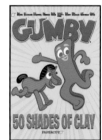

GUMBY #1

MELOWY #1

BLUEBEARD

THE RED SHOES

THE LITTLE
MERMAID

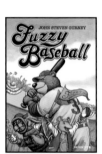

FUZZY BASEBALL #1

HOTEL
TRANSYLVANIA #1

THE LOUD HOUSE #1

MANOSAURS #1

THE ONLY LIVING
BOY #5

THE ONLY LIVING
GIRL #1

papercutz.com
Also available where ebooks are sold.

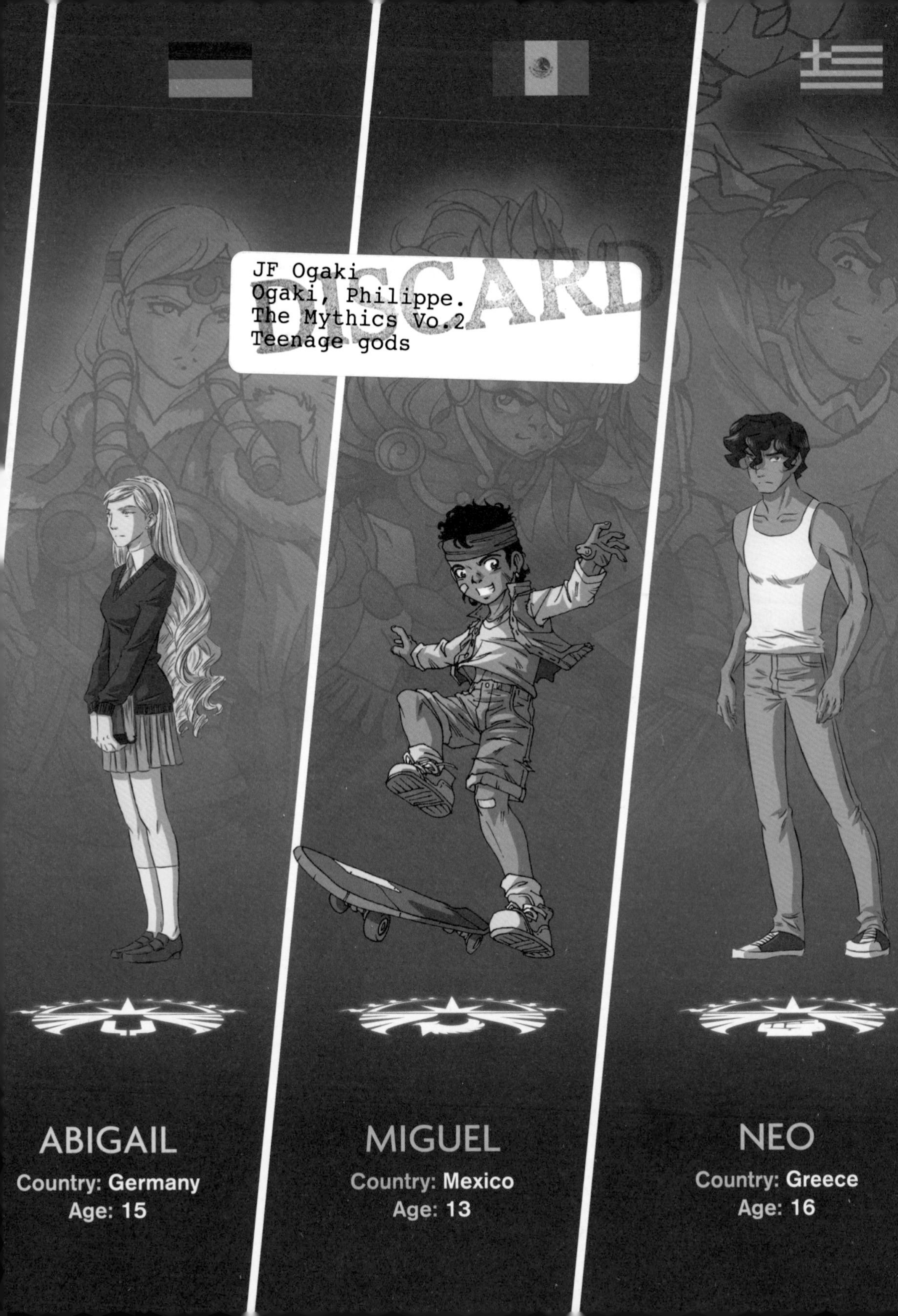
ABIGAIL
Country: Germany
Age: 15
MIGUEL
Country: Mexico
Age: 13
NEO
Country: Greece
Age: 16

Illustrations by Patricia Lyfoung and Patrick Sobral

2. TEENAGE GODS

**ALICE PICARD • JÉRÔME ALQUIÉ • FRÉDÉRIC CHARVE
PATRICK SOBRAL • PATRICIA LYFOUNG
PHILIPPE OGAKI• FABIEN DALMASSO**

New York

Originally published in French under the following titles:
Les Mythics, volume 2, de P. Sobral, P. Lyfoung, P. Ogaki and A. Picard
Les Mythics, volume 5, de P. Sobral, P. Lyfoung, P. Ogaki, F. Dalmasso and J. Alquié
Les Mythics, volume 6, de P. Sobral, P. Lyfoung, P. Ogaki and F. Charve
© Editions Delcourt, 2018/2019
English Translation and all other editorial material © 2020 Papercutz. All rights reserved.
Created by PATRICK SOBRAL, PATRICIA LYFOUNG, and PHILIPPE OGAKI

Part 1- Parvati
Script — PHILIPPE OGAKI
Art — ALICE PICARD
Color—MAGALI PAILLAT

Part 2- Miguel
Script —PATRICK SOBRAL with help from FABIEN DALMASSO
Art and Color — JÉRÔME ALQUIÉ

Part 3- Neo
Script —PHILIPPE OGAKI
Art —FRÉDÉRIC CHARVE
Color — MAGALI PAILLAT

Original editor — THIERRY JOOR

Special thanks to SÉVERINE AUPERT, LUCIE MASSENA, LINA DI FLAMMINIO, and JAYJAY
JACKSON

Papercutz books may be purchased for business or promotional use. For information on bulk
purchases please contact Macmillan Corporate and Premium Sales Department at (800) 221-7945
x5442

Translation — ELIZABETH S.TIERI
Lettering — WILSON RAMOS JR.
Production — BIG BIRD ZATRYB
Managing Editor — JEFF WHITMAN
Editorial Intern — ERIC STORMS
JIM SALICRUP
Editor-in-Chief

PB ISBN: 978-1-5458-0485-8
HC ISBN: 978-1-5458-0484-1

Printed in China
December 2020

Distributed by Macmillan
First Papercutz Printing

THE MYTHICS

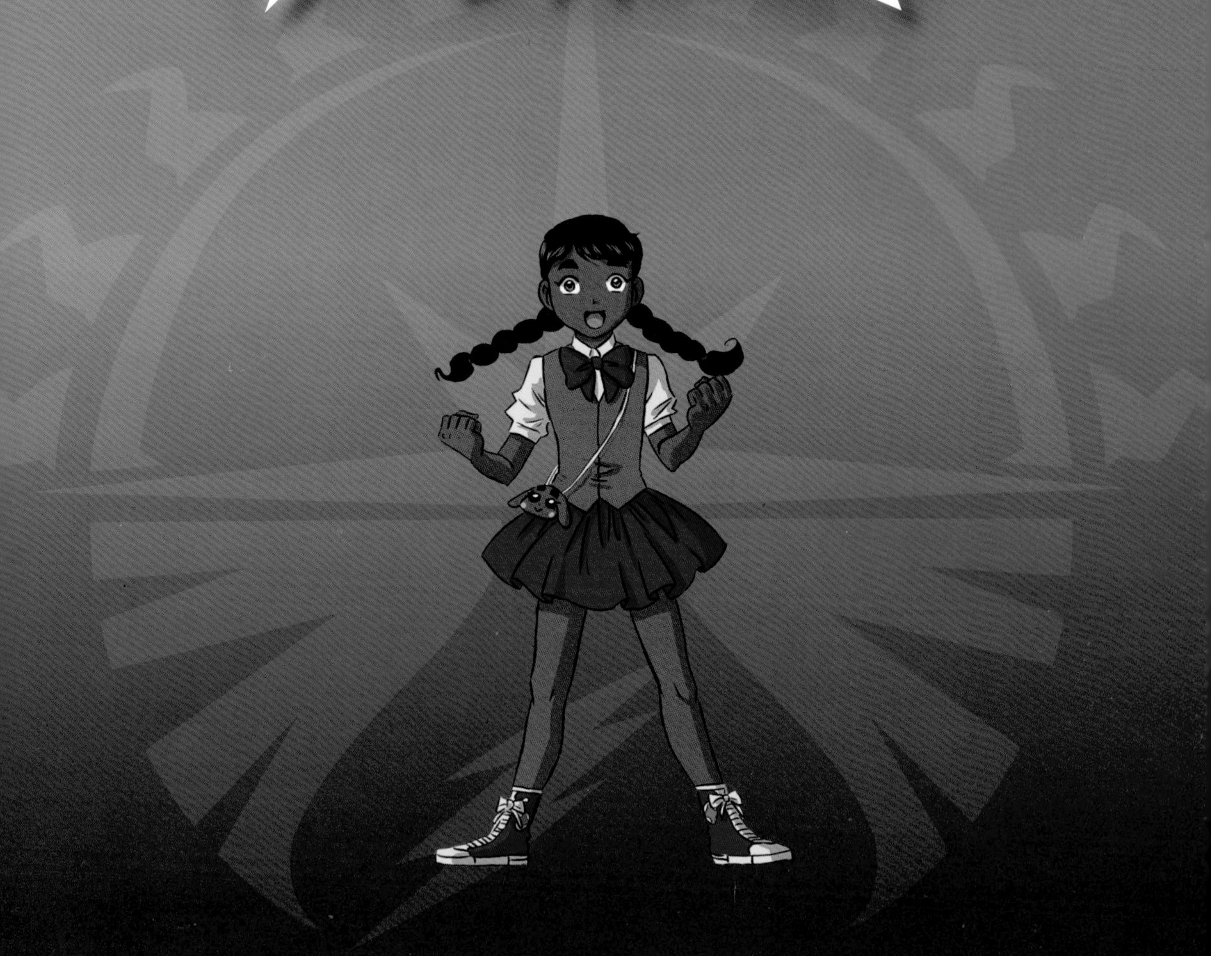

PART 4: PARVATI

Story by
PHILIPPE OGAKI

Art by
ALICE PICARD

Color by
MAGALI PAILLAT

A new album in the epic adventure that is THE MYTHICS. Thanks to you, dear readers, all the MYTHICS fans who have become loyal followers of this saga—thanks for having confidence in us. Thank you also to Fabien Dalmasso who was in charge of the difficult part of editing this script and an enormous thank you to Jérôme Alquié who agreed to give a body to my story; collaborating with him was a treat. And obviously, let's not forget Patricia Lyfoung, Philippe Ogaki and Delcourt, all at the core of this superb epic and all in this together for crazy adventures. What a path we've taken... And what a path still to come. But the best is yet to come!
—*Patrick Sobral*

A great THANK YOU to Patrick, Fabien, Philippe, and Jérôme for this beautiful volume of THE MYTHICS! Merci to the team at Delcourt who supported us since the beginning and thanks to whom we live this beautiful mythic adventure! Thanks to Fred for accepting to join us in the adventures of the Mythics! Thanks to Magali for the superb colors!
And thanks to you, our readers, for having this book in your hands... And for making this adventure mythic! Without you, we couldn't make a living from this beautiful profession!
—*Patricia Lyfoung*

I would like to thank the entire team of wonderful authors and friends who gave so much energy to bring life to the Mythics. I thank you, the reader as well, for your enthusiasm to accompany our young heroes in their adventures! I would like to thank all the people who went out of their way so that the Mythics could start their great adventures! In particular, Fred, who knew how to give life to Neo.
—*Philippe Ogaki*

Thanks to THE MYTHICS team, in particular Patricia, Philippe, and Thierry for having confidence in me and for their availability and help. Thanks to Magali for the work just in time.
—*Frederic Charve*

Thanks to all the readers who followed us during this season 1, looking forward to the next!
—*Magali Paillat*

Thanks to the entire Mythics team for their attention and their unfailing support. This was a marvelous adventure.
—*Fabien Dalmasso*

Thanks to the entire Mythics team, to the heart of Delcourt, and among the authors Patricia Lyfoung and Philippe Ogaki. And especially to Thierry Joor my director of the collection and of course Patrick Sobral, the genius author with whom collaboration was a true pleasure of apprenticeship and exchange. Your feedback and your advice were always precious and respectful, you are the best, gentlemen, don't change anything! Also a special thank you among the authors to Fabien Dalmasso who perfectly prepared my storyboard work and the final boards with very precise descriptions of each of the scenes.

Thanks to my family who accompanied me on each adventure, Cricri my better half that I love, Rémi, Maéline and Antonin, my three loves as well as my parents and my closest friends who always support me. Thanks to all my friends, you know who you are, Arnaud, Jean-Sé, Yvan, Jess, Lydie and everyone I'm forgetting...
And thanks to you, for reading this book, because it's obvious that we're only doing this work to bring pleasure and amusement to the public, and that we only exist thanks to you!
I hope that this book fascinates you as much as it did me while making it with the entire THE MYTHICS team.
—*Jérôme Alquié*

PREVIOUSLY IN THE MYTHICS

An ancient evil returned to earth after being banished to Mars for millennia. The old gods who thought they had defeated Evil must find new young protectors on earth. Six children from all over the world were chosen…

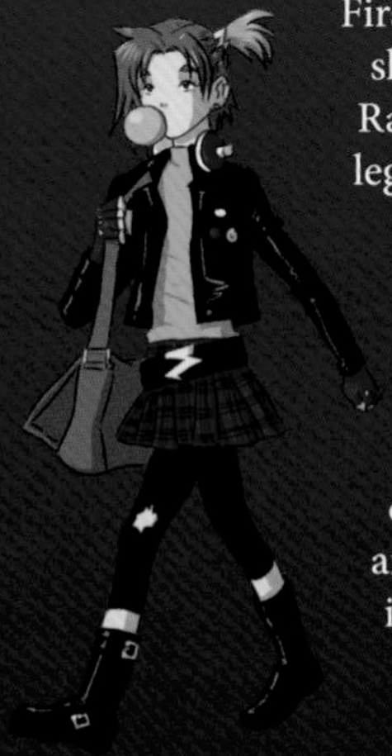

First, *Yuko*, a Japanese schoolgirl in a rock band discovered she had electrifying lightning powers. She met her ancestor, Raijin, the god of lighting himself, who led Yuko to the legendary weapon. Yuko learned to hone her newfound powers of electricity to defeat Fujin, the evil god of wind, before he could destroy all of Japan with nuclear warfare.

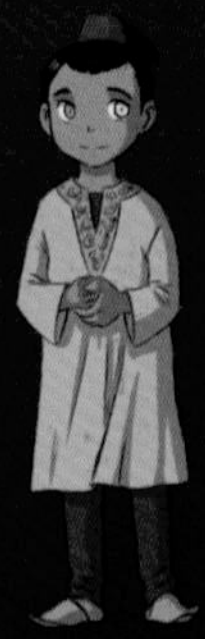

Meanwhile, in Egypt, young *Amir*, a recently orphaned boy taking over his father's successful company and landholdings, encountered Horus, the Sun and Moon god. Horus and Amir struggled to vanquish Evil in the form of Seth (aided by Amir's wicked half-brother) after they reanimated all the dead mummies in an attempt to take over the world in Evil's image.

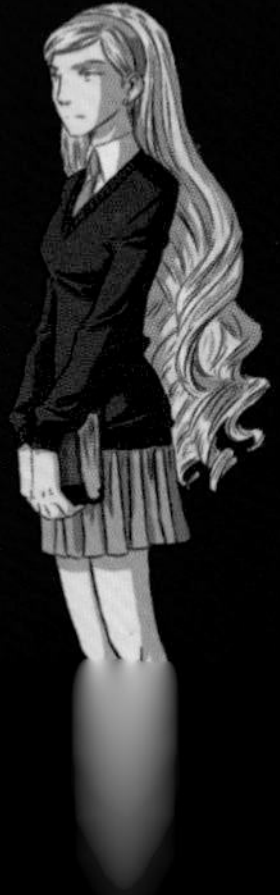

Then, a young Opera hopeful, *Abigail*, faced a blizzard freezing all of Germany orchestrated by Loki. The evil god of mischief was disguised as a wolf in sheep's clothing in the form of Abigail's charismatic professor. Under the guidance of Freya, the Norse god of beauty, Abigail learned to find her voice, and her supersonic vocal powers to wield her mythic weapon to stop Evil in its tracks.

Using their powers and strengths, these teenagers might just have what it takes to be the new Gods of today. Now, meet the next three adolescents that, along with Yuko, Amir, and Abigail, may be Earth's

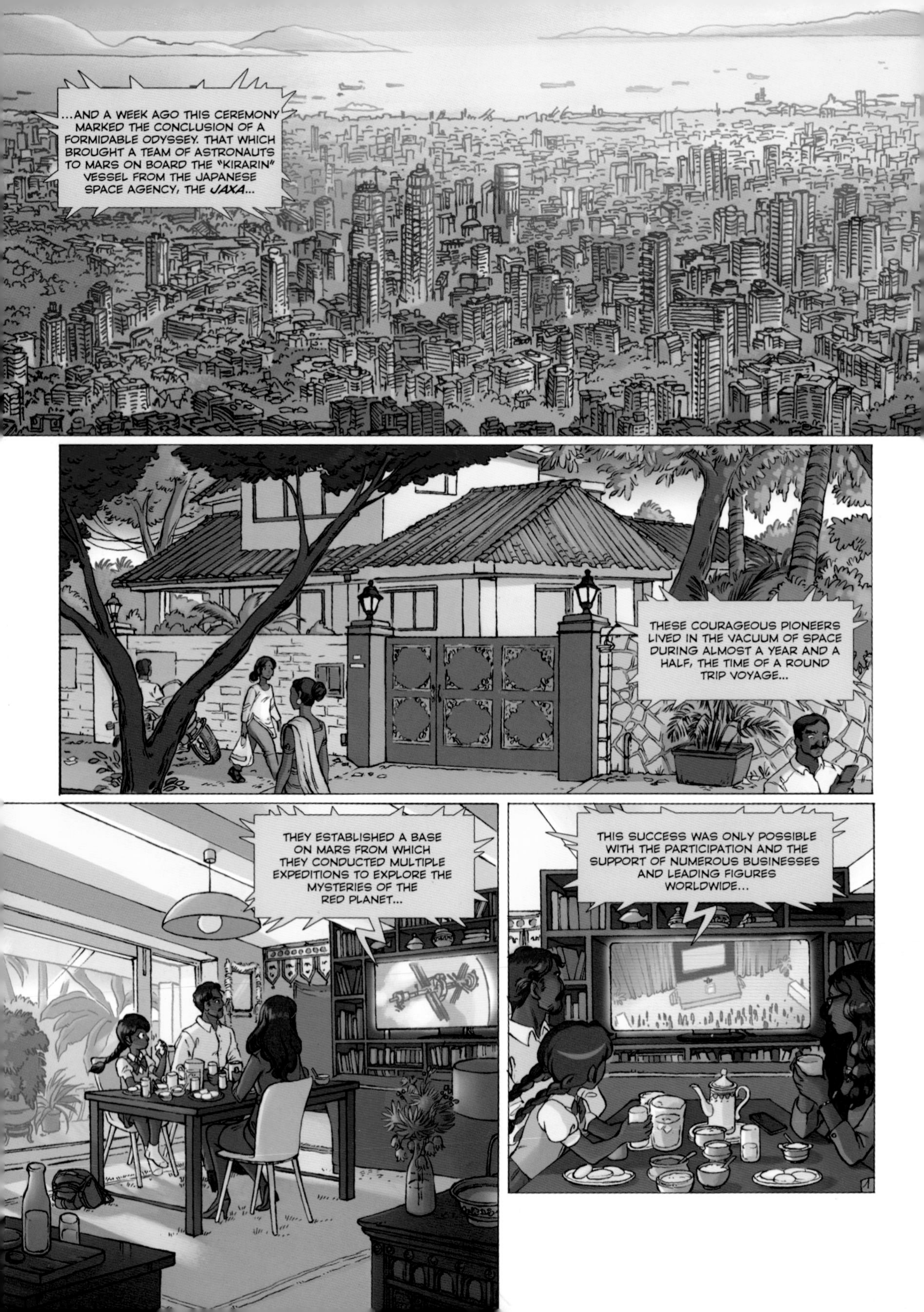
...AND A WEEK AGO THIS CEREMONY MARKED THE CONCLUSION OF A FORMIDABLE ODYSSEY. THAT WHICH BROUGHT A TEAM OF ASTRONAUTS TO MARS ON BOARD THE "KIRARIN" VESSEL FROM THE JAPANESE SPACE AGENCY, THE *JAXA*...
THESE COURAGEOUS PIONEERS LIVED IN THE VACUUM OF SPACE DURING ALMOST A YEAR AND A HALF, THE TIME OF A ROUND TRIP VOYAGE...
THEY ESTABLISHED A BASE ON MARS FROM WHICH THEY CONDUCTED MULTIPLE EXPEDITIONS TO EXPLORE THE MYSTERIES OF THE RED PLANET...
THIS SUCCESS WAS ONLY POSSIBLE WITH THE PARTICIPATION AND THE SUPPORT OF NUMEROUS BUSINESSES AND LEADING FIGURES WORLDWIDE...

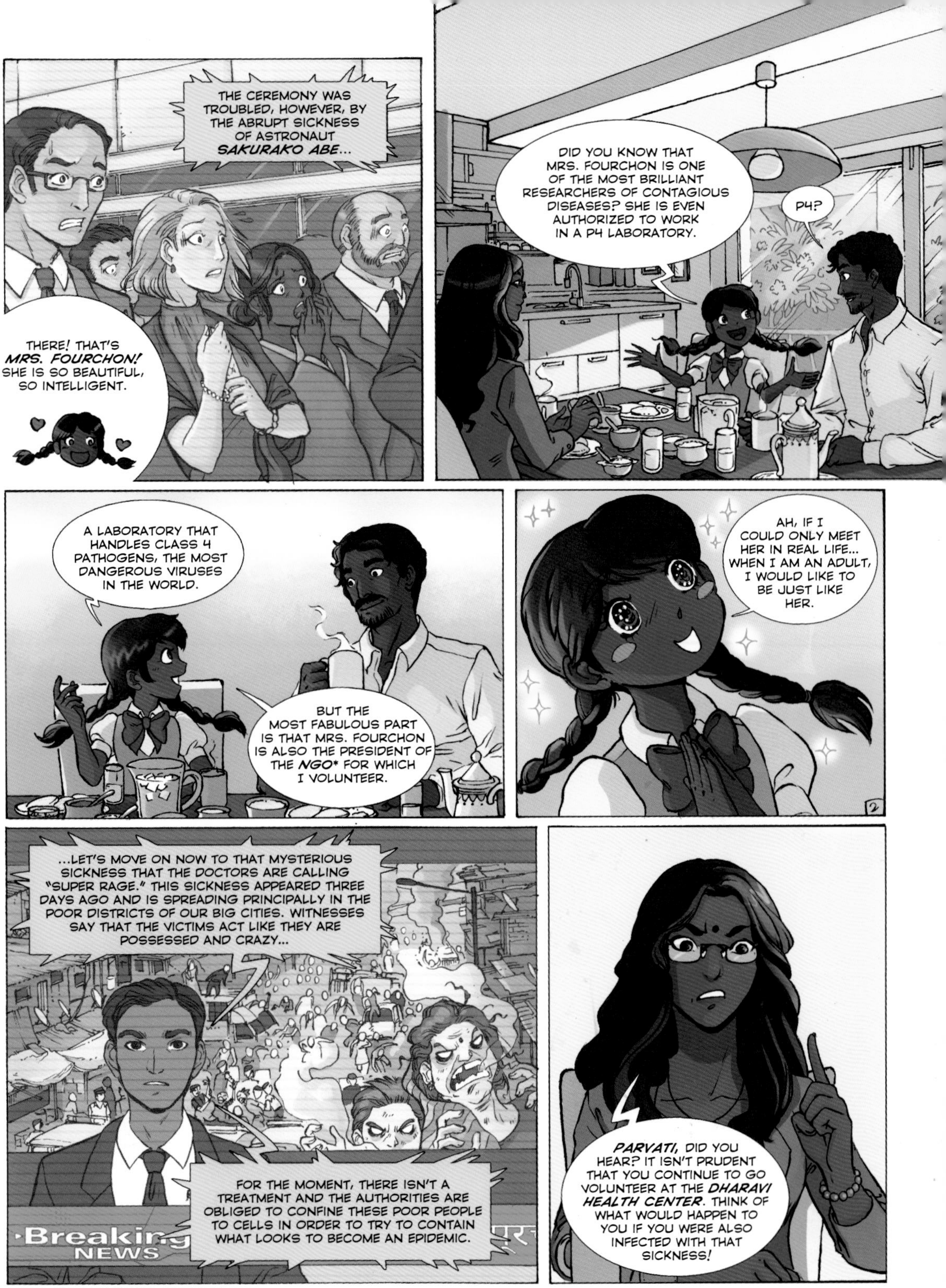

THE CEREMONY WAS TROUBLED, HOWEVER, BY THE ABRUPT SICKNESS OF ASTRONAUT *SAKURAKO ABE*...
THERE! THAT'S *MRS. FOURCHON!* SHE IS SO BEAUTIFUL, SO INTELLIGENT.
DID YOU KNOW THAT MRS. FOURCHON IS ONE OF THE MOST BRILLIANT RESEARCHERS OF CONTAGIOUS DISEASES? SHE IS EVEN AUTHORIZED TO WORK IN A P4 LABORATORY.
P4?
A LABORATORY THAT HANDLES CLASS 4 PATHOGENS, THE MOST DANGEROUS VIRUSES IN THE WORLD.
BUT THE MOST FABULOUS PART IS THAT MRS. FOURCHON IS ALSO THE PRESIDENT OF THE *NGO** FOR WHICH I VOLUNTEER.
AH, IF I COULD ONLY MEET HER IN REAL LIFE... WHEN I AM AN ADULT, I WOULD LIKE TO BE JUST LIKE HER.
...LET'S MOVE ON NOW TO THAT MYSTERIOUS SICKNESS THAT THE DOCTORS ARE CALLING "SUPER RAGE." THIS SICKNESS APPEARED THREE DAYS AGO AND IS SPREADING PRINCIPALLY IN THE POOR DISTRICTS OF OUR BIG CITIES. WITNESSES SAY THAT THE VICTIMS ACT LIKE THEY ARE POSSESSED AND CRAZY...
FOR THE MOMENT, THERE ISN'T A TREATMENT AND THE AUTHORITIES ARE OBLIGED TO CONFINE THESE POOR PEOPLE TO CELLS IN ORDER TO TRY TO CONTAIN WHAT LOOKS TO BECOME AN EPIDEMIC.
Breaking NEWS
PARVATI, DID YOU HEAR? IT ISN'T PRUDENT THAT YOU CONTINUE TO GO VOLUNTEER AT THE *DHARAVI HEALTH CENTER*. THINK OF WHAT WOULD HAPPEN TO YOU IF YOU WERE ALSO INFECTED WITH THAT SICKNESS!

*NON-GOVERNMENTAL ORGANIZATION

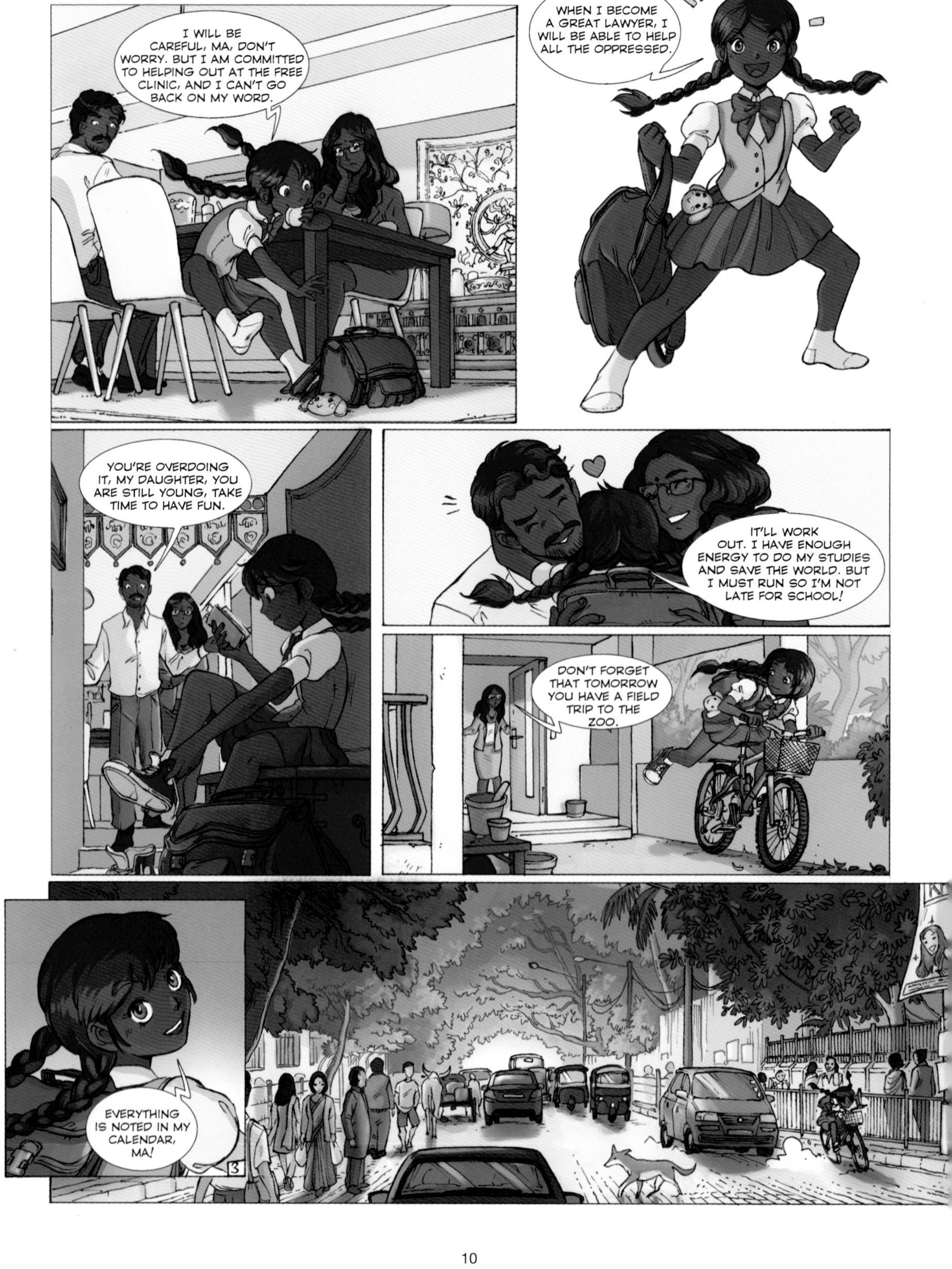
I WILL BE CAREFUL, MA, DON'T WORRY. BUT I AM COMMITTED TO HELPING OUT AT THE FREE CLINIC, AND I CAN'T GO BACK ON MY WORD.
WHEN I BECOME A GREAT LAWYER, I WILL BE ABLE TO HELP ALL THE OPPRESSED.
YOU'RE OVERDOING IT, MY DAUGHTER, YOU ARE STILL YOUNG, TAKE TIME TO HAVE FUN.
IT'LL WORK OUT. I HAVE ENOUGH ENERGY TO DO MY STUDIES AND SAVE THE WORLD. BUT I MUST RUN SO I'M NOT LATE FOR SCHOOL!
DON'T FORGET THAT TOMORROW YOU HAVE A FIELD TRIP TO THE ZOO.
EVERYTHING IS NOTED IN MY CALENDAR, MA!

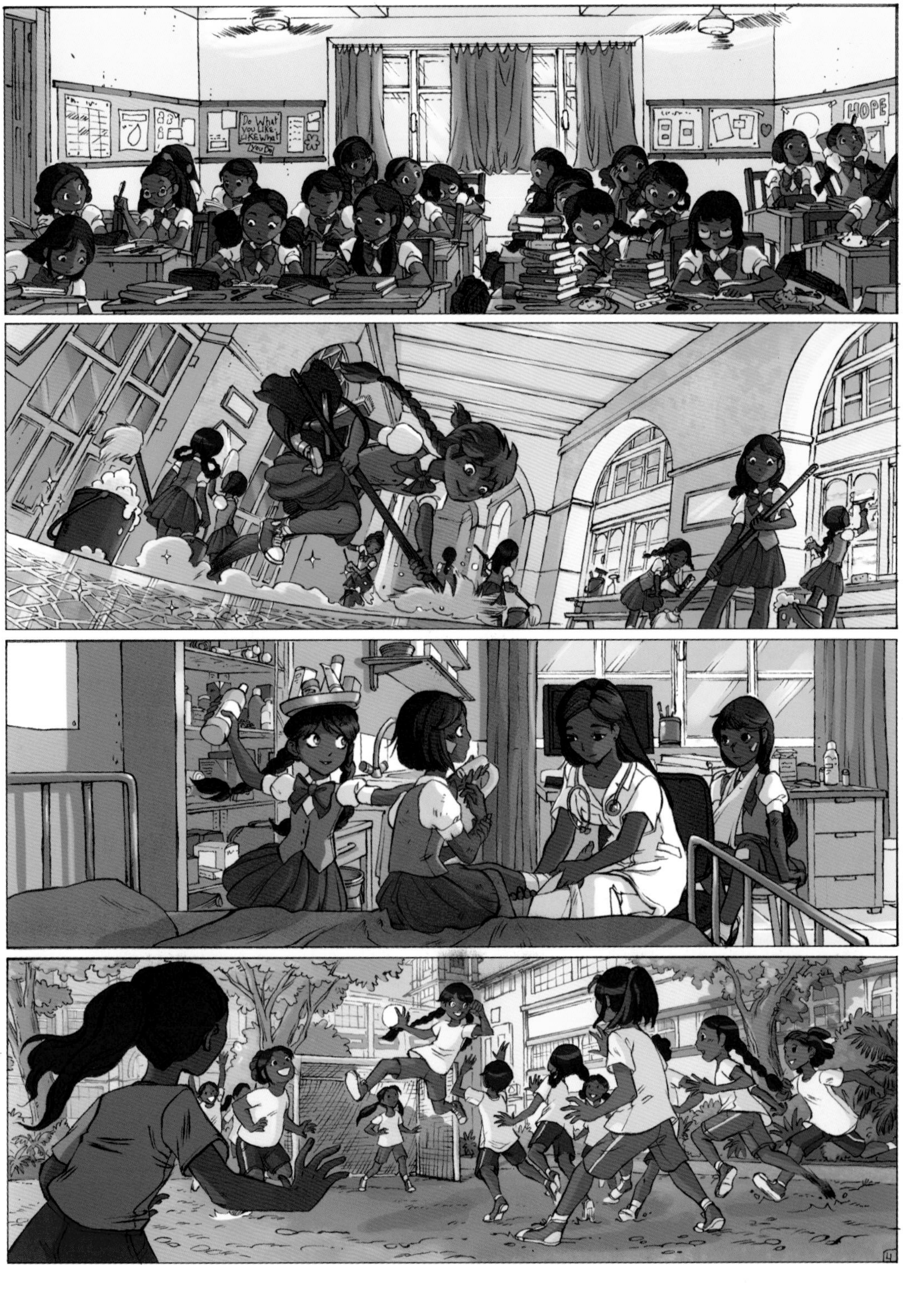
Do What You Like. LIKE What You Do
HOPE

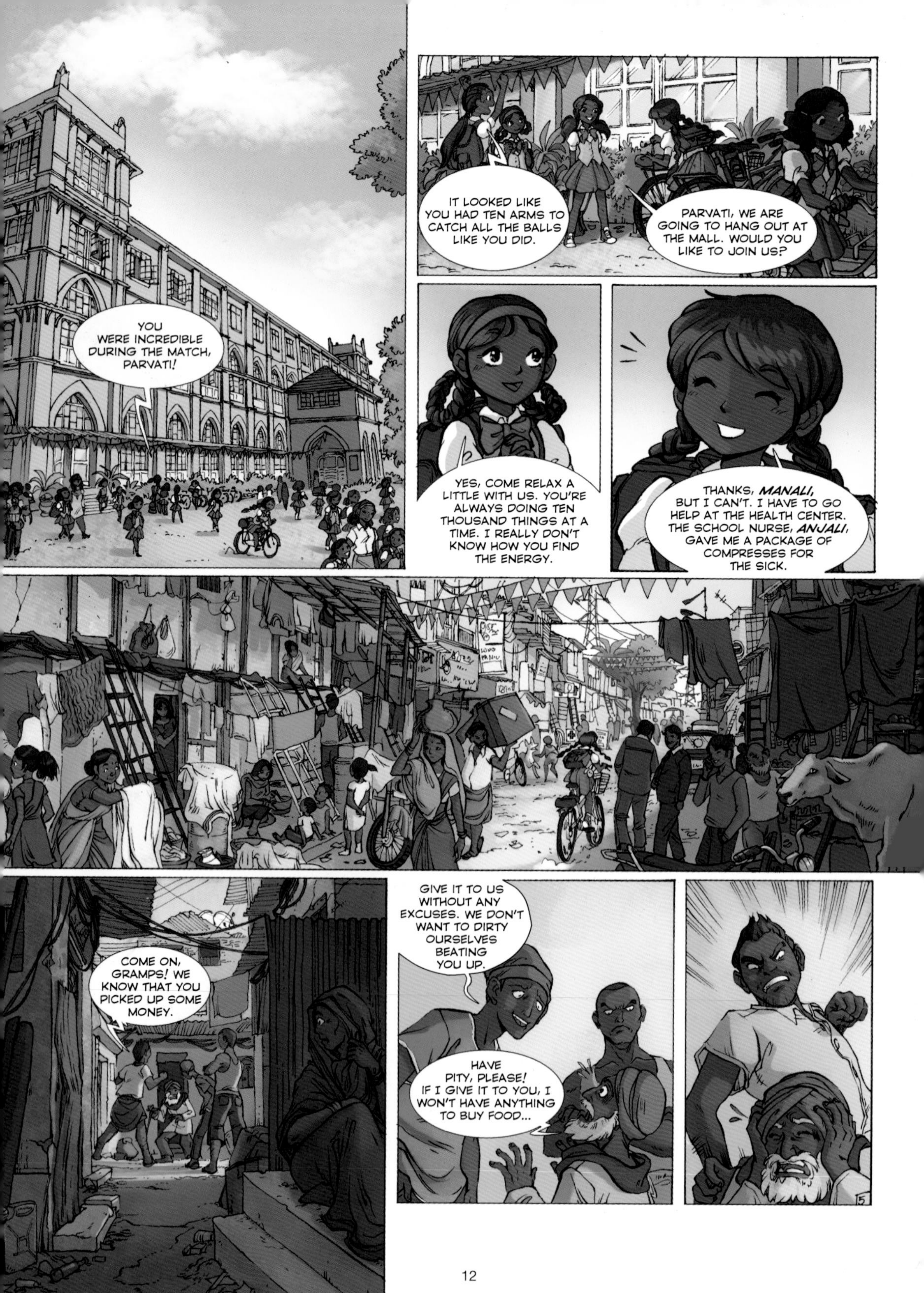
YOU WERE INCREDIBLE DURING THE MATCH, PARVATI!
IT LOOKED LIKE YOU HAD TEN ARMS TO CATCH ALL THE BALLS LIKE YOU DID.
PARVATI, WE ARE GOING TO HANG OUT AT THE MALL. WOULD YOU LIKE TO JOIN US?
YES, COME RELAX A LITTLE WITH US. YOU'RE ALWAYS DOING TEN THOUSAND THINGS AT A TIME. I REALLY DON'T KNOW HOW YOU FIND THE ENERGY.
THANKS, MANALI, BUT I CAN'T. I HAVE TO GO HELP AT THE HEALTH CENTER. THE SCHOOL NURSE, ANJALI, GAVE ME A PACKAGE OF COMPRESSES FOR THE SICK.
COME ON, GRAMPS! WE KNOW THAT YOU PICKED UP SOME MONEY.
GIVE IT TO US WITHOUT ANY EXCUSES. WE DON'T WANT TO DIRTY OURSELVES BEATING YOU UP.
HAVE PITY, PLEASE! IF I GIVE IT TO YOU, I WON'T HAVE ANYTHING TO BUY FOOD...

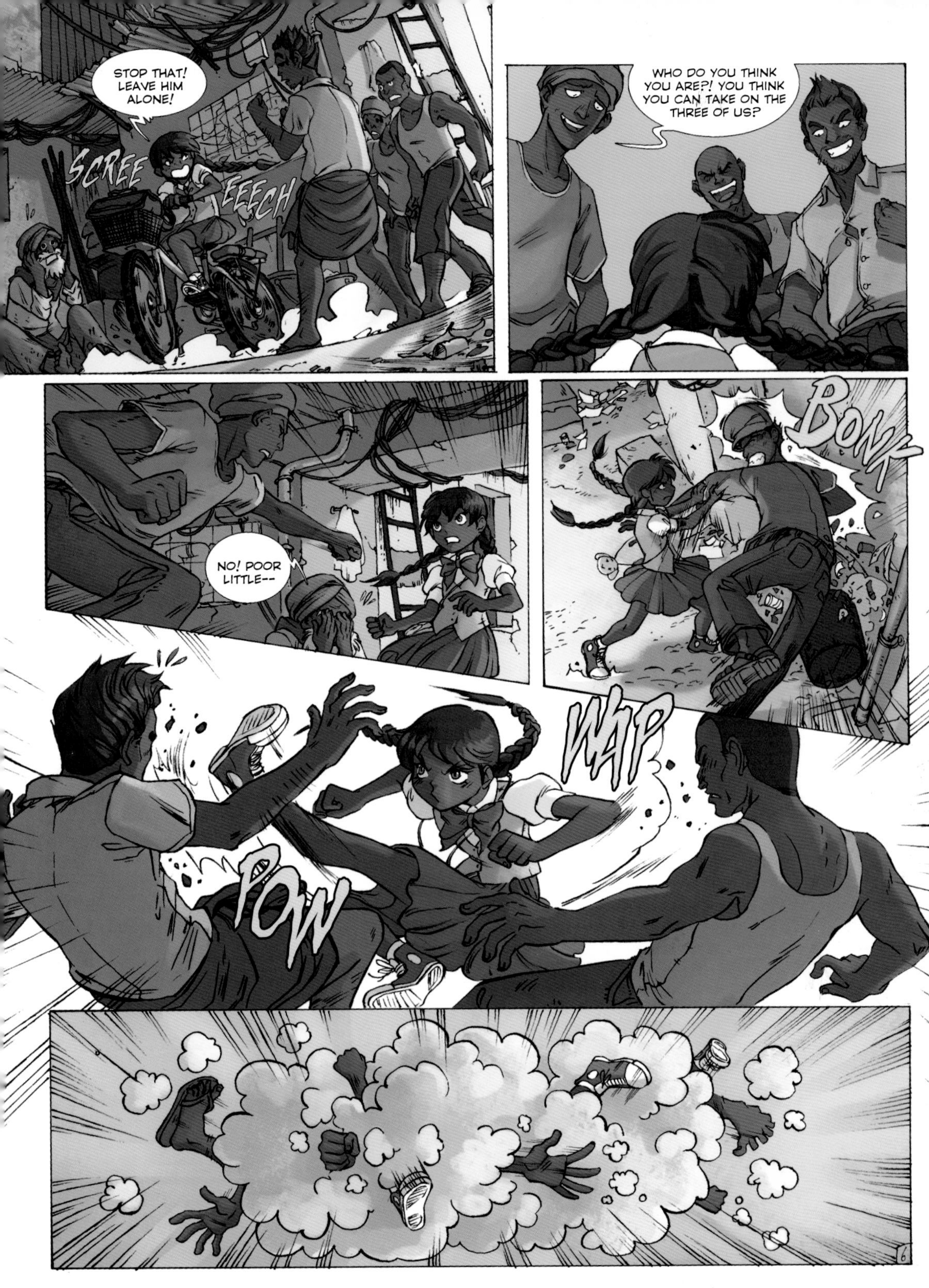
STOP THAT! LEAVE HIM ALONE!
SCREEEEECH
WHO DO YOU THINK YOU ARE?! YOU THINK YOU CAN TAKE ON THE THREE OF US?
NO! POOR LITTLE--
BONK
WAP
POW

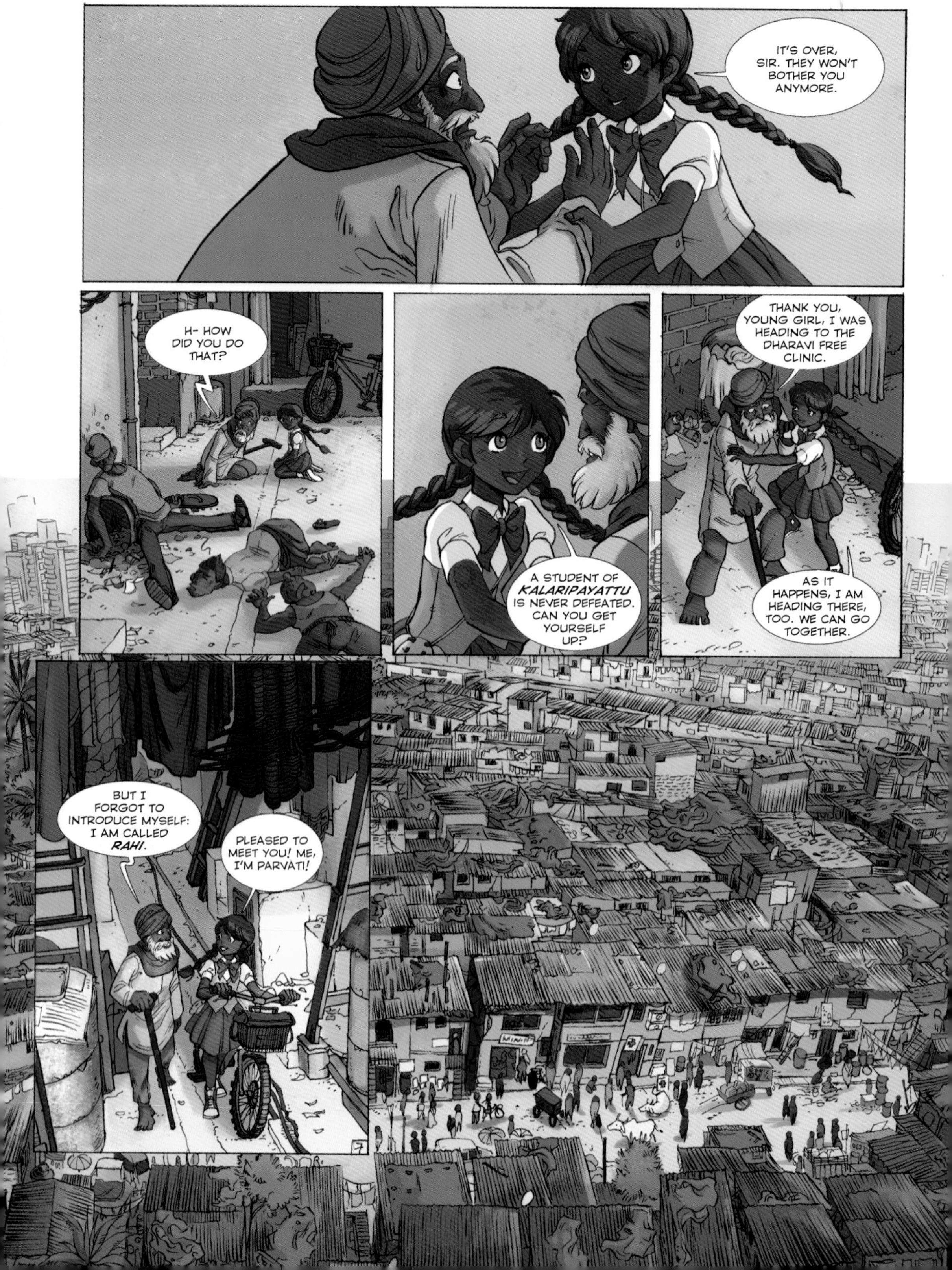

IT'S OVER, SIR. THEY WON'T BOTHER YOU ANYMORE.
H- HOW DID YOU DO THAT?
A STUDENT OF KALARIPAYATTU IS NEVER DEFEATED. CAN YOU GET YOURSELF UP?
THANK YOU, YOUNG GIRL, I WAS HEADING TO THE DHARAVI FREE CLINIC.
AS IT HAPPENS, I AM HEADING THERE, TOO. WE CAN GO TOGETHER.
BUT I FORGOT TO INTRODUCE MYSELF: I AM CALLED RAHI.
PLEASED TO MEET YOU! ME, I'M PARVATI!

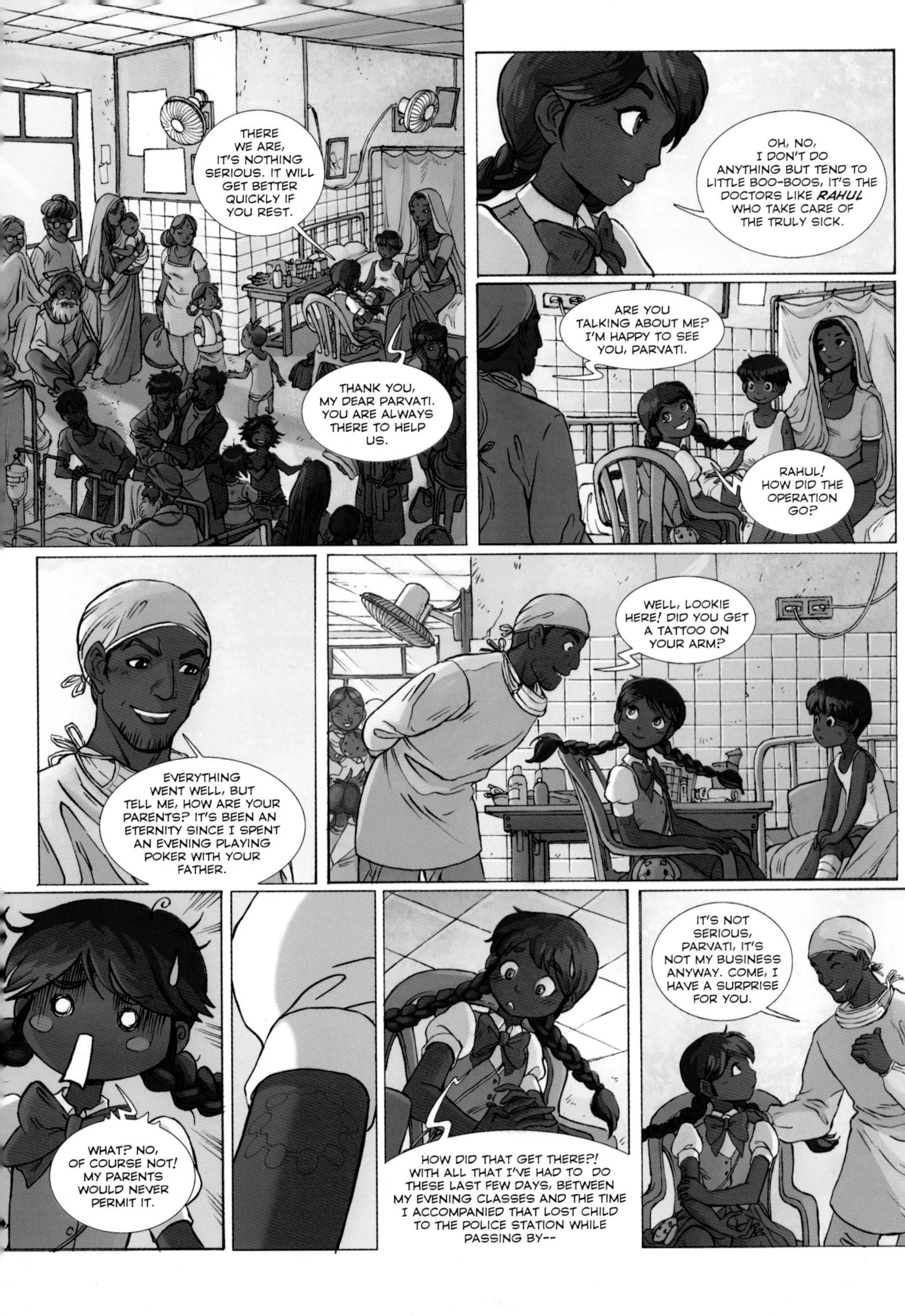
THERE WE ARE, IT'S NOTHING SERIOUS. IT WILL GET BETTER QUICKLY IF YOU REST.
THANK YOU, MY DEAR PARVATI. YOU ARE ALWAYS THERE TO HELP US.
OH, NO, I DON'T DO ANYTHING BUT TEND TO LITTLE BOO-BOOS, IT'S THE DOCTORS LIKE RAHUL WHO TAKE CARE OF THE TRULY SICK.
ARE YOU TALKING ABOUT ME? I'M HAPPY TO SEE YOU, PARVATI.
RAHUL! HOW DID THE OPERATION GO?
EVERYTHING WENT WELL, BUT TELL ME, HOW ARE YOUR PARENTS? IT'S BEEN AN ETERNITY SINCE I SPENT AN EVENING PLAYING POKER WITH YOUR FATHER.
WELL, LOOKIE HERE! DID YOU GET A TATTOO ON YOUR ARM?
WHAT? NO, OF COURSE NOT! MY PARENTS WOULD NEVER PERMIT IT.
HOW DID THAT GET THERE?! WITH ALL THAT I'VE HAD TO DO THESE LAST FEW DAYS, BETWEEN MY EVENING CLASSES AND THE TIME I ACCOMPANIED THAT LOST CHILD TO THE POLICE STATION WHILE PASSING BY--
IT'S NOT SERIOUS, PARVATI, IT'S NOT MY BUSINESS ANYWAY. COME, I HAVE A SURPRISE FOR YOU.

EXCUSE ME, MRS. FOURCHON, I PRESENT TO YOU THE SHINING STAR OF OUR VOLUNTEERS: PARVATI PATEL.

PLEASED TO MEET YOU, MISS PATEL.

NAMASTE*! IT'S REALLY YOU! MRS. FOURCHON, I AM YOUR GREATEST ADMIRER. TO BE ABLE TO MEET YOU WAS ONE OF MY DREAMS. BY WHAT MIRACLE IS THIS POSSIBLE?

UH, WELL, THE NGO THAT I CHAIR SPONSORS A GREAT PART OF THIS LITTLE CLINIC DIRECTED MASTERFULLY BY RAHUL.

WHEN I CAN, I LIKE TO MEET THE FOOT SOLDIERS AND TO BE ABLE TO OBSERVE THE RESULTS THAT THEY ARE ACHIEVING. SO, NATURALLY, HERE I AM TODAY.

THAT'S TERRIFIC! THANKS TO YOU, WE ARE ABLE TO HELP PEOPLE HERE.

NO, IT'S THANKS TO YOU! I AM TRULY HAPPY TO SEE THAT THERE ARE YOUNG GIRLS LIKE YOU WHO ARE FULL OF LIFE AND WHO MAKE SURE THAT THE WORLD BECOMES MORE BEAUTIFUL AND MORE JUST.

COUNT ON ME, I WILL REDOUBLE EFFORTS!

FOR THAT, IT WOULD BE NECESSARY FOR YOU TO DOUBLE YOURSELF! YOU'RE ALREADY DOING SO MUCH!

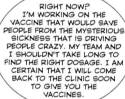

RIGHT NOW? I'M WORKING ON THE VACCINE THAT WOULD SAVE PEOPLE FROM THE MYSTERIOUS SICKNESS THAT IS DRIVING PEOPLE CRAZY. MY TEAM AND I SHOULDN'T TAKE LONG TO FIND THE RIGHT DOSAGE. I AM CERTAIN THAT I WILL COME BACK TO THE CLINIC SOON TO GIVE YOU THE VACCINES.

HA HA HA HA HA HA HA HA HA!!

PARDON MY INDISCRETION, MRS. FOURCHON, BUT I'M DYING TO KNOW WHAT YOU'RE WORKING ON RIGHT NOW.

YOU ARE TRULY TERRIFIC!

*"HELLO" IN HINDI.

16

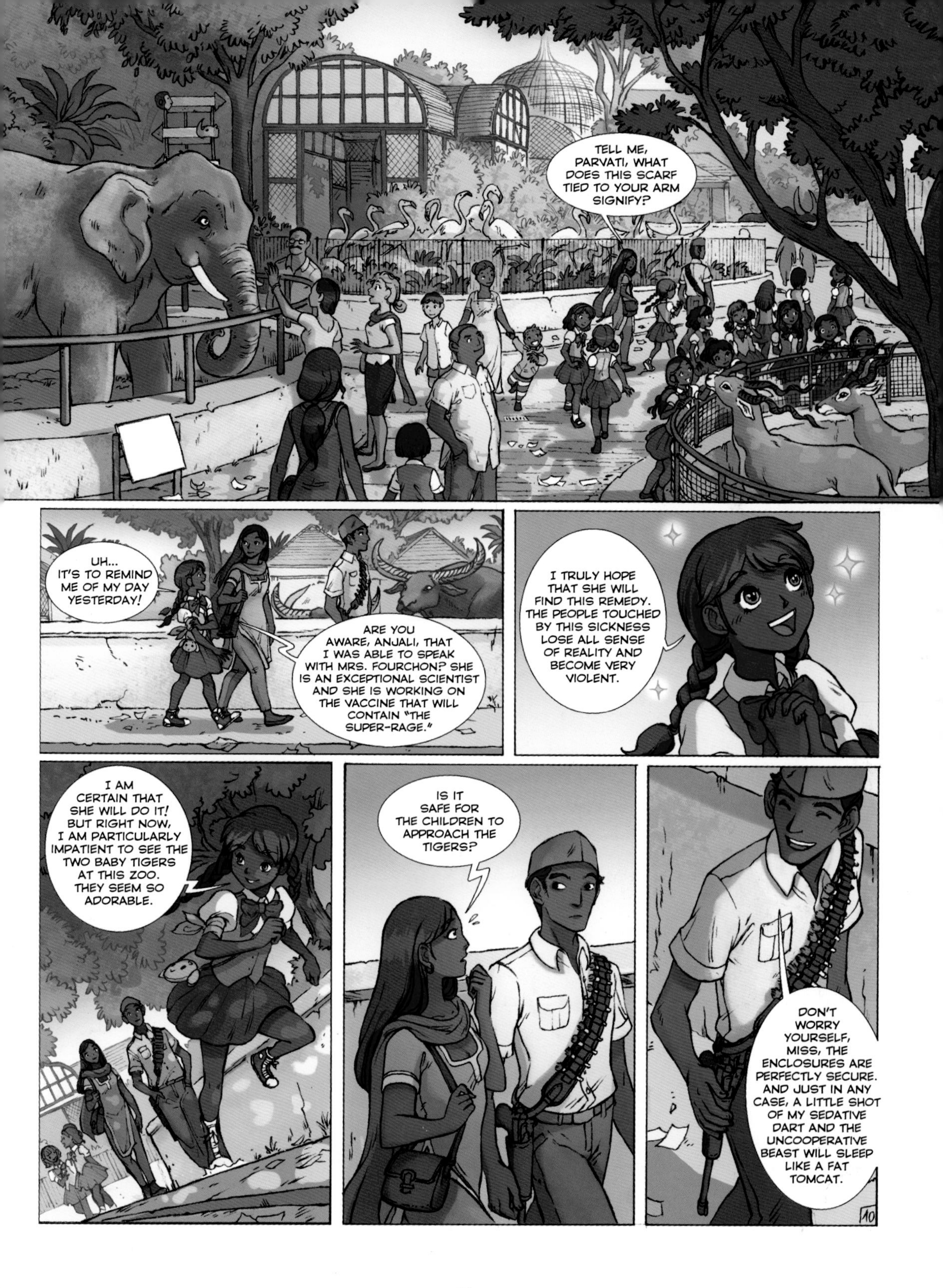
TELL ME, PARVATI, WHAT DOES THIS SCARF TIED TO YOUR ARM SIGNIFY?
UH... IT'S TO REMIND ME OF MY DAY YESTERDAY!
ARE YOU AWARE, ANJALI, THAT I WAS ABLE TO SPEAK WITH MRS. FOURCHON? SHE IS AN EXCEPTIONAL SCIENTIST AND SHE IS WORKING ON THE VACCINE THAT WILL CONTAIN "THE SUPER-RAGE."
I TRULY HOPE THAT SHE WILL FIND THIS REMEDY. THE PEOPLE TOUCHED BY THIS SICKNESS LOSE ALL SENSE OF REALITY AND BECOME VERY VIOLENT.
I AM CERTAIN THAT SHE WILL DO IT! BUT RIGHT NOW, I AM PARTICULARLY IMPATIENT TO SEE THE TWO BABY TIGERS AT THIS ZOO. THEY SEEM SO ADORABLE.
IS IT SAFE FOR THE CHILDREN TO APPROACH THE TIGERS?
DON'T WORRY YOURSELF, MISS, THE ENCLOSURES ARE PERFECTLY SECURE. AND JUST IN ANY CASE, A LITTLE SHOT OF MY SEDATIVE DART AND THE UNCOOPERATIVE BEAST WILL SLEEP LIKE A FAT TOMCAT.
10

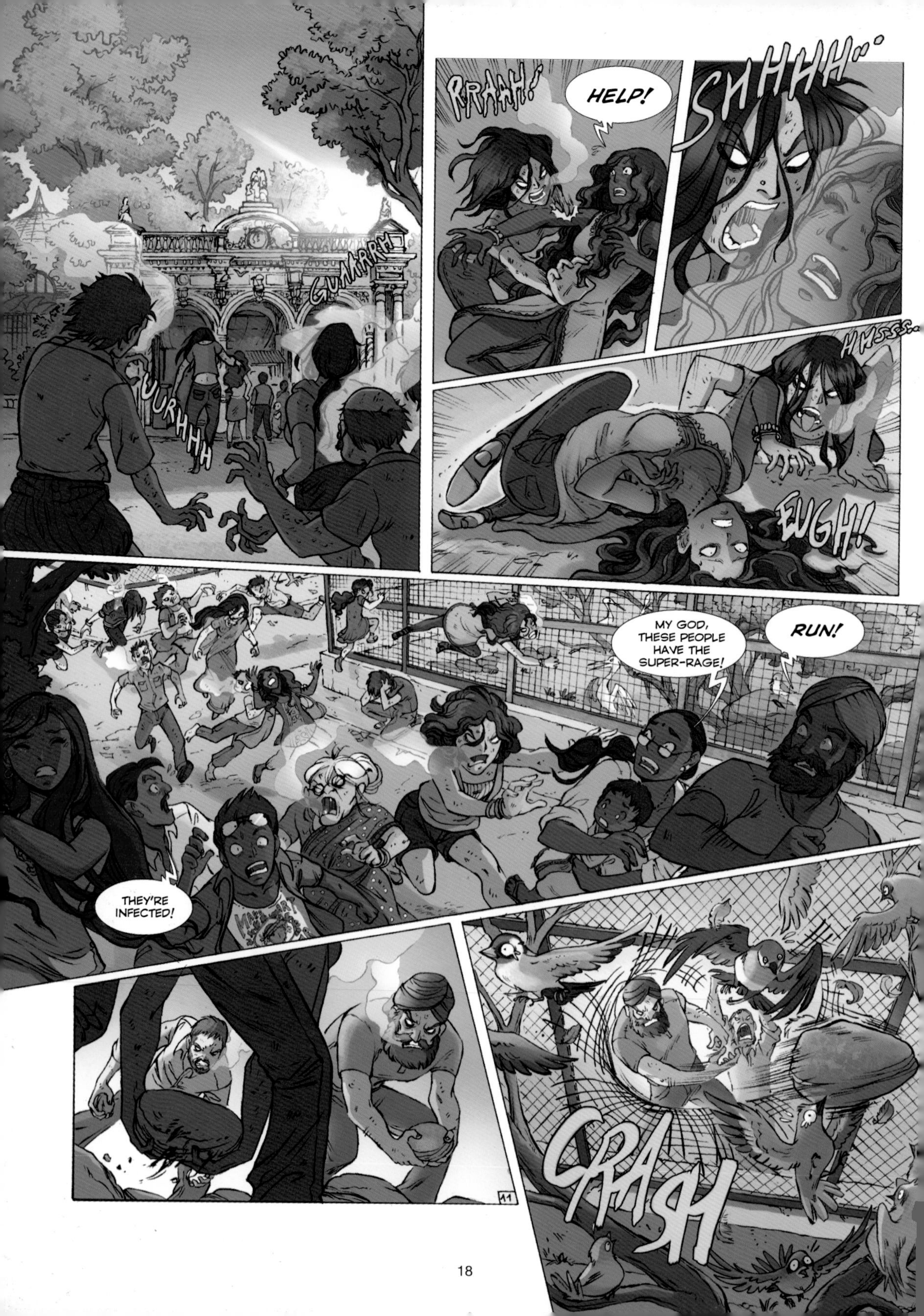
GUNRRR!
UURHHH
RRAAH!
HELP!
SHHHH..
HHSSSS..
EUGH!
MY GOD, THESE PEOPLE HAVE THE SUPER-RAGE!
RUN!
THEY'RE INFECTED!
CRASH

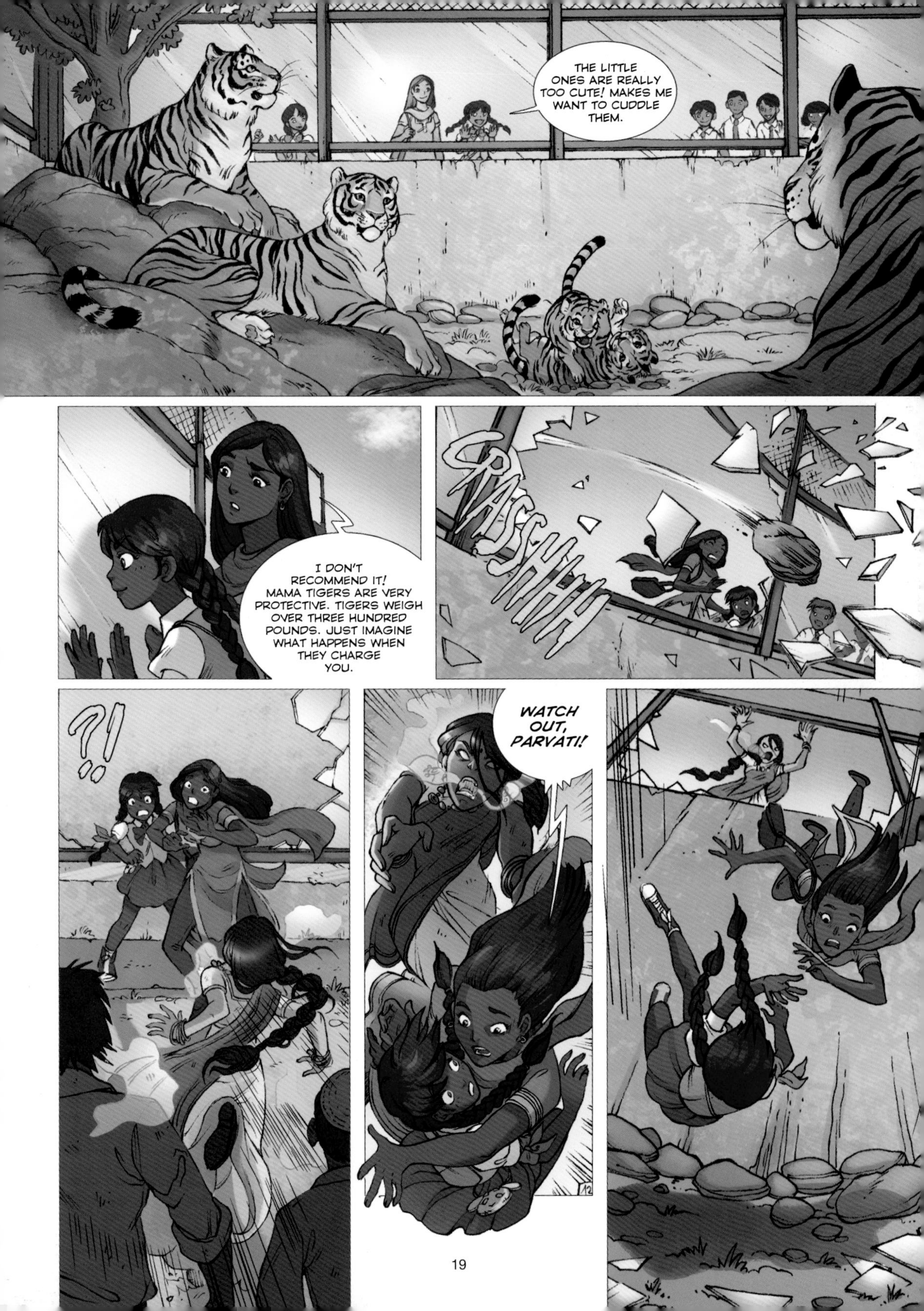
THE LITTLE ONES ARE REALLY TOO CUTE! MAKES ME WANT TO CUDDLE THEM.
I DON'T RECOMMEND IT! MAMA TIGERS ARE VERY PROTECTIVE. TIGERS WEIGH OVER THREE HUNDRED POUNDS. JUST IMAGINE WHAT HAPPENS WHEN THEY CHARGE YOU.
CRASSHHH
?!
WATCH OUT, PARVATI!

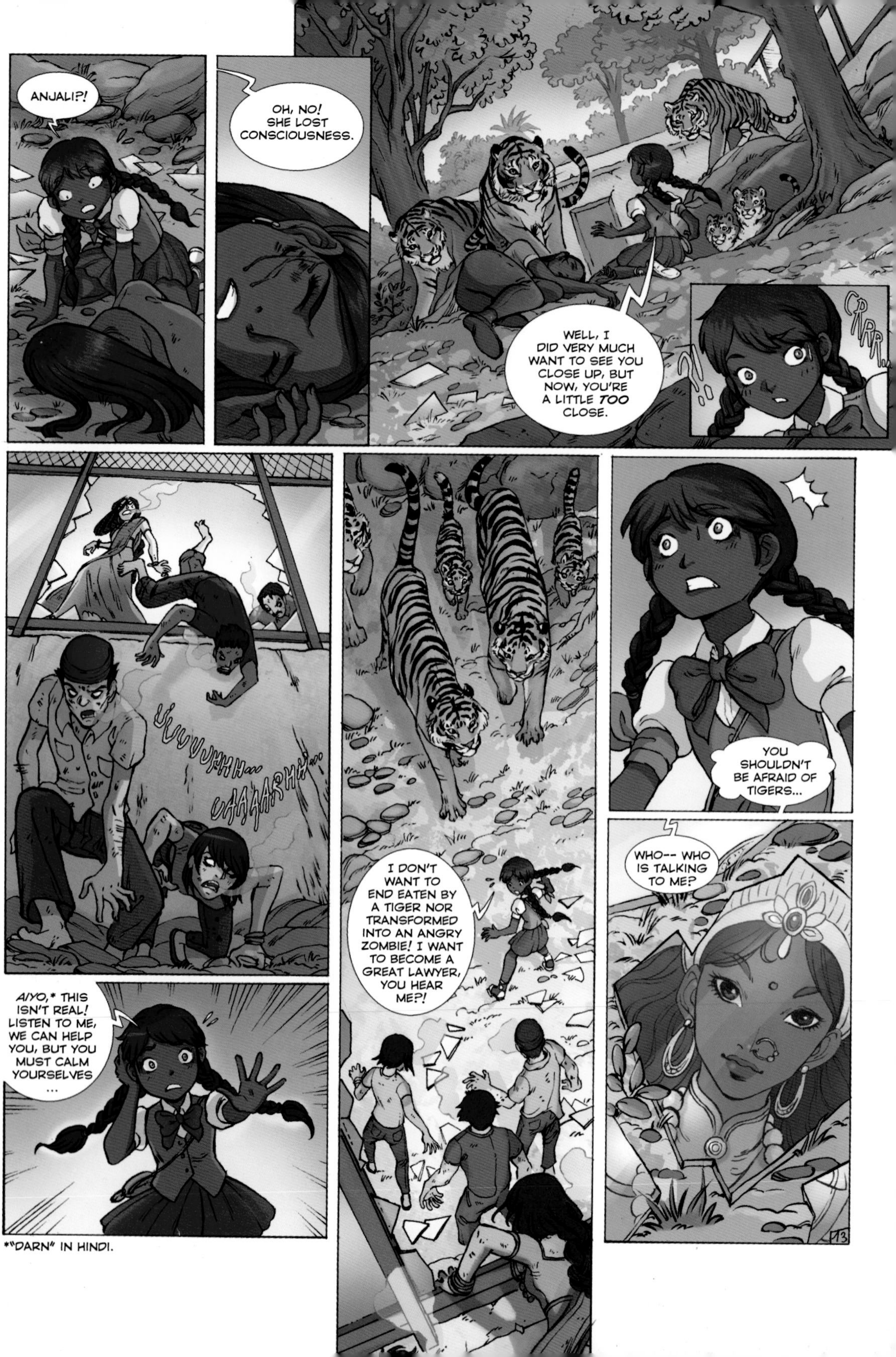

ANJALI?!
OH, NO! SHE LOST CONSCIOUSNESS.
WELL, I DID VERY MUCH WANT TO SEE YOU CLOSE UP, BUT NOW, YOU'RE A LITTLE *TOO* CLOSE.
CRRR...
UUUUUHHH...
UAAAARHH...
YOU SHOULDN'T BE AFRAID OF TIGERS...
*AIYO,** THIS ISN'T REAL! LISTEN TO ME, WE CAN HELP YOU, BUT YOU MUST CALM YOURSELVES ...
I DON'T WANT TO END EATEN BY A TIGER NOR TRANSFORMED INTO AN ANGRY ZOMBIE! I WANT TO BECOME A GREAT LAWYER, YOU HEAR ME?!
WHO-- WHO IS TALKING TO ME?

*"DARN" IN HINDI.

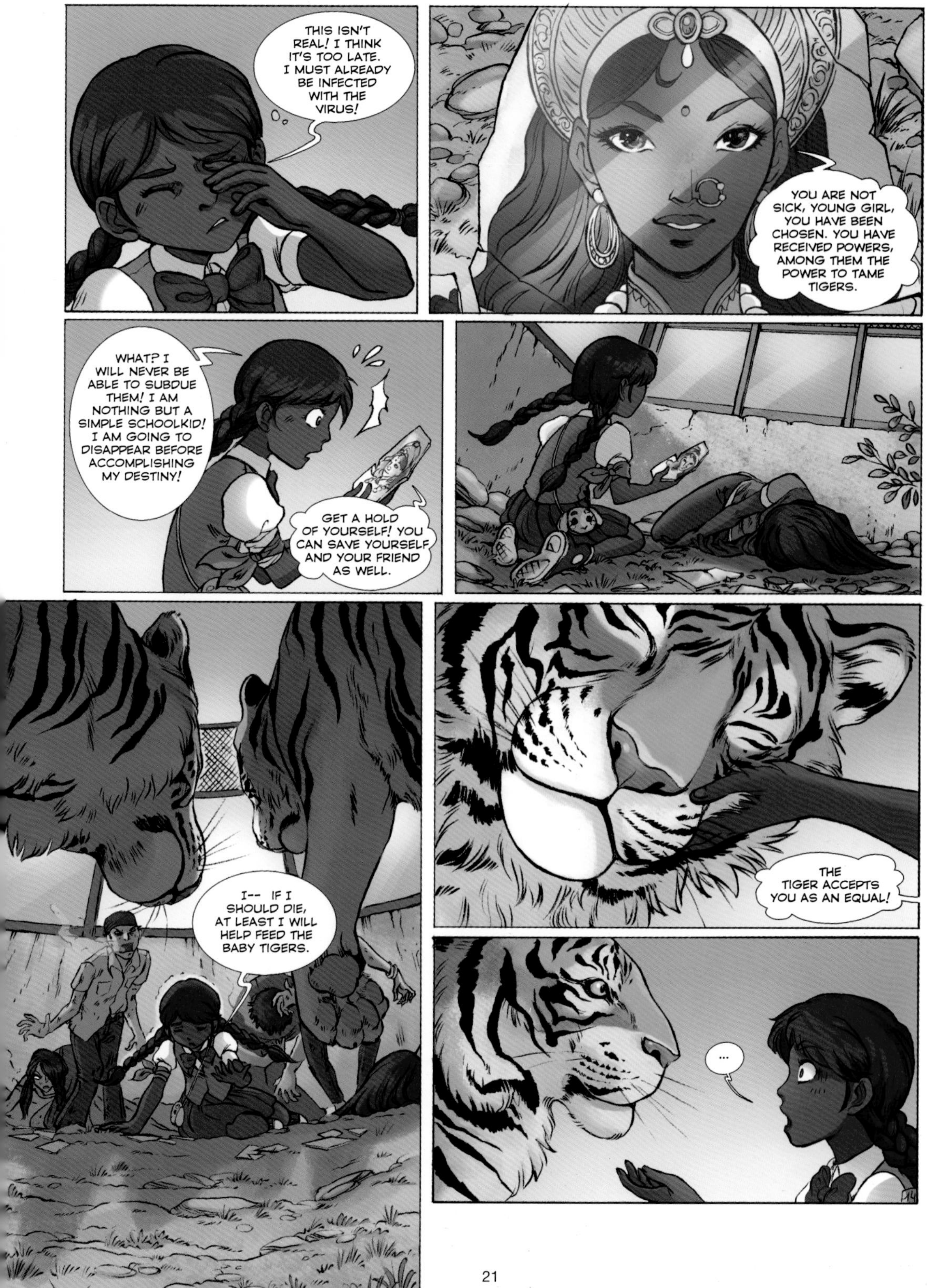
THIS ISN'T REAL! I THINK IT'S TOO LATE. I MUST ALREADY BE INFECTED WITH THE VIRUS!
YOU ARE NOT SICK, YOUNG GIRL, YOU HAVE BEEN CHOSEN. YOU HAVE RECEIVED POWERS, AMONG THEM THE POWER TO TAME TIGERS.
WHAT? I WILL NEVER BE ABLE TO SUBDUE THEM! I AM NOTHING BUT A SIMPLE SCHOOLKID! I AM GOING TO DISAPPEAR BEFORE ACCOMPLISHING MY DESTINY!
GET A HOLD OF YOURSELF! YOU CAN SAVE YOURSELF AND YOUR FRIEND AS WELL.
I-- IF I SHOULD DIE, AT LEAST I WILL HELP FEED THE BABY TIGERS.
THE TIGER ACCEPTS YOU AS AN EQUAL!
...

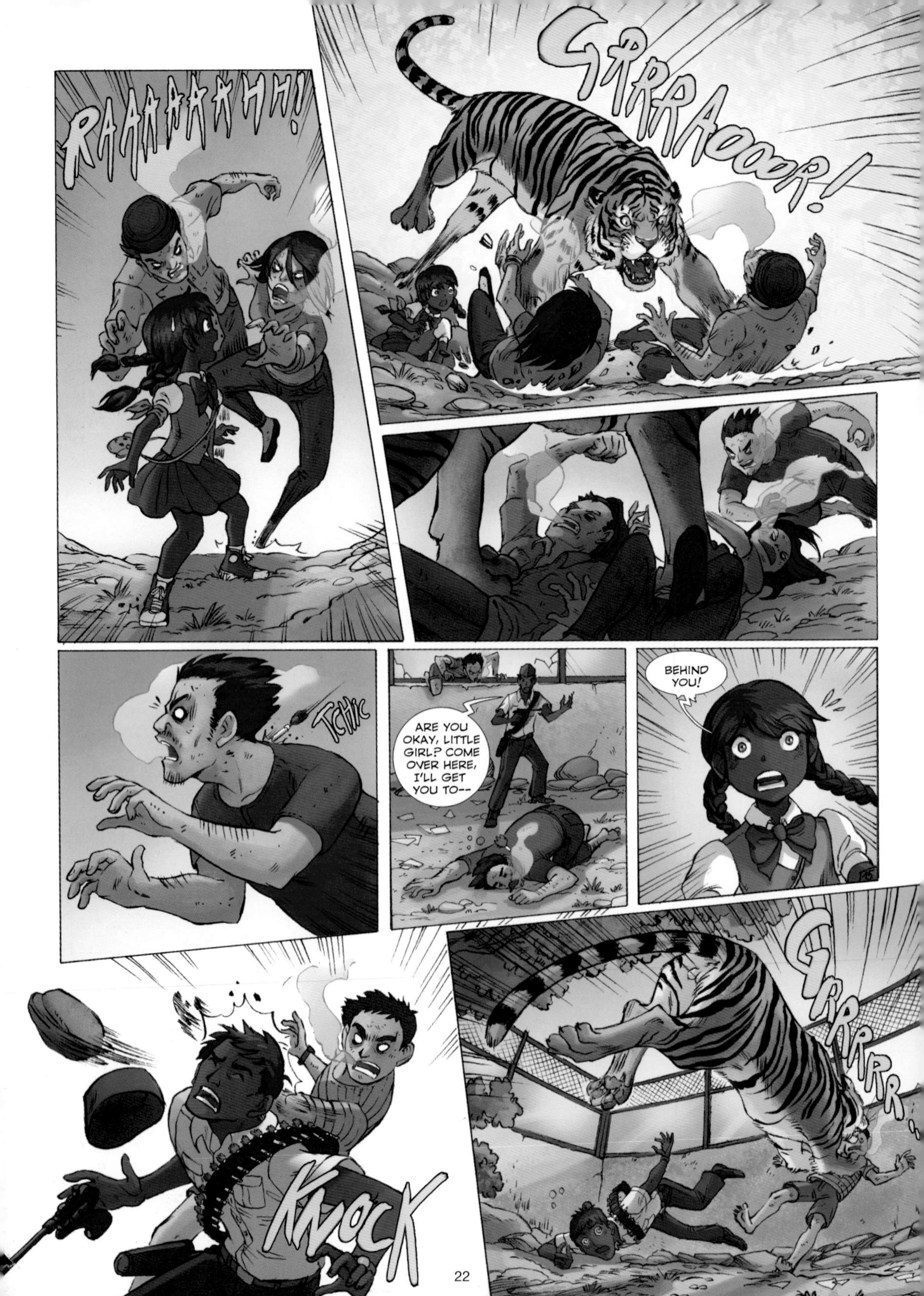
RAAAAAAHH!
GRRRAOOOR!
TCHIC
ARE YOU OKAY, LITTLE GIRL? COME OVER HERE, I'LL GET YOU TO--
BEHIND YOU!
KNOCK
GRRRRR...

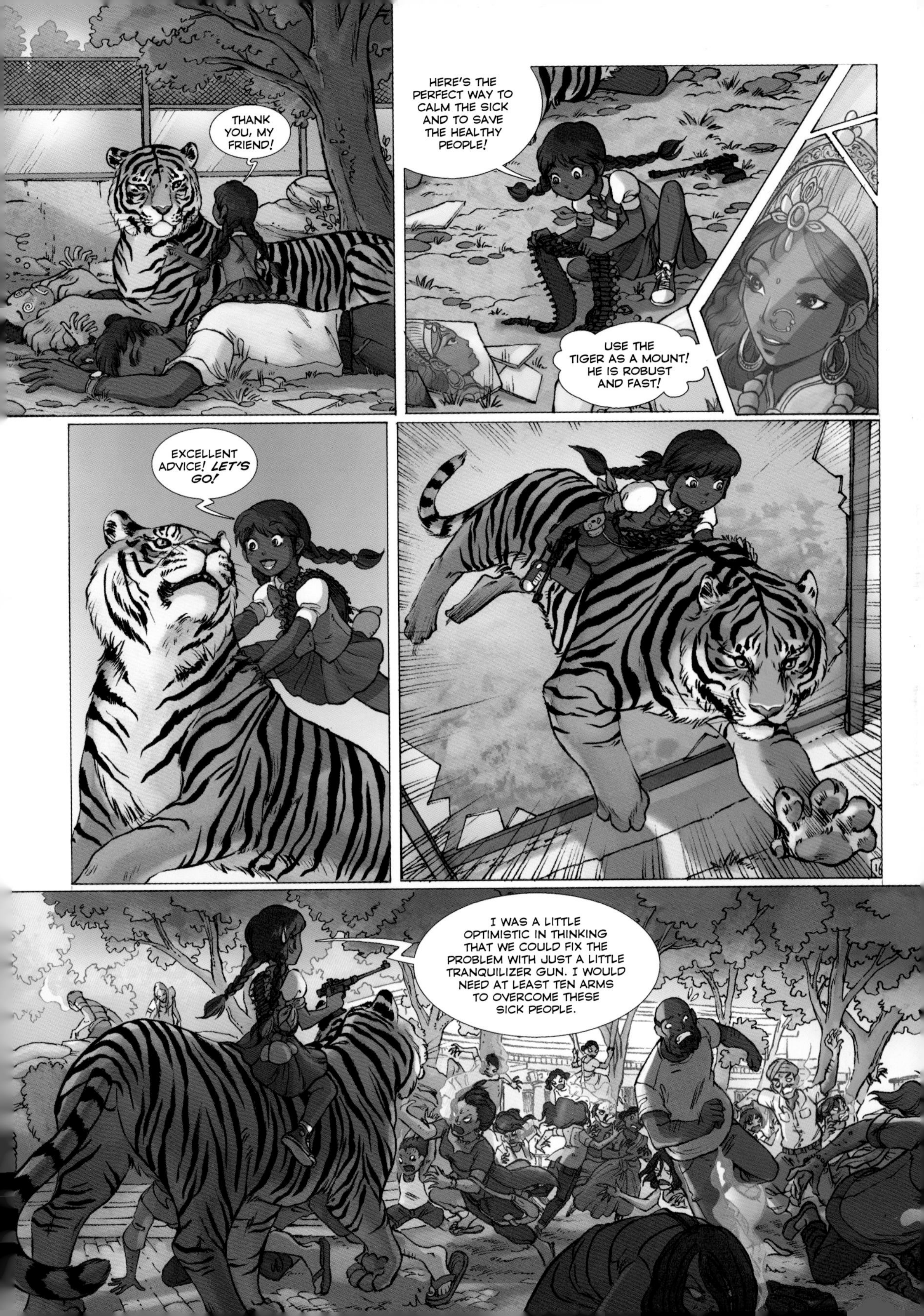
THANK YOU, MY FRIEND!
HERE'S THE PERFECT WAY TO CALM THE SICK AND TO SAVE THE HEALTHY PEOPLE!
USE THE TIGER AS A MOUNT! HE IS ROBUST AND FAST!
EXCELLENT ADVICE! LET'S GO!
I WAS A LITTLE OPTIMISTIC IN THINKING THAT WE COULD FIX THE PROBLEM WITH JUST A LITTLE TRANQUILIZER GUN. I WOULD NEED AT LEAST TEN ARMS TO OVERCOME THESE SICK PEOPLE.

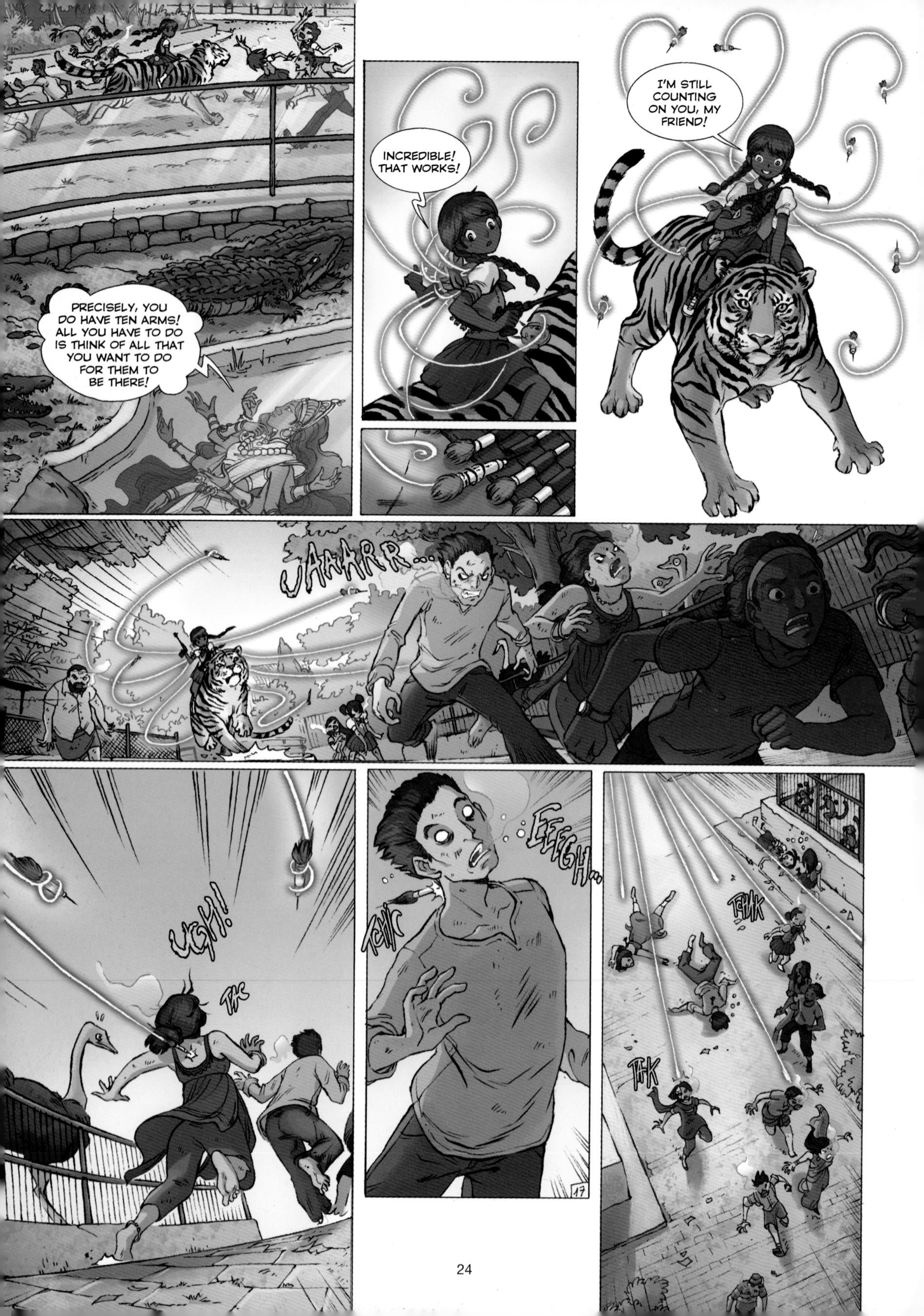
PRECISELY, YOU DO HAVE TEN ARMS! ALL YOU HAVE TO DO IS THINK OF ALL THAT YOU WANT TO DO FOR THEM TO BE THERE!
INCREDIBLE! THAT WORKS!
I'M STILL COUNTING ON YOU, MY FRIEND!
JAAARRR...
UGH!
THC
TCHK
EEEGH...
TCHK
THK
17

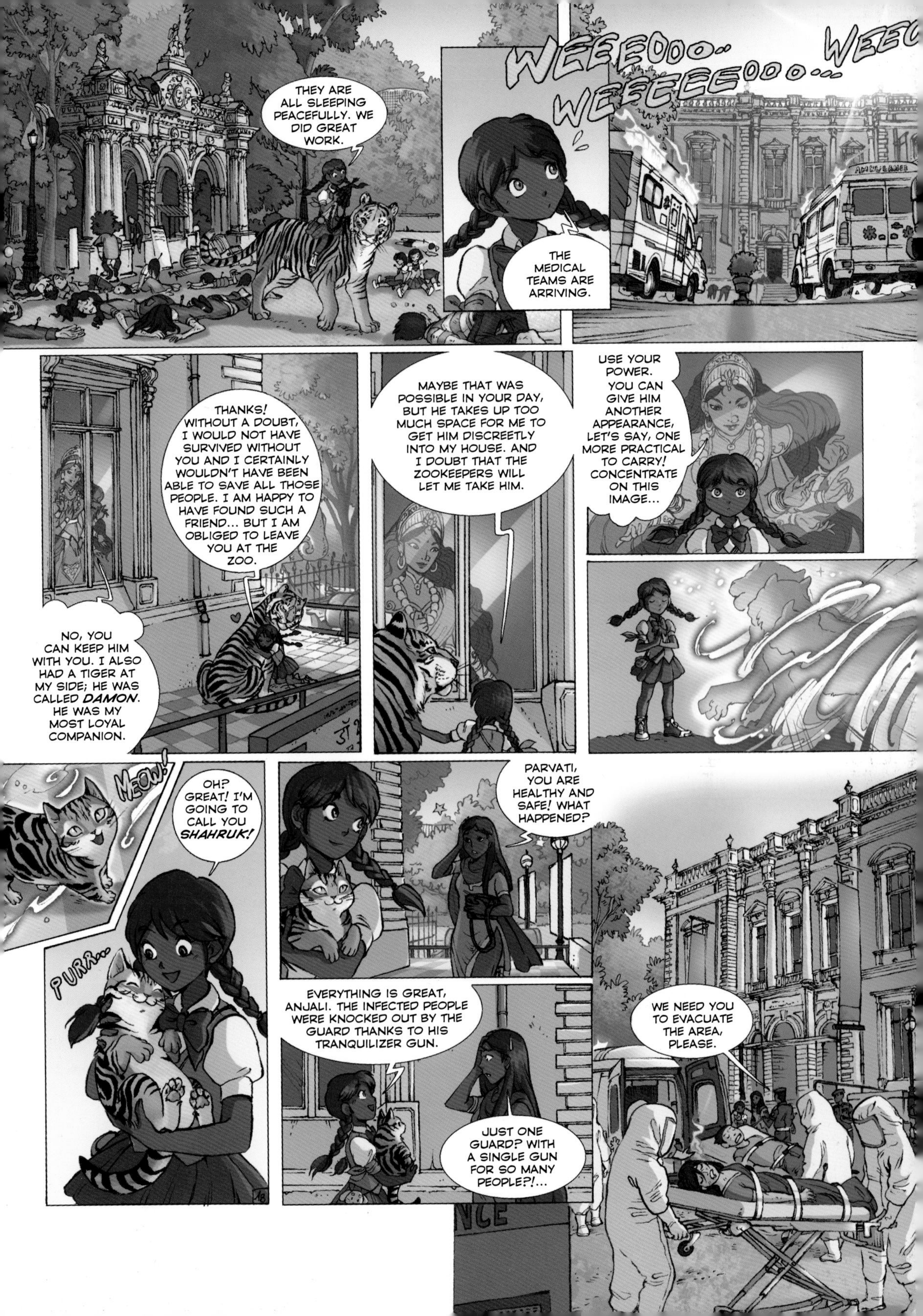

THEY ARE ALL SLEEPING PEACEFULLY. WE DID GREAT WORK.
THE MEDICAL TEAMS ARE ARRIVING.
WEEEOOO... WEEEEEOOO... WEEO
THANKS! WITHOUT A DOUBT, I WOULD NOT HAVE SURVIVED WITHOUT YOU AND I CERTAINLY WOULDN'T HAVE BEEN ABLE TO SAVE ALL THOSE PEOPLE. I AM HAPPY TO HAVE FOUND SUCH A FRIEND... BUT I AM OBLIGED TO LEAVE YOU AT THE ZOO.
NO, YOU CAN KEEP HIM WITH YOU. I ALSO HAD A TIGER AT MY SIDE; HE WAS CALLED DAMON. HE WAS MY MOST LOYAL COMPANION.
MAYBE THAT WAS POSSIBLE IN YOUR DAY, BUT HE TAKES UP TOO MUCH SPACE FOR ME TO GET HIM DISCREETLY INTO MY HOUSE. AND I DOUBT THAT THE ZOOKEEPERS WILL LET ME TAKE HIM.
USE YOUR POWER. YOU CAN GIVE HIM ANOTHER APPEARANCE, LET'S SAY, ONE MORE PRACTICAL TO CARRY! CONCENTRATE ON THIS IMAGE...
MEOW!
OH? GREAT! I'M GOING TO CALL YOU SHAHRUK!
PURR...
PARVATI, YOU ARE HEALTHY AND SAFE! WHAT HAPPENED?
EVERYTHING IS GREAT, ANJALI. THE INFECTED PEOPLE WERE KNOCKED OUT BY THE GUARD THANKS TO HIS TRANQUILIZER GUN.
JUST ONE GUARD? WITH A SINGLE GUN FOR SO MANY PEOPLE?!...
WE NEED YOU TO EVACUATE THE AREA, PLEASE.

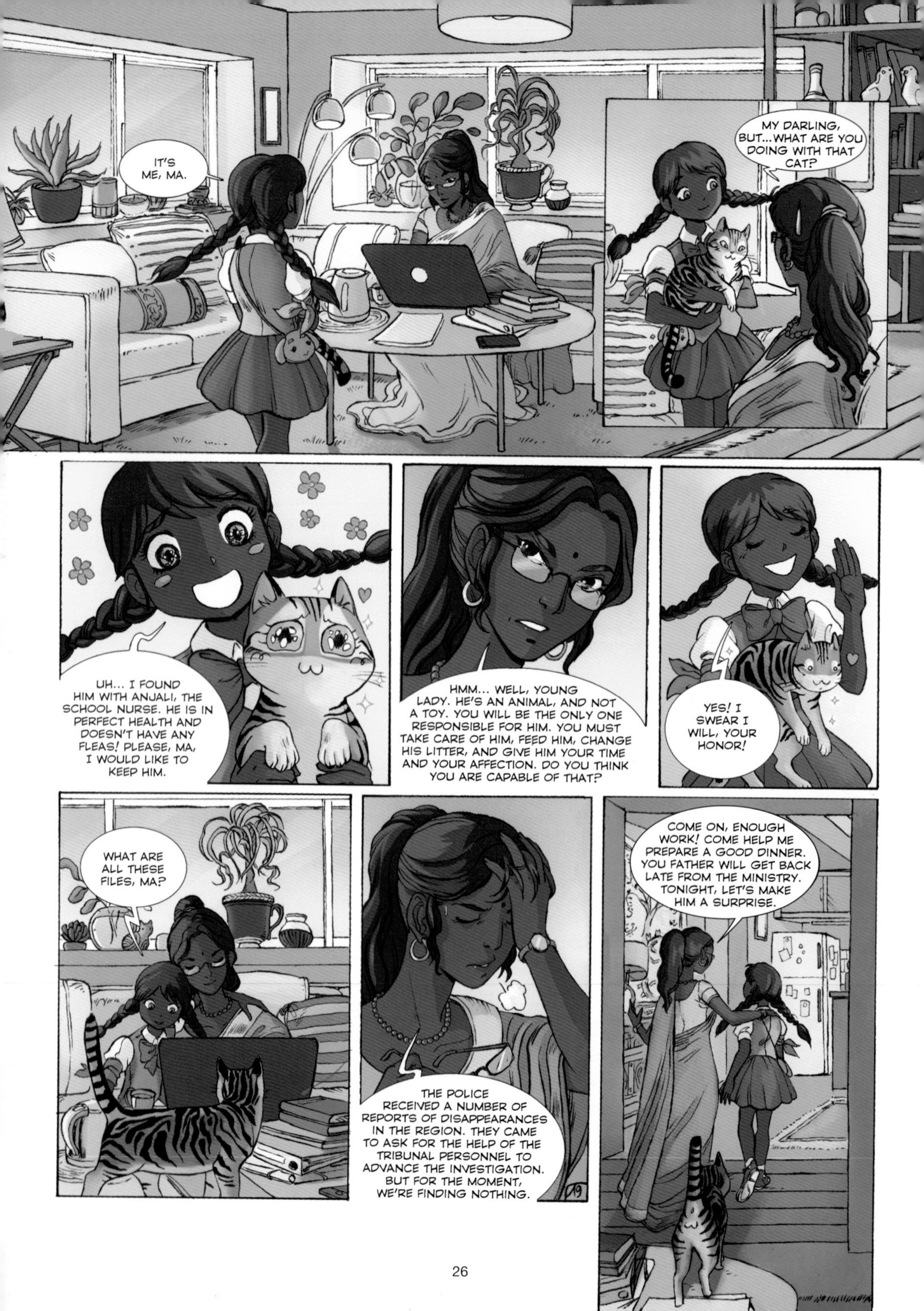
IT'S ME, MA.
MY DARLING, BUT...WHAT ARE YOU DOING WITH THAT CAT?
UH... I FOUND HIM WITH ANJALI, THE SCHOOL NURSE. HE IS IN PERFECT HEALTH AND DOESN'T HAVE ANY FLEAS! PLEASE, MA, I WOULD LIKE TO KEEP HIM.
HMM... WELL, YOUNG LADY. HE'S AN ANIMAL, AND NOT A TOY. YOU WILL BE THE ONLY ONE RESPONSIBLE FOR HIM. YOU MUST TAKE CARE OF HIM, FEED HIM, CHANGE HIS LITTER, AND GIVE HIM YOUR TIME AND YOUR AFFECTION. DO YOU THINK YOU ARE CAPABLE OF THAT?
YES! I SWEAR I WILL, YOUR HONOR!
WHAT ARE ALL THESE FILES, MA?
THE POLICE RECEIVED A NUMBER OF REPORTS OF DISAPPEARANCES IN THE REGION. THEY CAME TO ASK FOR THE HELP OF THE TRIBUNAL PERSONNEL TO ADVANCE THE INVESTIGATION. BUT FOR THE MOMENT, WE'RE FINDING NOTHING.
COME ON, ENOUGH WORK! COME HELP ME PREPARE A GOOD DINNER. YOU FATHER WILL GET BACK LATE FROM THE MINISTRY. TONIGHT, LET'S MAKE HIM A SURPRISE.

...THESE POWERS SEEM VERY PRACTICAL, BUT I WOULD VERY MUCH LIKE TO UNDERSTAND HOW THEY CAME TO ME.
AND YOU'RE TELLING ME THAT IT HAS SOMETHING TO DO WITH THIS TATTOO?
I AM **DURGA** AND YOU ARE MY DESCENDANT. THE TATTOO IS THE MARK OF THE HERO. IF IT APPEARS, IT MEANS THAT EVIL HAS COME BACK TO THE EARTH.
FROM WHAT INFORMATION I HAVE FOUND, YOU ARE ONE OF OUR MAJOR DEITIES. YOU BATTLED NUMEROUS DEMONS. YOU ARE THE POSSESSOR OF THE TEN SACRED WEAPONS... AND YOU EVEN HAVE A FESTIVAL IN YOUR HONOR, IN CALCUTTA AND IN BENGAL!
OH, MOTHER OF THE WORLD, I AM HONORED TO BE YOUR DESCENDANT.
I AM JUST AS HONORED AS YOU, PARVATI! DESTINY COULDN'T HAVE CHOSEN BETTER THAN A YOUNG GIRL SUCH AS YOURSELF: DARING, STRONG, AND INTELLIGENT.
I AM READY TO FIGHT THIS EVIL. TELL ME WHAT I MUST DO.
BEFORE THAT, IT'S NECESSARY THAT YOU GET ME OUT OF THE SPIRIT WORLD. GIVE ME A LITTLE OF YOUR ENERGY SO THAT I CAN MATERIALIZE MYSELF INTO THE REAL WORLD.
OPEN YOUR HEART AND THE GIFT WILL GIVE ITSELF.
YOU ARE TOO CUTE LIKE THAT!
NAMASTE, SHAHRUK!
20
? PooF

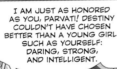

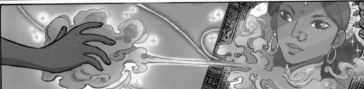

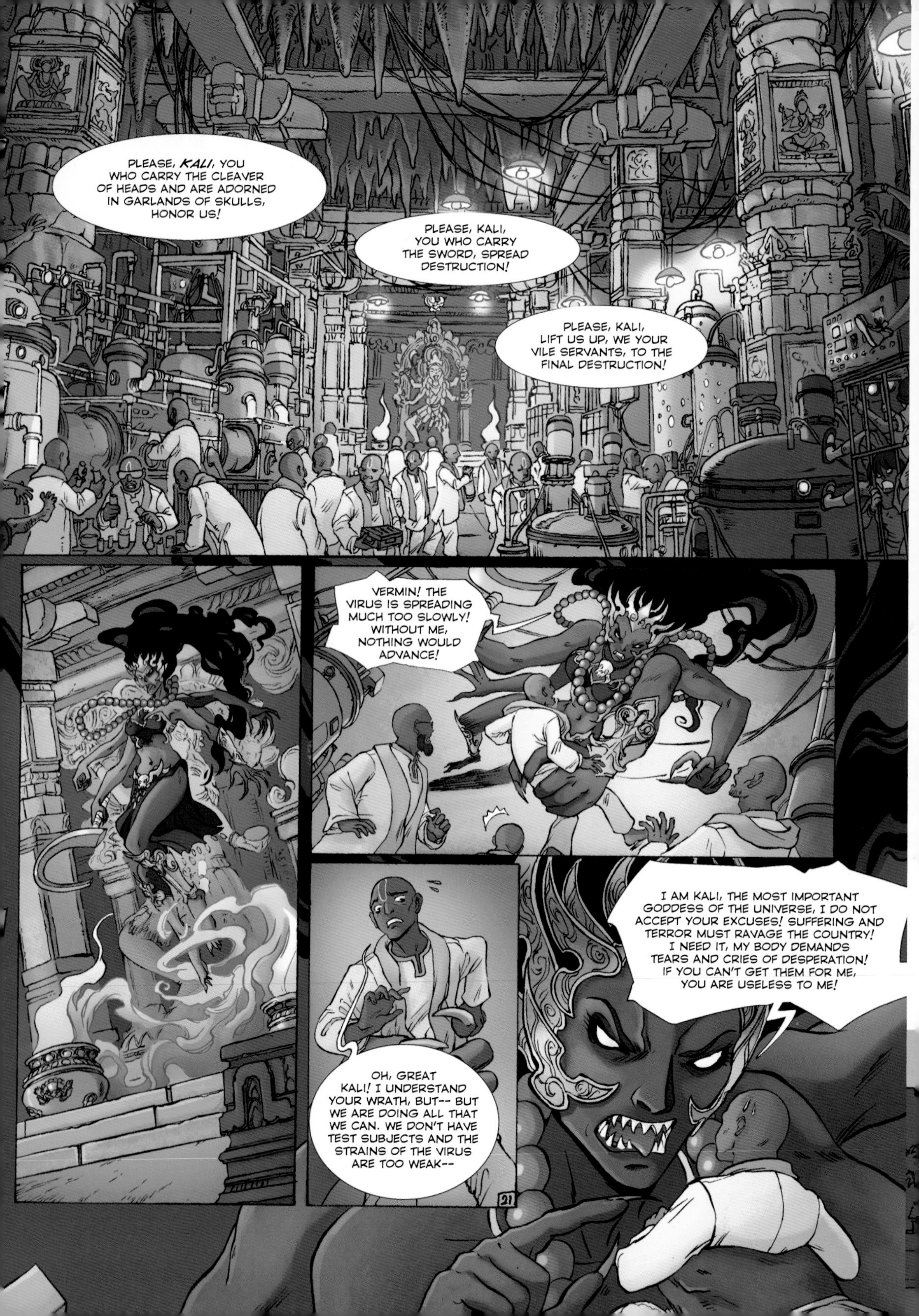

PLEASE, KALI, YOU WHO CARRY THE CLEAVER OF HEADS AND ARE ADORNED IN GARLANDS OF SKULLS, HONOR US!
PLEASE, KALI, YOU WHO CARRY THE SWORD, SPREAD DESTRUCTION!
PLEASE, KALI, LIFT US UP, WE YOUR VILE SERVANTS, TO THE FINAL DESTRUCTION!
VERMIN! THE VIRUS IS SPREADING MUCH TOO SLOWLY! WITHOUT ME, NOTHING WOULD ADVANCE!
I AM KALI, THE MOST IMPORTANT GODDESS OF THE UNIVERSE, I DO NOT ACCEPT YOUR EXCUSES! SUFFERING AND TERROR MUST RAVAGE THE COUNTRY! I NEED IT, MY BODY DEMANDS TEARS AND CRIES OF DESPERATION! IF YOU CAN'T GET THEM FOR ME, YOU ARE USELESS TO ME!
OH, GREAT KALI! I UNDERSTAND YOUR WRATH, BUT-- BUT WE ARE DOING ALL THAT WE CAN. WE DON'T HAVE TEST SUBJECTS AND THE STRAINS OF THE VIRUS ARE TOO WEAK--

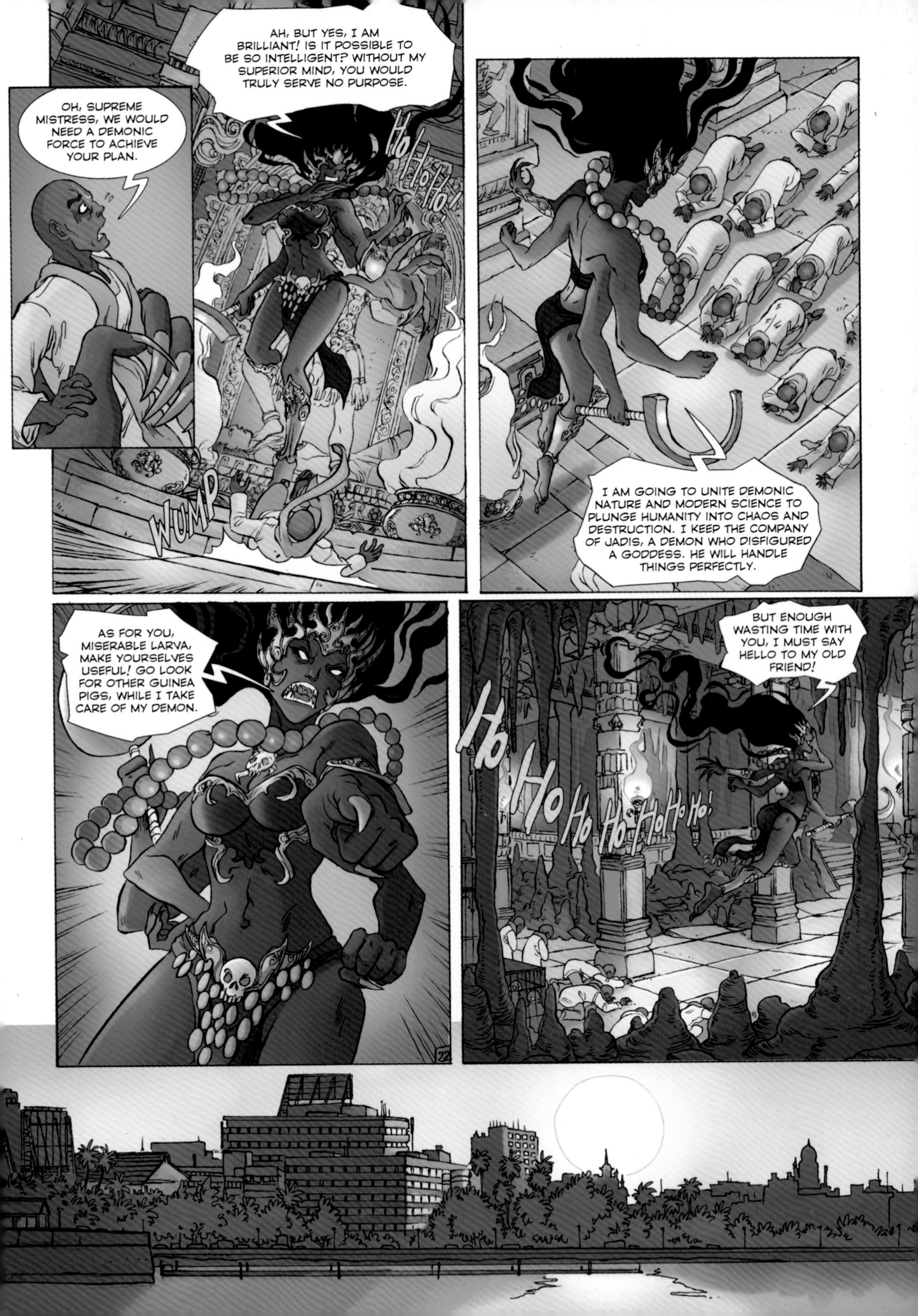
OH, SUPREME MISTRESS, WE WOULD NEED A DEMONIC FORCE TO ACHIEVE YOUR PLAN.
AH, BUT YES, I AM BRILLIANT! IS IT POSSIBLE TO BE SO INTELLIGENT? WITHOUT MY SUPERIOR MIND, YOU WOULD TRULY SERVE NO PURPOSE.
HO! HO! HO!
WUMP
I AM GOING TO UNITE DEMONIC NATURE AND MODERN SCIENCE TO PLUNGE HUMANITY INTO CHAOS AND DESTRUCTION. I KEEP THE COMPANY OF JADIS, A DEMON WHO DISFIGURED A GODDESS. HE WILL HANDLE THINGS PERFECTLY.
AS FOR YOU, MISERABLE LARVA, MAKE YOURSELVES USEFUL! GO LOOK FOR OTHER GUINEA PIGS, WHILE I TAKE CARE OF MY DEMON.
BUT ENOUGH WASTING TIME WITH YOU, I MUST SAY HELLO TO MY OLD FRIEND!
HO HO HO HO HO HO HO HO!
22

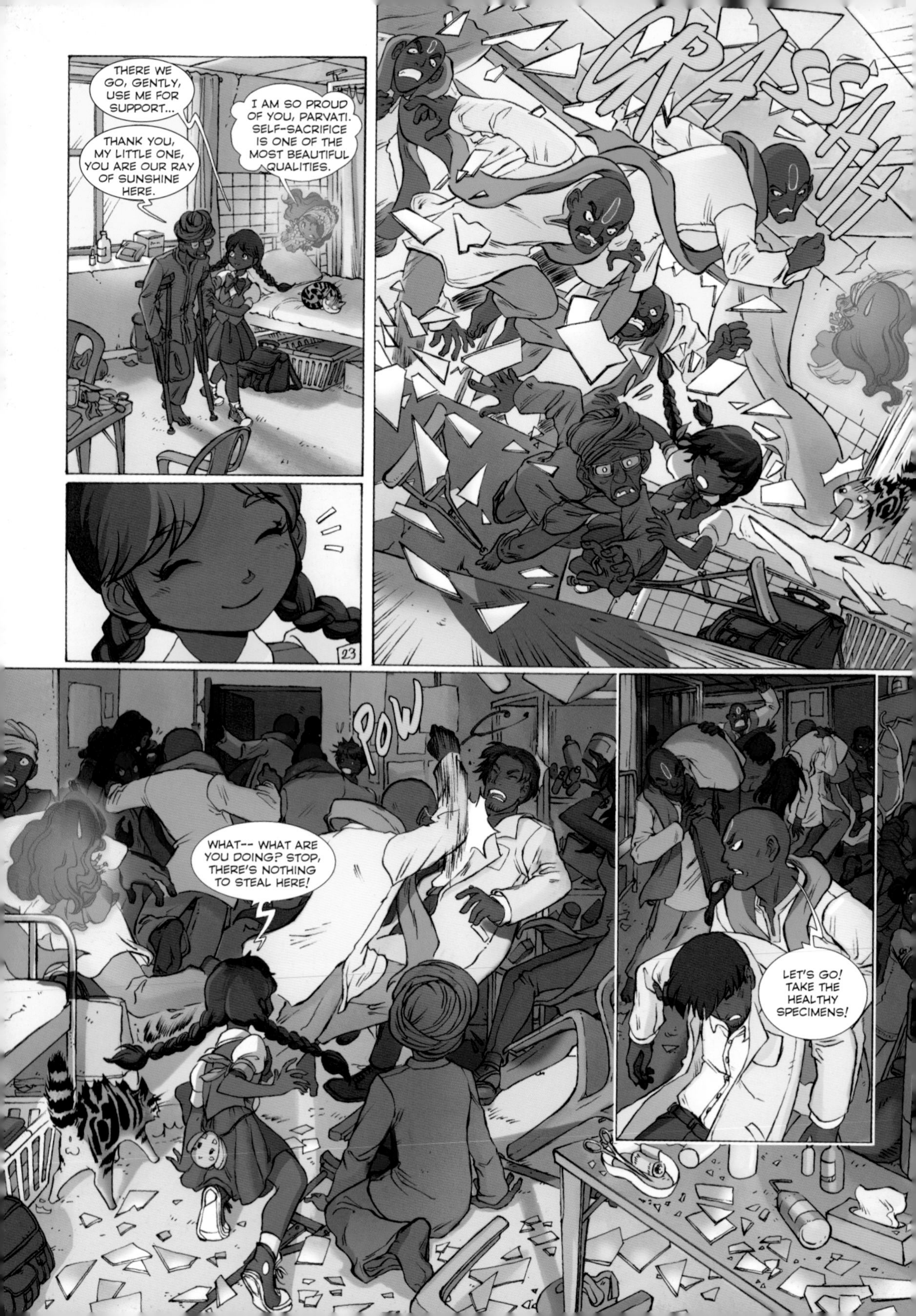
THERE WE GO, GENTLY, USE ME FOR SUPPORT...
THANK YOU, MY LITTLE ONE, YOU ARE OUR RAY OF SUNSHINE HERE.
I AM SO PROUD OF YOU, PARVATI. SELF-SACRIFICE IS ONE OF THE MOST BEAUTIFUL QUALITIES.
CRASSHHH
POW
WHAT-- WHAT ARE YOU DOING? STOP, THERE'S NOTHING TO STEAL HERE!
LET'S GO! TAKE THE HEALTHY SPECIMENS!

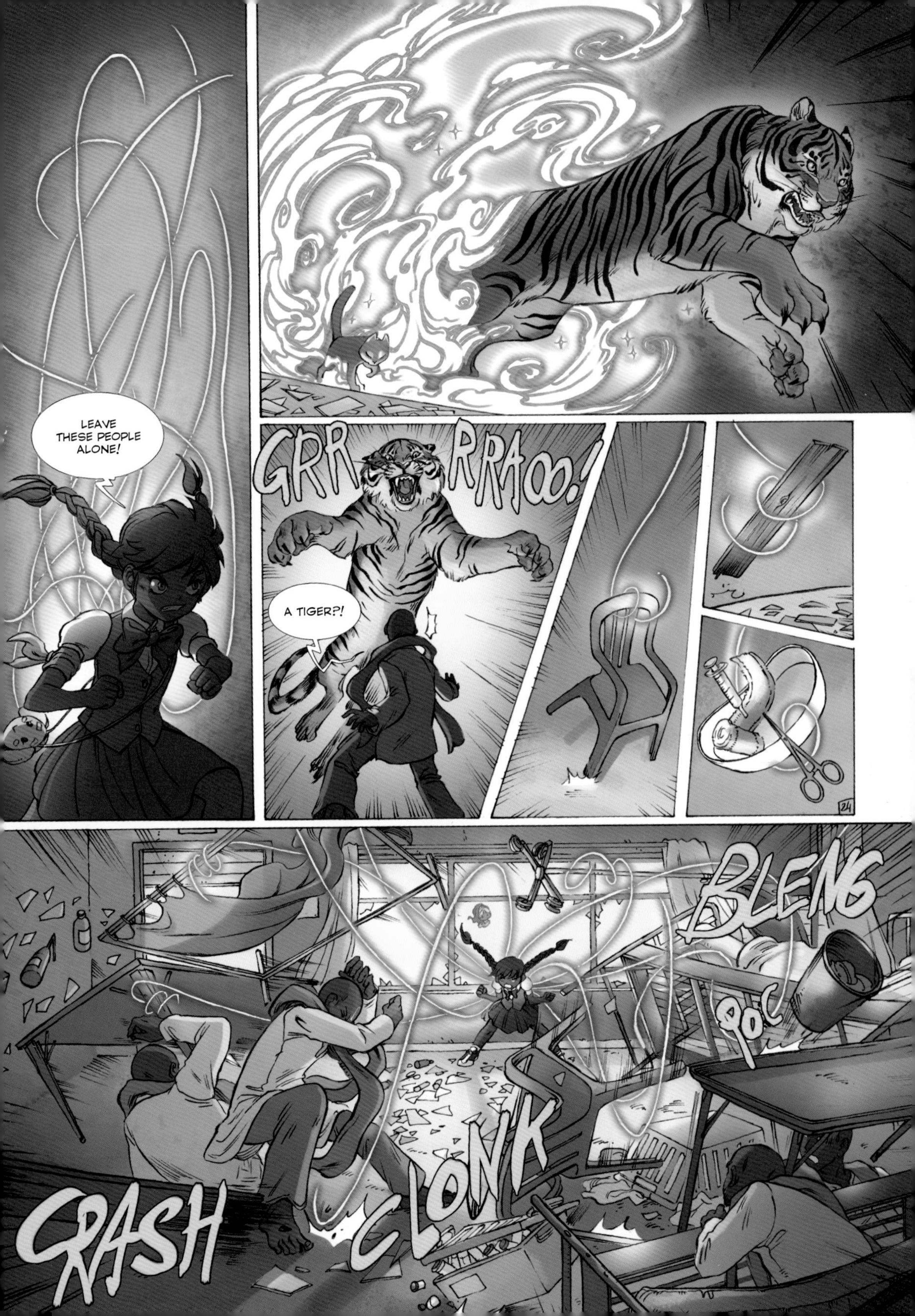
LEAVE THESE PEOPLE ALONE!
GRR RRAOO!
A TIGER?!
24
BLENG
POC
CRASH
CLONK

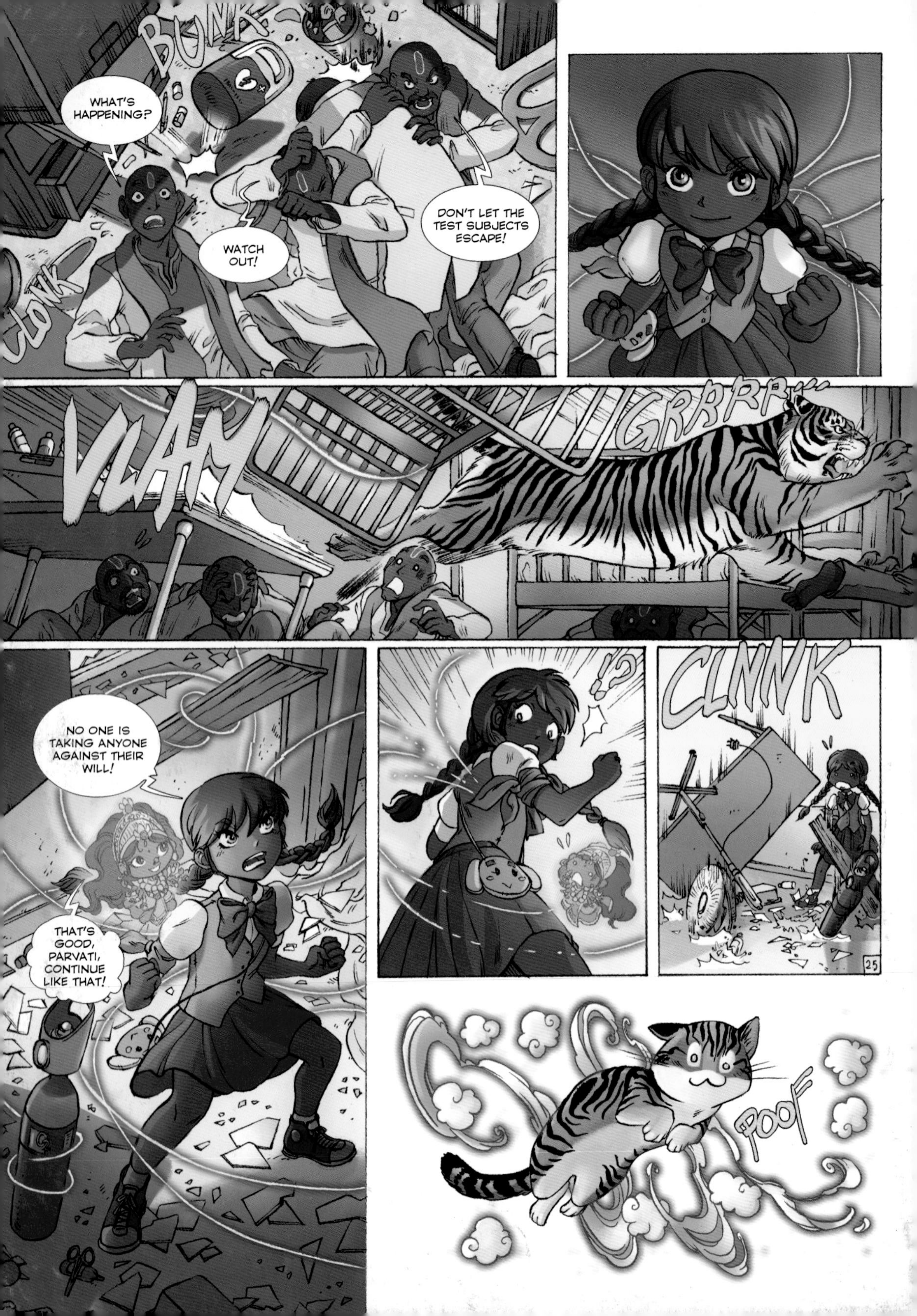
BUNK
WHAT'S HAPPENING?
CLONK
WATCH OUT!
DON'T LET THE TEST SUBJECTS ESCAPE!
VLAM
GRRRR...
NO ONE IS TAKING ANYONE AGAINST THEIR WILL!
THAT'S GOOD, PARVATI, CONTINUE LIKE THAT!
!?
CLNNK
25
POOF

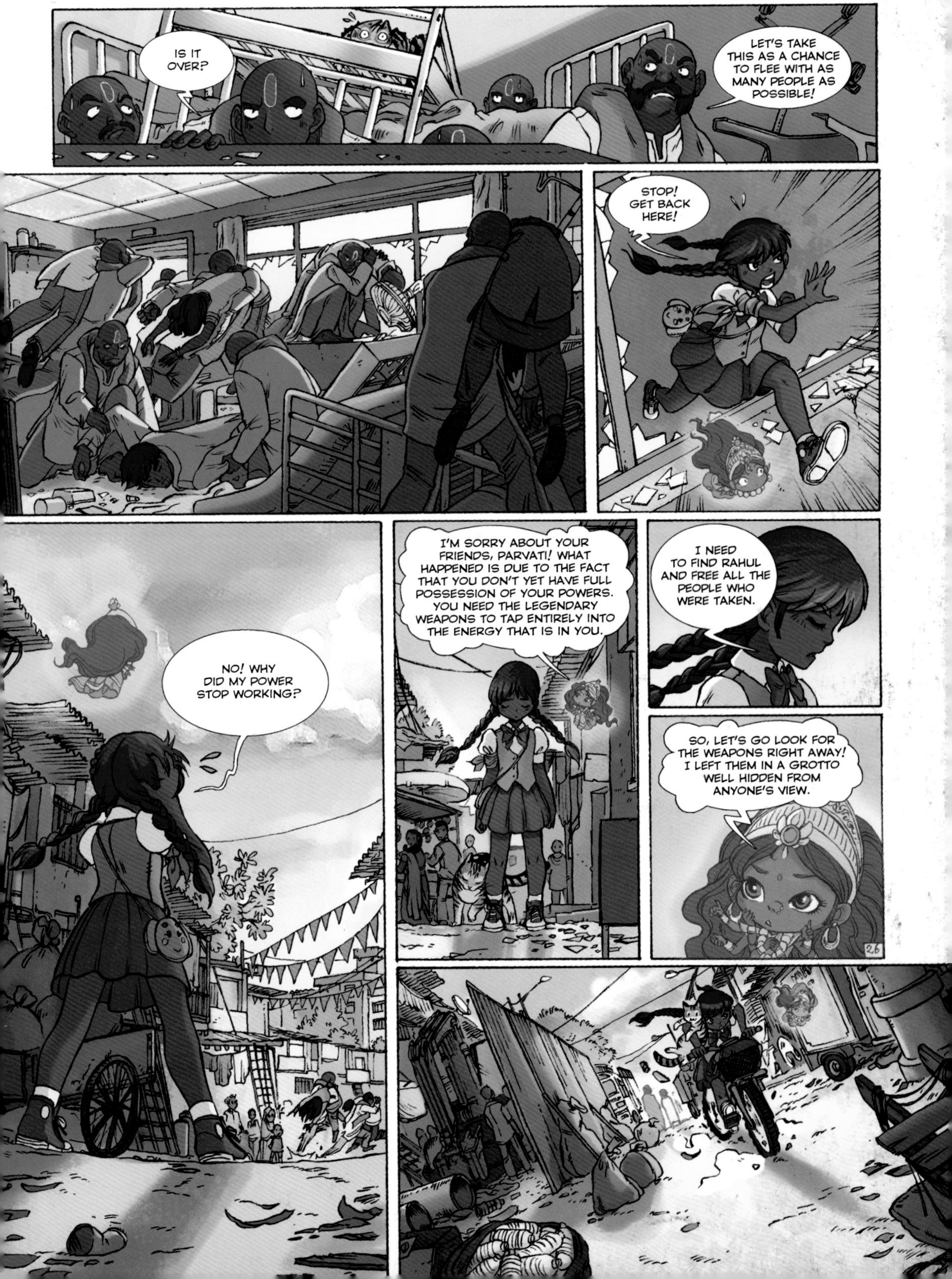
IS IT OVER?
LET'S TAKE THIS AS A CHANCE TO FLEE WITH AS MANY PEOPLE AS POSSIBLE!
STOP! GET BACK HERE!
NO! WHY DID MY POWER STOP WORKING?
I'M SORRY ABOUT YOUR FRIENDS, PARVATI! WHAT HAPPENED IS DUE TO THE FACT THAT YOU DON'T YET HAVE FULL POSSESSION OF YOUR POWERS. YOU NEED THE LEGENDARY WEAPONS TO TAP ENTIRELY INTO THE ENERGY THAT IS IN YOU.
I NEED TO FIND RAHUL AND FREE ALL THE PEOPLE WHO WERE TAKEN.
SO, LET'S GO LOOK FOR THE WEAPONS RIGHT AWAY! I LEFT THEM IN A GROTTO WELL HIDDEN FROM ANYONE'S VIEW.
26

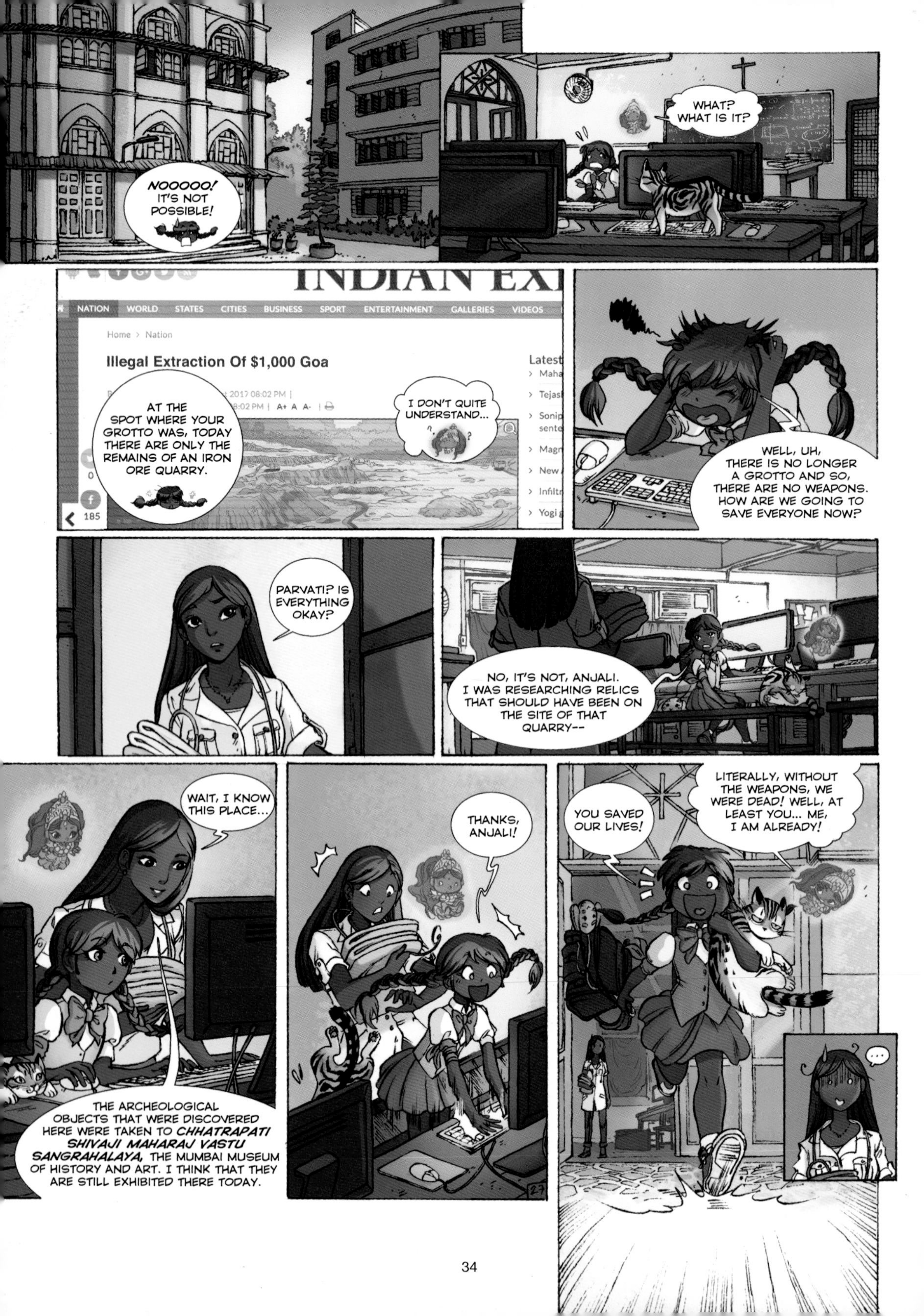
NOOOOO! IT'S NOT POSSIBLE!
WHAT? WHAT IS IT?
INDIAN EX
NATION WORLD STATES CITIES BUSINESS SPORT ENTERTAINMENT GALLERIES VIDEOS
Home > Nation
Illegal Extraction Of $1,000 Goa
AT THE SPOT WHERE YOUR GROTTO WAS, TODAY THERE ARE ONLY THE REMAINS OF AN IRON ORE QUARRY.
I DON'T QUITE UNDERSTAND...
WELL, UH, THERE IS NO LONGER A GROTTO AND SO, THERE ARE NO WEAPONS. HOW ARE WE GOING TO SAVE EVERYONE NOW?
PARVATI? IS EVERYTHING OKAY?
NO, IT'S NOT, ANJALI. I WAS RESEARCHING RELICS THAT SHOULD HAVE BEEN ON THE SITE OF THAT QUARRY--
WAIT, I KNOW THIS PLACE...
THE ARCHEOLOGICAL OBJECTS THAT WERE DISCOVERED HERE WERE TAKEN TO CHHATRAPATI SHIVAJI MAHARAJ VASTU SANGRAHALAYA, THE MUMBAI MUSEUM OF HISTORY AND ART. I THINK THAT THEY ARE STILL EXHIBITED THERE TODAY.
THANKS, ANJALI!
YOU SAVED OUR LIVES!
LITERALLY, WITHOUT THE WEAPONS, WE WERE DEAD! WELL, AT LEAST YOU... ME, I AM ALREADY!
...

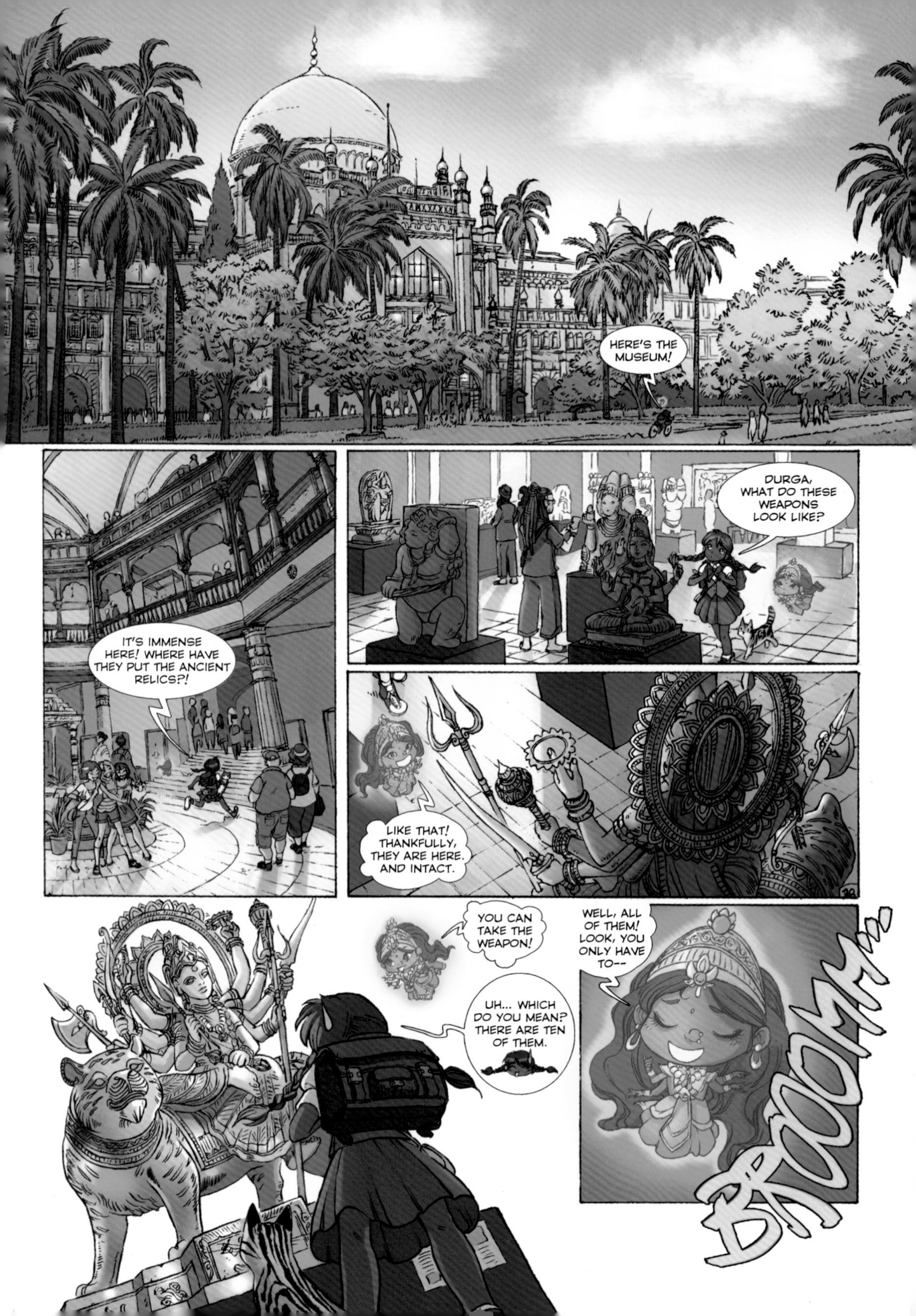
HERE'S THE MUSEUM!
IT'S IMMENSE HERE! WHERE HAVE THEY PUT THE ANCIENT RELICS?!
DURGA, WHAT DO THESE WEAPONS LOOK LIKE?
LIKE THAT! THANKFULLY, THEY ARE HERE. AND INTACT.
YOU CAN TAKE THE WEAPON!
UH... WHICH DO YOU MEAN? THERE ARE TEN OF THEM.
WELL, ALL OF THEM! LOOK, YOU ONLY HAVE TO--
BROOOM...

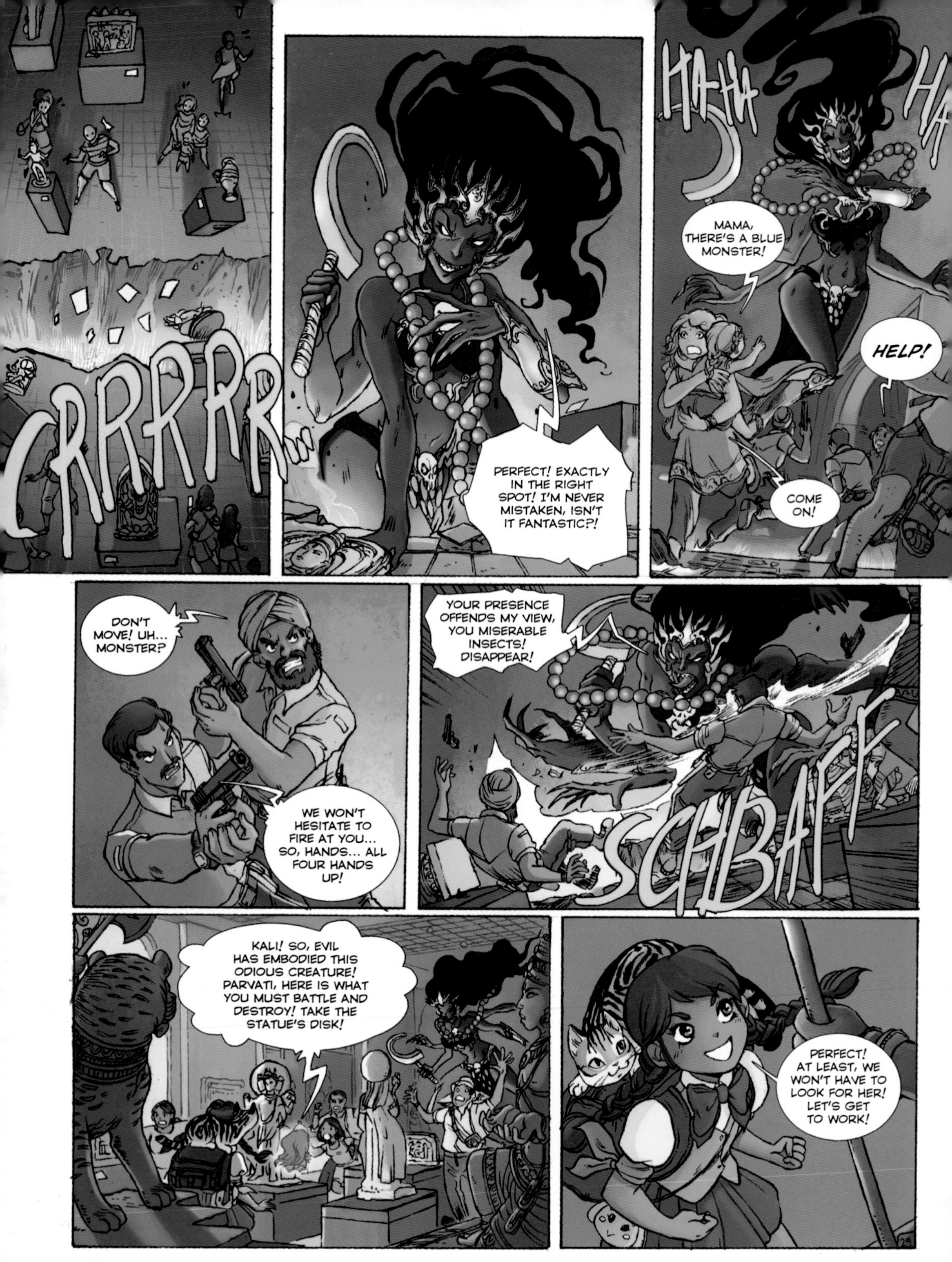
CRRRRR...
PERFECT! EXACTLY IN THE RIGHT SPOT! I'M NEVER MISTAKEN, ISN'T IT FANTASTIC?!
HAHA HA
MAMA, THERE'S A BLUE MONSTER!
HELP!
COME ON!
DON'T MOVE! UH... MONSTER?
WE WON'T HESITATE TO FIRE AT YOU... SO, HANDS... ALL FOUR HANDS UP!
YOUR PRESENCE OFFENDS MY VIEW, YOU MISERABLE INSECTS! DISAPPEAR!
SCHBAFF
KALI! SO, EVIL HAS EMBODIED THIS ODIOUS CREATURE! PARVATI, HERE IS WHAT YOU MUST BATTLE AND DESTROY! TAKE THE STATUE'S DISK!
PERFECT! AT LEAST, WE WON'T HAVE TO LOOK FOR HER! LET'S GET TO WORK!

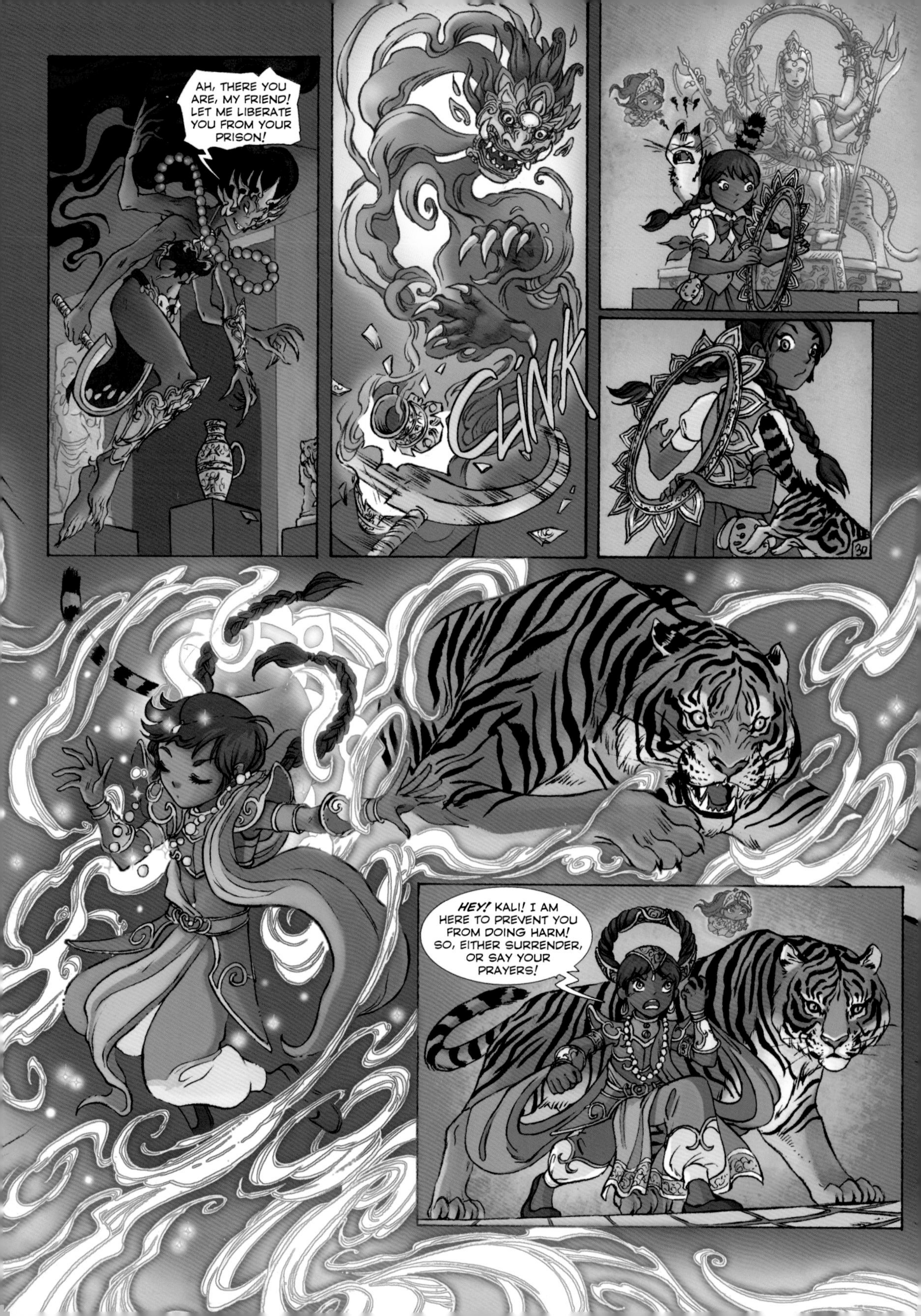

AH, THERE YOU ARE, MY FRIEND! LET ME LIBERATE YOU FROM YOUR PRISON!
CLINK
HEY! KALI! I AM HERE TO PREVENT YOU FROM DOING HARM! SO, EITHER SURRENDER, OR SAY YOUR PRAYERS!

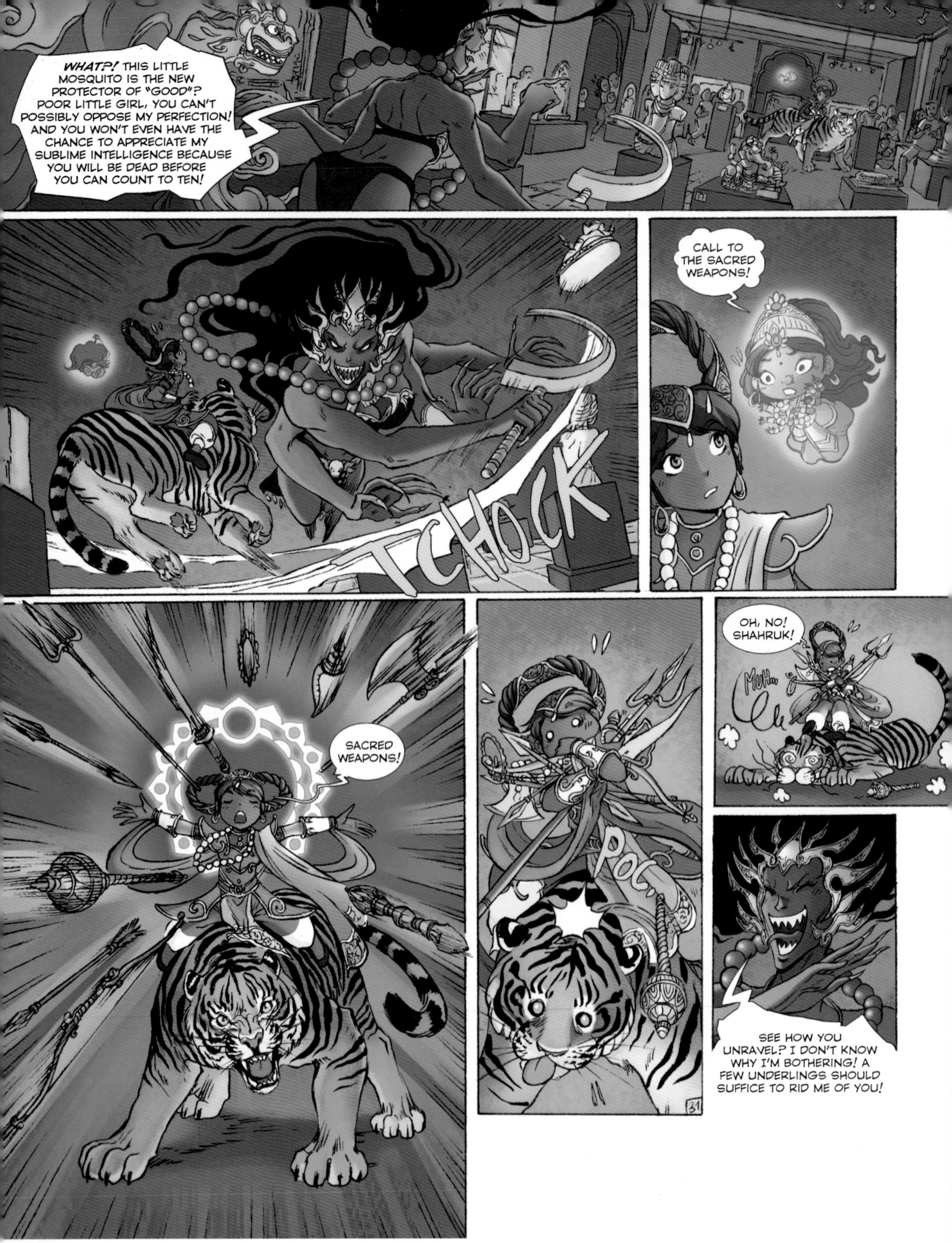
WHAT?! THIS LITTLE MOSQUITO IS THE NEW PROTECTOR OF "GOOD"? POOR LITTLE GIRL, YOU CAN'T POSSIBLY OPPOSE MY PERFECTION! AND YOU WON'T EVEN HAVE THE CHANCE TO APPRECIATE MY SUBLIME INTELLIGENCE BECAUSE YOU WILL BE DEAD BEFORE YOU CAN COUNT TO TEN!
TCHOCK
CALL TO THE SACRED WEAPONS!
SACRED WEAPONS!
POC
OH, NO! SHAHRUK!
MUH...
SEE HOW YOU UNRAVEL? I DON'T KNOW WHY I'M BOTHERING! A FEW UNDERLINGS SHOULD SUFFICE TO RID ME OF YOU!
31

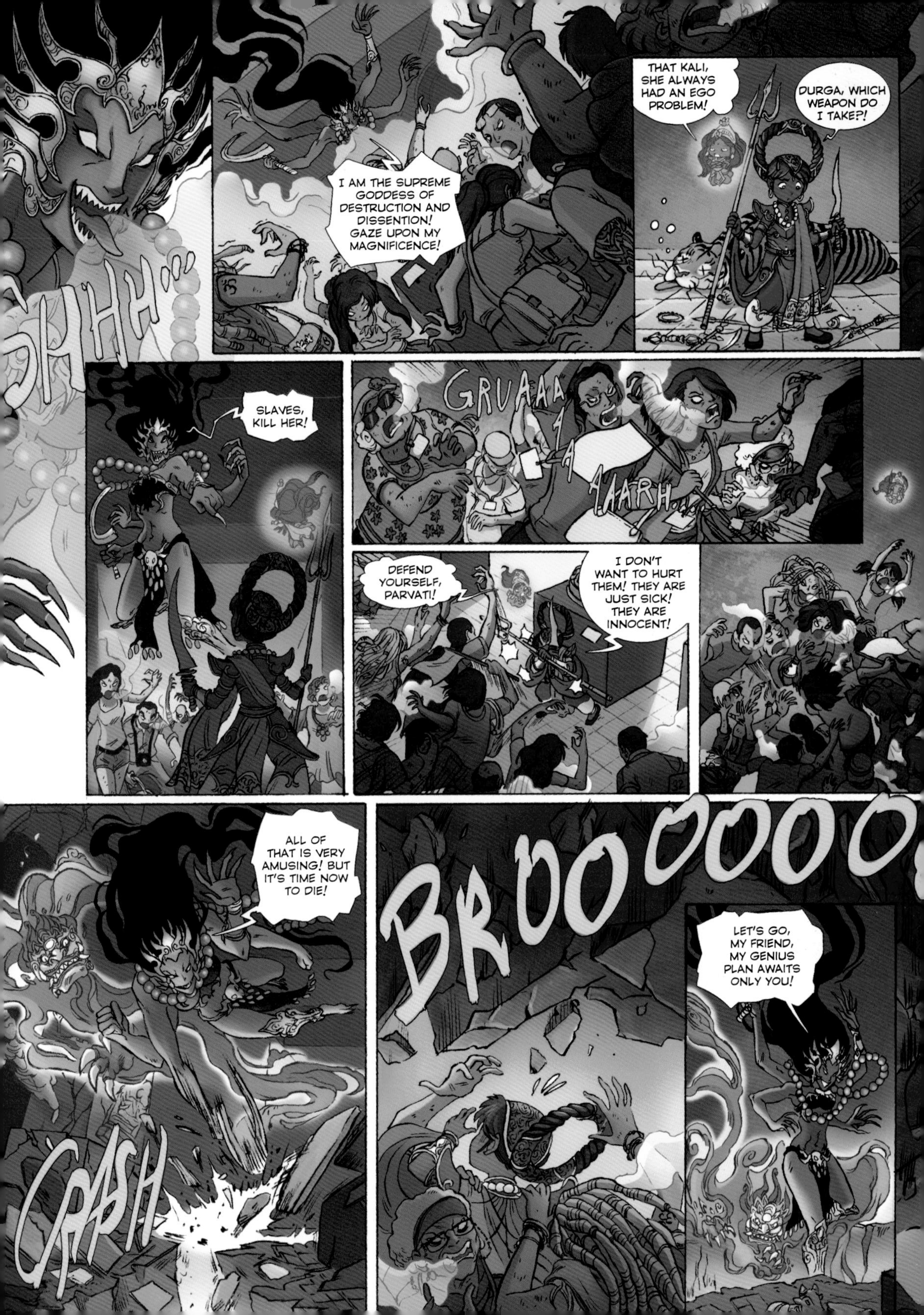
SHHH...
I AM THE SUPREME GODDESS OF DESTRUCTION AND DISSENTION! GAZE UPON MY MAGNIFICENCE!
THAT KALI, SHE ALWAYS HAD AN EGO PROBLEM!
DURGA, WHICH WEAPON DO I TAKE?!
SLAVES, KILL HER!
GRUAAAAAAAARH...
DEFEND YOURSELF, PARVATI!
I DON'T WANT TO HURT THEM! THEY ARE JUST SICK! THEY ARE INNOCENT!
ALL OF THAT IS VERY AMUSING! BUT IT'S TIME NOW TO DIE!
CRASH
BROOOOOOO
LET'S GO, MY FRIEND, MY GENIUS PLAN AWAITS ONLY YOU!

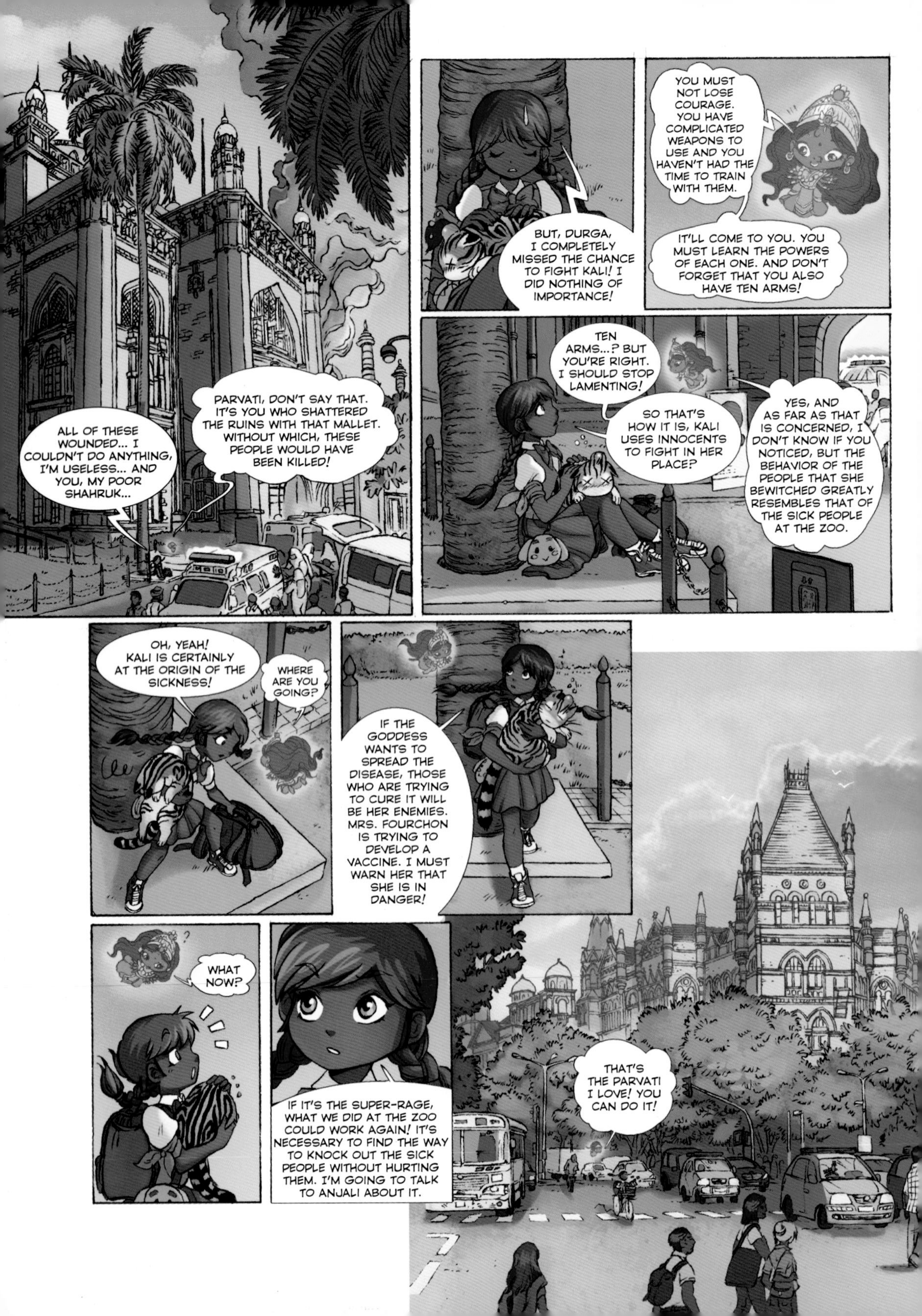
ALL OF THESE WOUNDED... I COULDN'T DO ANYTHING, I'M USELESS... AND YOU, MY POOR SHAHRUK...
PARVATI, DON'T SAY THAT. IT'S YOU WHO SHATTERED THE RUINS WITH THAT MALLET. WITHOUT WHICH, THESE PEOPLE WOULD HAVE BEEN KILLED!
BUT, DURGA, I COMPLETELY MISSED THE CHANCE TO FIGHT KALI! I DID NOTHING OF IMPORTANCE!
YOU MUST NOT LOSE COURAGE. YOU HAVE COMPLICATED WEAPONS TO USE AND YOU HAVEN'T HAD THE TIME TO TRAIN WITH THEM.
IT'LL COME TO YOU. YOU MUST LEARN THE POWERS OF EACH ONE. AND DON'T FORGET THAT YOU ALSO HAVE TEN ARMS!
TEN ARMS...? BUT YOU'RE RIGHT. I SHOULD STOP LAMENTING!
SO THAT'S HOW IT IS, KALI USES INNOCENTS TO FIGHT IN HER PLACE?
YES, AND AS FAR AS THAT IS CONCERNED, I DON'T KNOW IF YOU NOTICED, BUT THE BEHAVIOR OF THE PEOPLE THAT SHE BEWITCHED GREATLY RESEMBLES THAT OF THE SICK PEOPLE AT THE ZOO.
OH, YEAH! KALI IS CERTAINLY AT THE ORIGIN OF THE SICKNESS!
WHERE ARE YOU GOING?
IF THE GODDESS WANTS TO SPREAD THE DISEASE, THOSE WHO ARE TRYING TO CURE IT WILL BE HER ENEMIES. MRS. FOURCHON IS TRYING TO DEVELOP A VACCINE. I MUST WARN HER THAT SHE IS IN DANGER!
WHAT NOW?
IF IT'S THE SUPER-RAGE, WHAT WE DID AT THE ZOO COULD WORK AGAIN! IT'S NECESSARY TO FIND THE WAY TO KNOCK OUT THE SICK PEOPLE WITHOUT HURTING THEM. I'M GOING TO TALK TO ANJALI ABOUT IT.
THAT'S THE PARVATI I LOVE! YOU CAN DO IT!

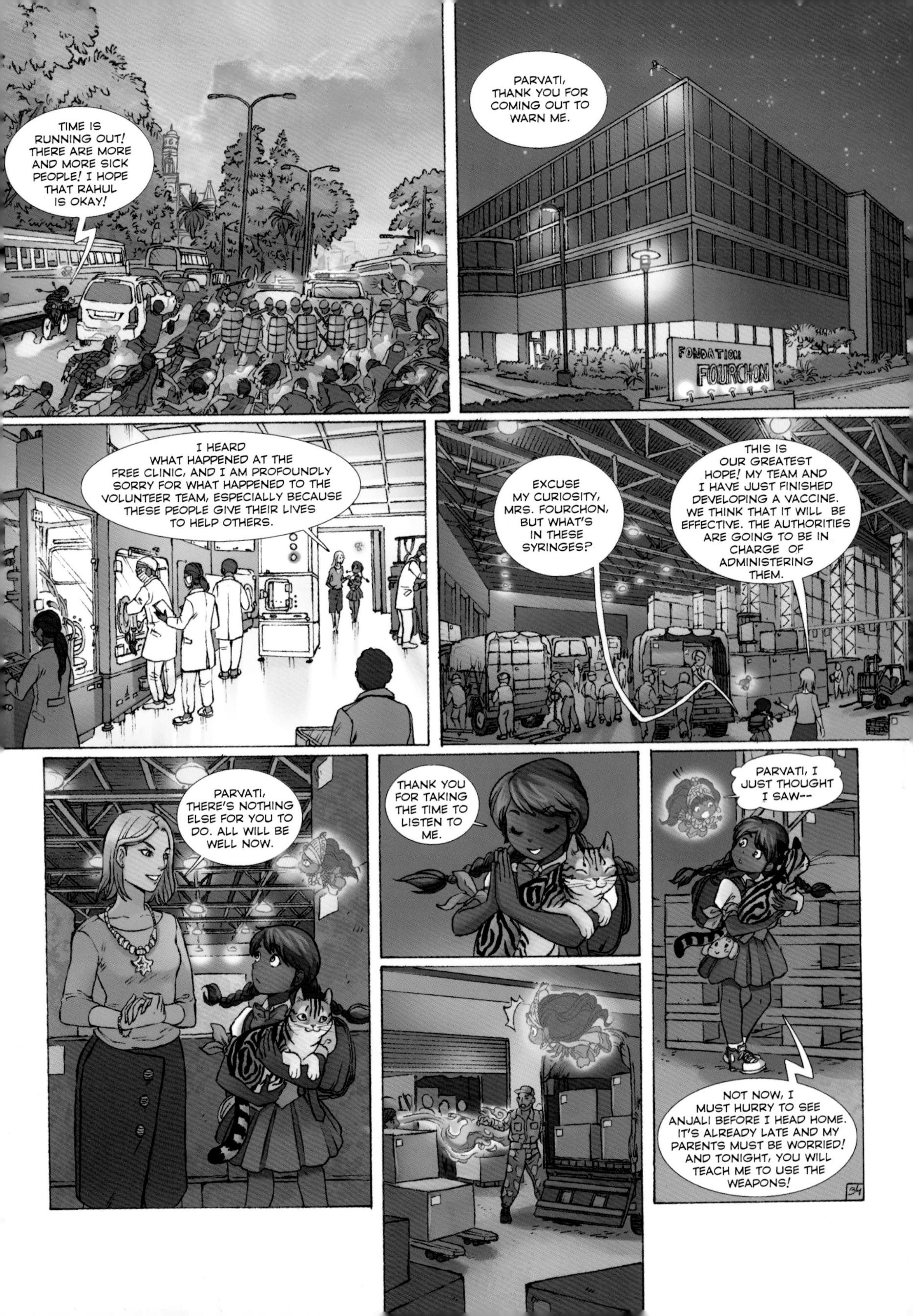

TIME IS RUNNING OUT! THERE ARE MORE AND MORE SICK PEOPLE! I HOPE THAT RAHUL IS OKAY!
PARVATI, THANK YOU FOR COMING OUT TO WARN ME.
FONDATION FOURCHON
I HEARD WHAT HAPPENED AT THE FREE CLINIC, AND I AM PROFOUNDLY SORRY FOR WHAT HAPPENED TO THE VOLUNTEER TEAM, ESPECIALLY BECAUSE THESE PEOPLE GIVE THEIR LIVES TO HELP OTHERS.
EXCUSE MY CURIOSITY, MRS. FOURCHON, BUT WHAT'S IN THESE SYRINGES?
THIS IS OUR GREATEST HOPE! MY TEAM AND I HAVE JUST FINISHED DEVELOPING A VACCINE. WE THINK THAT IT WILL BE EFFECTIVE. THE AUTHORITIES ARE GOING TO BE IN CHARGE OF ADMINISTERING THEM.
PARVATI, THERE'S NOTHING ELSE FOR YOU TO DO. ALL WILL BE WELL NOW.
THANK YOU FOR TAKING THE TIME TO LISTEN TO ME.
PARVATI, I JUST THOUGHT I SAW--
NOT NOW, I MUST HURRY TO SEE ANJALI BEFORE I HEAD HOME. IT'S ALREADY LATE AND MY PARENTS MUST BE WORRIED! AND TONIGHT, YOU WILL TEACH ME TO USE THE WEAPONS!
34

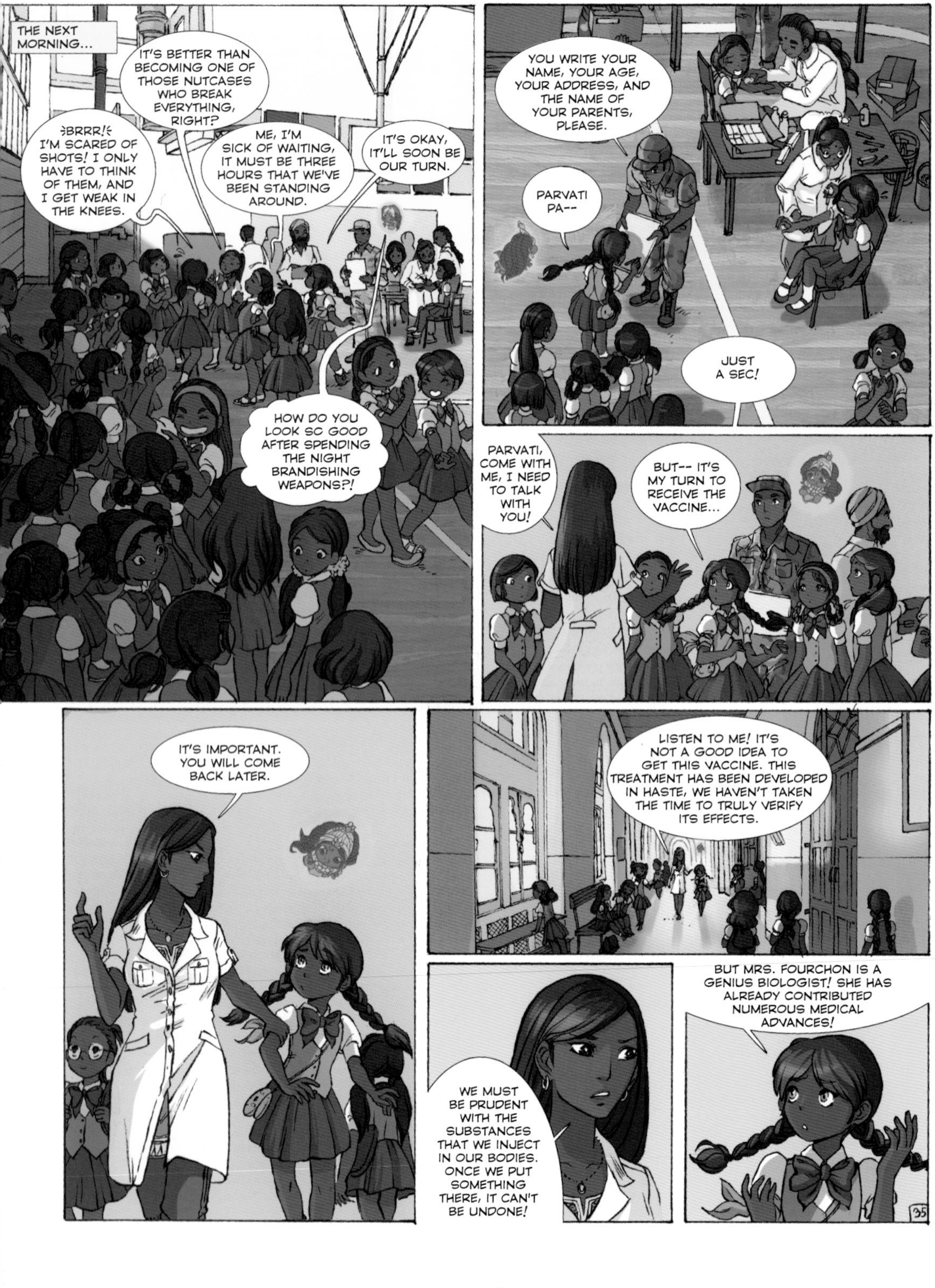
THE NEXT MORNING...
IT'S BETTER THAN BECOMING ONE OF THOSE NUTCASES WHO BREAK EVERYTHING, RIGHT?
BRRR! I'M SCARED OF SHOTS! I ONLY HAVE TO THINK OF THEM, AND I GET WEAK IN THE KNEES.
ME, I'M SICK OF WAITING, IT MUST BE THREE HOURS THAT WE'VE BEEN STANDING AROUND.
IT'S OKAY, IT'LL SOON BE OUR TURN.
HOW DO YOU LOOK SC GOOD AFTER SPENDING THE NIGHT BRANDISHING WEAPONS?!
YOU WRITE YOUR NAME, YOUR AGE, YOUR ADDRESS, AND THE NAME OF YOUR PARENTS, PLEASE.
PARVATI PA--
JUST A SEC!
PARVATI, COME WITH ME, I NEED TO TALK WITH YOU!
BUT-- IT'S MY TURN TO RECEIVE THE VACCINE...
IT'S IMPORTANT. YOU WILL COME BACK LATER.
LISTEN TO ME! IT'S NOT A GOOD IDEA TO GET THIS VACCINE. THIS TREATMENT HAS BEEN DEVELOPED IN HASTE, WE HAVEN'T TAKEN THE TIME TO TRULY VERIFY ITS EFFECTS.
WE MUST BE PRUDENT WITH THE SUBSTANCES THAT WE INJECT IN OUR BODIES. ONCE WE PUT SOMETHING THERE, IT CAN'T BE UNDONE!
BUT MRS. FOURCHON IS A GENIUS BIOLOGIST! SHE HAS ALREADY CONTRIBUTED NUMEROUS MEDICAL ADVANCES!
35

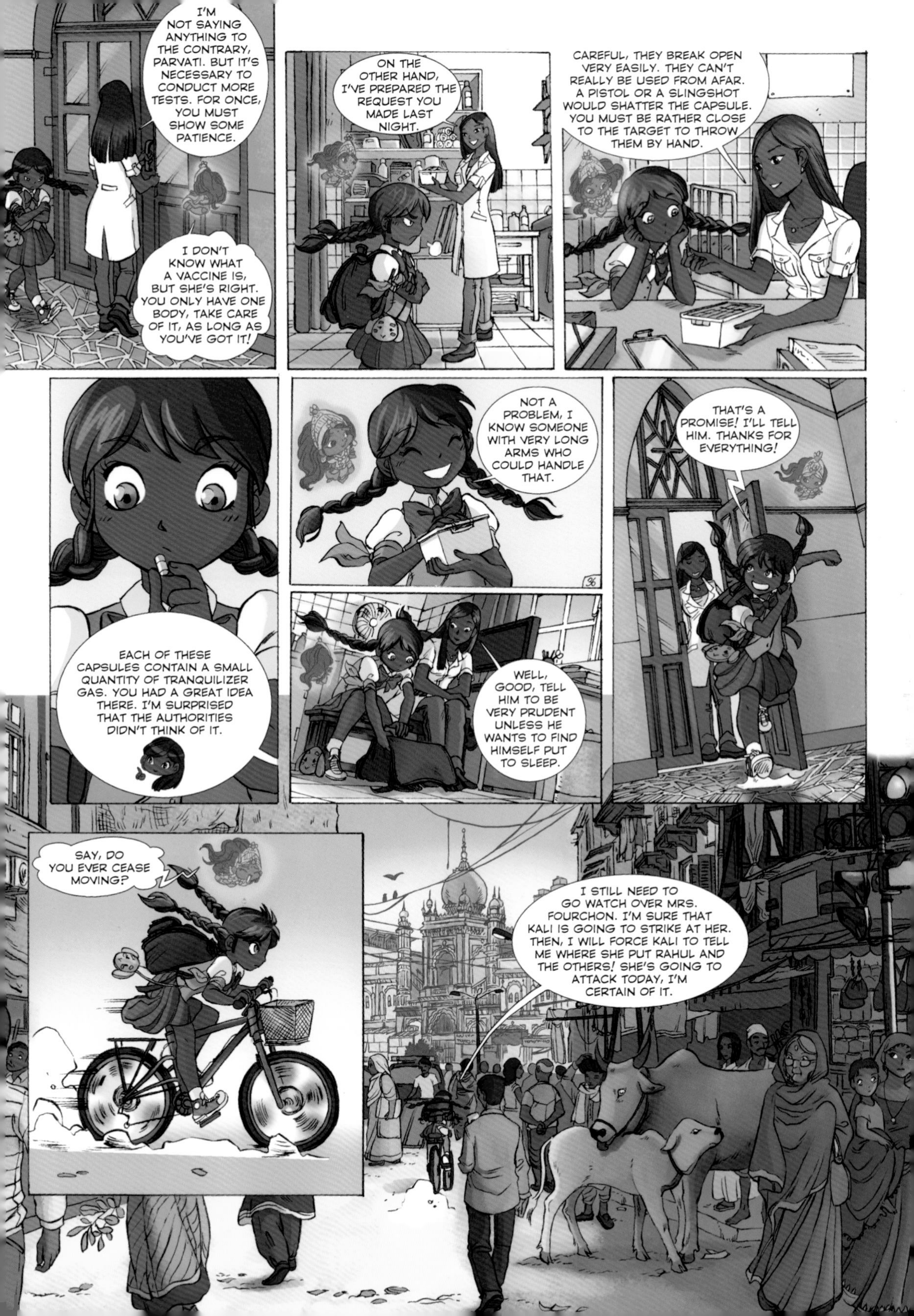
I'M NOT SAYING ANYTHING TO THE CONTRARY, PARVATI. BUT IT'S NECESSARY TO CONDUCT MORE TESTS. FOR ONCE, YOU MUST SHOW SOME PATIENCE.
I DON'T KNOW WHAT A VACCINE IS, BUT SHE'S RIGHT. YOU ONLY HAVE ONE BODY, TAKE CARE OF IT, AS LONG AS YOU'VE GOT IT!
ON THE OTHER HAND, I'VE PREPARED THE REQUEST YOU MADE LAST NIGHT.
CAREFUL, THEY BREAK OPEN VERY EASILY. THEY CAN'T REALLY BE USED FROM AFAR. A PISTOL OR A SLINGSHOT WOULD SHATTER THE CAPSULE. YOU MUST BE RATHER CLOSE TO THE TARGET TO THROW THEM BY HAND.
EACH OF THESE CAPSULES CONTAIN A SMALL QUANTITY OF TRANQUILIZER GAS. YOU HAD A GREAT IDEA THERE. I'M SURPRISED THAT THE AUTHORITIES DIDN'T THINK OF IT.
NOT A PROBLEM, I KNOW SOMEONE WITH VERY LONG ARMS WHO COULD HANDLE THAT.
WELL, GOOD, TELL HIM TO BE VERY PRUDENT UNLESS HE WANTS TO FIND HIMSELF PUT TO SLEEP.
THAT'S A PROMISE! I'LL TELL HIM. THANKS FOR EVERYTHING!
SAY, DO YOU EVER CEASE MOVING?
I STILL NEED TO GO WATCH OVER MRS. FOURCHON. I'M SURE THAT KALI IS GOING TO STRIKE AT HER. THEN, I WILL FORCE KALI TO TELL ME WHERE SHE PUT RAHUL AND THE OTHERS! SHE'S GOING TO ATTACK TODAY, I'M CERTAIN OF IT.

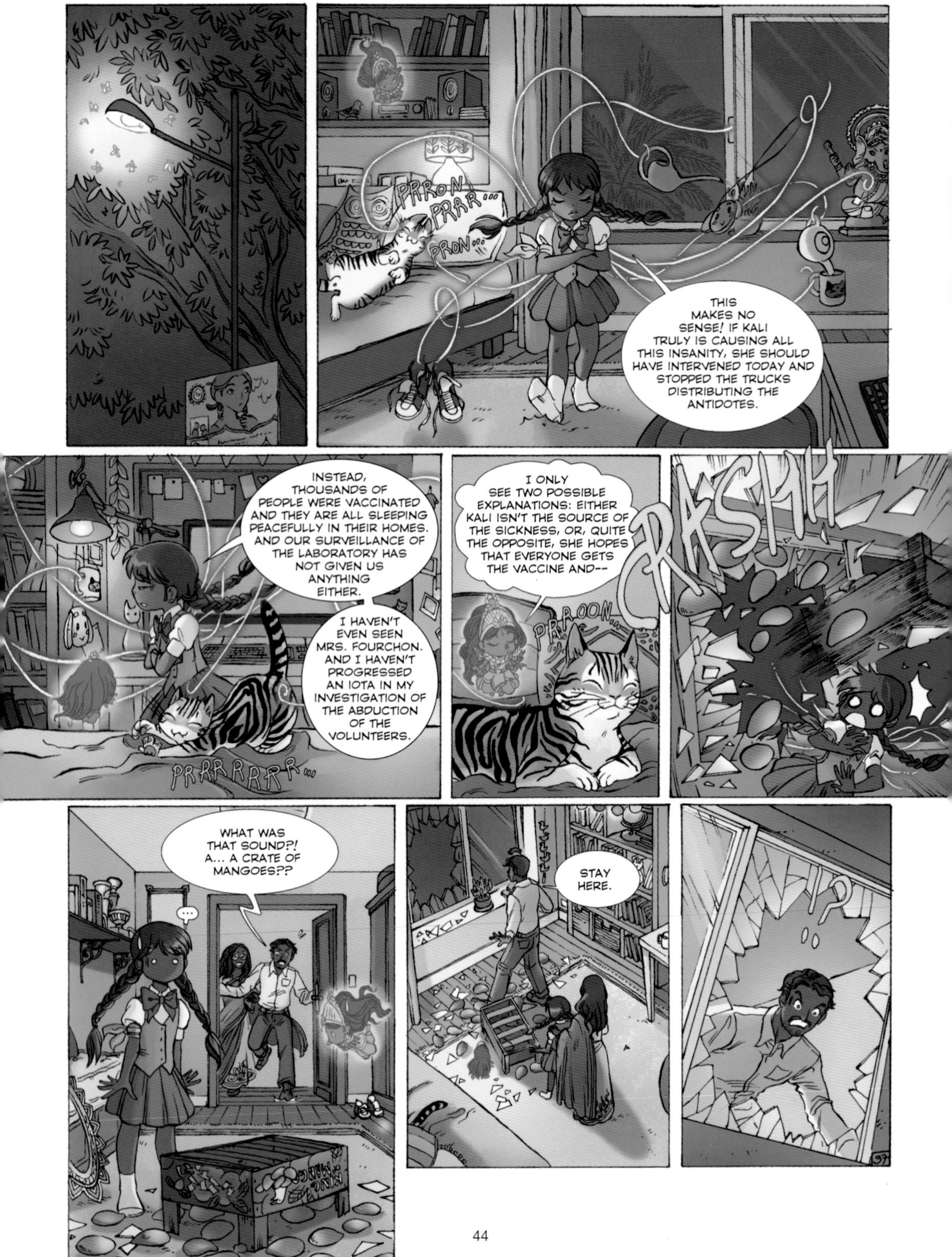
PRRON PRAR... PRON...
THIS MAKES NO SENSE! IF KALI TRULY IS CAUSING ALL THIS INSANITY, SHE SHOULD HAVE INTERVENED TODAY AND STOPPED THE TRUCKS DISTRIBUTING THE ANTIDOTES.
INSTEAD, THOUSANDS OF PEOPLE WERE VACCINATED AND THEY ARE ALL SLEEPING PEACEFULLY IN THEIR HOMES. AND OUR SURVEILLANCE OF THE LABORATORY HAS NOT GIVEN US ANYTHING EITHER.
I HAVEN'T EVEN SEEN MRS. FOURCHON. AND I HAVEN'T PROGRESSED AN IOTA IN MY INVESTIGATION OF THE ABDUCTION OF THE VOLUNTEERS.
PRRRRRRR...
I ONLY SEE TWO POSSIBLE EXPLANATIONS: EITHER KALI ISN'T THE SOURCE OF THE SICKNESS, OR, QUITE THE OPPOSITE, SHE HOPES THAT EVERYONE GETS THE VACCINE AND--
PRROON...
CRASHH
WHAT WAS THAT SOUND?! A... A CRATE OF MANGOES??
...
STAY HERE.
!?

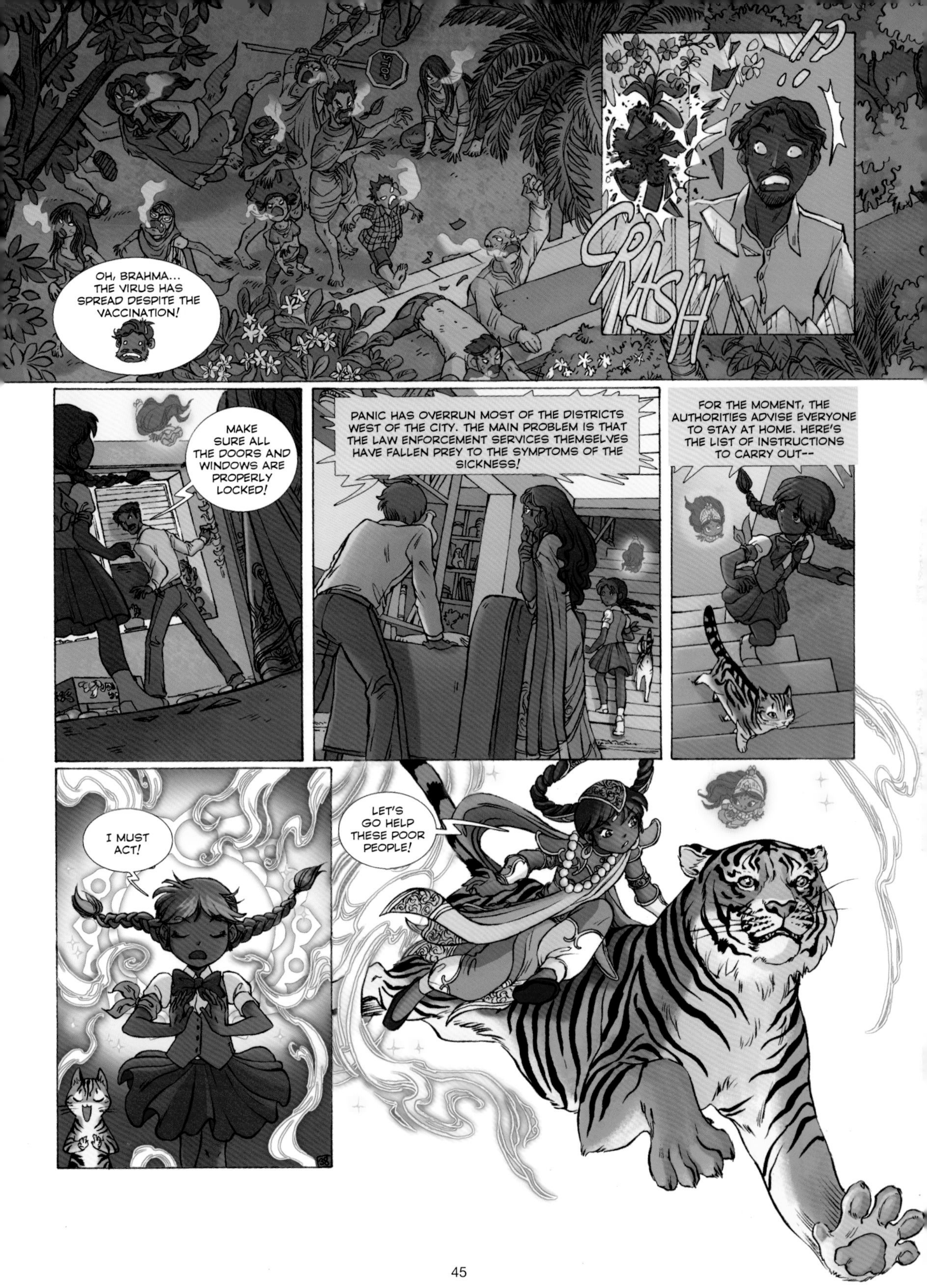
OH, BRAHMA... THE VIRUS HAS SPREAD DESPITE THE VACCINATION!
STOP
!?
CRASH
MAKE SURE ALL THE DOORS AND WINDOWS ARE PROPERLY LOCKED!
PANIC HAS OVERRUN MOST OF THE DISTRICTS WEST OF THE CITY. THE MAIN PROBLEM IS THAT THE LAW ENFORCEMENT SERVICES THEMSELVES HAVE FALLEN PREY TO THE SYMPTOMS OF THE SICKNESS!
FOR THE MOMENT, THE AUTHORITIES ADVISE EVERYONE TO STAY AT HOME. HERE'S THE LIST OF INSTRUCTIONS TO CARRY OUT--
I MUST ACT!
LET'S GO HELP THESE POOR PEOPLE!

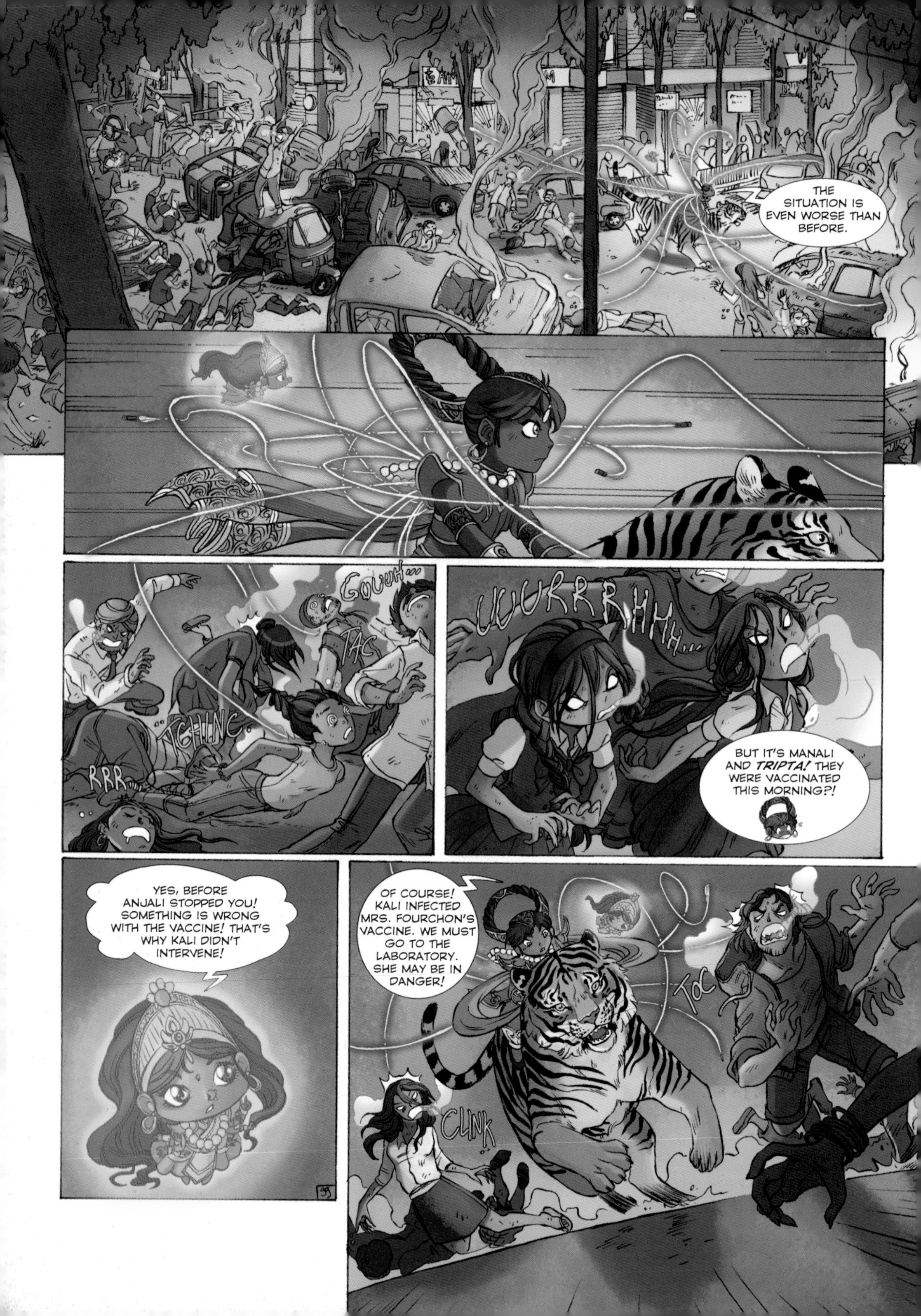
THE SITUATION IS EVEN WORSE THAN BEFORE.
GOUUH...
TAC
TCHING
RRR...
UUURRRRHHH...
BUT IT'S MANALI AND TRIPTA! THEY WERE VACCINATED THIS MORNING?!
YES, BEFORE ANJALI STOPPED YOU! SOMETHING IS WRONG WITH THE VACCINE! THAT'S WHY KALI DIDN'T INTERVENE!
OF COURSE! KALI INFECTED MRS. FOURCHON'S VACCINE. WE MUST GO TO THE LABORATORY. SHE MAY BE IN DANGER!
TOC
CLINK

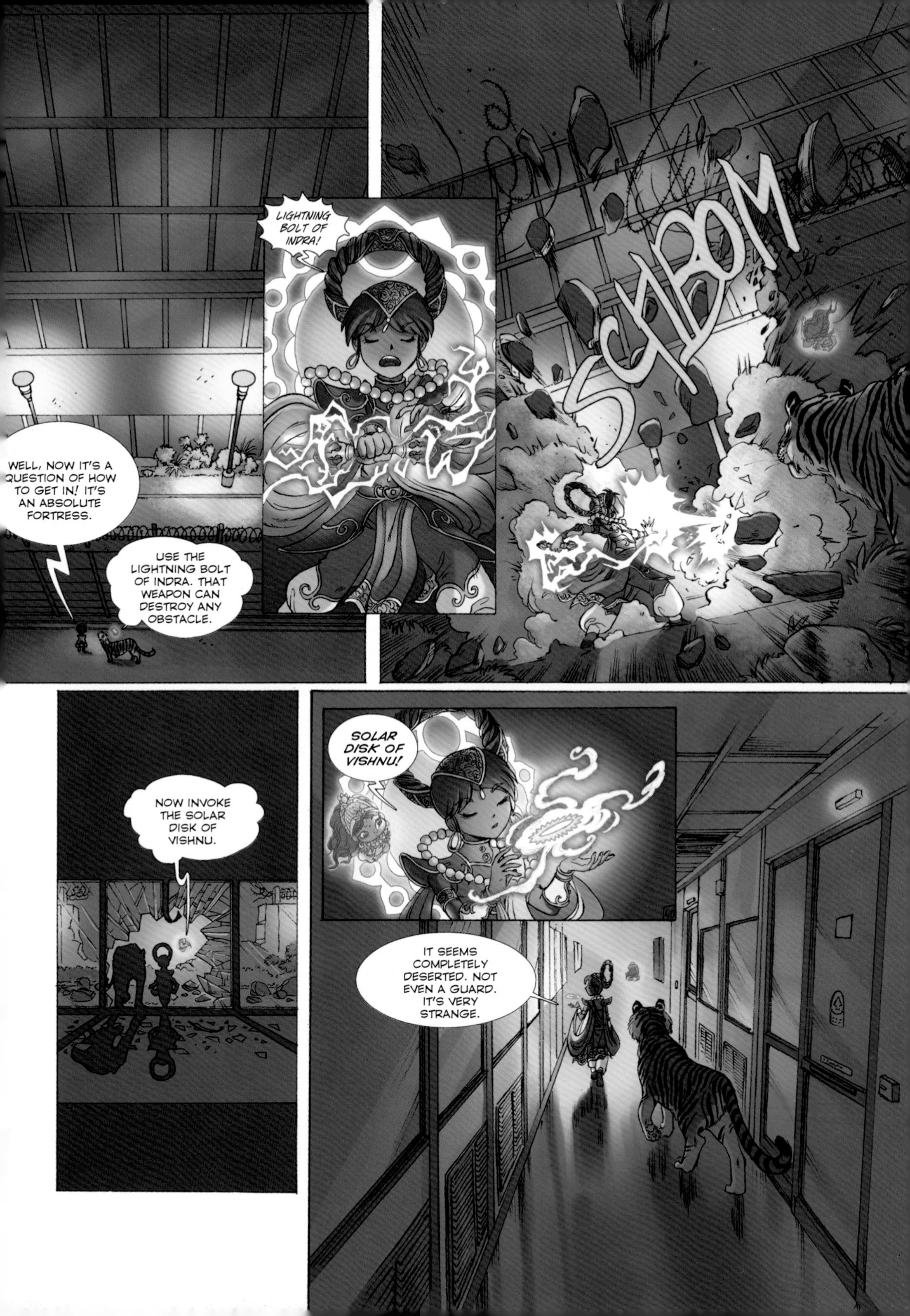
WELL, NOW IT'S A QUESTION OF HOW TO GET IN! IT'S AN ABSOLUTE FORTRESS.
USE THE LIGHTNING BOLT OF INDRA. THAT WEAPON CAN DESTROY ANY OBSTACLE.
LIGHTNING BOLT OF INDRA!
SCHBOOM!
NOW INVOKE THE SOLAR DISK OF VISHNU.
SOLAR DISK OF VISHNU!
IT SEEMS COMPLETELY DESERTED. NOT EVEN A GUARD. IT'S VERY STRANGE.

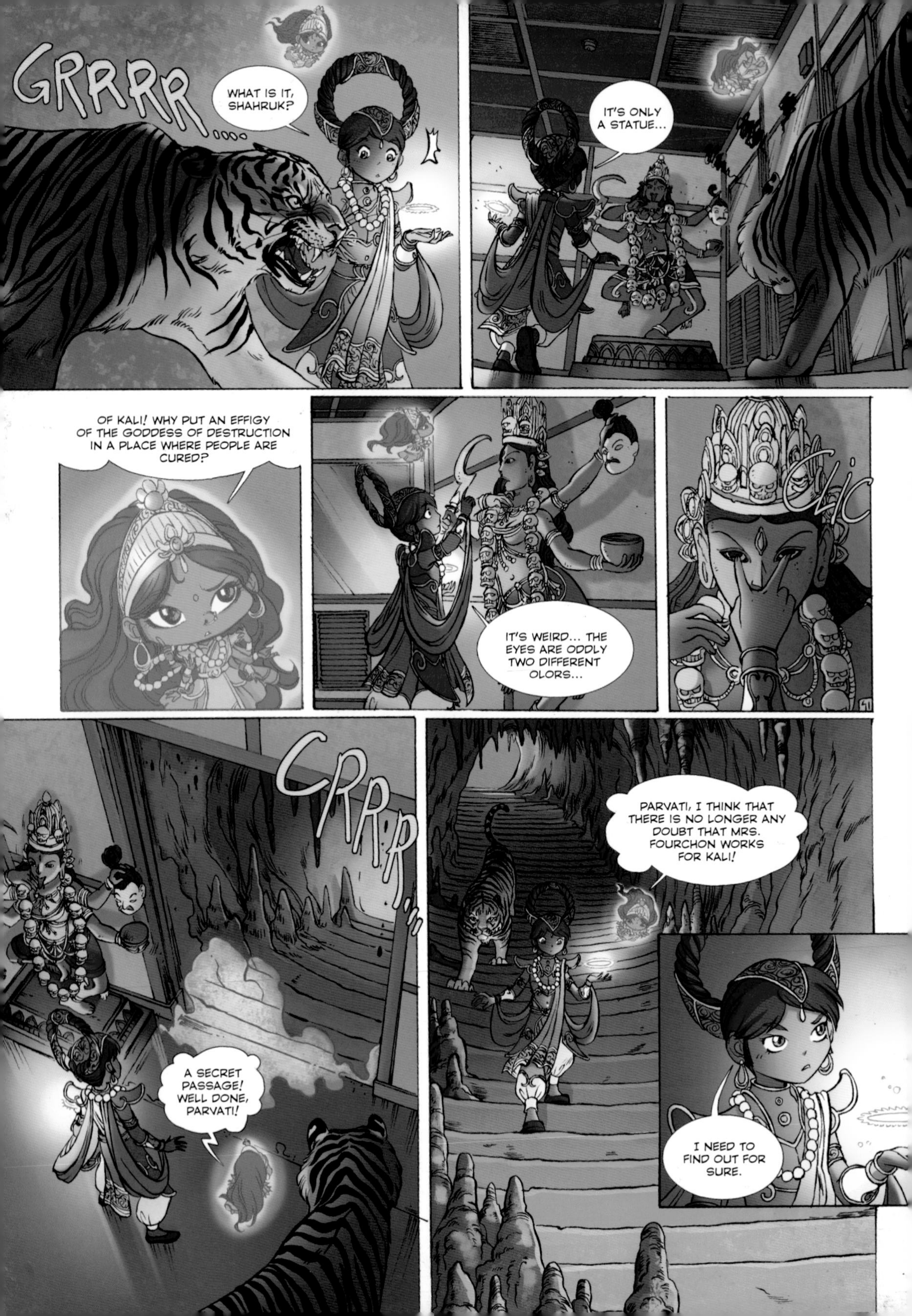
GRRRR...
WHAT IS IT, SHAHRUK?
!
IT'S ONLY A STATUE...
OF KALI! WHY PUT AN EFFIGY OF THE GODDESS OF DESTRUCTION IN A PLACE WHERE PEOPLE ARE CURED?
IT'S WEIRD... THE EYES ARE ODDLY TWO DIFFERENT OLORS...
CLIC
CRRR...
A SECRET PASSAGE! WELL DONE, PARVATI!
PARVATI, I THINK THAT THERE IS NO LONGER ANY DOUBT THAT MRS. FOURCHON WORKS FOR KALI!
I NEED TO FIND OUT FOR SURE.

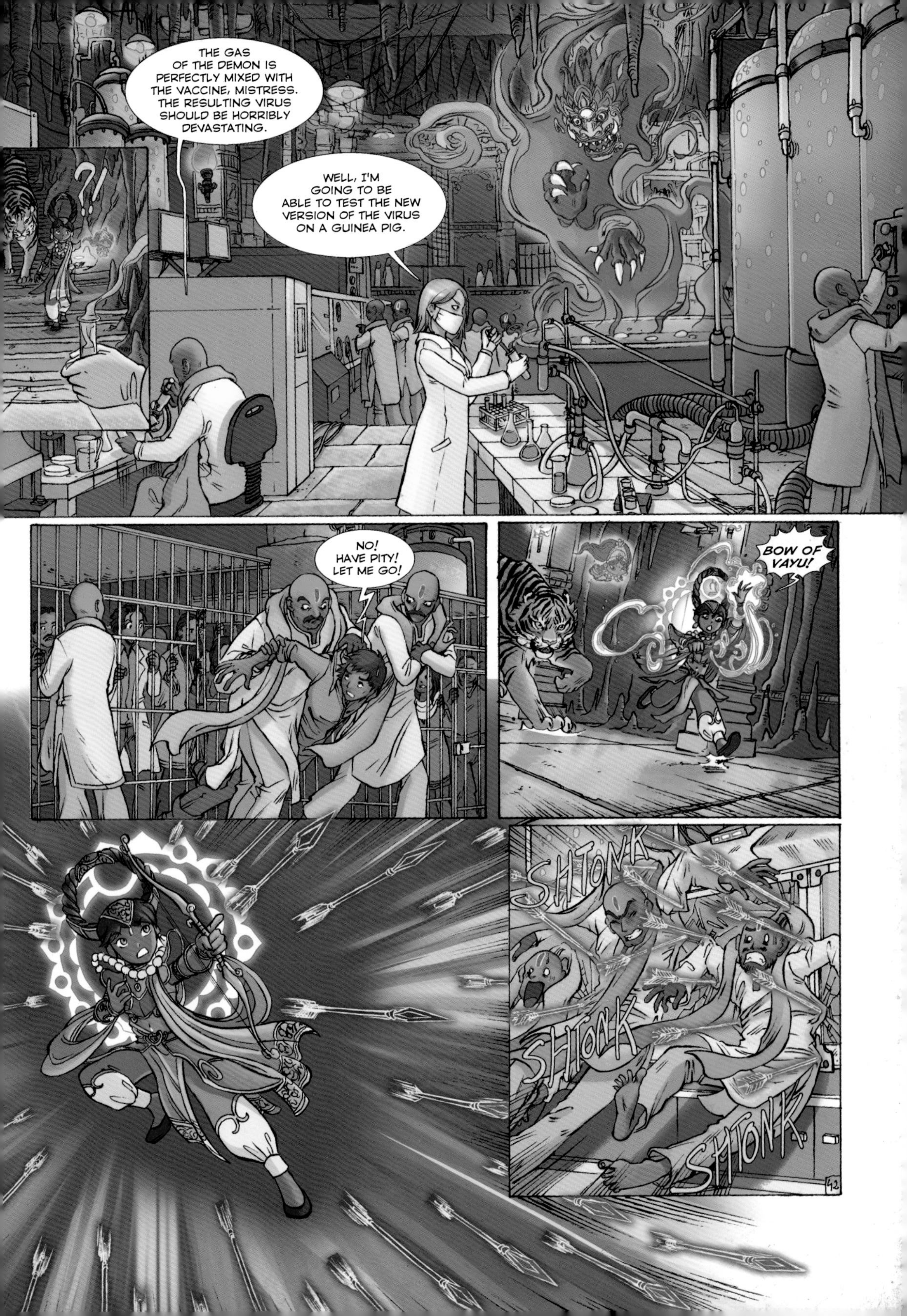
THE GAS OF THE DEMON IS PERFECTLY MIXED WITH THE VACCINE, MISTRESS. THE RESULTING VIRUS SHOULD BE HORRIBLY DEVASTATING.
?!
WELL, I'M GOING TO BE ABLE TO TEST THE NEW VERSION OF THE VIRUS ON A GUINEA PIG.
NO! HAVE PITY! LET ME GO!
BOW OF VAYU!
SHTONK
SHTONK
SHTONK
42

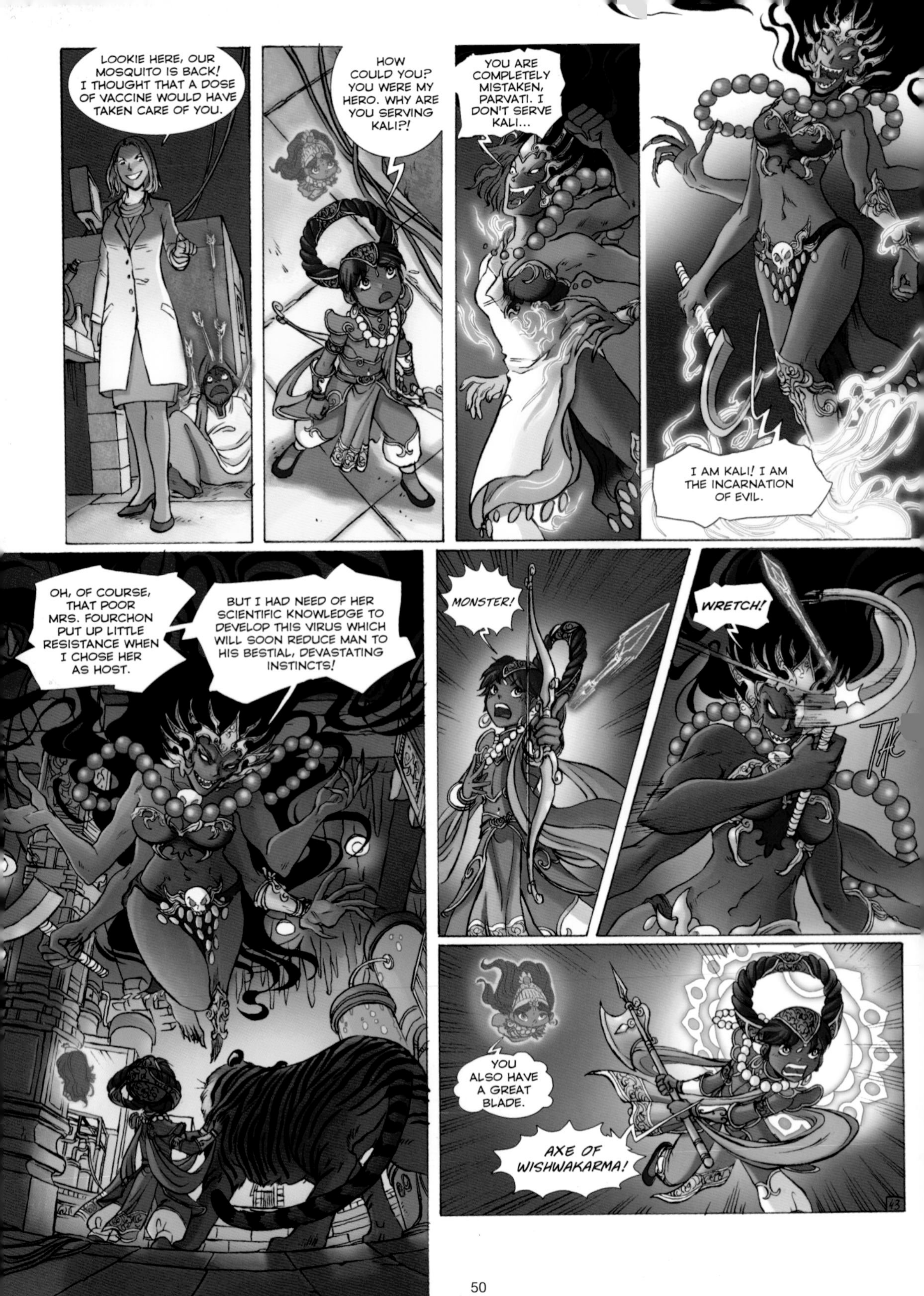

LOOKIE HERE, OUR MOSQUITO IS BACK! I THOUGHT THAT A DOSE OF VACCINE WOULD HAVE TAKEN CARE OF YOU.
HOW COULD YOU? YOU WERE MY HERO. WHY ARE YOU SERVING KALI?!
YOU ARE COMPLETELY MISTAKEN, PARVATI. I DON'T SERVE KALI...
I AM KALI! I AM THE INCARNATION OF EVIL.
OH, OF COURSE, THAT POOR MRS. FOURCHON PUT UP LITTLE RESISTANCE WHEN I CHOSE HER AS HOST.
BUT I HAD NEED OF HER SCIENTIFIC KNOWLEDGE TO DEVELOP THIS VIRUS WHICH WILL SOON REDUCE MAN TO HIS BESTIAL, DEVASTATING INSTINCTS!
MONSTER!
WRETCH!
YOU ALSO HAVE A GREAT BLADE.
AXE OF WISHWAKARMA!
43

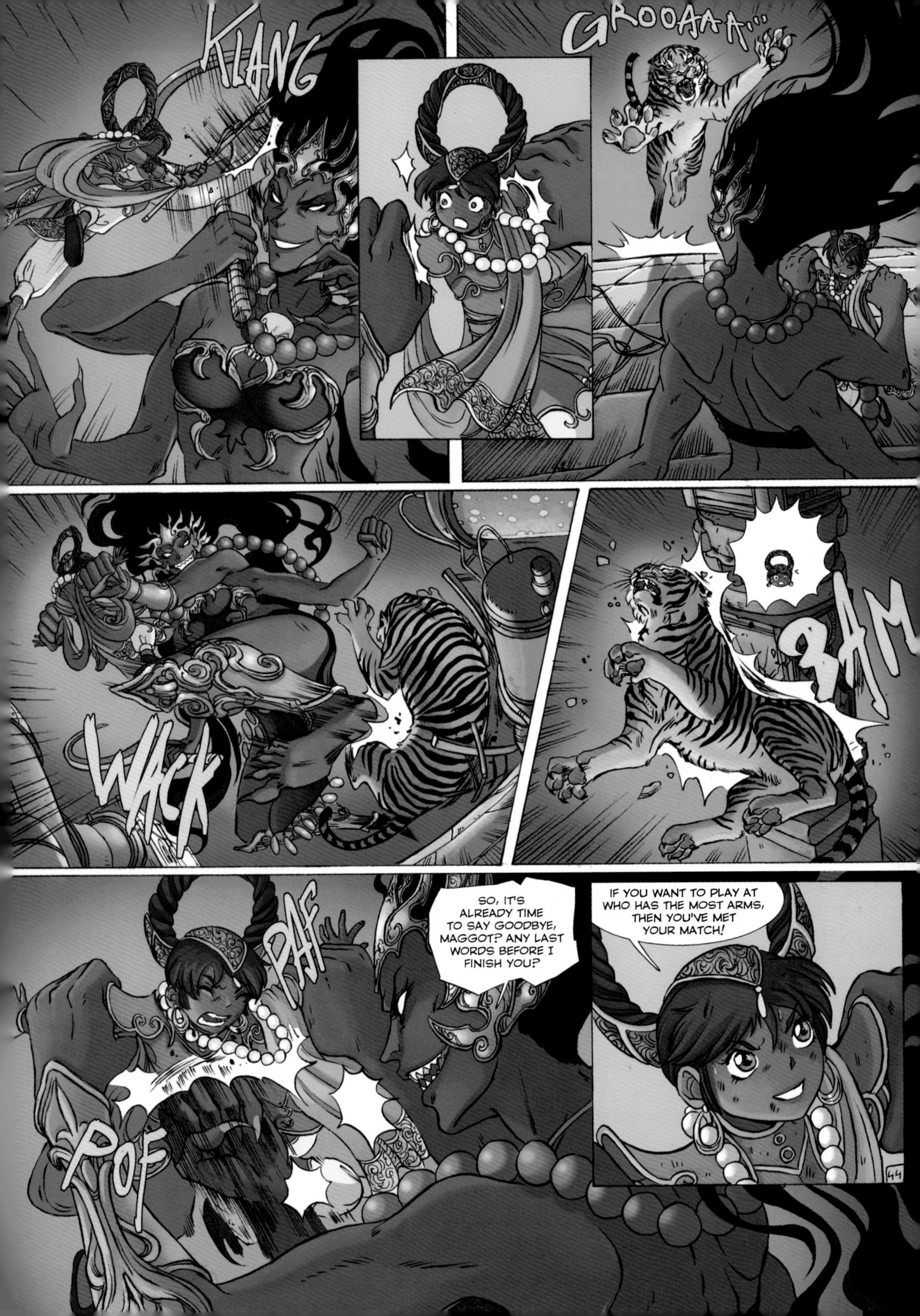
KLANG
GROOAAA...
WACK
BAM
PAF
POF
SO, IT'S ALREADY TIME TO SAY GOODBYE, MAGGOT? ANY LAST WORDS BEFORE I FINISH YOU?
IF YOU WANT TO PLAY AT WHO HAS THE MOST ARMS, THEN YOU'VE MET YOUR MATCH!
44

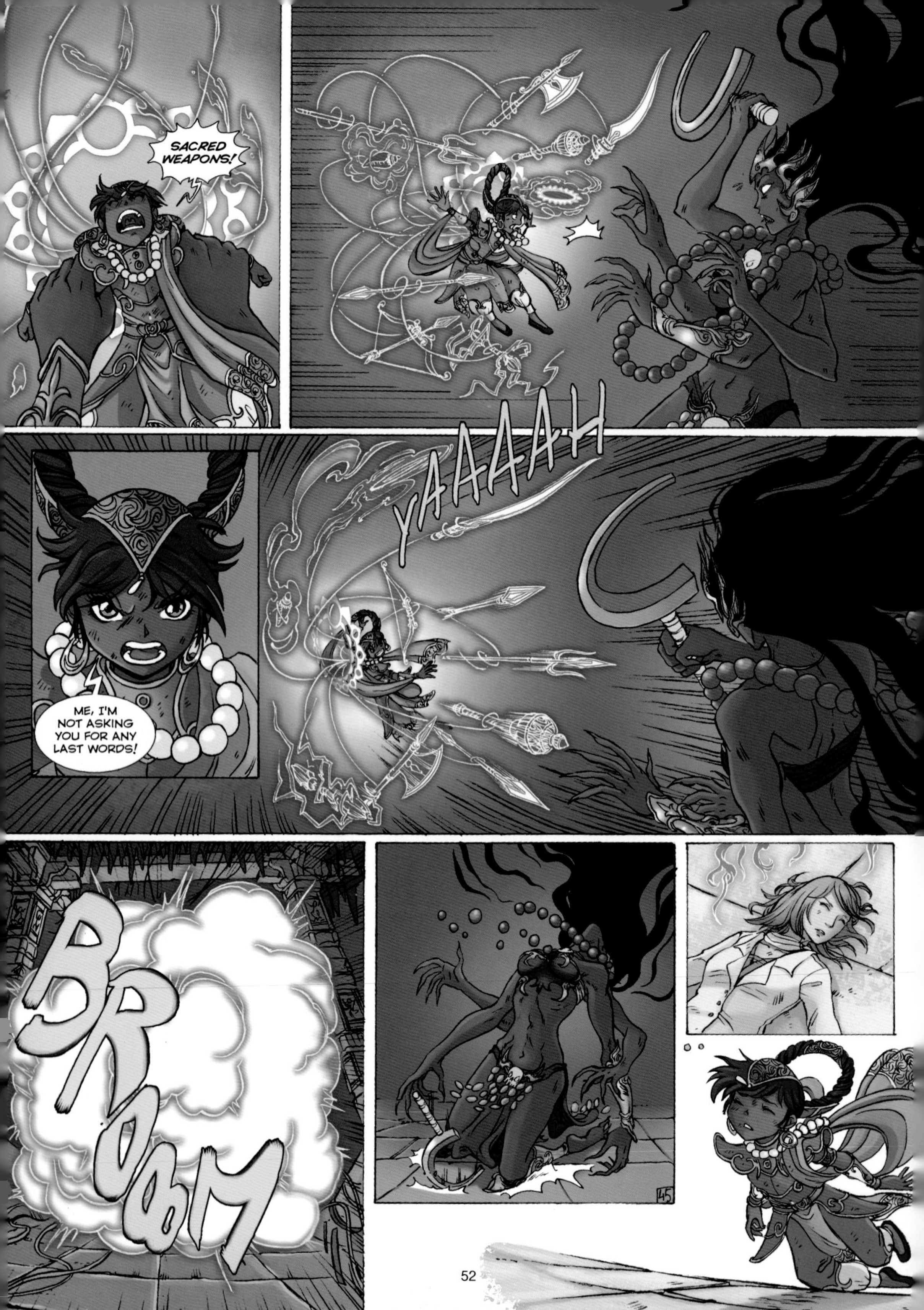
SACRED WEAPONS!
YAAAAH
ME, I'M NOT ASKING YOU FOR ANY LAST WORDS!
BROOM
45

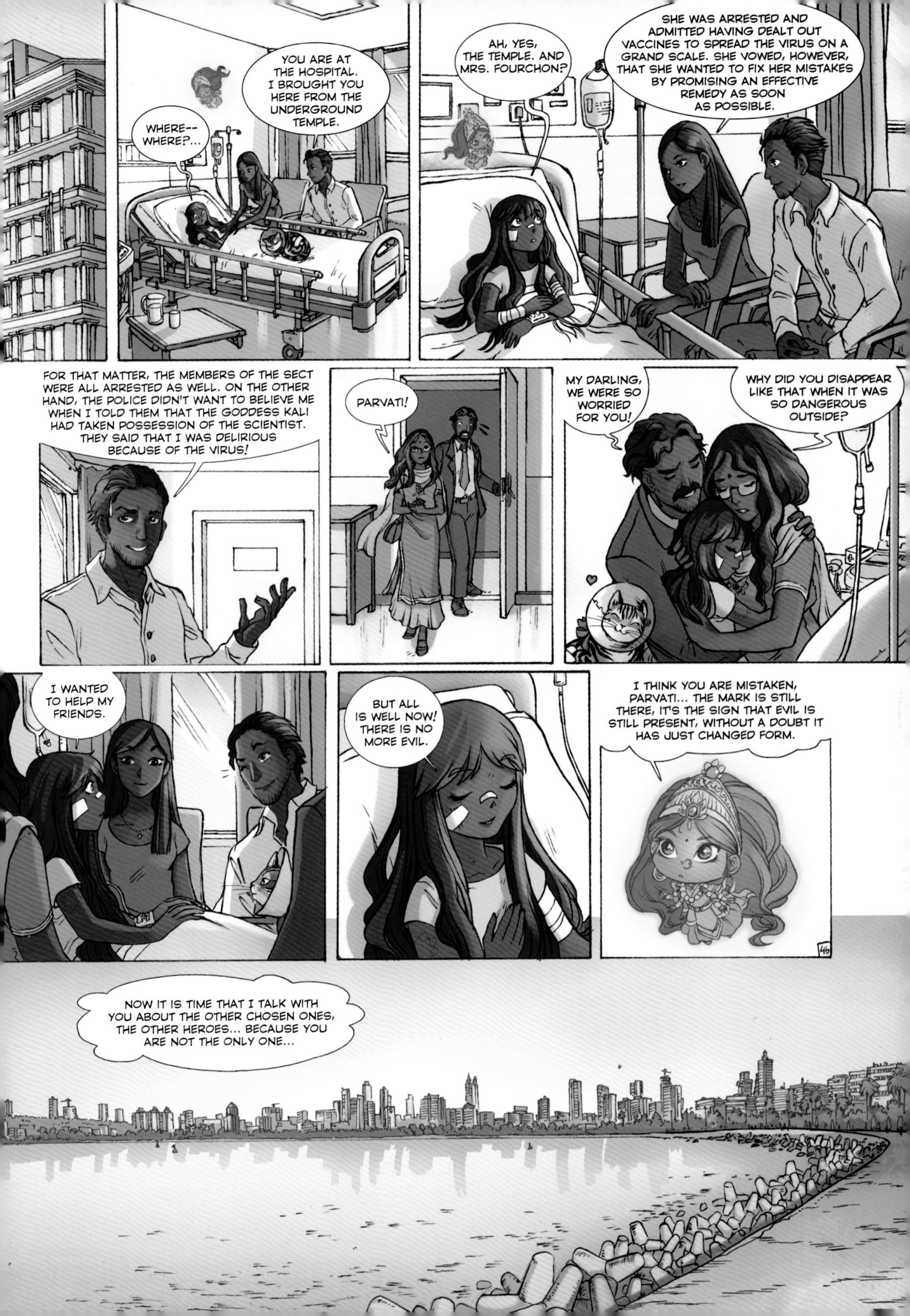

WHERE-- WHERE?...
YOU ARE AT THE HOSPITAL. I BROUGHT YOU HERE FROM THE UNDERGROUND TEMPLE.
AH, YES, THE TEMPLE. AND MRS. FOURCHON?
SHE WAS ARRESTED AND ADMITTED HAVING DEALT OUT VACCINES TO SPREAD THE VIRUS ON A GRAND SCALE. SHE VOWED, HOWEVER, THAT SHE WANTED TO FIX HER MISTAKES BY PROMISING AN EFFECTIVE REMEDY AS SOON AS POSSIBLE.
FOR THAT MATTER, THE MEMBERS OF THE SECT WERE ALL ARRESTED AS WELL. ON THE OTHER HAND, THE POLICE DIDN'T WANT TO BELIEVE ME WHEN I TOLD THEM THAT THE GODDESS KALI HAD TAKEN POSSESSION OF THE SCIENTIST. THEY SAID THAT I WAS DELIRIOUS BECAUSE OF THE VIRUS!
PARVATI!
MY DARLING, WE WERE SO WORRIED FOR YOU!
WHY DID YOU DISAPPEAR LIKE THAT WHEN IT WAS SO DANGEROUS OUTSIDE?
I WANTED TO HELP MY FRIENDS.
BUT ALL IS WELL NOW! THERE IS NO MORE EVIL.
I THINK YOU ARE MISTAKEN, PARVATI... THE MARK IS STILL THERE, IT'S THE SIGN THAT EVIL IS STILL PRESENT, WITHOUT A DOUBT IT HAS JUST CHANGED FORM.
46
NOW IT IS TIME THAT I TALK WITH YOU ABOUT THE OTHER CHOSEN ONES, THE OTHER HEROES... BECAUSE YOU ARE NOT THE ONLY ONE...

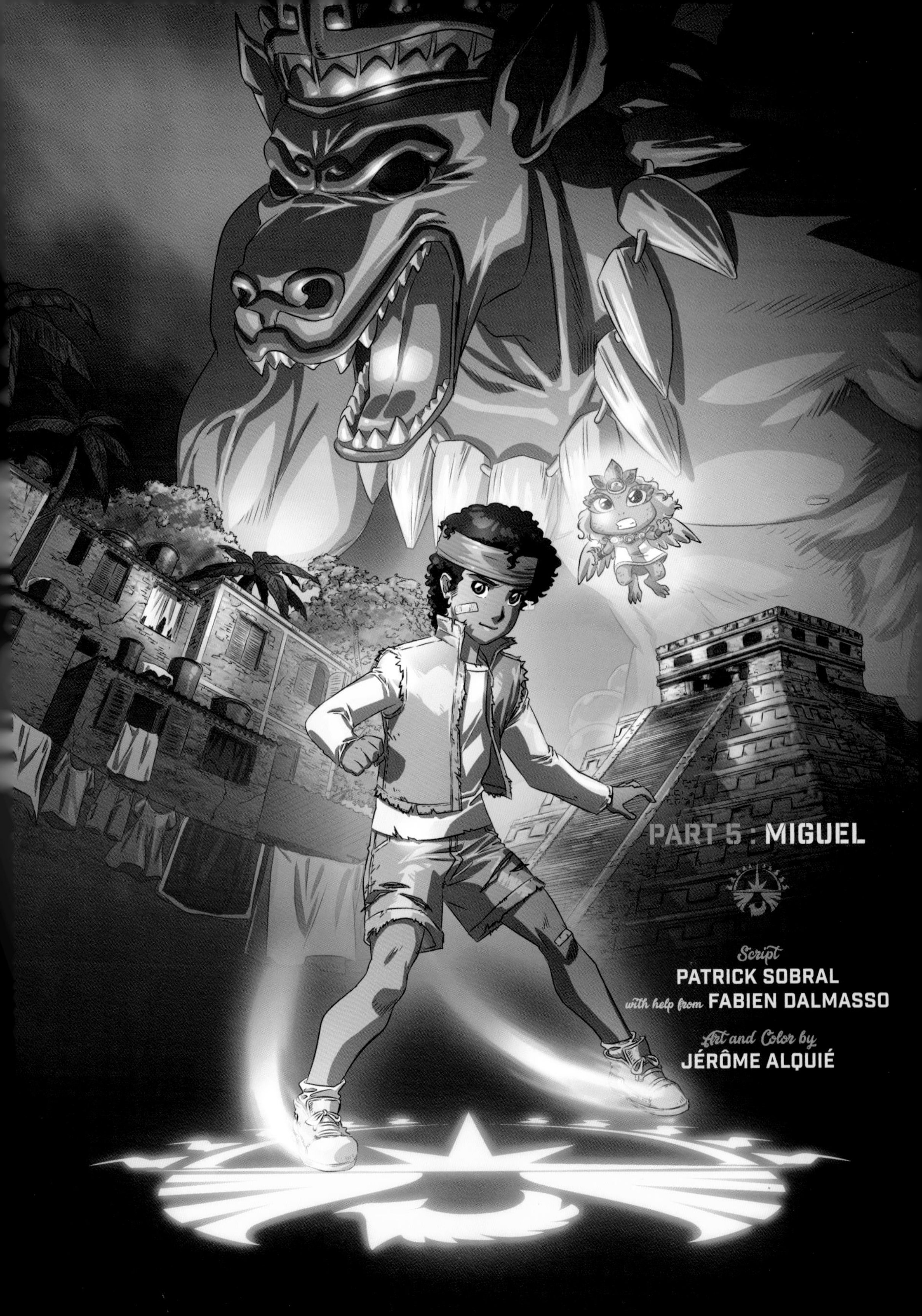
PART 5 : MIGUEL
Script
PATRICK SOBRAL
with help from FABIEN DALMASSO
Art and Color by
JÉRÔME ALQUIÉ

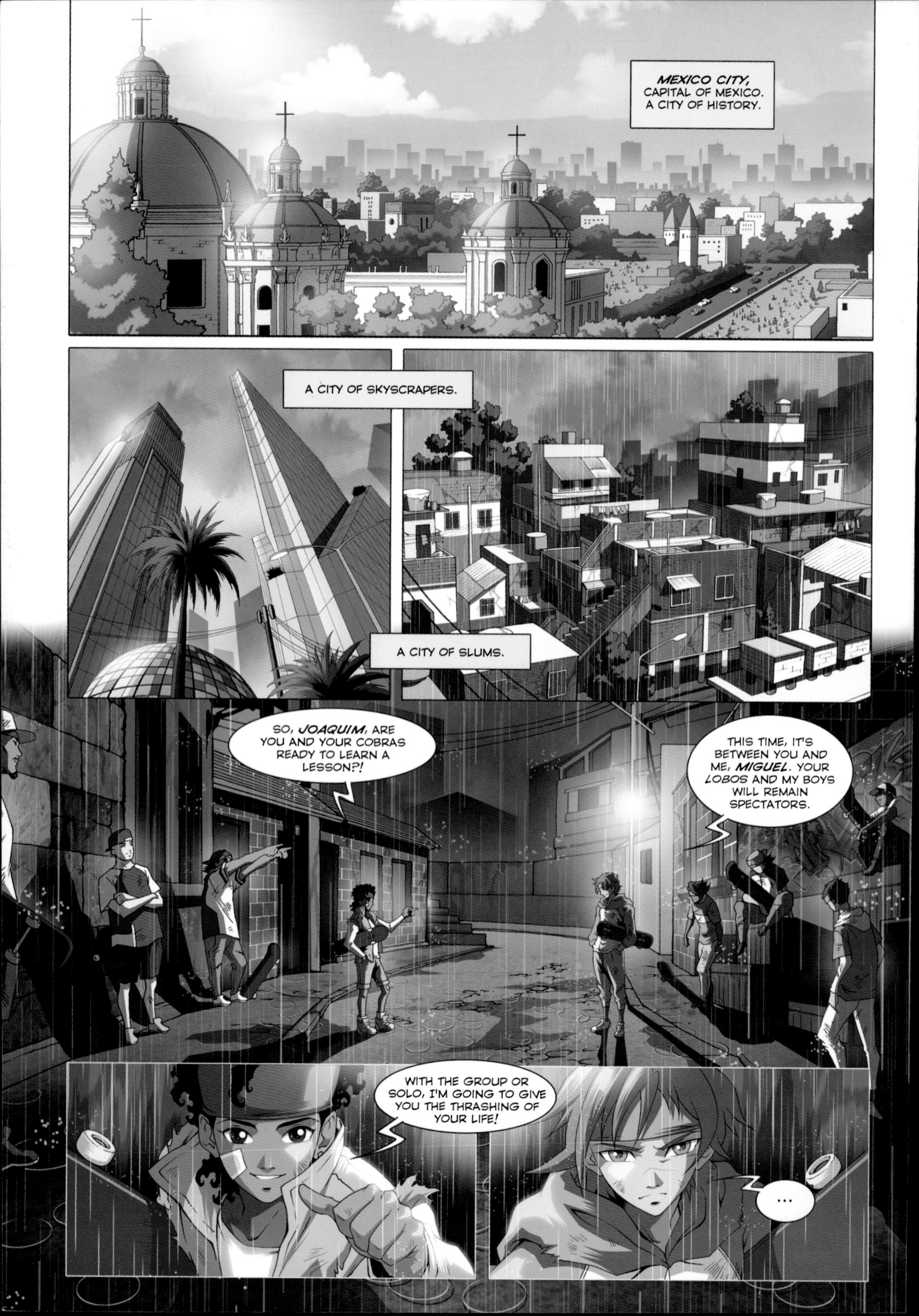
MEXICO CITY,
CAPITAL OF MEXICO.
A CITY OF HISTORY.
A CITY OF SKYSCRAPERS.
A CITY OF SLUMS.
SO, JOAQUIM, ARE YOU AND YOUR COBRAS READY TO LEARN A LESSON?!
THIS TIME, IT'S BETWEEN YOU AND ME, MIGUEL. YOUR LOBOS AND MY BOYS WILL REMAIN SPECTATORS.
WITH THE GROUP OR SOLO, I'M GOING TO GIVE YOU THE THRASHING OF YOUR LIFE!
...

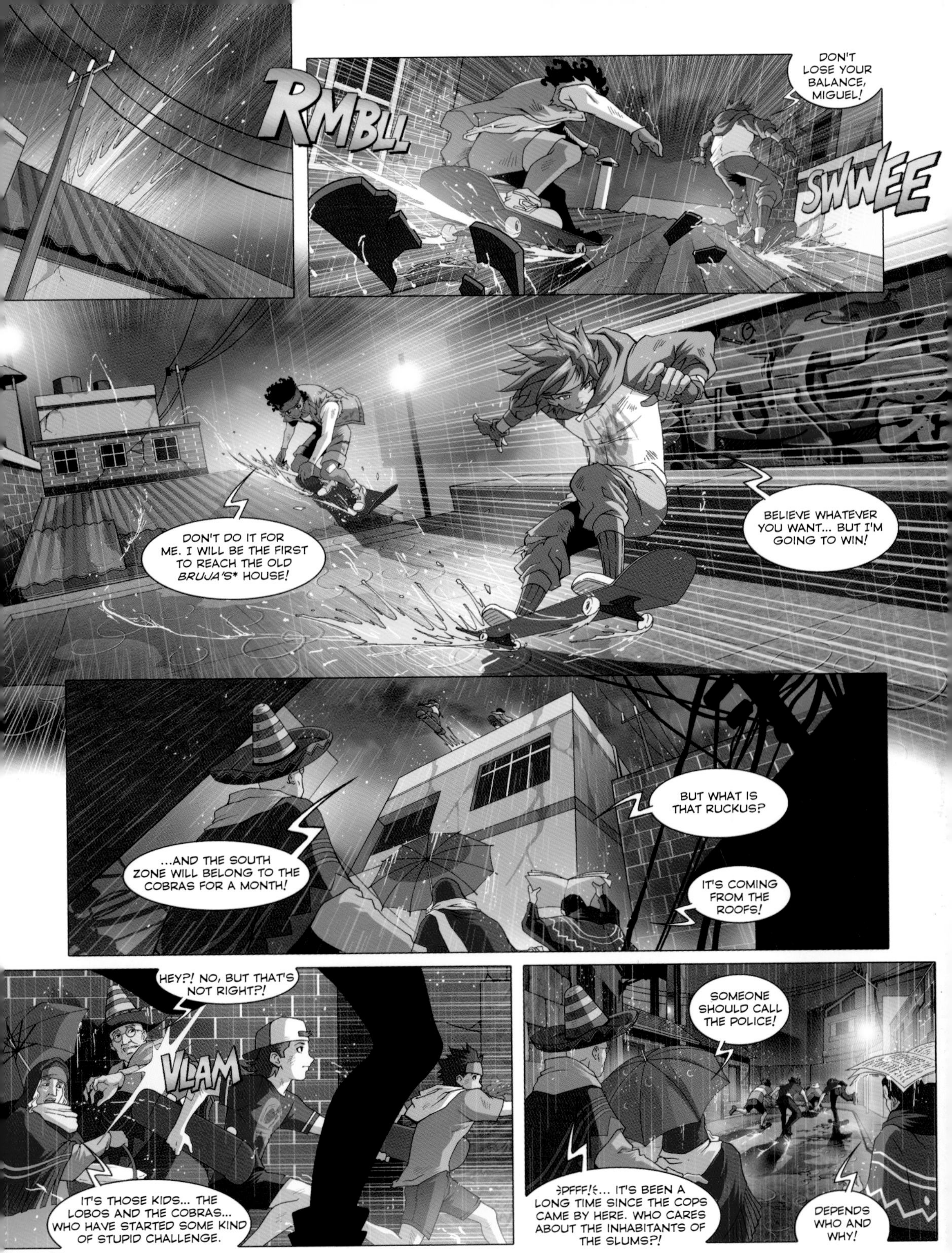
RMBLL
DON'T LOSE YOUR BALANCE, MIGUEL!
SWWEE
DON'T DO IT FOR ME. I WILL BE THE FIRST TO REACH THE OLD *BRUJA'S** HOUSE!
BELIEVE WHATEVER YOU WANT... BUT I'M GOING TO WIN!
...AND THE SOUTH ZONE WILL BELONG TO THE COBRAS FOR A MONTH!
BUT WHAT IS THAT RUCKUS?
IT'S COMING FROM THE ROOFS!
HEY?! NO, BUT THAT'S NOT RIGHT?!
VLAM
IT'S THOSE KIDS... THE LOBOS AND THE COBRAS... WHO HAVE STARTED SOME KIND OF STUPID CHALLENGE.
SOMEONE SHOULD CALL THE POLICE!
¡PFFF!¡... IT'S BEEN A LONG TIME SINCE THE COPS CAME BY HERE. WHO CARES ABOUT THE INHABITANTS OF THE SLUMS?!
DEPENDS WHO AND WHY!

*SPANISH FOR "WITCH."

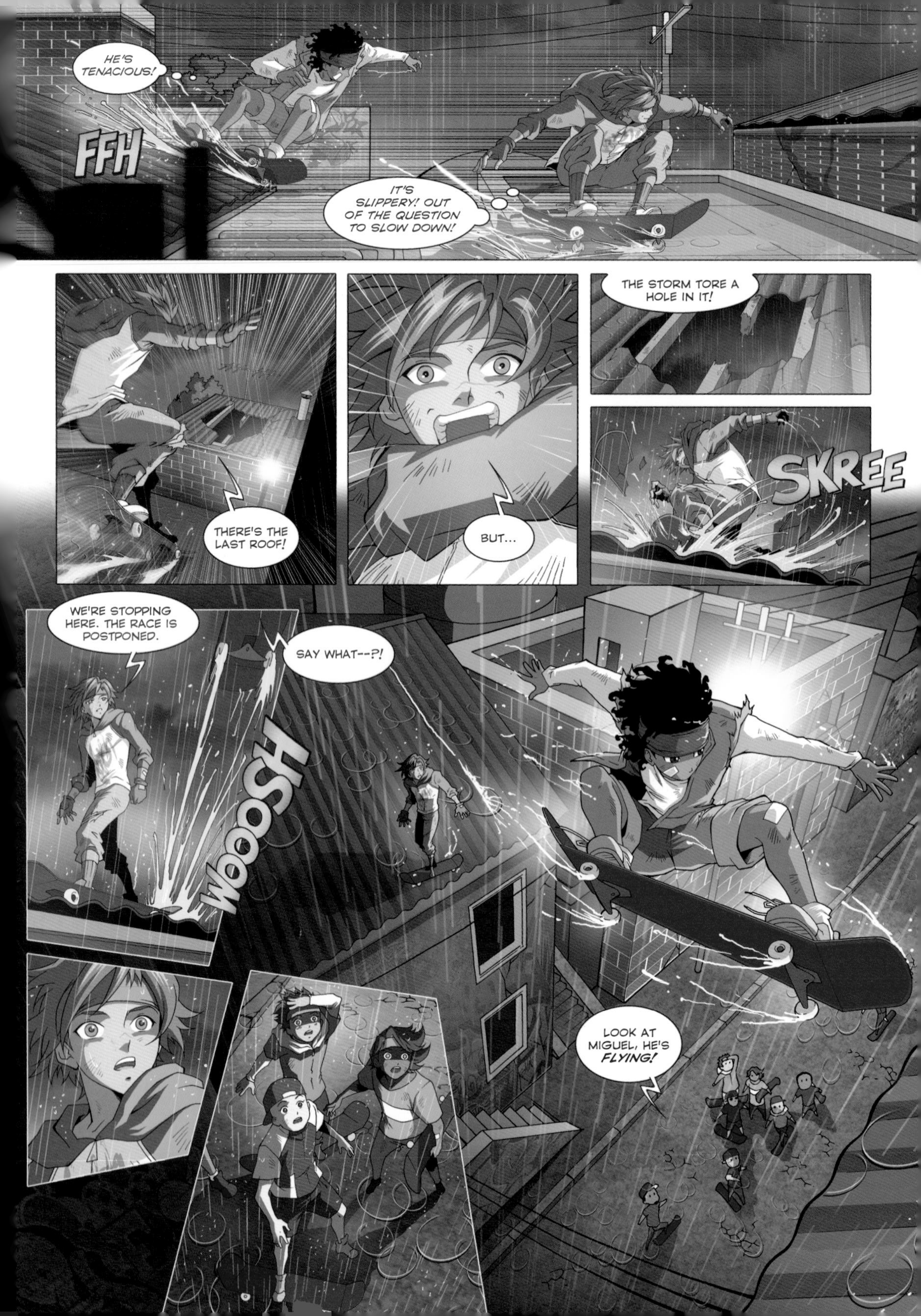
HE'S TENACIOUS!
FFH
IT'S SLIPPERY! OUT OF THE QUESTION TO SLOW DOWN!
THERE'S THE LAST ROOF!
BUT...
THE STORM TORE A HOLE IN IT!
SKREE
WE'RE STOPPING HERE. THE RACE IS POSTPONED.
SAY WHAT--?!
WOOOOSH
LOOK AT MIGUEL, HE'S *FLYING!*

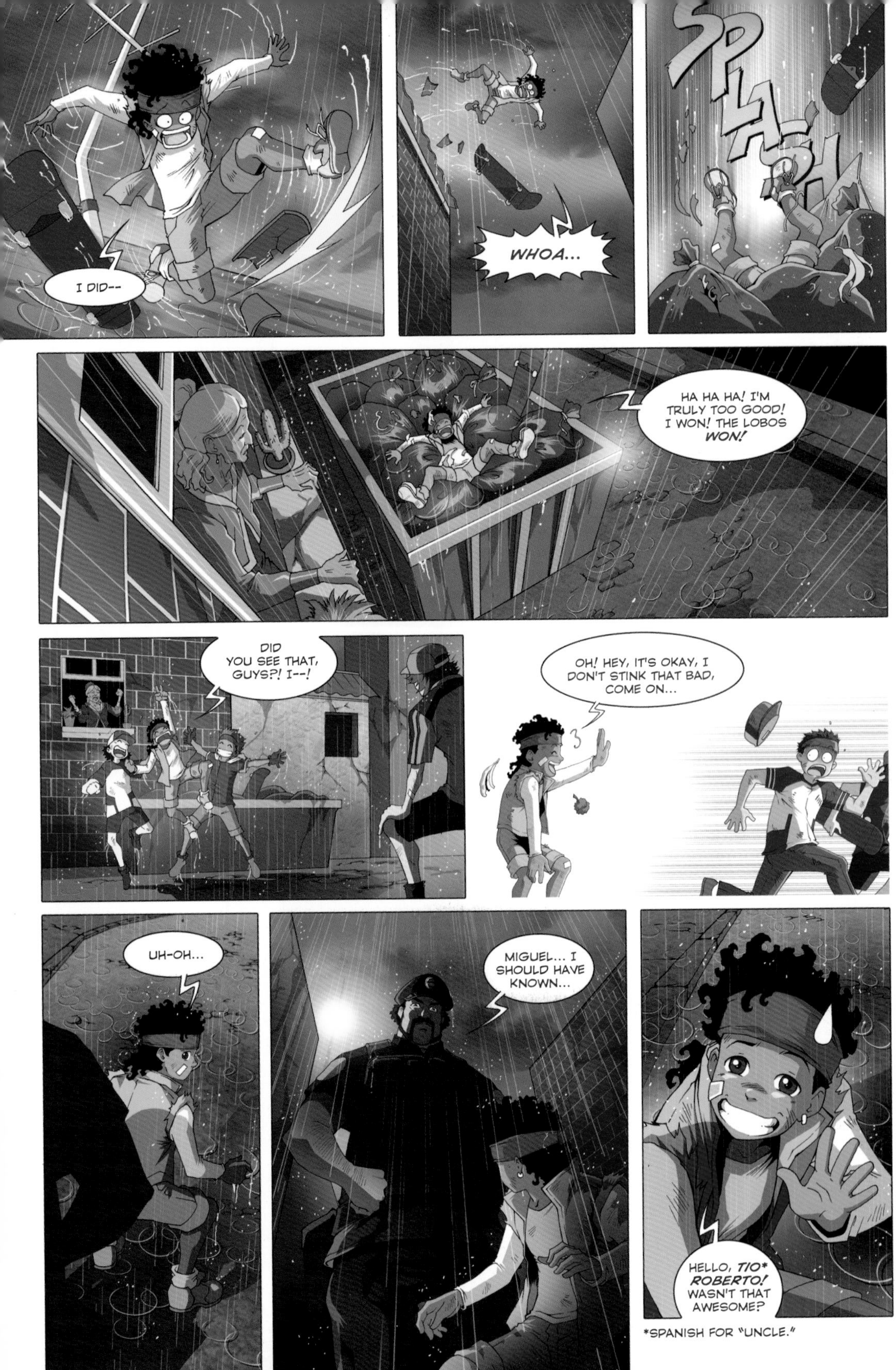
I DID--
WHOA...
SPLASH
HA HA HA! I'M TRULY TOO GOOD! I WON! THE LOBOS WON!
DID YOU SEE THAT, GUYS?! I--!
OH! HEY, IT'S OKAY, I DON'T STINK THAT BAD, COME ON...
UH-OH...
MIGUEL... I SHOULD HAVE KNOWN...
HELLO, TIO* ROBERTO! WASN'T THAT AWESOME?

*SPANISH FOR "UNCLE."

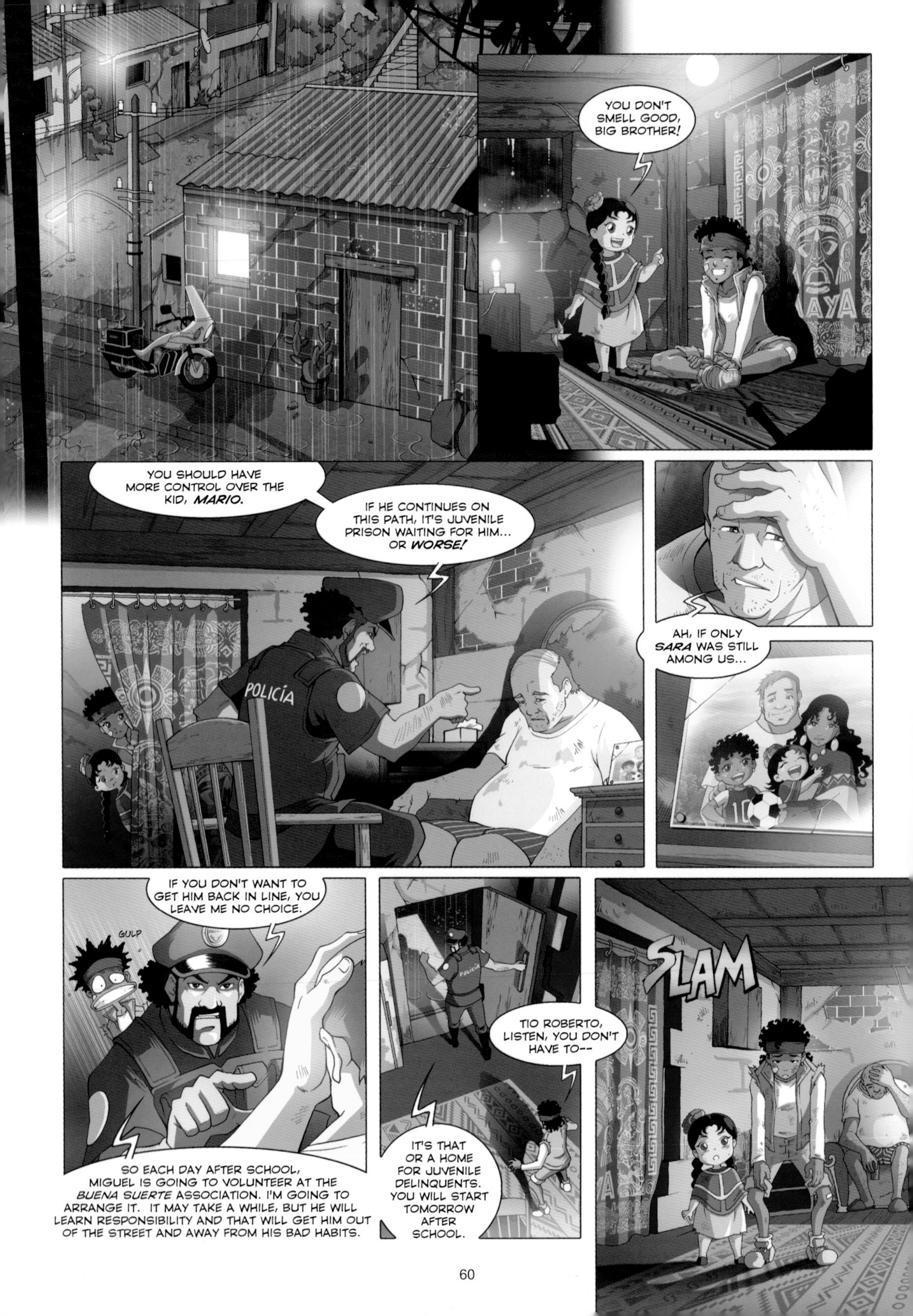
YOU DON'T SMELL GOOD, BIG BROTHER!
YOU SHOULD HAVE MORE CONTROL OVER THE KID, MARIO.
IF HE CONTINUES ON THIS PATH, IT'S JUVENILE PRISON WAITING FOR HIM... OR WORSE!
POLICÍA
AH, IF ONLY SARA WAS STILL AMONG US...
IF YOU DON'T WANT TO GET HIM BACK IN LINE, YOU LEAVE ME NO CHOICE.
GULP
SO EACH DAY AFTER SCHOOL, MIGUEL IS GOING TO VOLUNTEER AT THE BUENA SUERTE ASSOCIATION. I'M GOING TO ARRANGE IT. IT MAY TAKE A WHILE, BUT HE WILL LEARN RESPONSIBILITY AND THAT WILL GET HIM OUT OF THE STREET AND AWAY FROM HIS BAD HABITS.
TIO ROBERTO, LISTEN, YOU DON'T HAVE TO--
IT'S THAT OR A HOME FOR JUVENILE DELINQUENTS. YOU WILL START TOMORROW AFTER SCHOOL.
SLAM

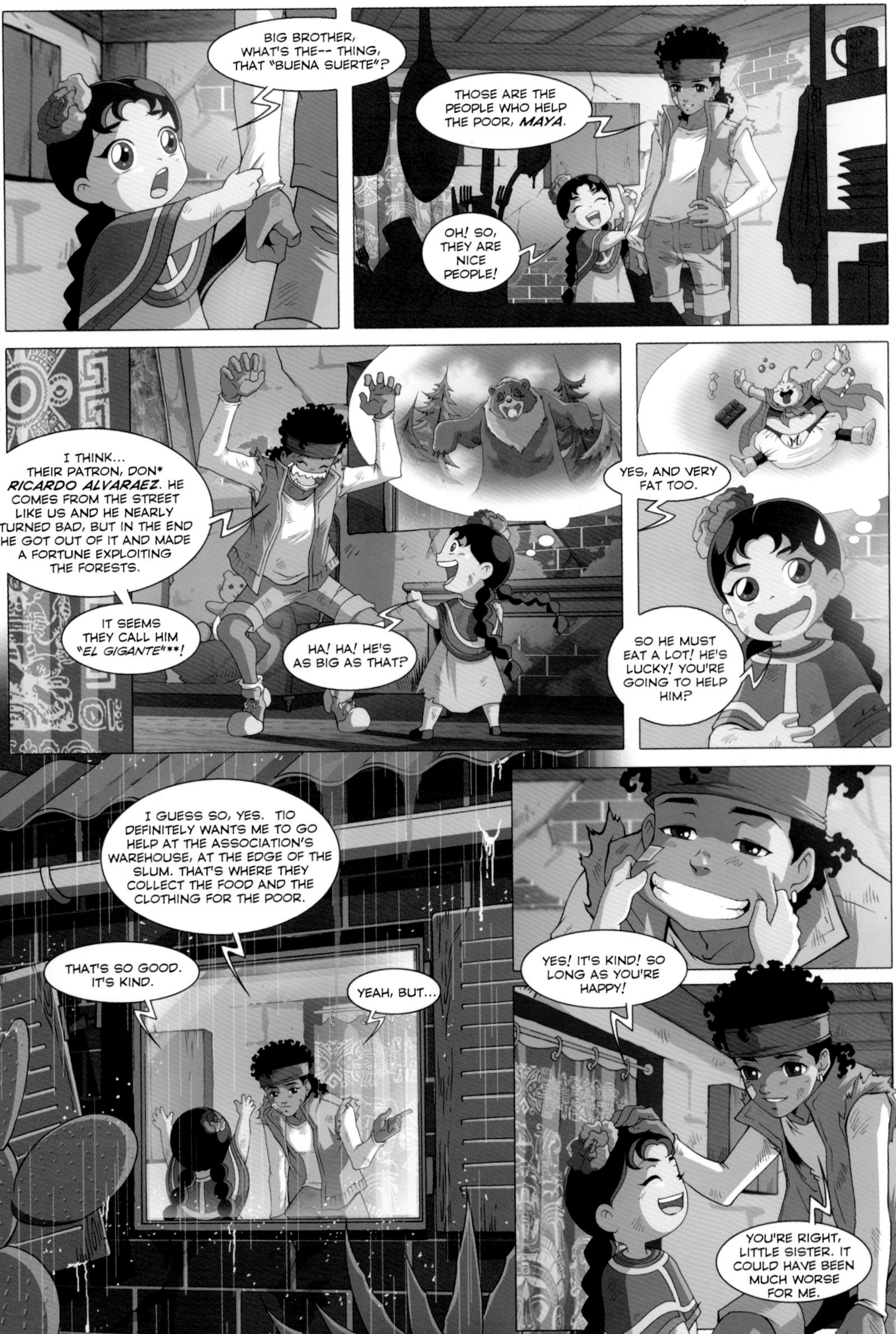

BIG BROTHER, WHAT'S THE-- THING, THAT "BUENA SUERTE"?
THOSE ARE THE PEOPLE WHO HELP THE POOR, MAYA.
OH! SO, THEY ARE NICE PEOPLE!
I THINK... THEIR PATRON, DON* RICARDO ALVARAEZ. HE COMES FROM THE STREET LIKE US AND HE NEARLY TURNED BAD, BUT IN THE END HE GOT OUT OF IT AND MADE A FORTUNE EXPLOITING THE FORESTS.
IT SEEMS THEY CALL HIM "EL GIGANTE"**!
HA! HA! HE'S AS BIG AS THAT?
YES, AND VERY FAT TOO.
SO HE MUST EAT A LOT! HE'S LUCKY! YOU'RE GOING TO HELP HIM?
I GUESS SO, YES. TIO DEFINITELY WANTS ME TO GO HELP AT THE ASSOCIATION'S WAREHOUSE, AT THE EDGE OF THE SLUM. THAT'S WHERE THEY COLLECT THE FOOD AND THE CLOTHING FOR THE POOR.
THAT'S SO GOOD. IT'S KIND.
YEAH, BUT...
YES! IT'S KIND! SO LONG AS YOU'RE HAPPY!
YOU'RE RIGHT, LITTLE SISTER. IT COULD HAVE BEEN MUCH WORSE FOR ME.

*A MARK OF ESTEEM FOR A PERSON OF SOCIAL DISTINCTION.
** SPANISH FOR "THE GIANT."

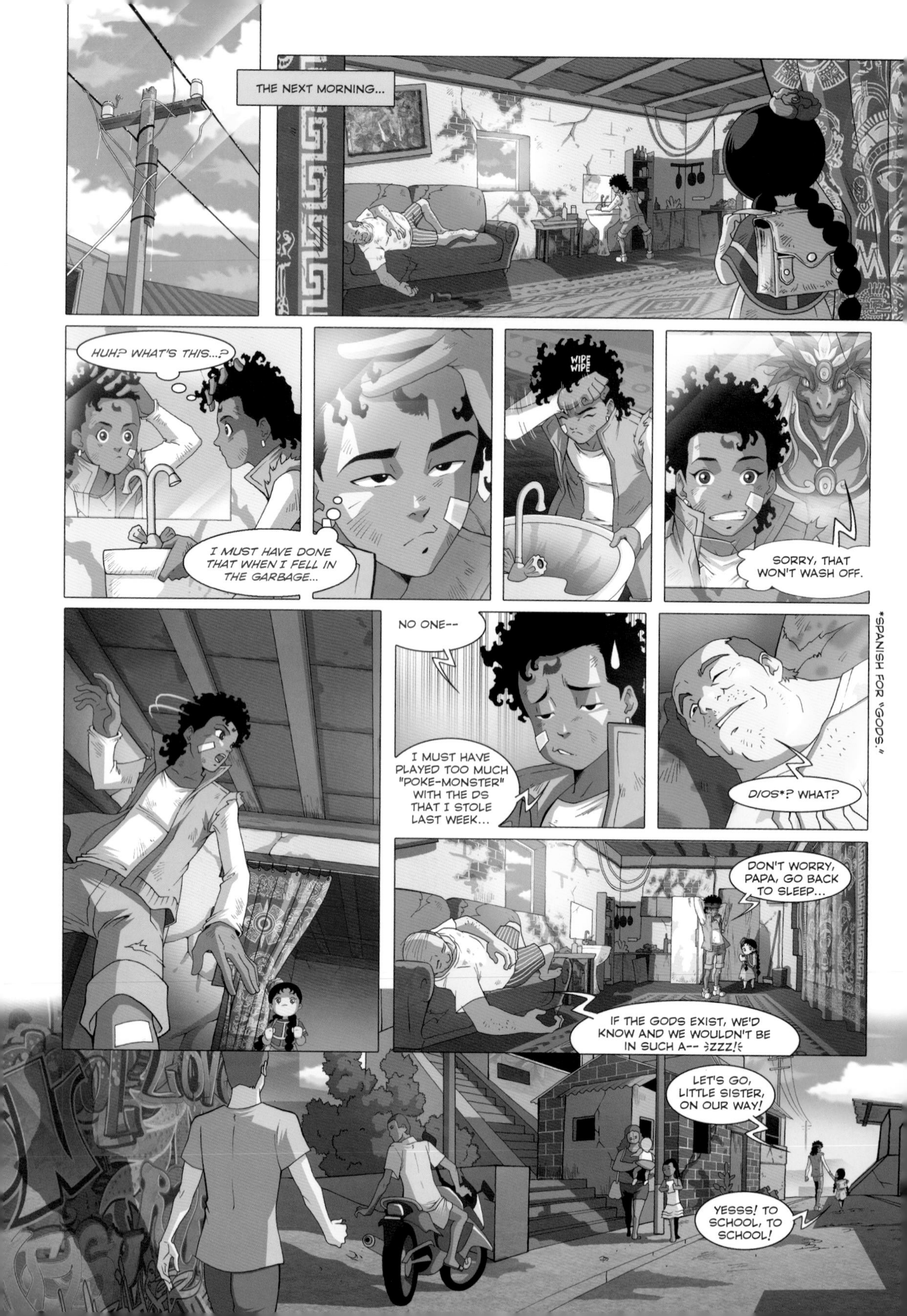
THE NEXT MORNING...
HUH? WHAT'S THIS...?
I MUST HAVE DONE THAT WHEN I FELL IN THE GARBAGE...
WIPE WIPE
SORRY, THAT WON'T WASH OFF.
NO ONE--
I MUST HAVE PLAYED TOO MUCH "POKE-MONSTER" WITH THE DS THAT I STOLE LAST WEEK...
DIOS*? WHAT?
*SPANISH FOR "GODS."
DON'T WORRY, PAPA, GO BACK TO SLEEP...
IF THE GODS EXIST, WE'D KNOW AND WE WOULDN'T BE IN SUCH A-- ZZZ!
LET'S GO, LITTLE SISTER, ON OUR WAY!
YESSS! TO SCHOOL, TO SCHOOL!

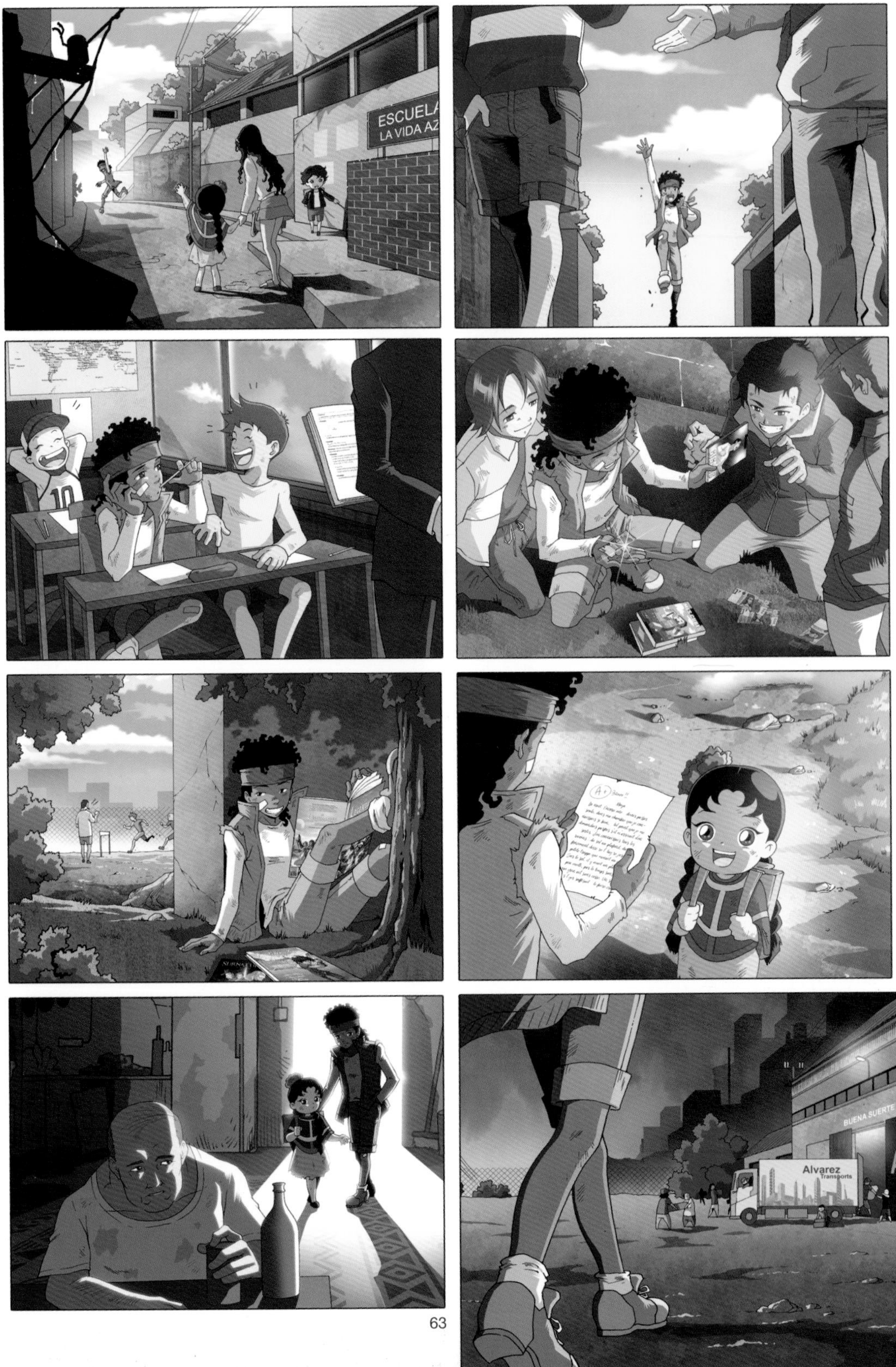
ESCUELA
LA VIDA AZ
BUENA SUERTE
Alvarez
Transports
A

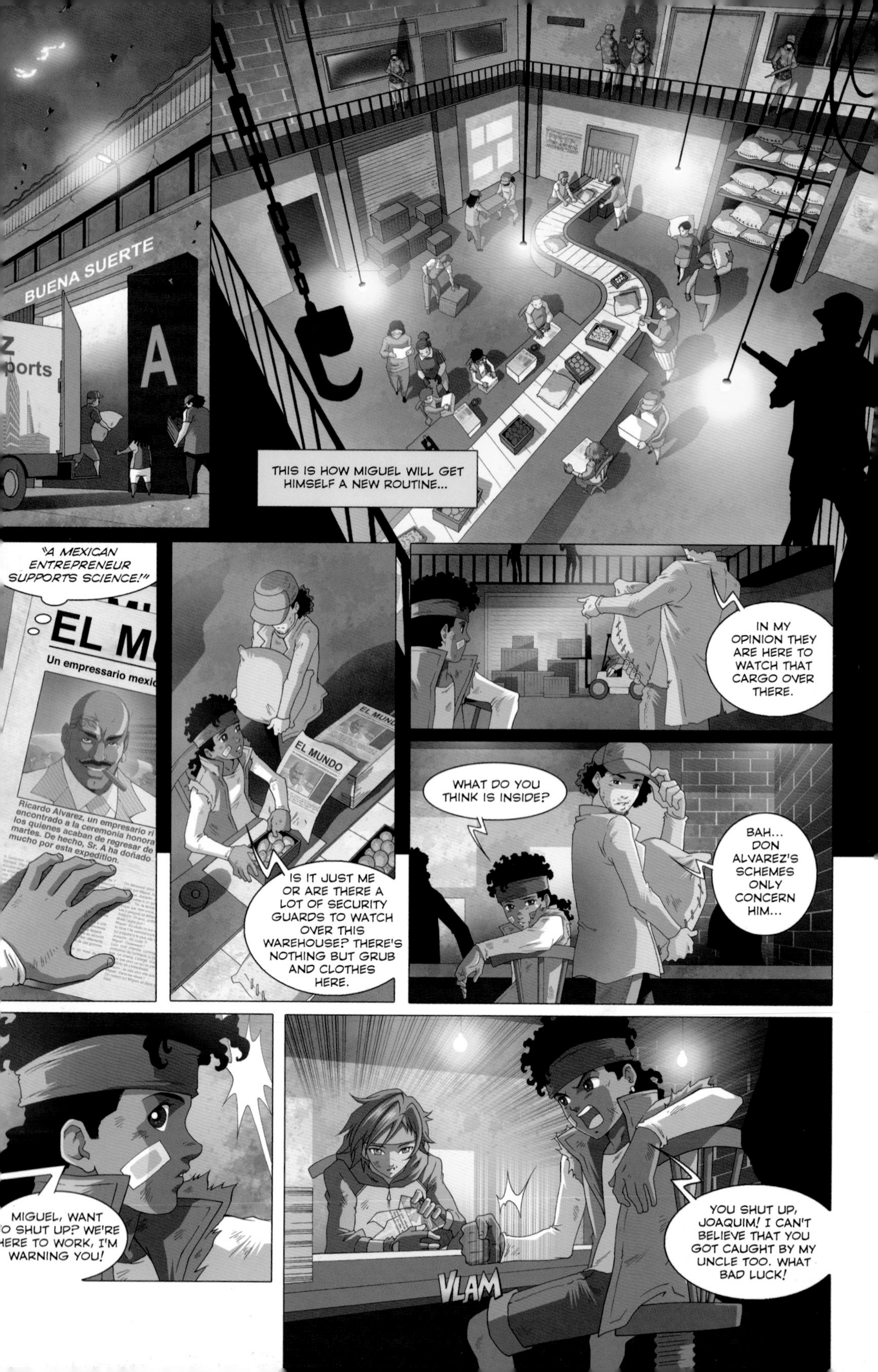
BUENA SUERTE
A
THIS IS HOW MIGUEL WILL GET HIMSELF A NEW ROUTINE...
"A MEXICAN ENTREPRENEUR SUPPORTS SCIENCE!"
EL MU
Un empressario mexic
Ricardo Alvarez, un empresario ri
encontrado a la ceremonia honora
los quienes acaban de regresar de
martes. De hecho, Sr. A ha doñado
mucho por esta expedition.
EL MUNDO
EL MUNDO
IS IT JUST ME OR ARE THERE A LOT OF SECURITY GUARDS TO WATCH OVER THIS WAREHOUSE? THERE'S NOTHING BUT GRUB AND CLOTHES HERE.
IN MY OPINION THEY ARE HERE TO WATCH THAT CARGO OVER THERE.
WHAT DO YOU THINK IS INSIDE?
BAH... DON ALVAREZ'S SCHEMES ONLY CONCERN HIM...
MIGUEL, WANT O SHUT UP? WE'RE HERE TO WORK, I'M WARNING YOU!
VLAM
YOU SHUT UP, JOAQUIM! I CAN'T BELIEVE THAT YOU GOT CAUGHT BY MY UNCLE TOO. WHAT BAD LUCK!

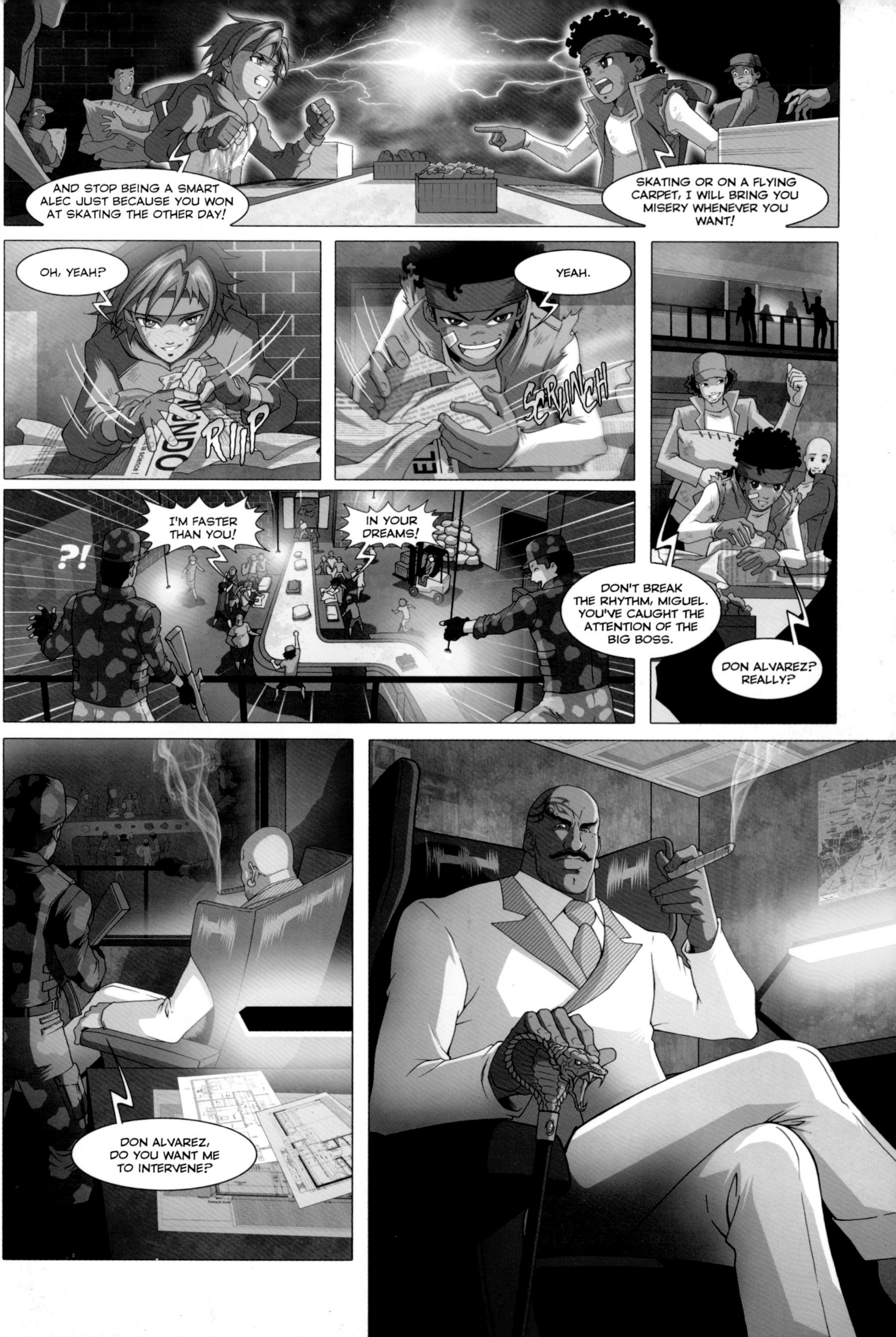
AND STOP BEING A SMART ALEC JUST BECAUSE YOU WON AT SKATING THE OTHER DAY!
SKATING OR ON A FLYING CARPET, I WILL BRING YOU MISERY WHENEVER YOU WANT!
OH, YEAH?
RIIP
YEAH.
SCRUNCH
?!
I'M FASTER THAN YOU!
IN YOUR DREAMS!
DON'T BREAK THE RHYTHM, MIGUEL. YOU'VE CAUGHT THE ATTENTION OF THE BIG BOSS.
DON ALVAREZ? REALLY?
DON ALVAREZ, DO YOU WANT ME TO INTERVENE?

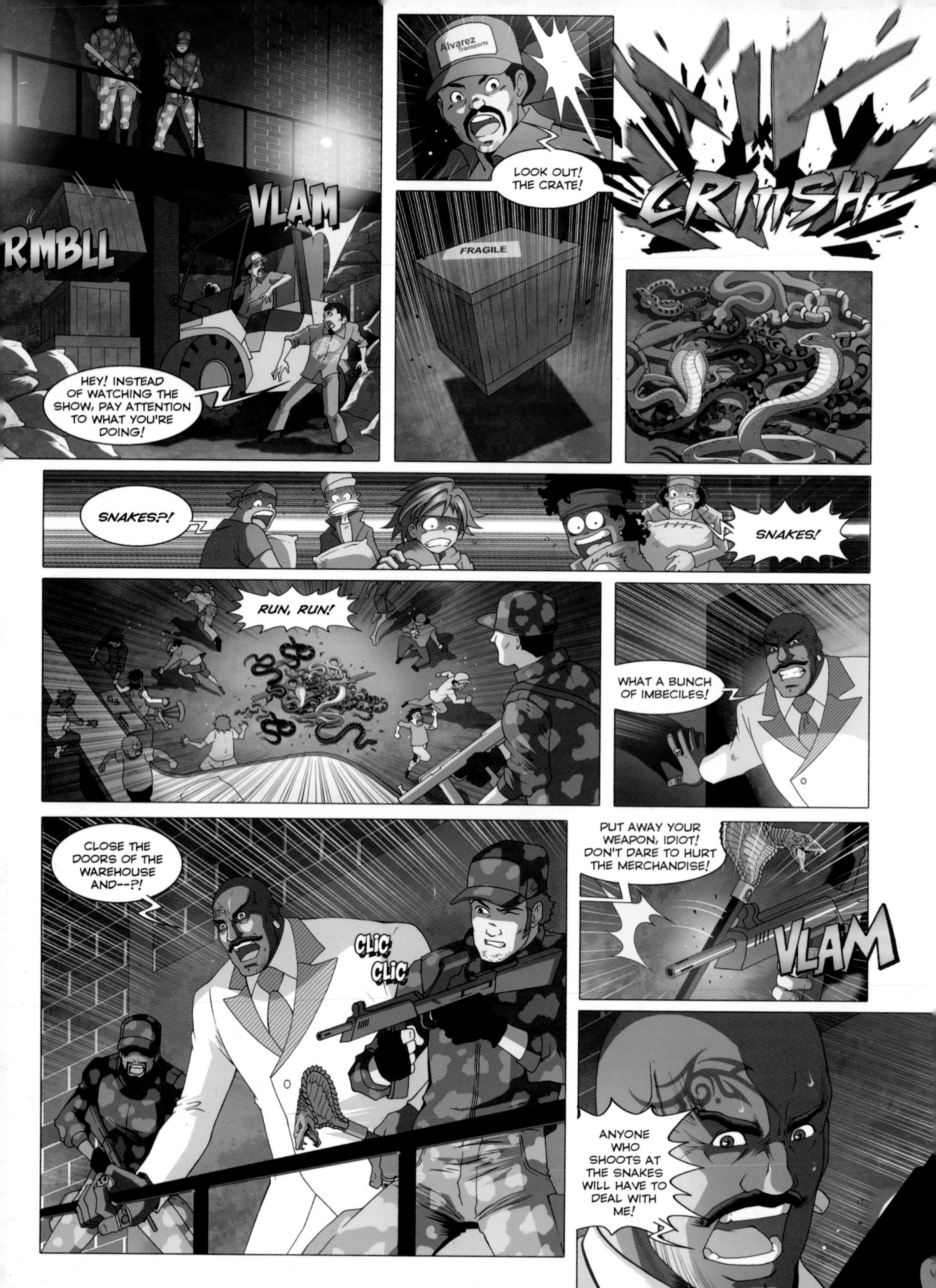

RMBLL
VLAM
HEY! INSTEAD OF WATCHING THE SHOW, PAY ATTENTION TO WHAT YOU'RE DOING!
Alvarez Transports
LOOK OUT! THE CRATE!
FRAGILE
CRUNSH
SNAKES?!
SNAKES!
RUN, RUN!
WHAT A BUNCH OF IMBECILES!
CLOSE THE DOORS OF THE WAREHOUSE AND--?!
CLIC
CLIC
PUT AWAY YOUR WEAPON, IDIOT! DON'T DARE TO HURT THE MERCHANDISE!
VLAM
ANYONE WHO SHOOTS AT THE SNAKES WILL HAVE TO DEAL WITH ME!

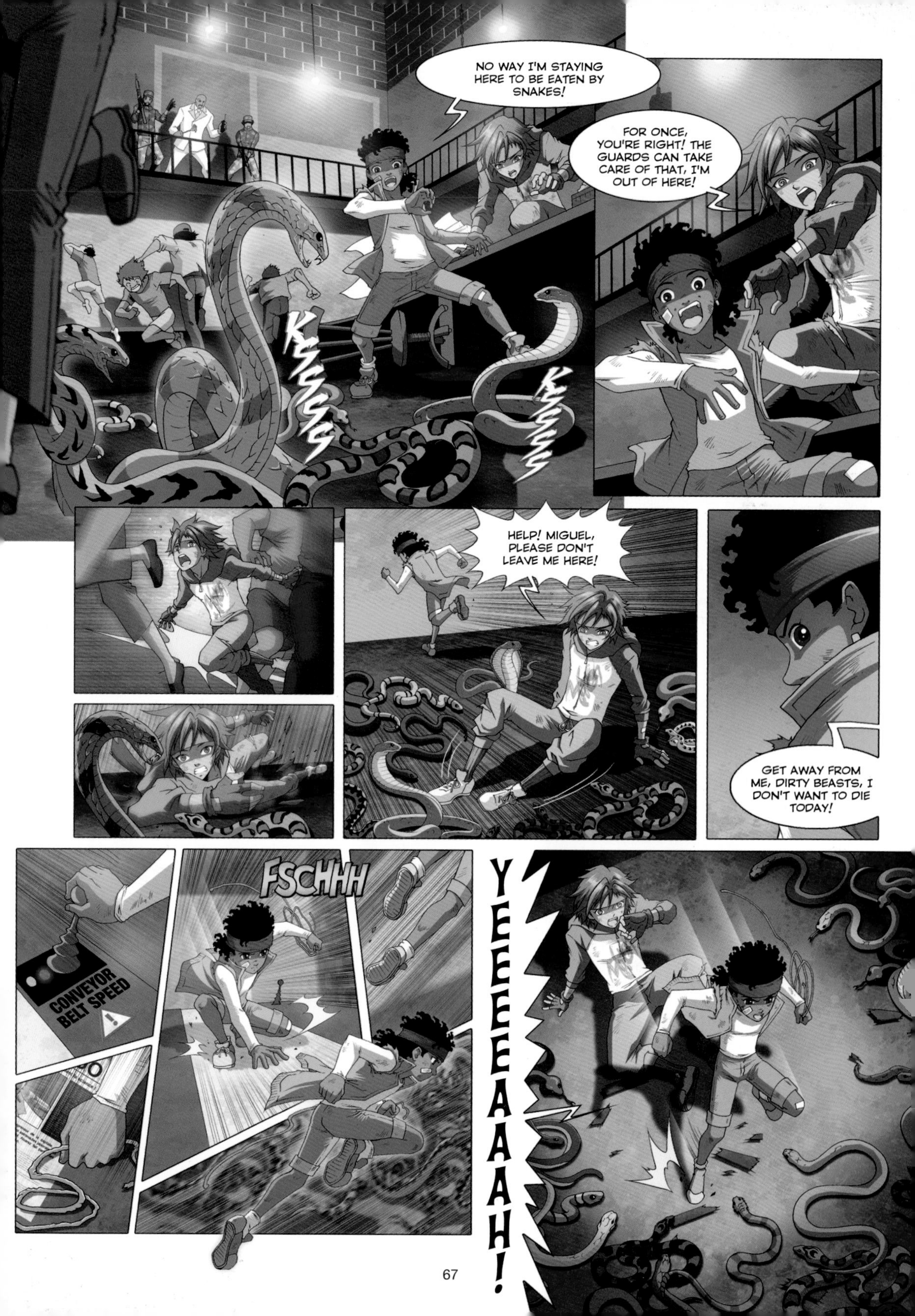
NO WAY I'M STAYING HERE TO BE EATEN BY SNAKES!
FOR ONCE, YOU'RE RIGHT! THE GUARDS CAN TAKE CARE OF THAT, I'M OUT OF HERE!
KSSSS
KSSSS
HELP! MIGUEL, PLEASE DON'T LEAVE ME HERE!
GET AWAY FROM ME, DIRTY BEASTS, I DON'T WANT TO DIE TODAY!
CONVEYOR BELT SPEED
FSCHHH
YEEEEAAAAH!

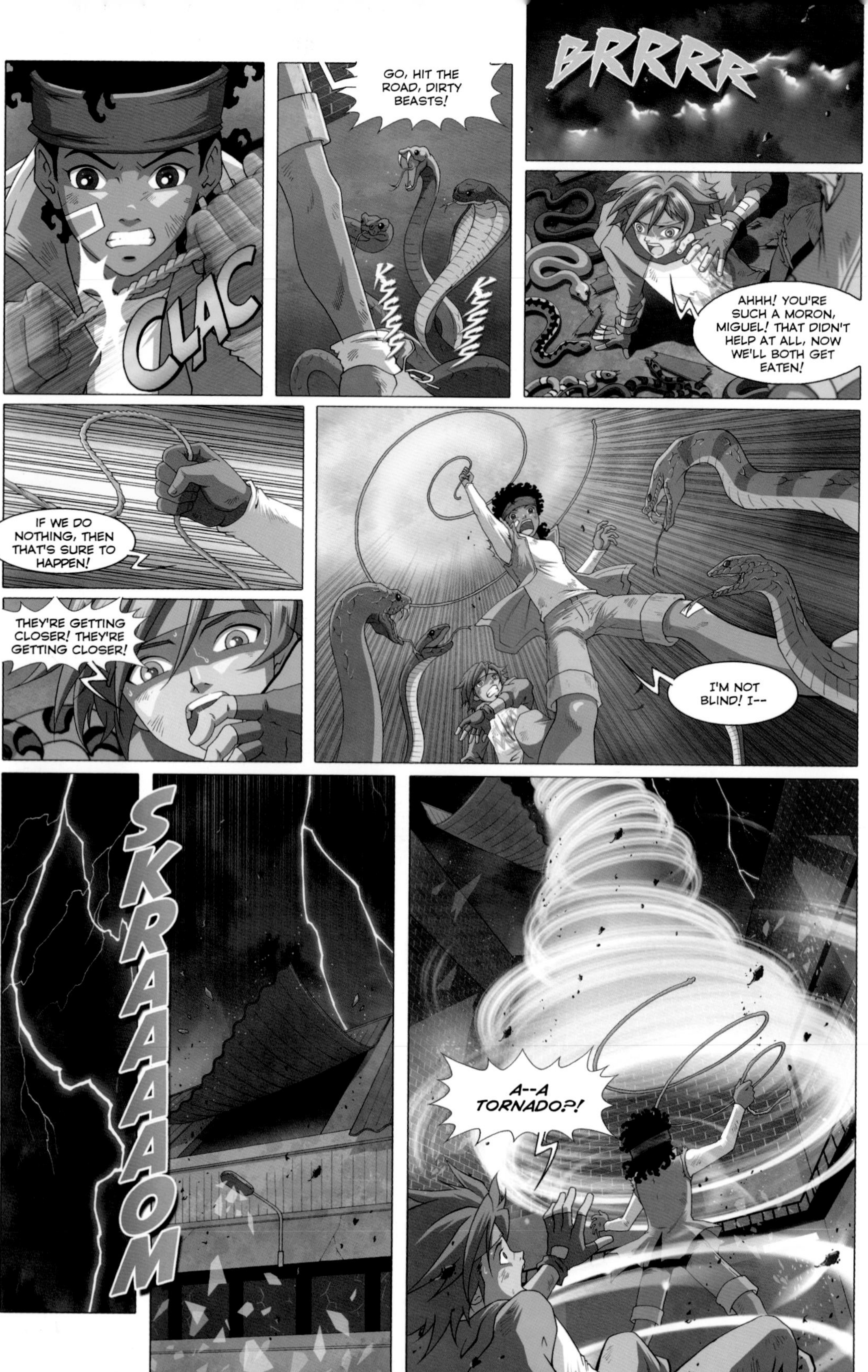
CLAC
GO, HIT THE ROAD, DIRTY BEASTS!
KSSSS
KSSSS
BRRRR
AHHH! YOU'RE SUCH A MORON, MIGUEL! THAT DIDN'T HELP AT ALL, NOW WE'LL BOTH GET EATEN!
IF WE DO NOTHING, THEN THAT'S SURE TO HAPPEN!
THEY'RE GETTING CLOSER! THEY'RE GETTING CLOSER!
I'M NOT BLIND! I--
SKRAAAAAOM
A--A TORNADO?!

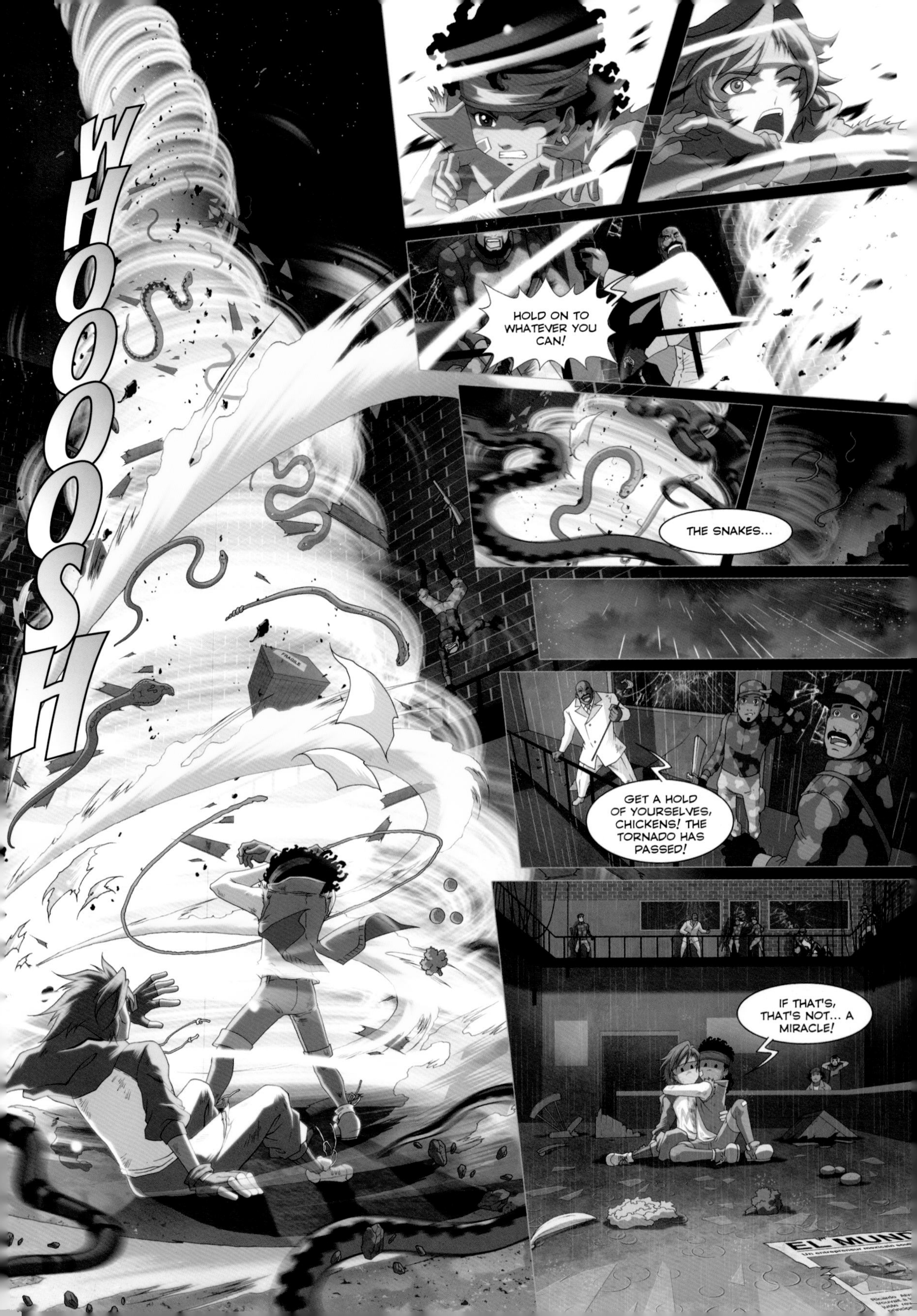
WHOOOOOSH
HOLD ON TO WHATEVER YOU CAN!
THE SNAKES...
GET A HOLD OF YOURSELVES, CHICKENS! THE TORNADO HAS PASSED!
IF THAT'S, THAT'S NOT... A MIRACLE!

LET ME GO, I'M NO BABY!

HEY!

PAF

THAT'S HOW YOU EXPRESS GRATITUDE?!

GET LOST, MIGUEL! I DIDN'T ASK YOU FOR ANYTHING!

CLAP CLAP

BRAVO, KIDS, BRAVO.

CLAP CLAP

UH, WELL, WE COULD SAY THAT LUCK--

WHAT AM I SAYING, LUCK?... IT'S CLEAR THAT THE GODS ARE WITH YOU, BOYS!

THE SNAKES ARE ALL DEAD...

EL GIGANTE IS GOING TO BE FURIOUS.

YOU ARE TOO GENEROUS, DON ALVAREZ. BUT... WHY ARE YOU GIVING ME THIS MONEY?

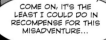

COME ON, IT'S THE LEAST I COULD DO IN RECOMPENSE FOR THIS MISADVENTURE...

IN FACT, COME SEE ME THE DAY AFTER TOMORROW AT THE WAREHOUSE, AT NOON. I WILL HAVE SOMETHING TO PROPOSE TO YOU.

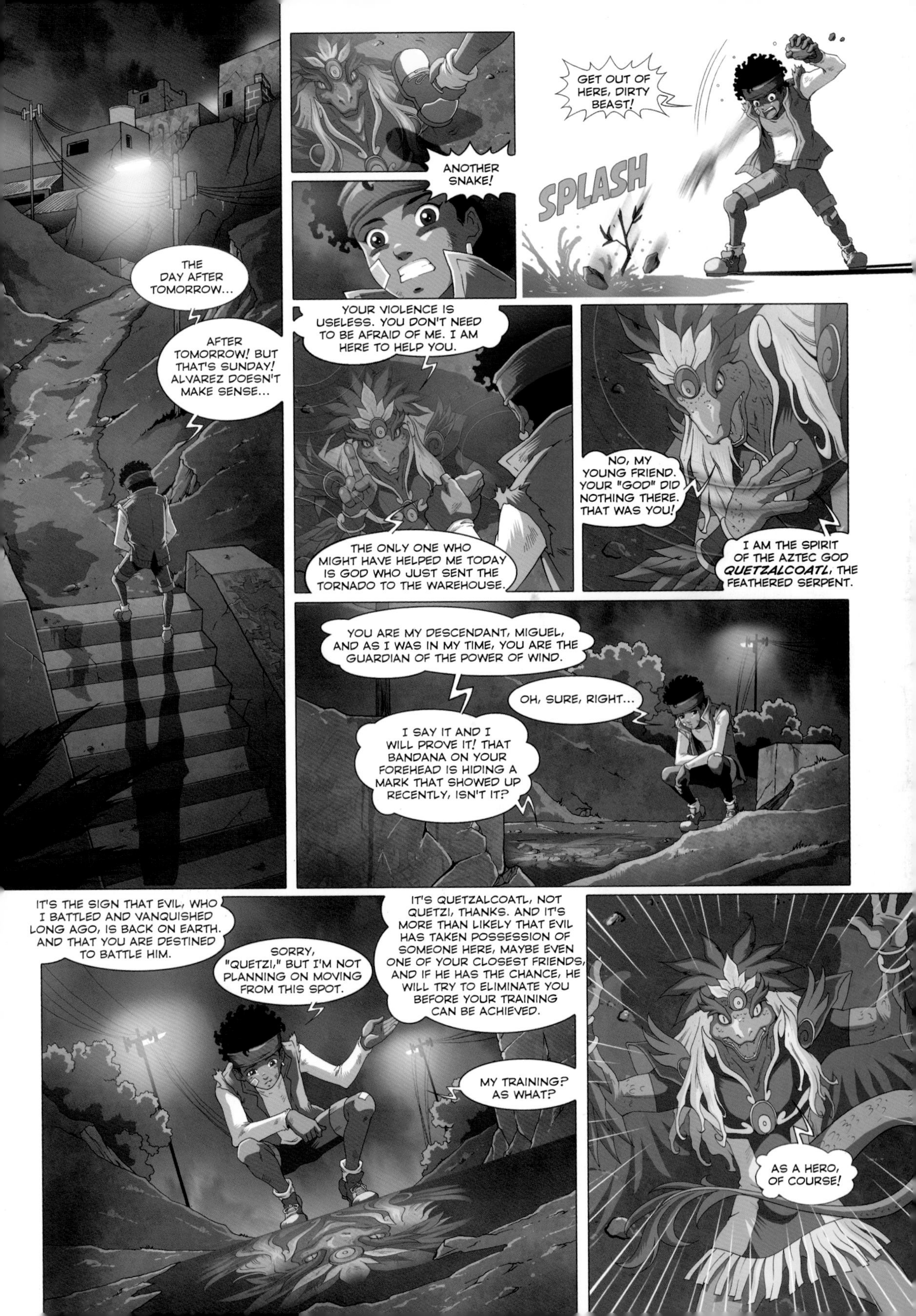

THE DAY AFTER TOMORROW...
AFTER TOMORROW! BUT THAT'S SUNDAY! ALVAREZ DOESN'T MAKE SENSE...
ANOTHER SNAKE!
GET OUT OF HERE, DIRTY BEAST!
SPLASH
YOUR VIOLENCE IS USELESS. YOU DON'T NEED TO BE AFRAID OF ME. I AM HERE TO HELP YOU.
THE ONLY ONE WHO MIGHT HAVE HELPED ME TODAY IS GOD WHO JUST SENT THE TORNADO TO THE WAREHOUSE.
NO, MY YOUNG FRIEND. YOUR "GOD" DID NOTHING THERE. THAT WAS YOU!
I AM THE SPIRIT OF THE AZTEC GOD *QUETZALCOATL*, THE FEATHERED SERPENT.
YOU ARE MY DESCENDANT, MIGUEL, AND AS I WAS IN MY TIME, YOU ARE THE GUARDIAN OF THE POWER OF WIND.
OH, SURE, RIGHT...
I SAY IT AND I WILL PROVE IT! THAT BANDANA ON YOUR FOREHEAD IS HIDING A MARK THAT SHOWED UP RECENTLY, ISN'T IT?
IT'S THE SIGN THAT EVIL, WHO I BATTLED AND VANQUISHED LONG AGO, IS BACK ON EARTH. AND THAT YOU ARE DESTINED TO BATTLE HIM.
SORRY, "QUETZI," BUT I'M NOT PLANNING ON MOVING FROM THIS SPOT.
IT'S QUETZALCOATL, NOT QUETZI, THANKS. AND IT'S MORE THAN LIKELY THAT EVIL HAS TAKEN POSSESSION OF SOMEONE HERE, MAYBE EVEN ONE OF YOUR CLOSEST FRIENDS, AND IF HE HAS THE CHANCE, HE WILL TRY TO ELIMINATE YOU BEFORE YOUR TRAINING CAN BE ACHIEVED.
MY TRAINING? AS WHAT?
AS A HERO, OF COURSE!

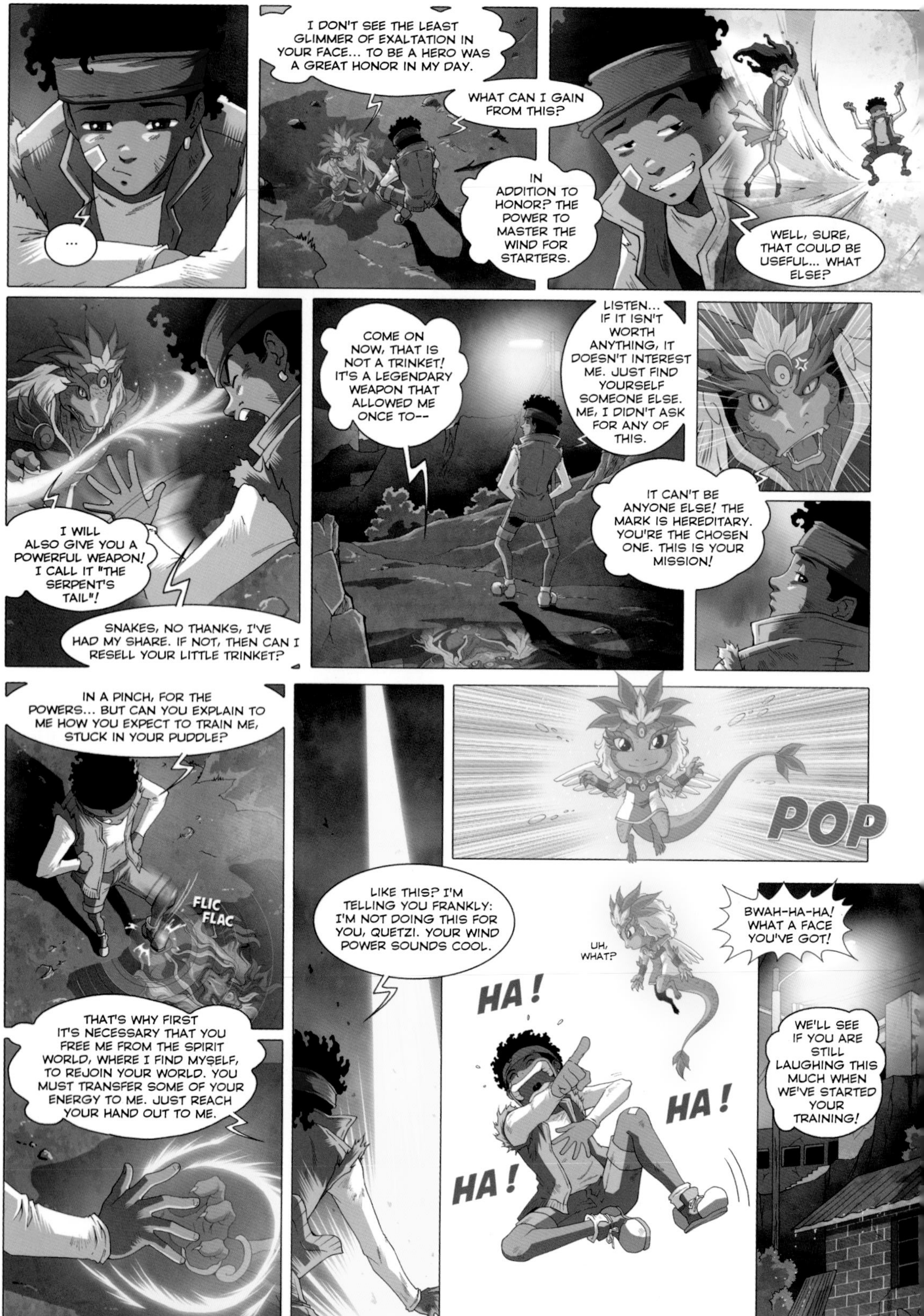
...
I DON'T SEE THE LEAST GLIMMER OF EXALTATION IN YOUR FACE... TO BE A HERO WAS A GREAT HONOR IN MY DAY.
WHAT CAN I GAIN FROM THIS?
IN ADDITION TO HONOR? THE POWER TO MASTER THE WIND FOR STARTERS.
WELL, SURE, THAT COULD BE USEFUL... WHAT ELSE?
I WILL ALSO GIVE YOU A POWERFUL WEAPON! I CALL IT "THE SERPENT'S TAIL"!
SNAKES, NO THANKS, I'VE HAD MY SHARE. IF NOT, THEN CAN I RESELL YOUR LITTLE TRINKET?
COME ON NOW, THAT IS NOT A TRINKET! IT'S A LEGENDARY WEAPON THAT ALLOWED ME ONCE TO--
LISTEN... IF IT ISN'T WORTH ANYTHING, IT DOESN'T INTEREST ME. JUST FIND YOURSELF SOMEONE ELSE. ME, I DIDN'T ASK FOR ANY OF THIS.
IT CAN'T BE ANYONE ELSE! THE MARK IS HEREDITARY. YOU'RE THE CHOSEN ONE. THIS IS YOUR MISSION!
IN A PINCH, FOR THE POWERS... BUT CAN YOU EXPLAIN TO ME HOW YOU EXPECT TO TRAIN ME, STUCK IN YOUR PUDDLE?
FLIC FLAC
THAT'S WHY FIRST IT'S NECESSARY THAT YOU FREE ME FROM THE SPIRIT WORLD, WHERE I FIND MYSELF, TO REJOIN YOUR WORLD. YOU MUST TRANSFER SOME OF YOUR ENERGY TO ME. JUST REACH YOUR HAND OUT TO ME.
POP
LIKE THIS? I'M TELLING YOU FRANKLY: I'M NOT DOING THIS FOR YOU, QUETZI. YOUR WIND POWER SOUNDS COOL.
UH, WHAT?
HA!
HA!
HA!
BWAH-HA-HA! WHAT A FACE YOU'VE GOT!
WE'LL SEE IF YOU ARE STILL LAUGHING THIS MUCH WHEN WE'VE STARTED YOUR TRAINING!

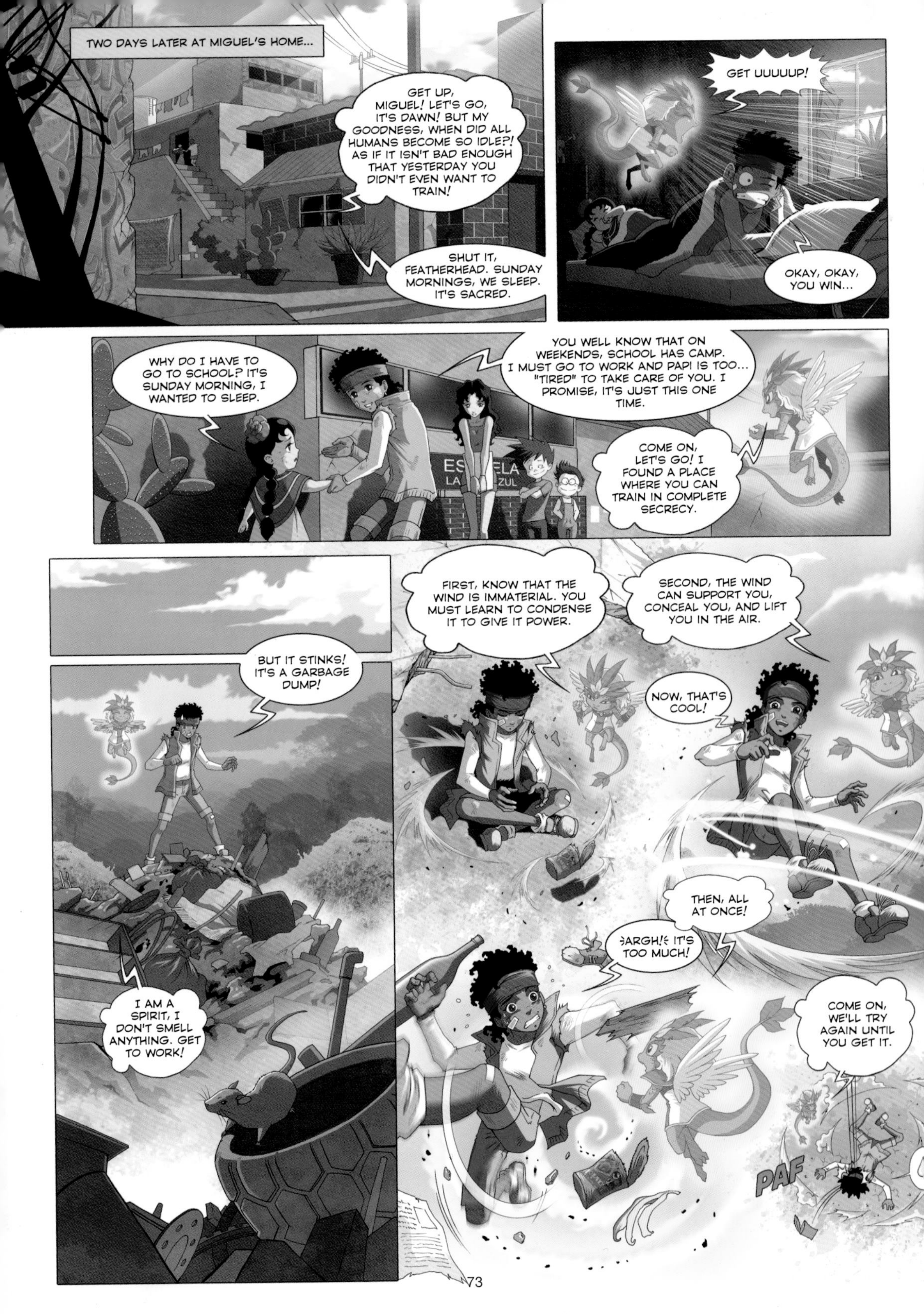
TWO DAYS LATER AT MIGUEL'S HOME...
GET UP, MIGUEL! LET'S GO, IT'S DAWN! BUT MY GOODNESS, WHEN DID ALL HUMANS BECOME SO IDLE?! AS IF IT ISN'T BAD ENOUGH THAT YESTERDAY YOU DIDN'T EVEN WANT TO TRAIN!
SHUT IT, FEATHERHEAD. SUNDAY MORNINGS, WE SLEEP. IT'S SACRED.
GET UUUUUP!
OKAY, OKAY, YOU WIN...
WHY DO I HAVE TO GO TO SCHOOL? IT'S SUNDAY MORNING, I WANTED TO SLEEP.
YOU WELL KNOW THAT ON WEEKENDS, SCHOOL HAS CAMP. I MUST GO TO WORK AND PAPI IS TOO... "TIRED" TO TAKE CARE OF YOU. I PROMISE, IT'S JUST THIS ONE TIME.
COME ON, LET'S GO! I FOUND A PLACE WHERE YOU CAN TRAIN IN COMPLETE SECRECY.
BUT IT STINKS! IT'S A GARBAGE DUMP!
I AM A SPIRIT, I DON'T SMELL ANYTHING. GET TO WORK!
FIRST, KNOW THAT THE WIND IS IMMATERIAL. YOU MUST LEARN TO CONDENSE IT TO GIVE IT POWER.
SECOND, THE WIND CAN SUPPORT YOU, CONCEAL YOU, AND LIFT YOU IN THE AIR.
NOW, THAT'S COOL!
THEN, ALL AT ONCE!
ARGH! IT'S TOO MUCH!
COME ON, WE'LL TRY AGAIN UNTIL YOU GET IT.
PAF

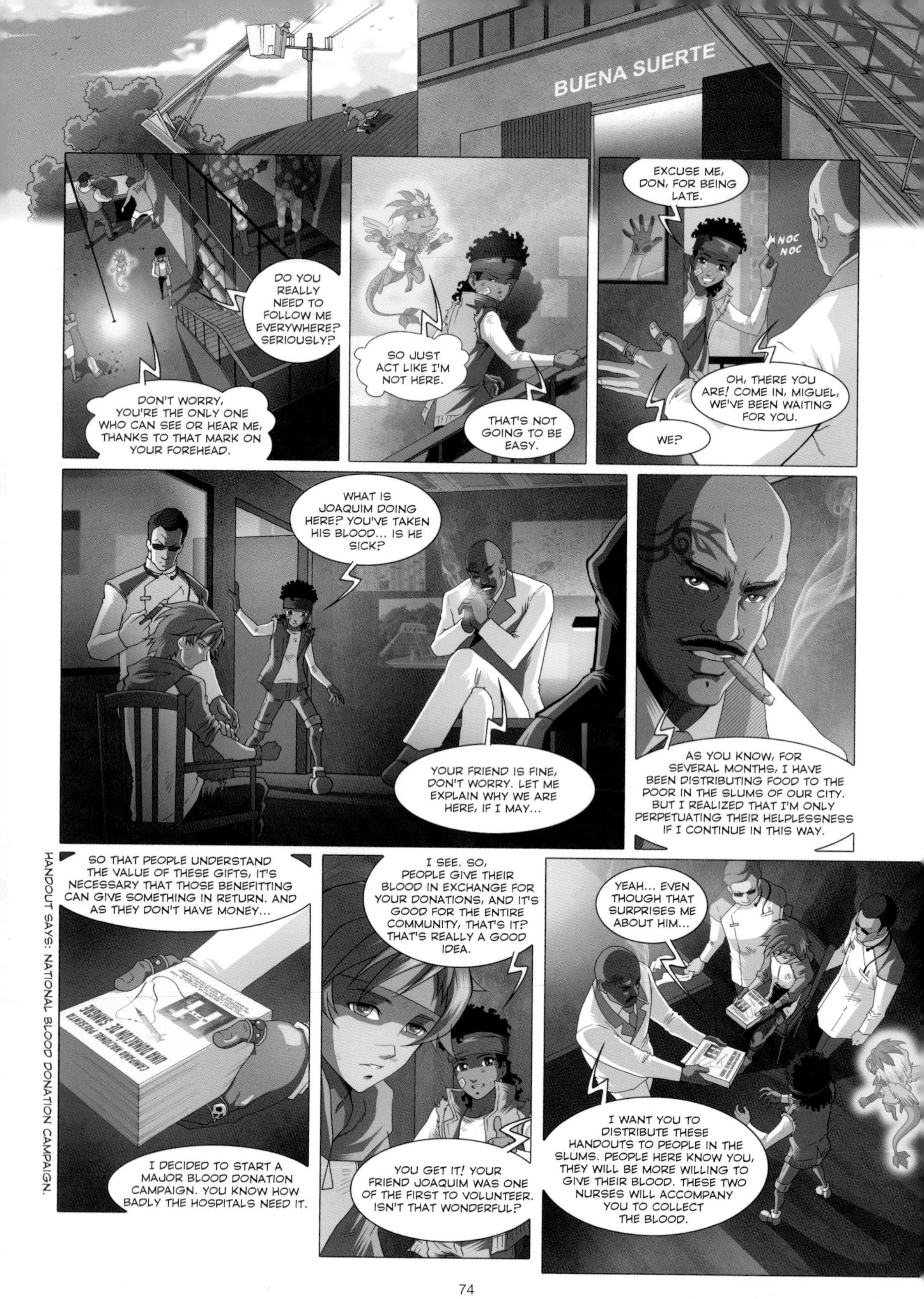
BUENA SUERTE
DO YOU REALLY NEED TO FOLLOW ME EVERYWHERE? SERIOUSLY?
DON'T WORRY, YOU'RE THE ONLY ONE WHO CAN SEE OR HEAR ME, THANKS TO THAT MARK ON YOUR FOREHEAD.
SO JUST ACT LIKE I'M NOT HERE.
THAT'S NOT GOING TO BE EASY.
EXCUSE ME, DON, FOR BEING LATE.
NOC NOC
OH, THERE YOU ARE! COME IN, MIGUEL, WE'VE BEEN WAITING FOR YOU.
WE?
WHAT IS JOAQUIM DOING HERE? YOU'VE TAKEN HIS BLOOD... IS HE SICK?
YOUR FRIEND IS FINE, DON'T WORRY. LET ME EXPLAIN WHY WE ARE HERE, IF I MAY...
AS YOU KNOW, FOR SEVERAL MONTHS, I HAVE BEEN DISTRIBUTING FOOD TO THE POOR IN THE SLUMS OF OUR CITY. BUT I REALIZED THAT I'M ONLY PERPETUATING THEIR HELPLESSNESS IF I CONTINUE IN THIS WAY.
SO THAT PEOPLE UNDERSTAND THE VALUE OF THESE GIFTS, IT'S NECESSARY THAT THOSE BENEFITTING CAN GIVE SOMETHING IN RETURN. AND AS THEY DON'T HAVE MONEY...
I DECIDED TO START A MAJOR BLOOD DONATION CAMPAIGN. YOU KNOW HOW BADLY THE HOSPITALS NEED IT.
HANDOUT SAYS: NATIONAL BLOOD DONATION CAMPAIGN.
I SEE. SO, PEOPLE GIVE THEIR BLOOD IN EXCHANGE FOR YOUR DONATIONS, AND IT'S GOOD FOR THE ENTIRE COMMUNITY, THAT'S IT? THAT'S REALLY A GOOD IDEA.
YOU GET IT! YOUR FRIEND JOAQUIM WAS ONE OF THE FIRST TO VOLUNTEER. ISN'T THAT WONDERFUL?
YEAH... EVEN THOUGH THAT SURPRISES ME ABOUT HIM...
I WANT YOU TO DISTRIBUTE THESE HANDOUTS TO PEOPLE IN THE SLUMS. PEOPLE HERE KNOW YOU, THEY WILL BE MORE WILLING TO GIVE THEIR BLOOD. THESE TWO NURSES WILL ACCOMPANY YOU TO COLLECT THE BLOOD.

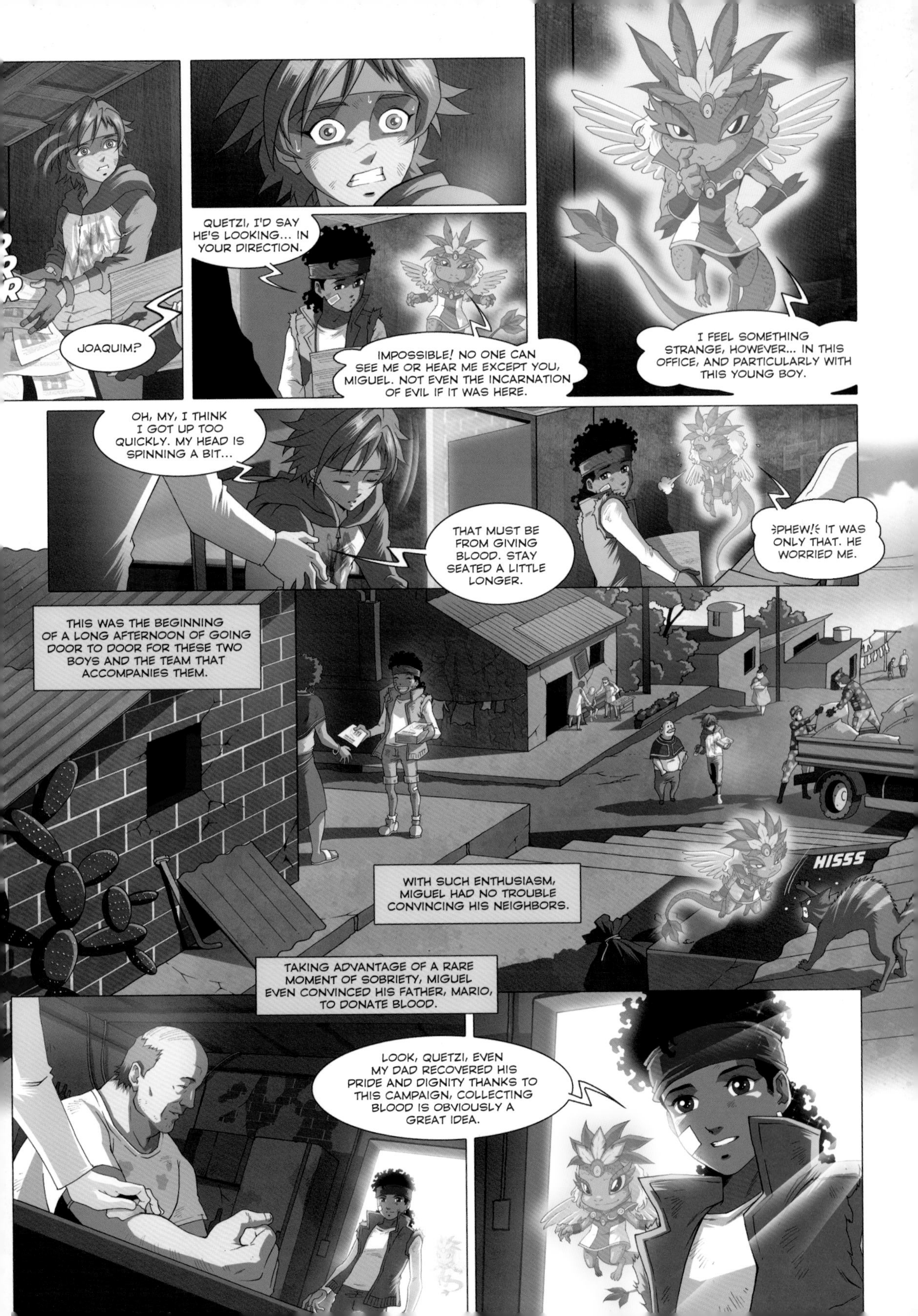

RRR
JOAQUIM?
QUETZI, I'D SAY HE'S LOOKING... IN YOUR DIRECTION.
IMPOSSIBLE! NO ONE CAN SEE ME OR HEAR ME EXCEPT YOU, MIGUEL. NOT EVEN THE INCARNATION OF EVIL IF IT WAS HERE.
I FEEL SOMETHING STRANGE, HOWEVER... IN THIS OFFICE, AND PARTICULARLY WITH THIS YOUNG BOY.
OH, MY, I THINK I GOT UP TOO QUICKLY. MY HEAD IS SPINNING A BIT...
THAT MUST BE FROM GIVING BLOOD. STAY SEATED A LITTLE LONGER.
PHEW! IT WAS ONLY THAT. HE WORRIED ME.
THIS WAS THE BEGINNING OF A LONG AFTERNOON OF GOING DOOR TO DOOR FOR THESE TWO BOYS AND THE TEAM THAT ACCOMPANIES THEM.
WITH SUCH ENTHUSIASM, MIGUEL HAD NO TROUBLE CONVINCING HIS NEIGHBORS.
HISSS
TAKING ADVANTAGE OF A RARE MOMENT OF SOBRIETY, MIGUEL EVEN CONVINCED HIS FATHER, MARIO, TO DONATE BLOOD.
LOOK, QUETZI, EVEN MY DAD RECOVERED HIS PRIDE AND DIGNITY THANKS TO THIS CAMPAIGN, COLLECTING BLOOD IS OBVIOUSLY A GREAT IDEA.

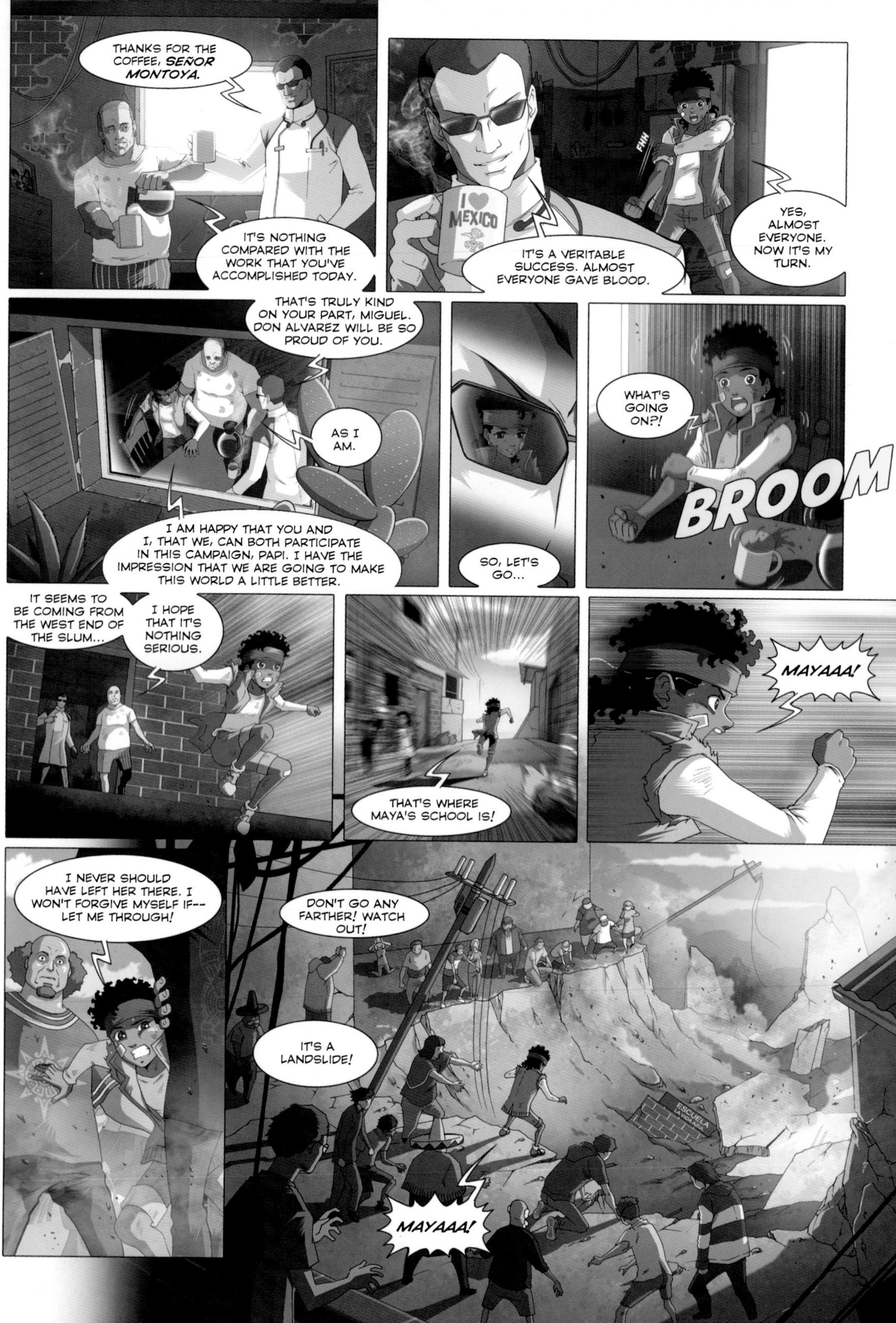
THANKS FOR THE COFFEE, *SEÑOR MONTOYA*.
IT'S NOTHING COMPARED WITH THE WORK THAT YOU'VE ACCOMPLISHED TODAY.
I ♥ MEXICO
IT'S A VERITABLE SUCCESS. ALMOST EVERYONE GAVE BLOOD.
FHH
YES, ALMOST EVERYONE. NOW IT'S MY TURN.
THAT'S TRULY KIND ON YOUR PART, MIGUEL. DON ALVAREZ WILL BE SO PROUD OF YOU.
AS I AM.
I AM HAPPY THAT YOU AND I, THAT WE, CAN BOTH PARTICIPATE IN THIS CAMPAIGN, PAPI. I HAVE THE IMPRESSION THAT WE ARE GOING TO MAKE THIS WORLD A LITTLE BETTER.
SO, LET'S GO...
WHAT'S GOING ON?!
BROOM
IT SEEMS TO BE COMING FROM THE WEST END OF THE SLUM...
I HOPE THAT IT'S NOTHING SERIOUS.
THAT'S WHERE MAYA'S SCHOOL IS!
MAYAAA!
I NEVER SHOULD HAVE LEFT HER THERE. I WON'T FORGIVE MYSELF IF-- LET ME THROUGH!
DON'T GO ANY FARTHER! WATCH OUT!
IT'S A LANDSLIDE!
ESCUELA
MAYAAA!

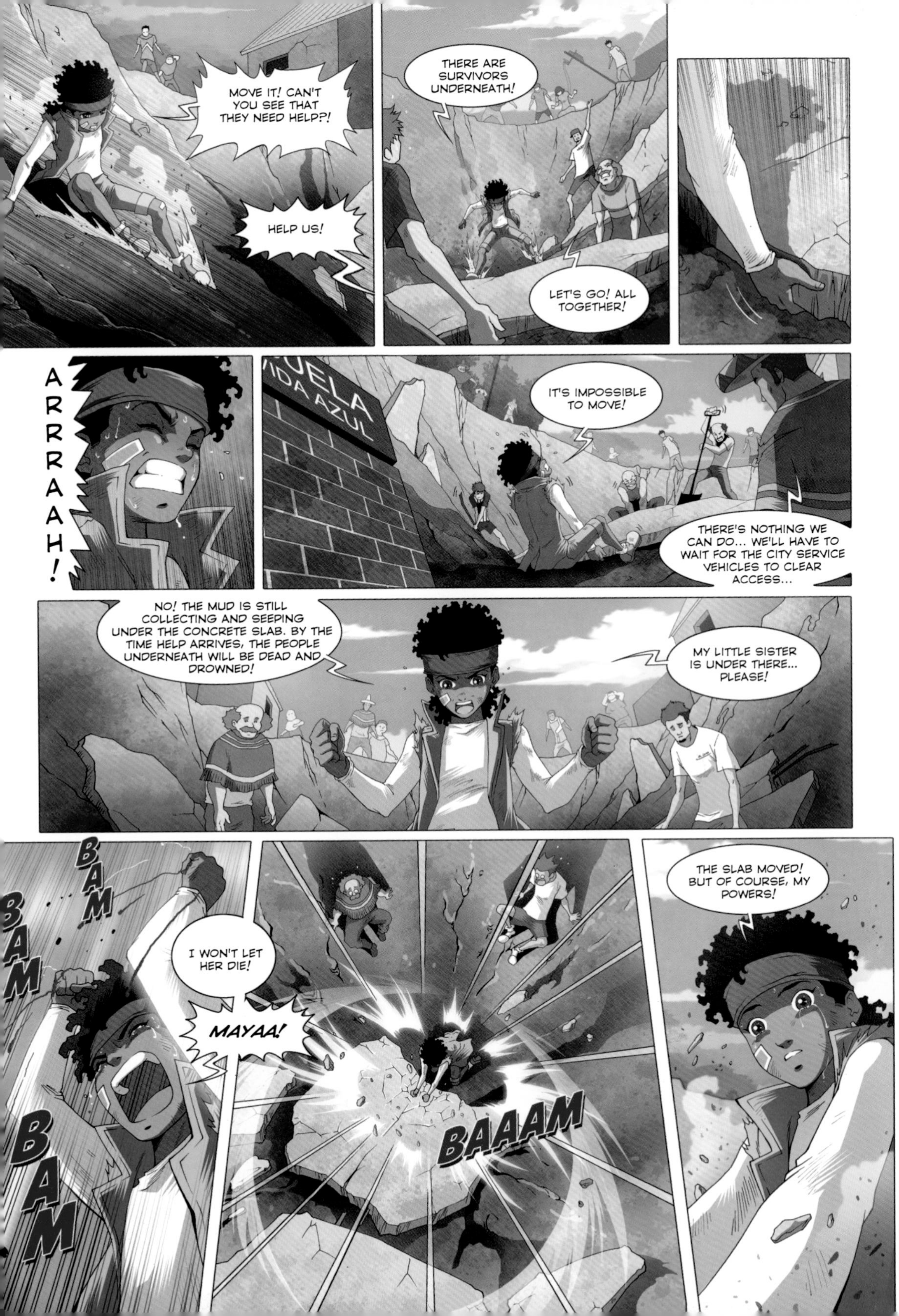
MOVE IT! CAN'T YOU SEE THAT THEY NEED HELP?!
HELP US!
THERE ARE SURVIVORS UNDERNEATH!
LET'S GO! ALL TOGETHER!
ARRRAAH!
UELA
VIDA AZUL
IT'S IMPOSSIBLE TO MOVE!
THERE'S NOTHING WE CAN DO... WE'LL HAVE TO WAIT FOR THE CITY SERVICE VEHICLES TO CLEAR ACCESS...
NO! THE MUD IS STILL COLLECTING AND SEEPING UNDER THE CONCRETE SLAB. BY THE TIME HELP ARRIVES, THE PEOPLE UNDERNEATH WILL BE DEAD AND DROWNED!
MY LITTLE SISTER IS UNDER THERE... PLEASE!
BAM
BAM
BAM
BAM
I WON'T LET HER DIE!
MAYAA!
BAAAM
THE SLAB MOVED! BUT OF COURSE, MY POWERS!

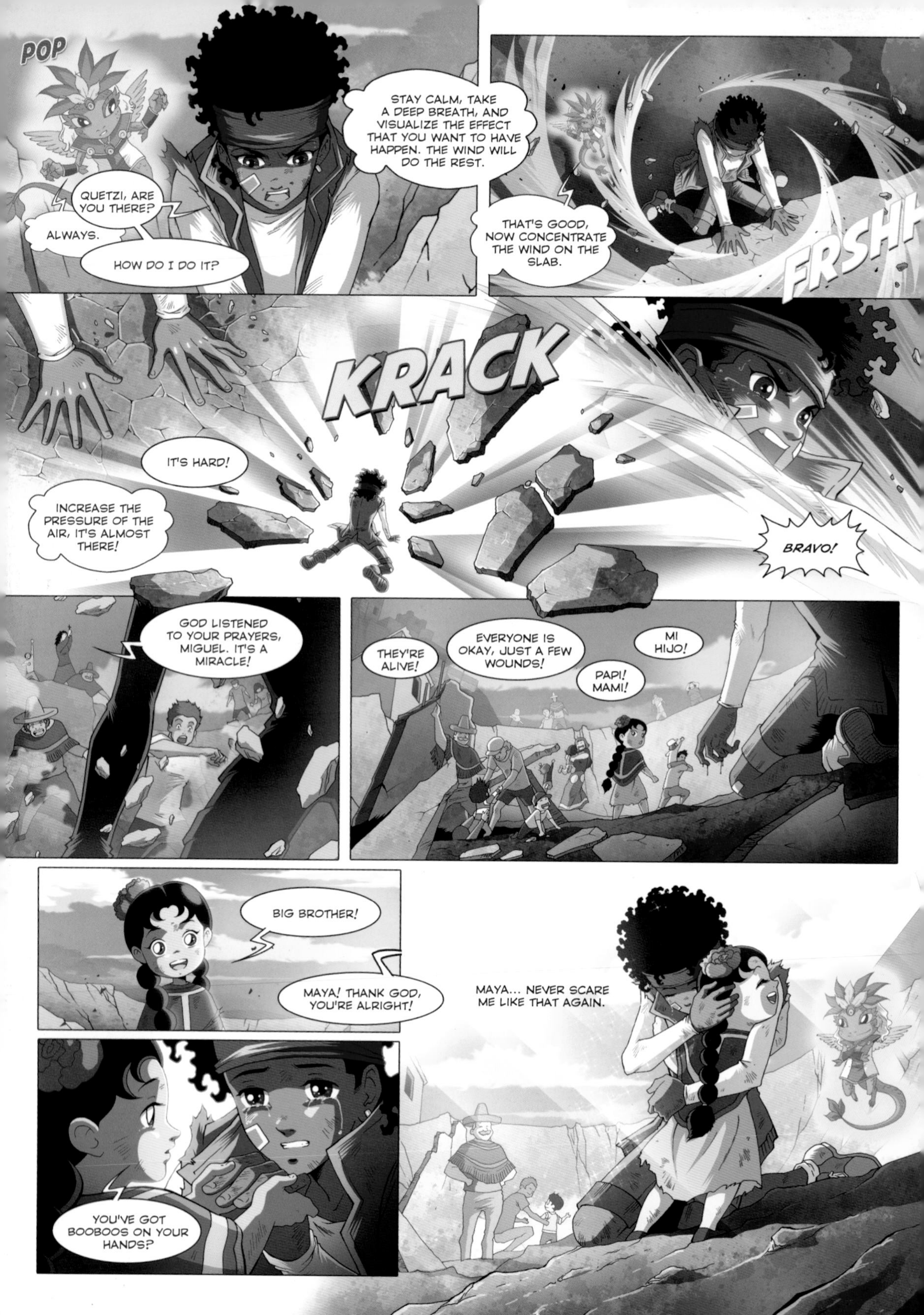
POP
QUETZI, ARE YOU THERE?
ALWAYS.
HOW DO I DO IT?
STAY CALM, TAKE A DEEP BREATH, AND VISUALIZE THE EFFECT THAT YOU WANT TO HAVE HAPPEN. THE WIND WILL DO THE REST.
THAT'S GOOD, NOW CONCENTRATE THE WIND ON THE SLAB.
FRSHH
KRACK
IT'S HARD!
INCREASE THE PRESSURE OF THE AIR, IT'S ALMOST THERE!
BRAVO!
GOD LISTENED TO YOUR PRAYERS, MIGUEL. IT'S A MIRACLE!
THEY'RE ALIVE!
EVERYONE IS OKAY, JUST A FEW WOUNDS!
MI HIJO!
PAPI! MAMI!
BIG BROTHER!
MAYA! THANK GOD, YOU'RE ALRIGHT!
MAYA... NEVER SCARE ME LIKE THAT AGAIN.
YOU'VE GOT BOOBOOS ON YOUR HANDS?

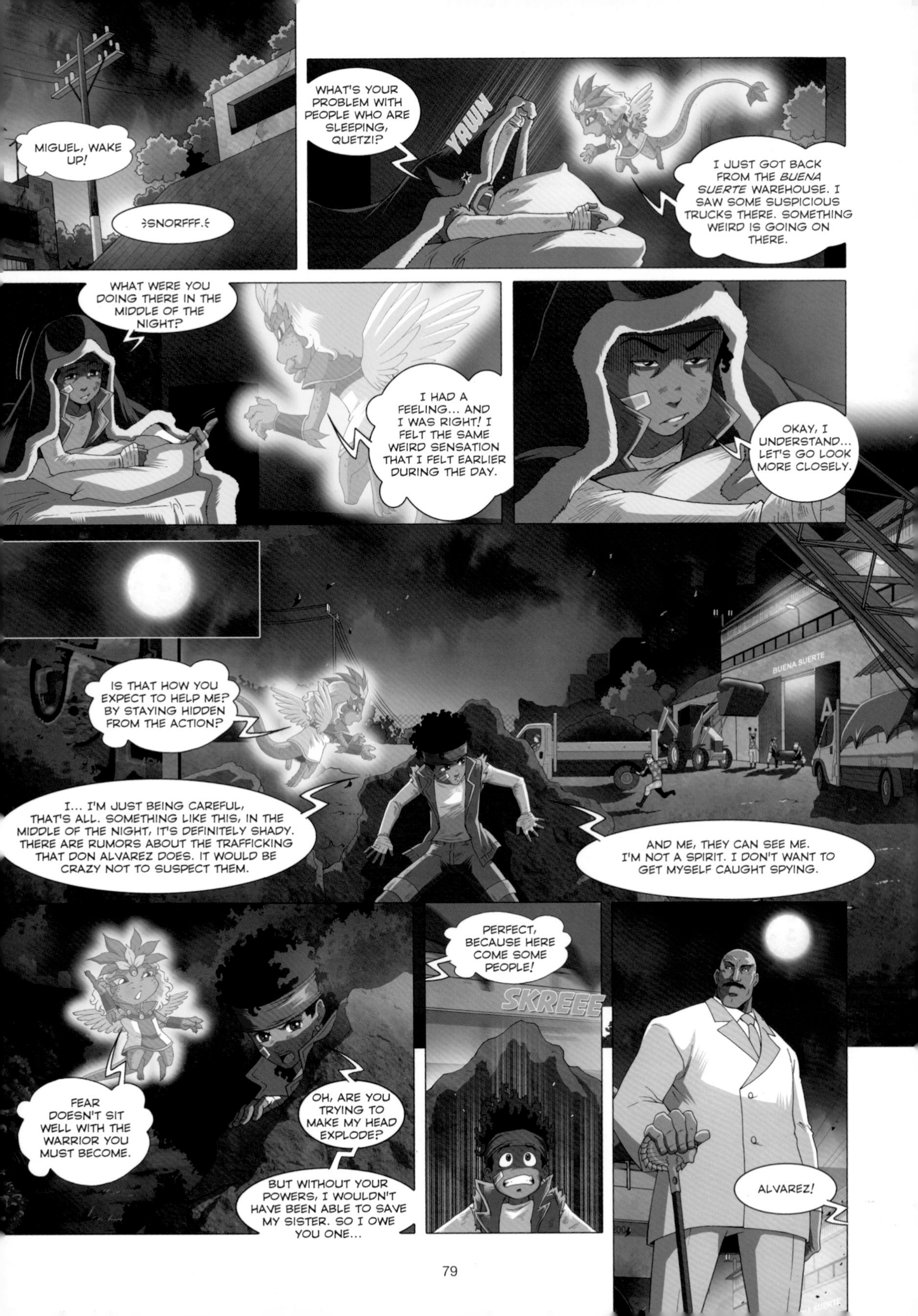
MIGUEL, WAKE UP!
SNORFFF.
YAWN
WHAT'S YOUR PROBLEM WITH PEOPLE WHO ARE SLEEPING, QUETZI?
I JUST GOT BACK FROM THE *BUENA SUERTE* WAREHOUSE. I SAW SOME SUSPICIOUS TRUCKS THERE. SOMETHING WEIRD IS GOING ON THERE.
WHAT WERE YOU DOING THERE IN THE MIDDLE OF THE NIGHT?
I HAD A FEELING... AND I WAS RIGHT! I FELT THE SAME WEIRD SENSATION THAT I FELT EARLIER DURING THE DAY.
OKAY, I UNDERSTAND... LET'S GO LOOK MORE CLOSELY.
BUENA SUERTE
IS THAT HOW YOU EXPECT TO HELP ME? BY STAYING HIDDEN FROM THE ACTION?
I... I'M JUST BEING CAREFUL, THAT'S ALL. SOMETHING LIKE THIS, IN THE MIDDLE OF THE NIGHT, IT'S DEFINITELY SHADY. THERE ARE RUMORS ABOUT THE TRAFFICKING THAT DON ALVAREZ DOES. IT WOULD BE CRAZY NOT TO SUSPECT THEM.
AND ME, THEY CAN SEE ME. I'M NOT A SPIRIT. I DON'T WANT TO GET MYSELF CAUGHT SPYING.
FEAR DOESN'T SIT WELL WITH THE WARRIOR YOU MUST BECOME.
OH, ARE YOU TRYING TO MAKE MY HEAD EXPLODE?
BUT WITHOUT YOUR POWERS, I WOULDN'T HAVE BEEN ABLE TO SAVE MY SISTER. SO I OWE YOU ONE...
PERFECT, BECAUSE HERE COME SOME PEOPLE!
SKREEE
ALVAREZ!

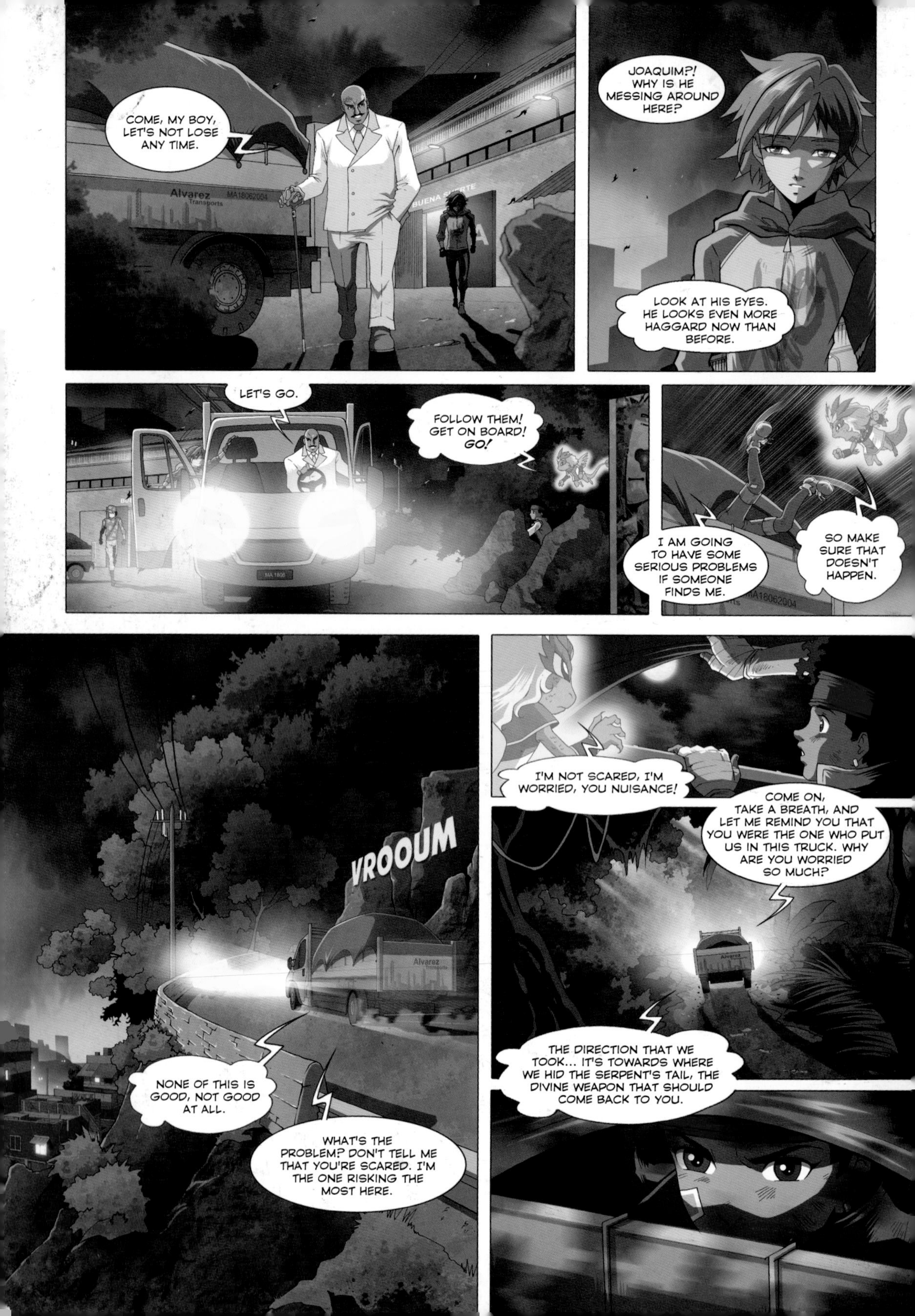
COME, MY BOY, LET'S NOT LOSE ANY TIME.
Alvarez Transports
MA18062004
BUENA SUERTE
JOAQUIM?! WHY IS HE MESSING AROUND HERE?
LOOK AT HIS EYES. HE LOOKS EVEN MORE HAGGARD NOW THAN BEFORE.
LET'S GO.
FOLLOW THEM! GET ON BOARD! GO!
I AM GOING TO HAVE SOME SERIOUS PROBLEMS IF SOMEONE FINDS ME.
SO MAKE SURE THAT DOESN'T HAPPEN.
VROOUM
Alvarez
NONE OF THIS IS GOOD, NOT GOOD AT ALL.
WHAT'S THE PROBLEM? DON'T TELL ME THAT YOU'RE SCARED. I'M THE ONE RISKING THE MOST HERE.
I'M NOT SCARED, I'M WORRIED, YOU NUISANCE!
COME ON, TAKE A BREATH, AND LET ME REMIND YOU THAT YOU WERE THE ONE WHO PUT US IN THIS TRUCK. WHY ARE YOU WORRIED SO MUCH?
THE DIRECTION THAT WE TOOK... IT'S TOWARDS WHERE WE HID THE SERPENT'S TAIL, THE DIVINE WEAPON THAT SHOULD COME BACK TO YOU.

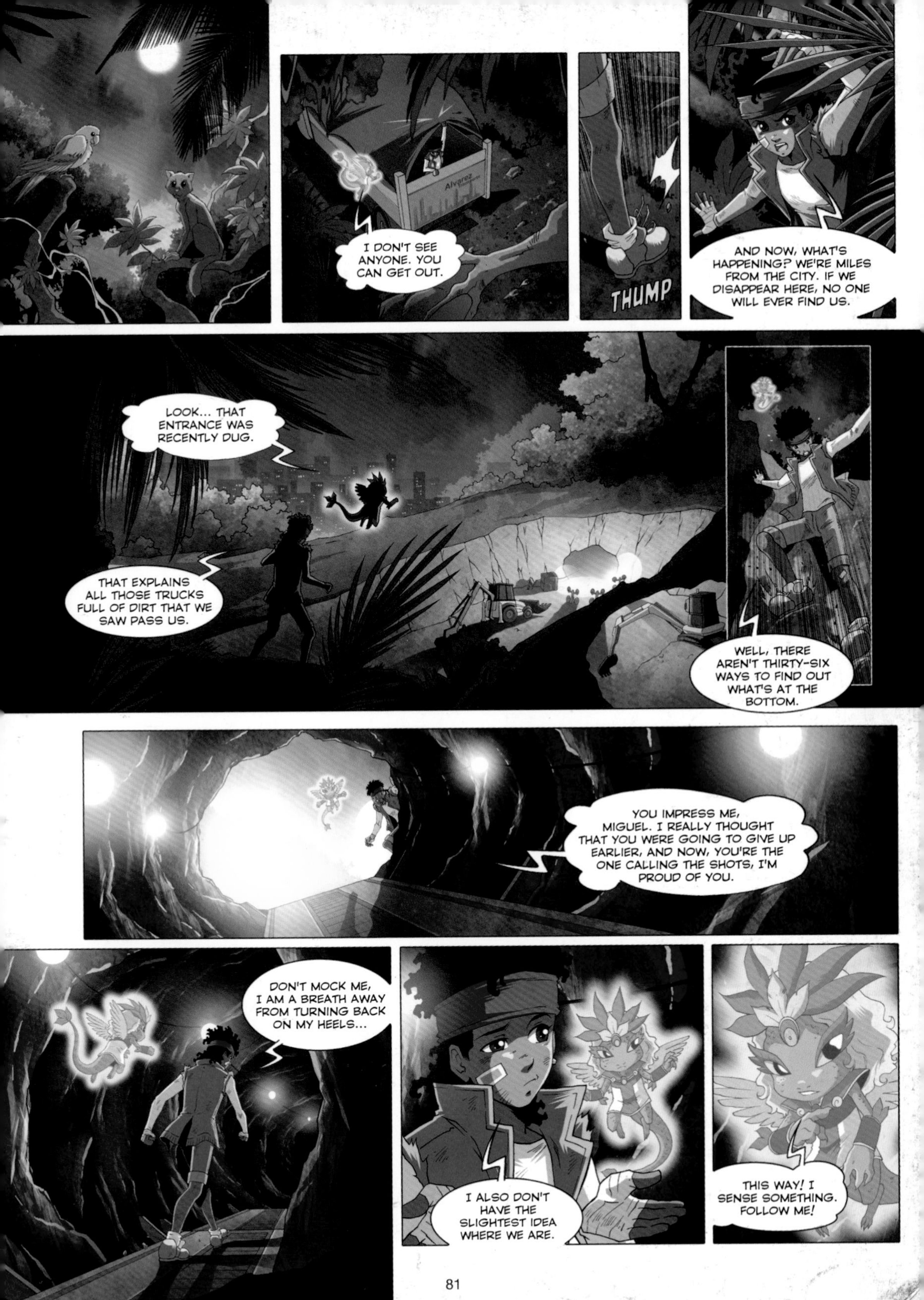

Alvarez
I DON'T SEE ANYONE. YOU CAN GET OUT.
THUMP
AND NOW, WHAT'S HAPPENING? WE'RE MILES FROM THE CITY. IF WE DISAPPEAR HERE, NO ONE WILL EVER FIND US.
LOOK... THAT ENTRANCE WAS RECENTLY DUG.
THAT EXPLAINS ALL THOSE TRUCKS FULL OF DIRT THAT WE SAW PASS US.
WELL, THERE AREN'T THIRTY-SIX WAYS TO FIND OUT WHAT'S AT THE BOTTOM.
YOU IMPRESS ME, MIGUEL. I REALLY THOUGHT THAT YOU WERE GOING TO GIVE UP EARLIER, AND NOW, YOU'RE THE ONE CALLING THE SHOTS, I'M PROUD OF YOU.
DON'T MOCK ME, I AM A BREATH AWAY FROM TURNING BACK ON MY HEELS...
I ALSO DON'T HAVE THE SLIGHTEST IDEA WHERE WE ARE.
THIS WAY! I SENSE SOMETHING. FOLLOW ME!

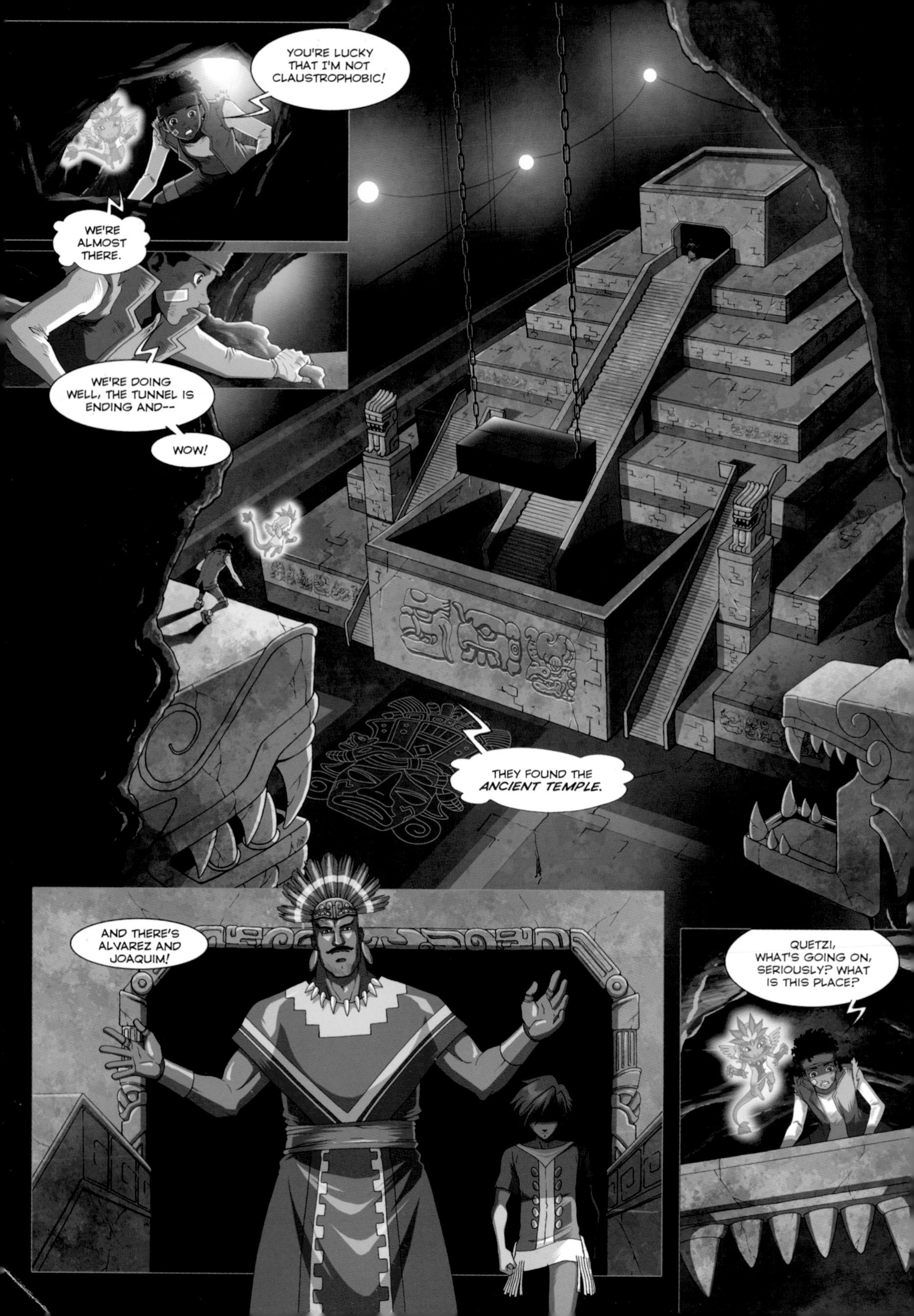
YOU'RE LUCKY THAT I'M NOT CLAUSTROPHOBIC!
WE'RE ALMOST THERE.
WE'RE DOING WELL, THE TUNNEL IS ENDING AND--
WOW!
THEY FOUND THE *ANCIENT TEMPLE*.
AND THERE'S ALVAREZ AND JOAQUIM!
QUETZI, WHAT'S GOING ON, SERIOUSLY? WHAT IS THIS PLACE?

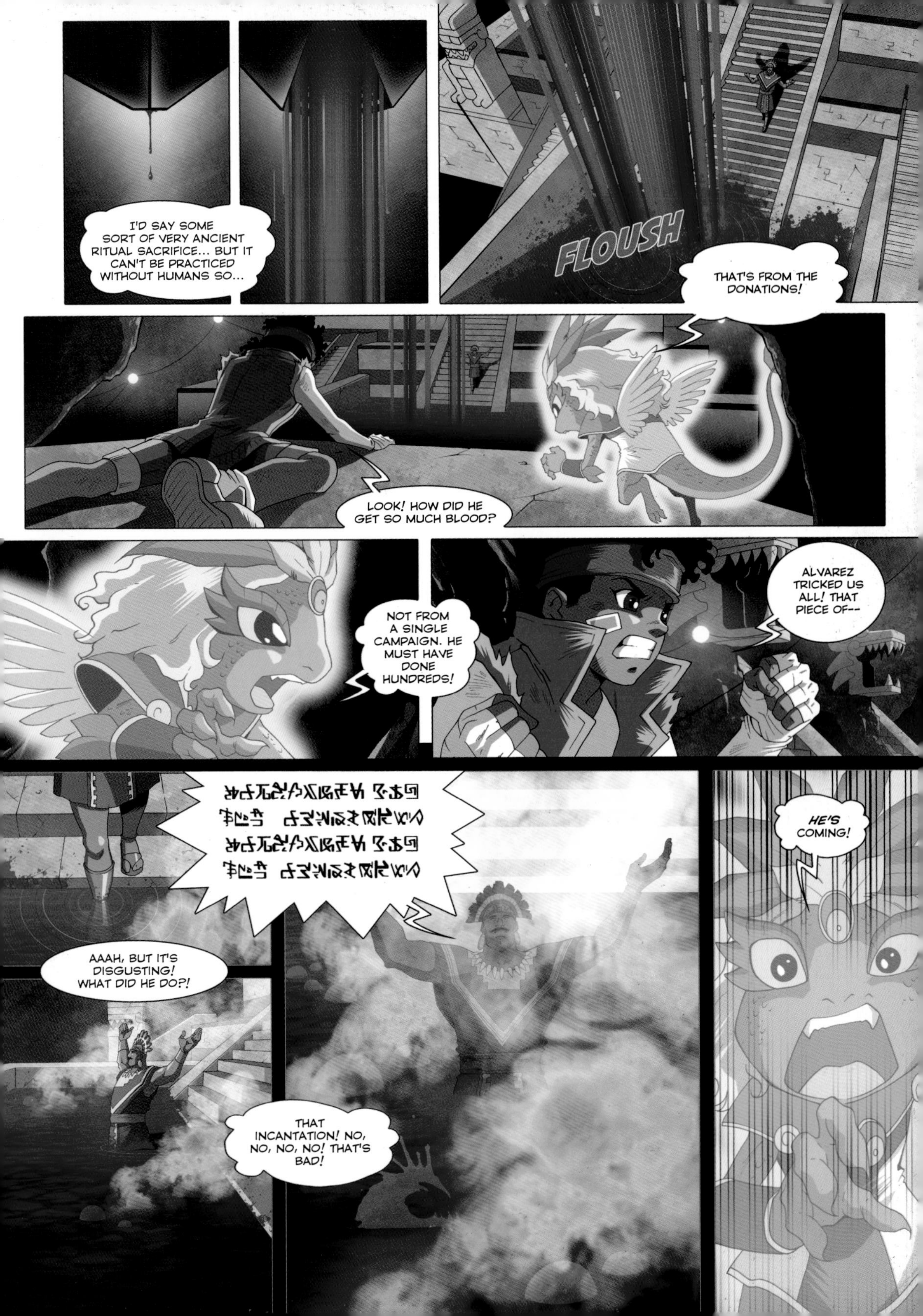
I'D SAY SOME SORT OF VERY ANCIENT RITUAL SACRIFICE... BUT IT CAN'T BE PRACTICED WITHOUT HUMANS SO...
FLOUSH
THAT'S FROM THE DONATIONS!
LOOK! HOW DID HE GET SO MUCH BLOOD?
NOT FROM A SINGLE CAMPAIGN. HE MUST HAVE DONE HUNDREDS!
ALVAREZ TRICKED US ALL! THAT PIECE OF--
AAAH, BUT IT'S DISGUSTING! WHAT DID HE DO?!
THAT INCANTATION! NO, NO, NO, NO! THAT'S BAD!
HE'S COMING!

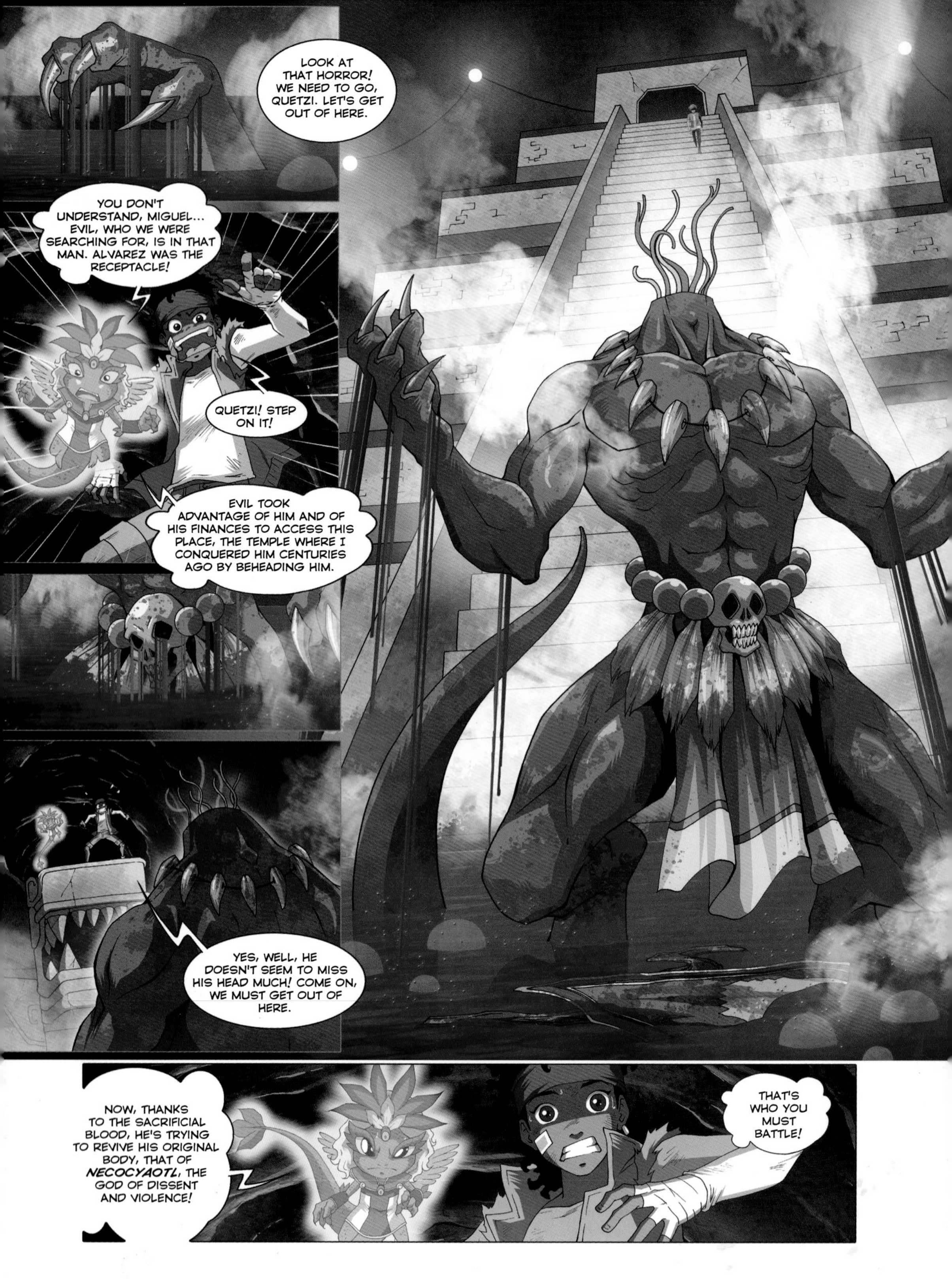
LOOK AT THAT HORROR! WE NEED TO GO, QUETZI. LET'S GET OUT OF HERE.
YOU DON'T UNDERSTAND, MIGUEL... EVIL, WHO WE WERE SEARCHING FOR, IS IN THAT MAN. ALVAREZ WAS THE RECEPTACLE!
QUETZI! STEP ON IT!
EVIL TOOK ADVANTAGE OF HIM AND OF HIS FINANCES TO ACCESS THIS PLACE, THE TEMPLE WHERE I CONQUERED HIM CENTURIES AGO BY BEHEADING HIM.
YES, WELL, HE DOESN'T SEEM TO MISS HIS HEAD MUCH! COME ON, WE MUST GET OUT OF HERE.
NOW, THANKS TO THE SACRIFICIAL BLOOD, HE'S TRYING TO REVIVE HIS ORIGINAL BODY, THAT OF NECOCYAOTL, THE GOD OF DISSENT AND VIOLENCE!
THAT'S WHO YOU MUST BATTLE!

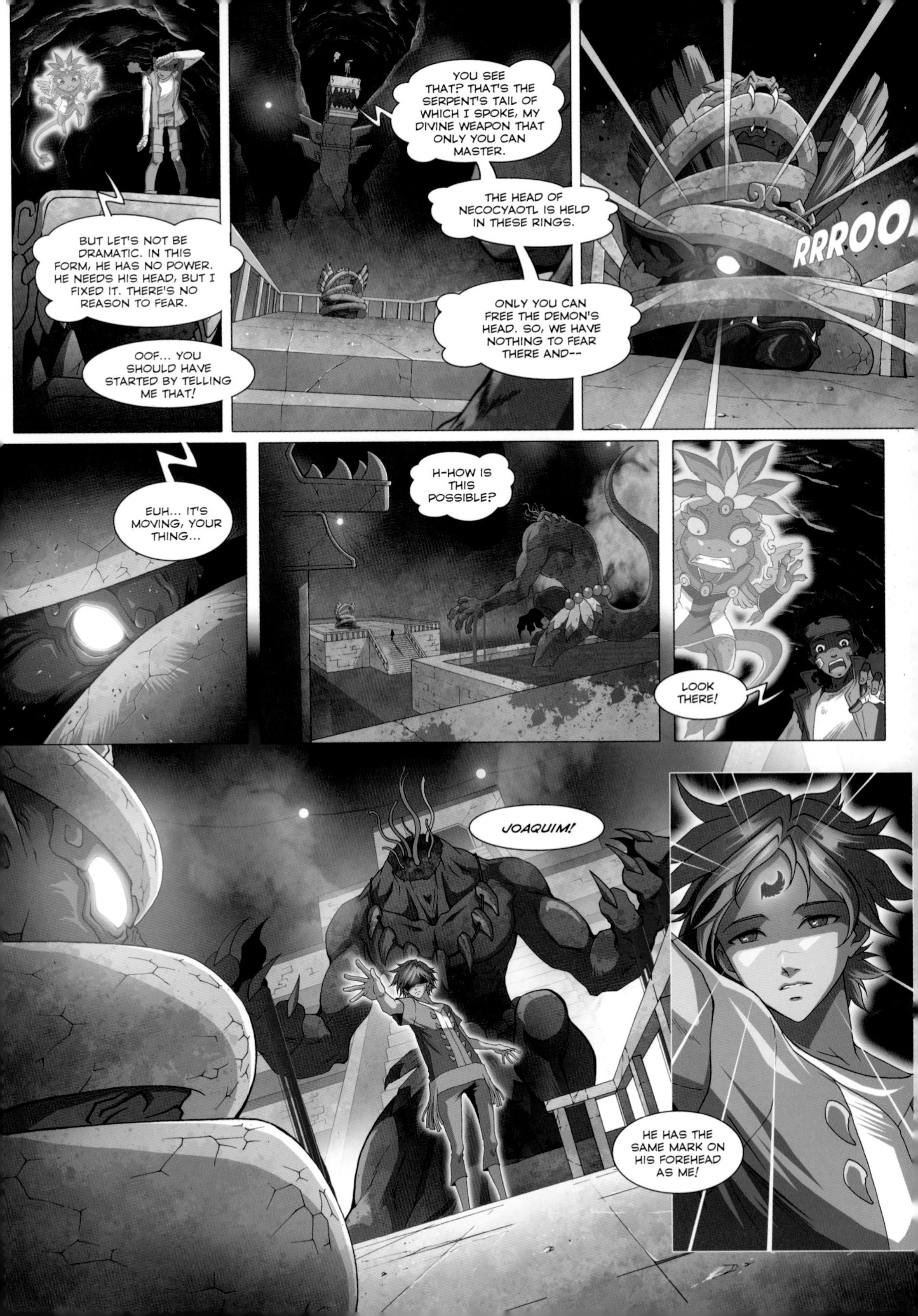
BUT LET'S NOT BE DRAMATIC. IN THIS FORM, HE HAS NO POWER. HE NEEDS HIS HEAD, BUT I FIXED IT. THERE'S NO REASON TO FEAR.
OOF... YOU SHOULD HAVE STARTED BY TELLING ME THAT!
YOU SEE THAT? THAT'S THE SERPENT'S TAIL OF WHICH I SPOKE, MY DIVINE WEAPON THAT ONLY YOU CAN MASTER.
THE HEAD OF NECOCYAOTL IS HELD IN THESE RINGS.
ONLY YOU CAN FREE THE DEMON'S HEAD. SO, WE HAVE NOTHING TO FEAR THERE AND--
RRROO
EUH... IT'S MOVING, YOUR THING...
H-HOW IS THIS POSSIBLE?
LOOK THERE!
JOAQUIM!
HE HAS THE SAME MARK ON HIS FOREHEAD AS ME!

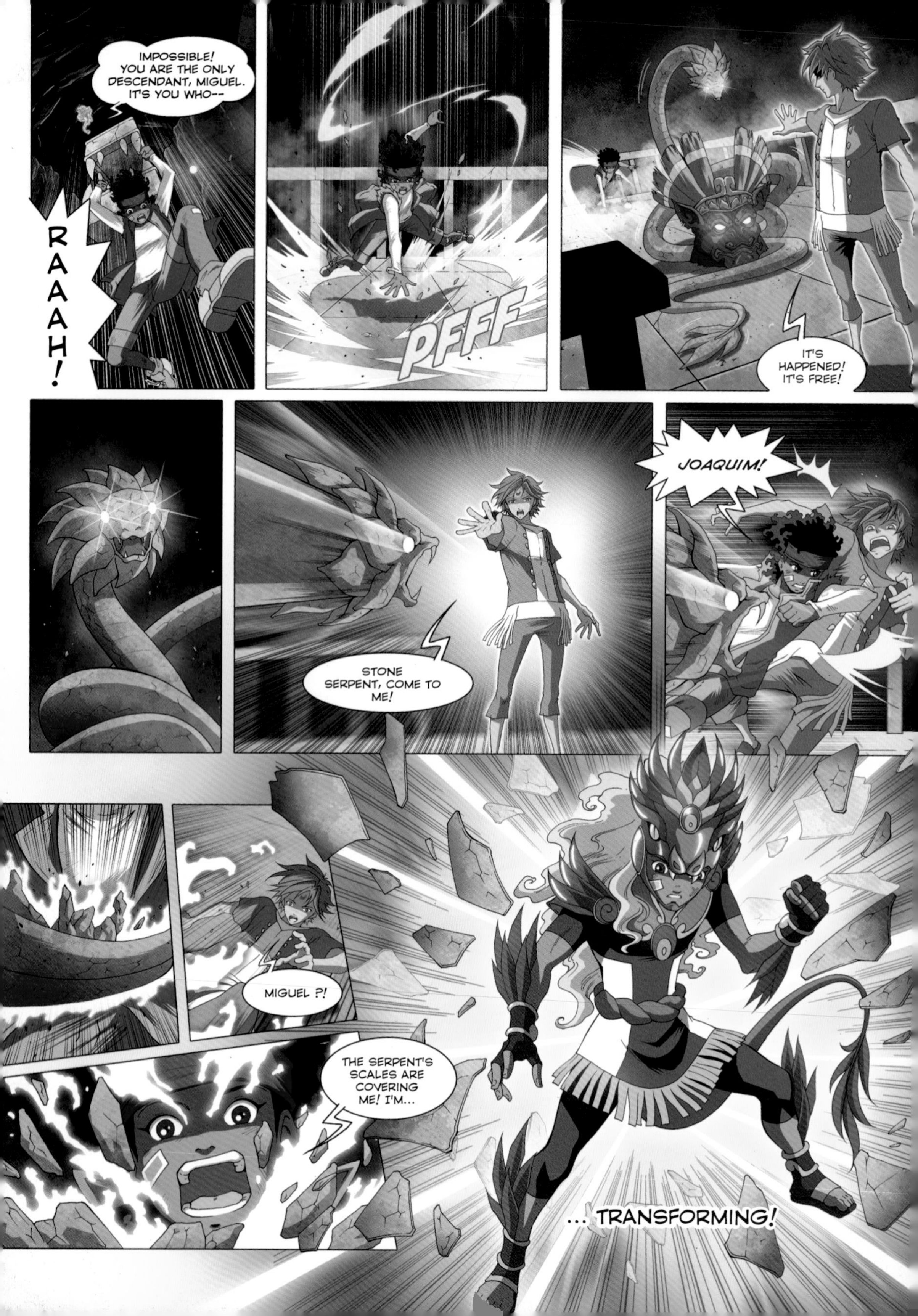
IMPOSSIBLE! YOU ARE THE ONLY DESCENDANT, MIGUEL. IT'S YOU WHO--
RAAAAH!
PFFF
IT'S HAPPENED! IT'S FREE!
STONE SERPENT, COME TO ME!
JOAQUIM!
MIGUEL ?!
THE SERPENT'S SCALES ARE COVERING ME! I'M...
... TRANSFORMING!

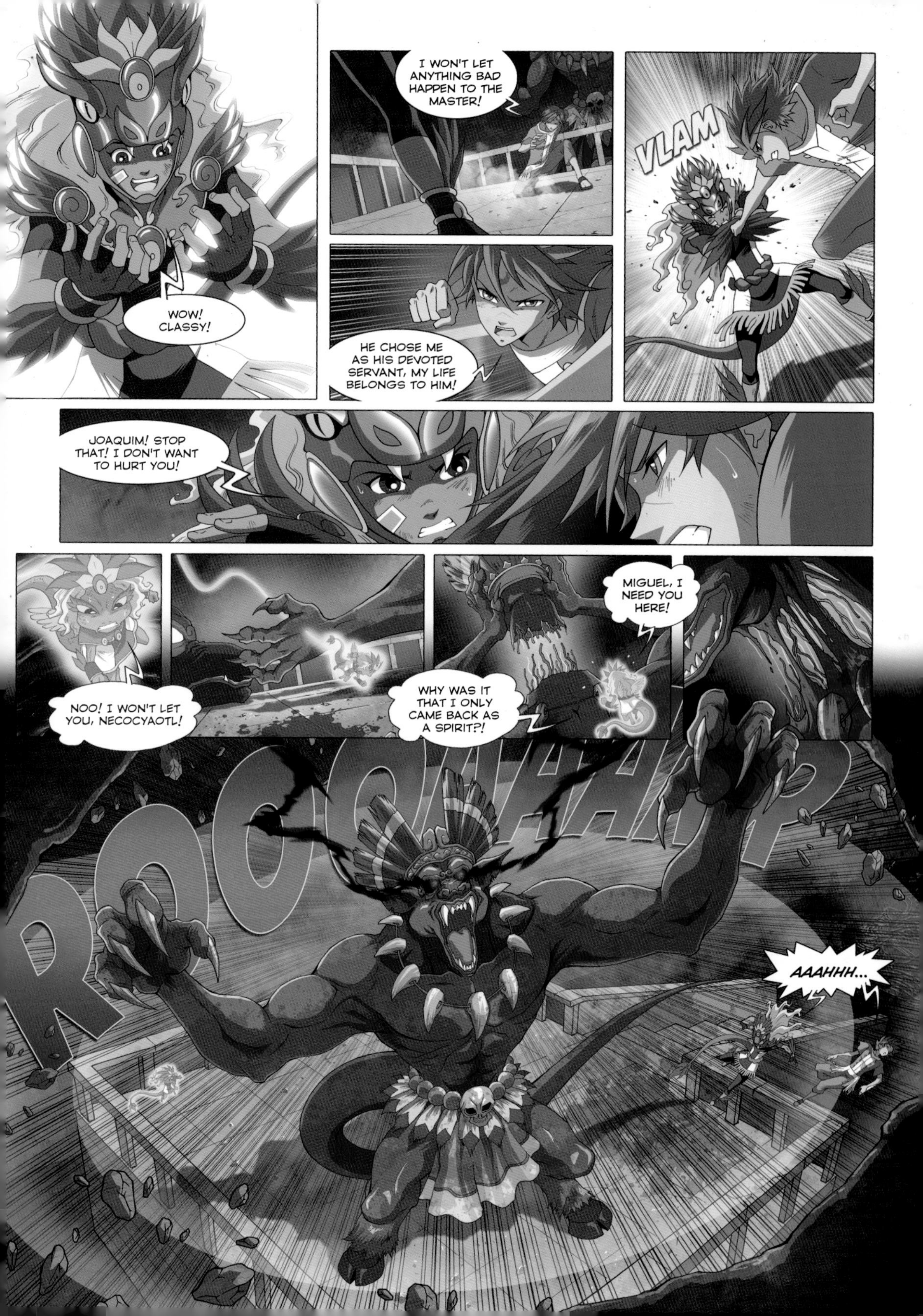
WOW! CLASSY!
I WON'T LET ANYTHING BAD HAPPEN TO THE MASTER!
HE CHOSE ME AS HIS DEVOTED SERVANT, MY LIFE BELONGS TO HIM!
VLAM
JOAQUIM! STOP THAT! I DON'T WANT TO HURT YOU!
NOO! I WON'T LET YOU, NECOCYAOTL!
WHY WAS IT THAT I ONLY CAME BACK AS A SPIRIT?!
MIGUEL, I NEED YOU HERE!
ROOOAAAARR
AAAHHH...

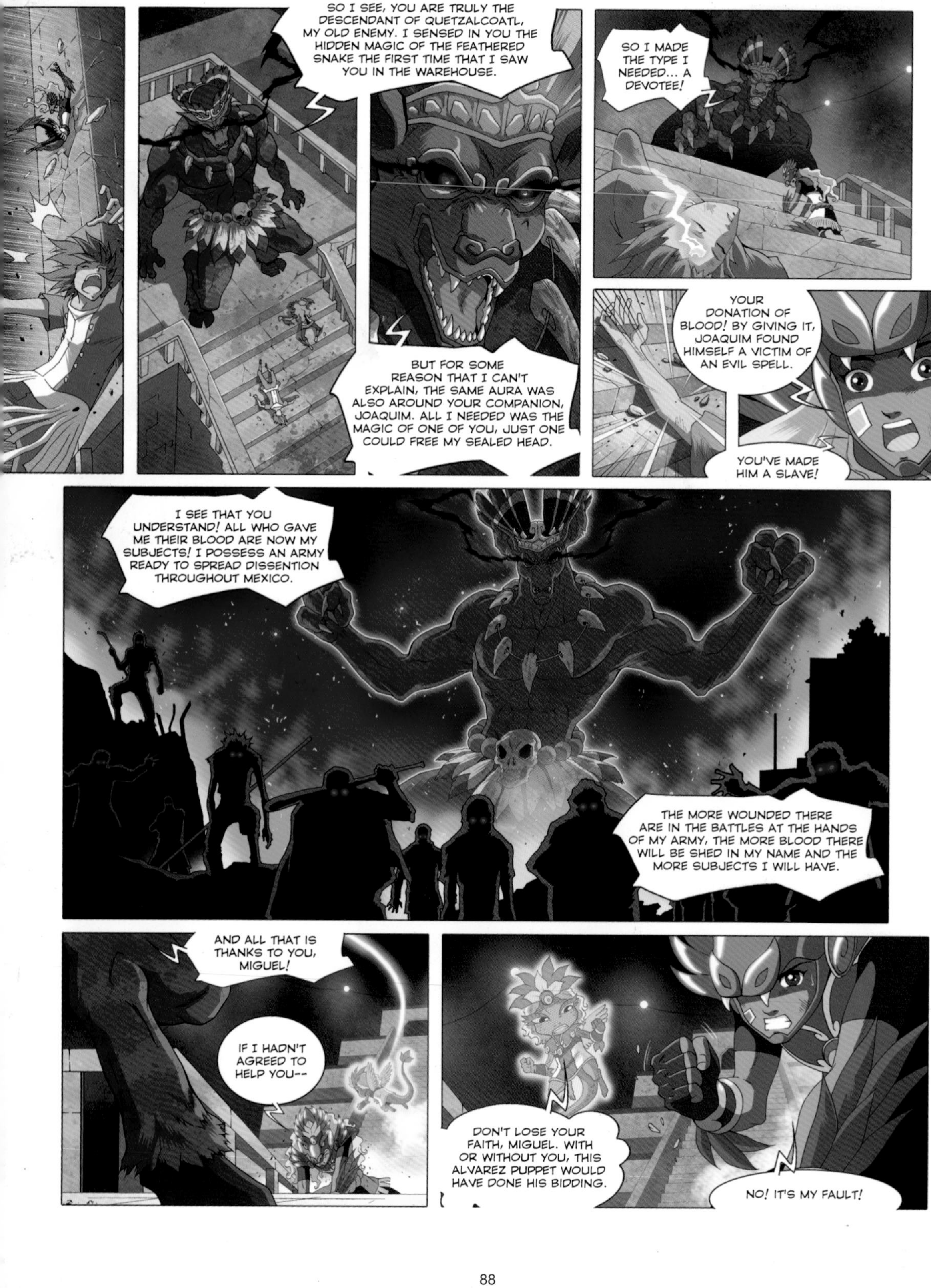
SO I SEE, YOU ARE TRULY THE DESCENDANT OF QUETZALCOATL, MY OLD ENEMY. I SENSED IN YOU THE HIDDEN MAGIC OF THE FEATHERED SNAKE THE FIRST TIME THAT I SAW YOU IN THE WAREHOUSE.
BUT FOR SOME REASON THAT I CAN'T EXPLAIN, THE SAME AURA WAS ALSO AROUND YOUR COMPANION, JOAQUIM. ALL I NEEDED WAS THE MAGIC OF ONE OF YOU, JUST ONE COULD FREE MY SEALED HEAD.
SO I MADE THE TYPE I NEEDED... A DEVOTEE!
YOUR DONATION OF BLOOD! BY GIVING IT, JOAQUIM FOUND HIMSELF A VICTIM OF AN EVIL SPELL.
YOU'VE MADE HIM A SLAVE!
I SEE THAT YOU UNDERSTAND! ALL WHO GAVE ME THEIR BLOOD ARE NOW MY SUBJECTS! I POSSESS AN ARMY READY TO SPREAD DISSENTION THROUGHOUT MEXICO.
THE MORE WOUNDED THERE ARE IN THE BATTLES AT THE HANDS OF MY ARMY, THE MORE BLOOD THERE WILL BE SHED IN MY NAME AND THE MORE SUBJECTS I WILL HAVE.
AND ALL THAT IS THANKS TO YOU, MIGUEL!
IF I HADN'T AGREED TO HELP YOU--
DON'T LOSE YOUR FAITH, MIGUEL. WITH OR WITHOUT YOU, THIS ALVAREZ PUPPET WOULD HAVE DONE HIS BIDDING.
NO! IT'S MY FAULT!

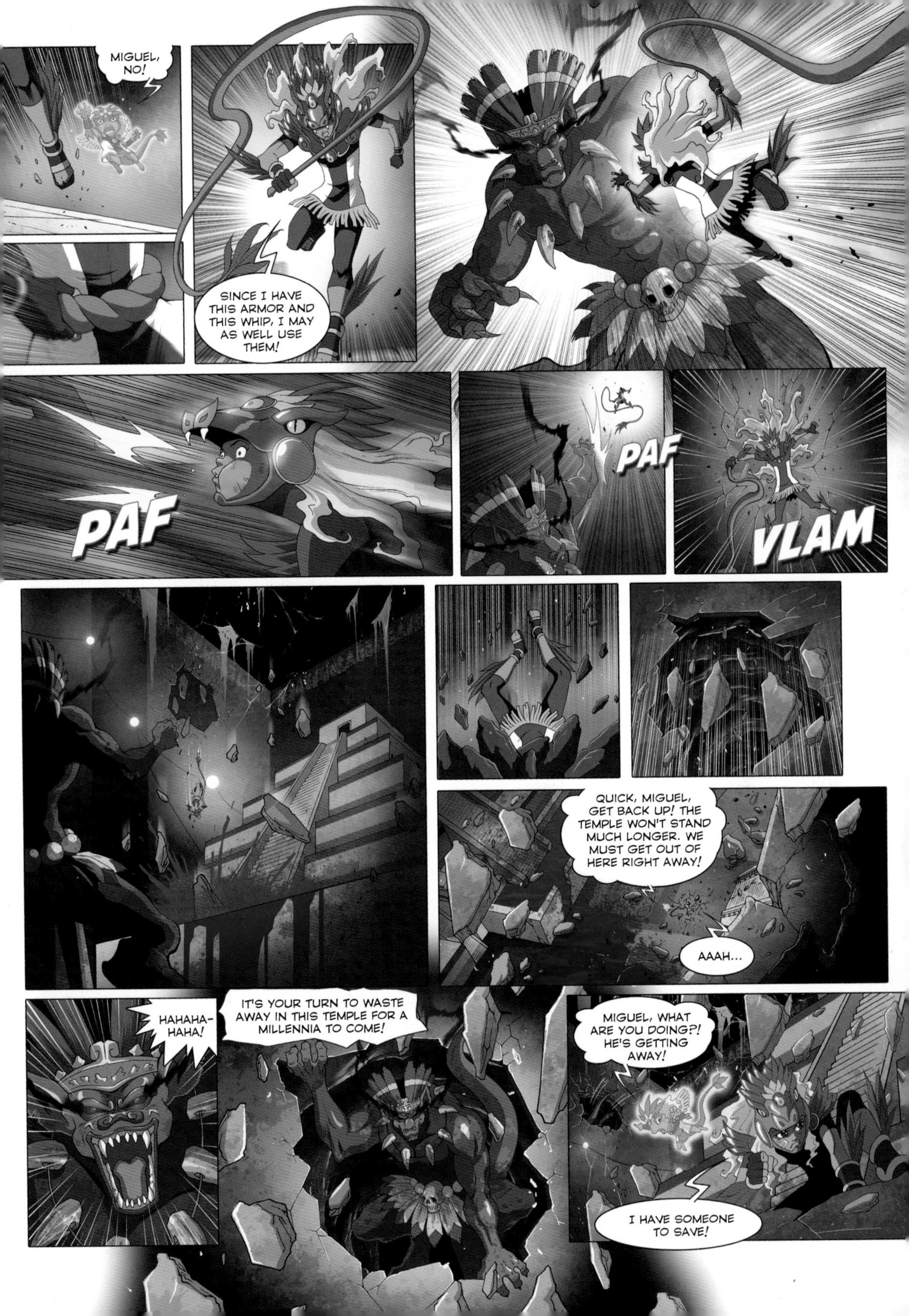
MIGUEL, NO!
SINCE I HAVE THIS ARMOR AND THIS WHIP, I MAY AS WELL USE THEM!
PAF
PAF
VLAM
QUICK, MIGUEL, GET BACK UP! THE TEMPLE WON'T STAND MUCH LONGER. WE MUST GET OUT OF HERE RIGHT AWAY!
AAAH...
HAHAHA-HAHA!
IT'S YOUR TURN TO WASTE AWAY IN THIS TEMPLE FOR A MILLENNIA TO COME!
MIGUEL, WHAT ARE YOU DOING?! HE'S GETTING AWAY!
I HAVE SOMEONE TO SAVE!

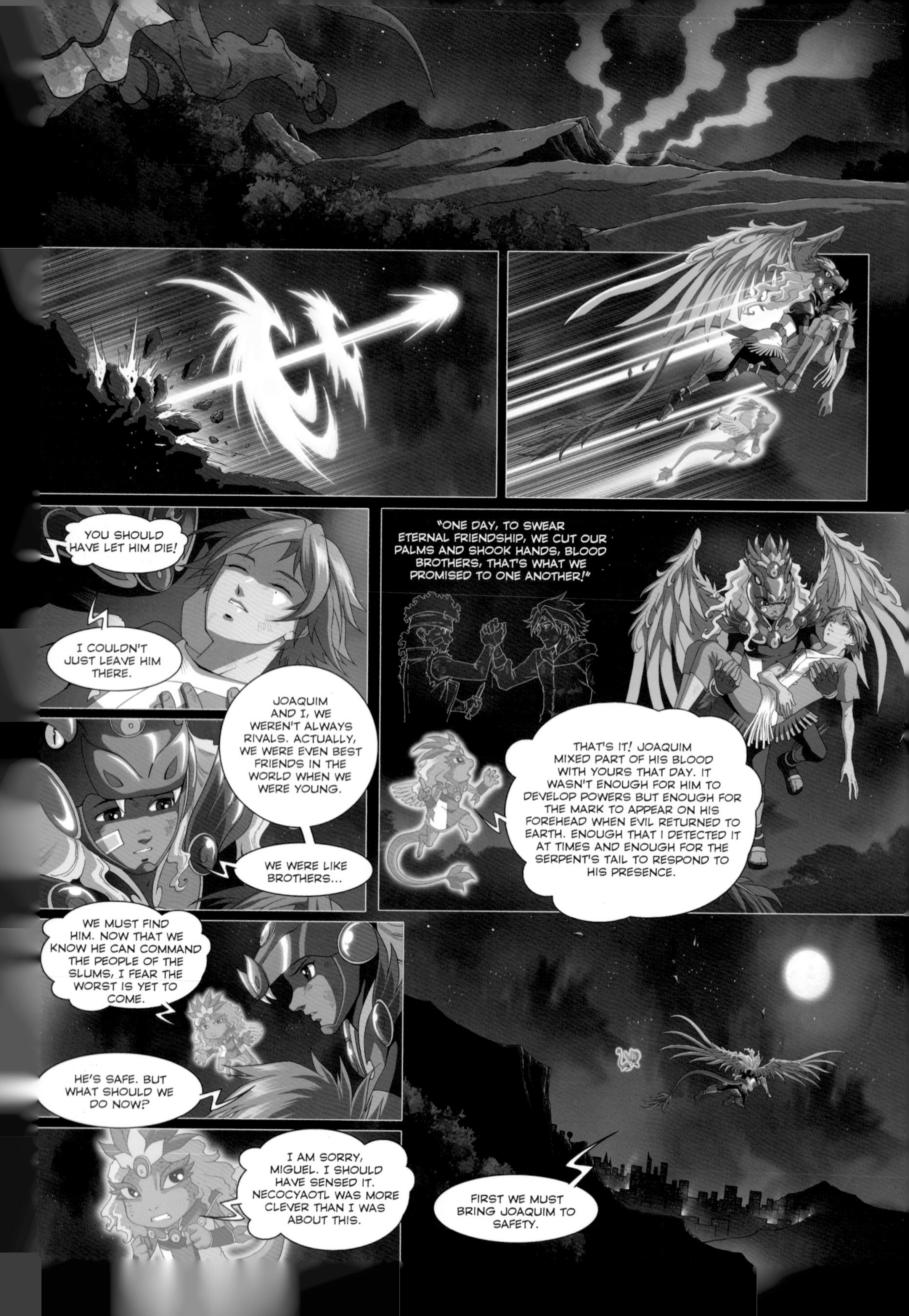
YOU SHOULD HAVE LET HIM DIE!
I COULDN'T JUST LEAVE HIM THERE.
JOAQUIM AND I, WE WEREN'T ALWAYS RIVALS. ACTUALLY, WE WERE EVEN BEST FRIENDS IN THE WORLD WHEN WE WERE YOUNG.
WE WERE LIKE BROTHERS...
"ONE DAY, TO SWEAR ETERNAL FRIENDSHIP, WE CUT OUR PALMS AND SHOOK HANDS, BLOOD BROTHERS, THAT'S WHAT WE PROMISED TO ONE ANOTHER!"
THAT'S IT! JOAQUIM MIXED PART OF HIS BLOOD WITH YOURS THAT DAY. IT WASN'T ENOUGH FOR HIM TO DEVELOP POWERS BUT ENOUGH FOR THE MARK TO APPEAR ON HIS FOREHEAD WHEN EVIL RETURNED TO EARTH. ENOUGH THAT I DETECTED IT AT TIMES AND ENOUGH FOR THE SERPENT'S TAIL TO RESPOND TO HIS PRESENCE.
WE MUST FIND HIM. NOW THAT WE KNOW HE CAN COMMAND THE PEOPLE OF THE SLUMS, I FEAR THE WORST IS YET TO COME.
HE'S SAFE. BUT WHAT SHOULD WE DO NOW?
I AM SORRY, MIGUEL. I SHOULD HAVE SENSED IT. NECOCYAOTL WAS MORE CLEVER THAN I WAS ABOUT THIS.
FIRST WE MUST BRING JOAQUIM TO SAFETY.

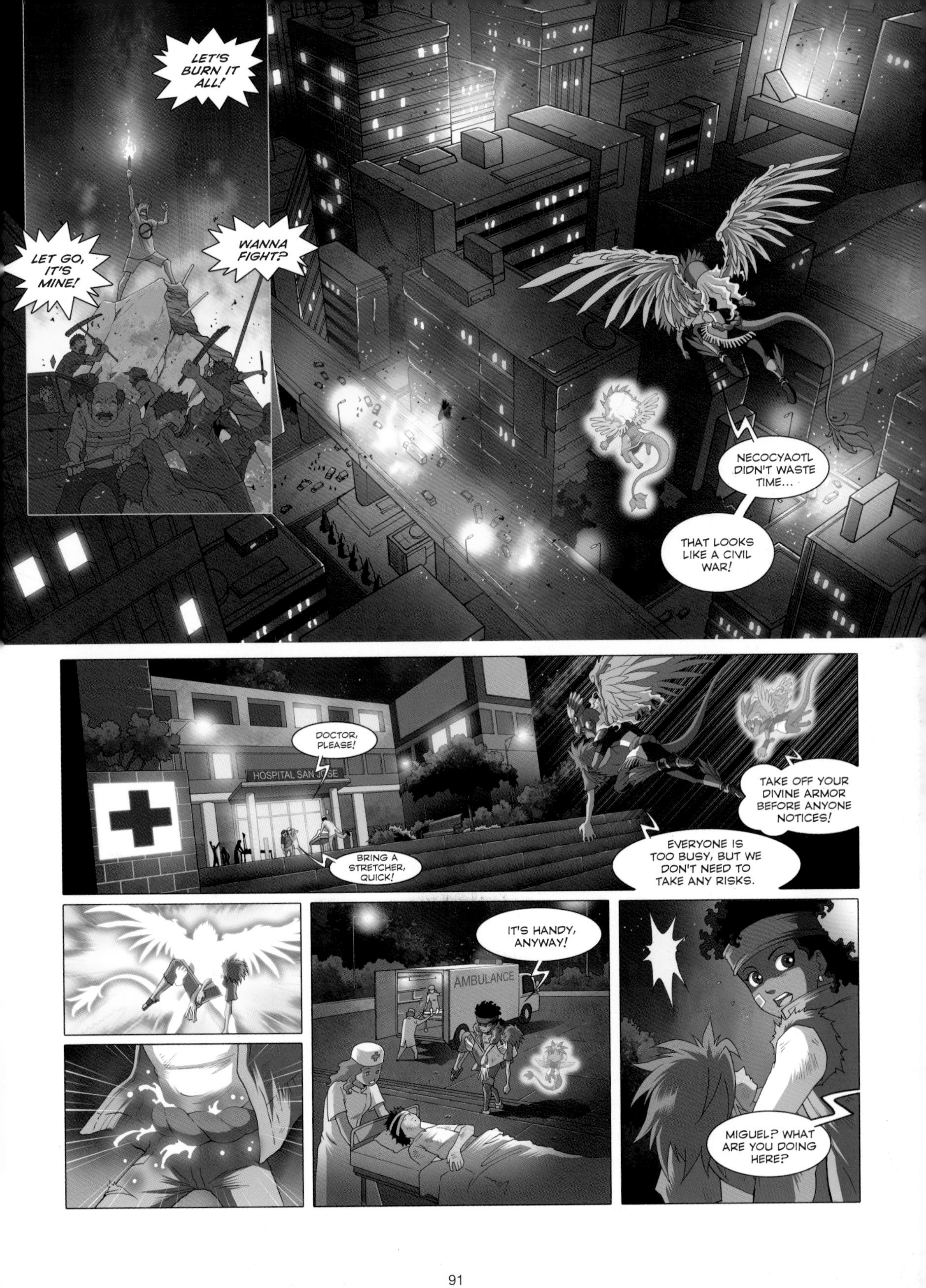
LET'S BURN IT ALL!
LET GO, IT'S MINE!
WANNA FIGHT?
NECOCYAOTL DIDN'T WASTE TIME...
THAT LOOKS LIKE A CIVIL WAR!
HOSPITAL SAN JOSE
DOCTOR, PLEASE!
BRING A STRETCHER, QUICK!
TAKE OFF YOUR DIVINE ARMOR BEFORE ANYONE NOTICES!
EVERYONE IS TOO BUSY, BUT WE DON'T NEED TO TAKE ANY RISKS.
IT'S HANDY, ANYWAY!
AMBULANCE
MIGUEL? WHAT ARE YOU DOING HERE?

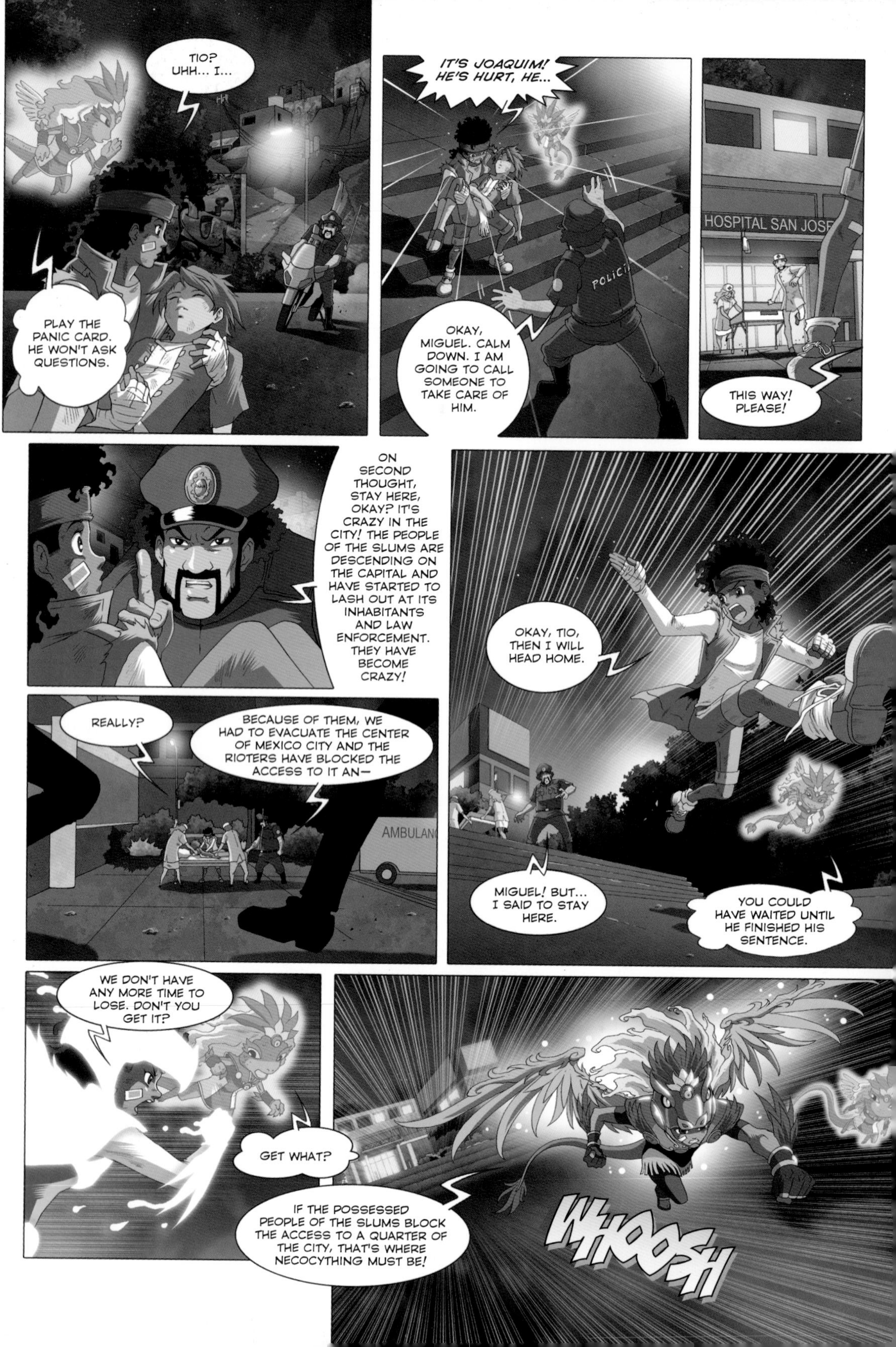
TIO? UHH... I...
PLAY THE PANIC CARD. HE WON'T ASK QUESTIONS.
IT'S JOAQUIM! HE'S HURT, HE...
POLICI
OKAY, MIGUEL. CALM DOWN. I AM GOING TO CALL SOMEONE TO TAKE CARE OF HIM.
HOSPITAL SAN JOSE
THIS WAY! PLEASE!
ON SECOND THOUGHT, STAY HERE, OKAY? IT'S CRAZY IN THE CITY! THE PEOPLE OF THE SLUMS ARE DESCENDING ON THE CAPITAL AND HAVE STARTED TO LASH OUT AT ITS INHABITANTS AND LAW ENFORCEMENT. THEY HAVE BECOME CRAZY!
REALLY?
BECAUSE OF THEM, WE HAD TO EVACUATE THE CENTER OF MEXICO CITY AND THE RIOTERS HAVE BLOCKED THE ACCESS TO IT AN—
AMBULANC
OKAY, TIO, THEN I WILL HEAD HOME.
MIGUEL! BUT... I SAID TO STAY HERE.
YOU COULD HAVE WAITED UNTIL HE FINISHED HIS SENTENCE.
WE DON'T HAVE ANY MORE TIME TO LOSE. DON'T YOU GET IT?
GET WHAT?
IF THE POSSESSED PEOPLE OF THE SLUMS BLOCK THE ACCESS TO A QUARTER OF THE CITY, THAT'S WHERE NECOCYTHING MUST BE!
WHOOSH

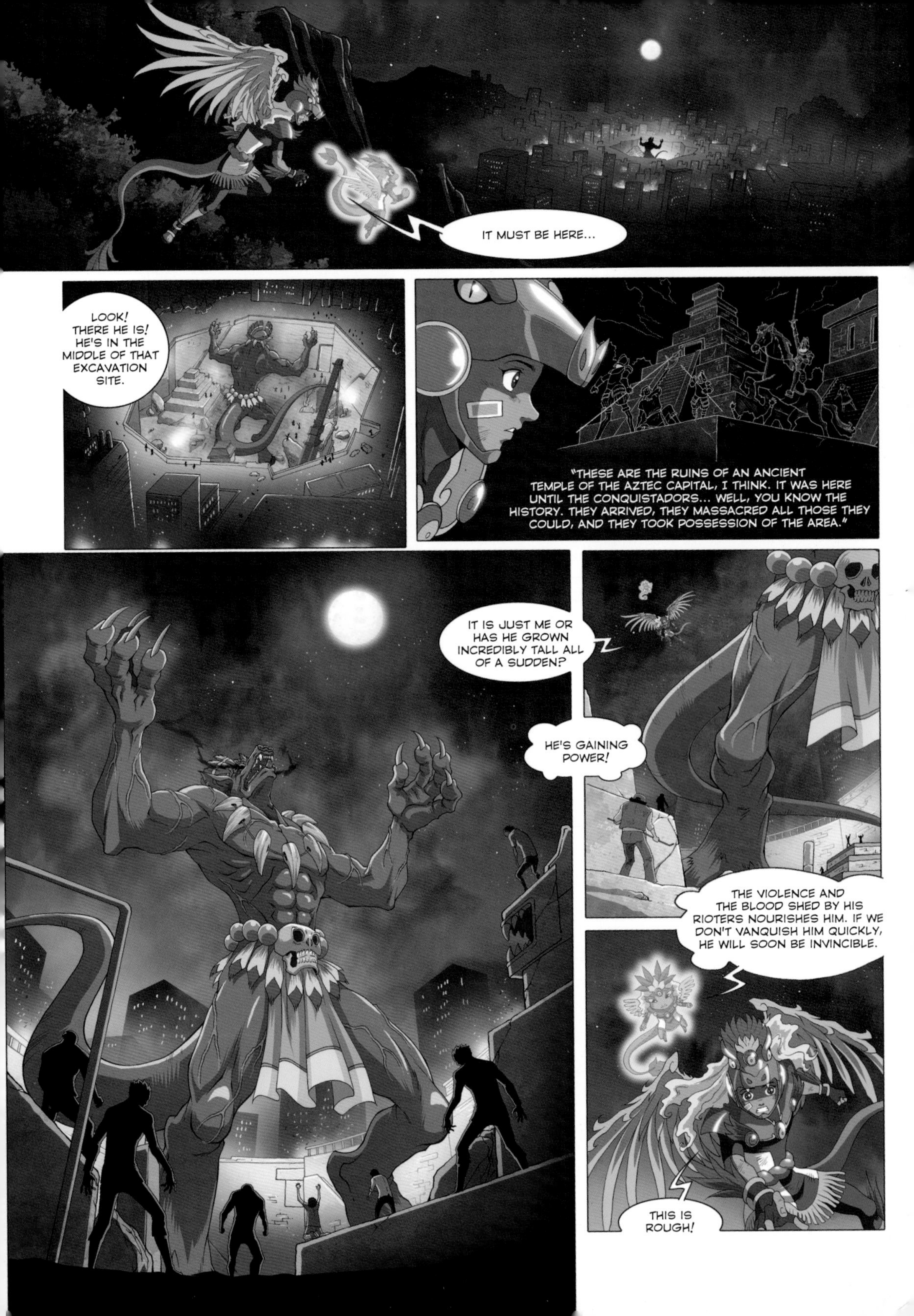
IT MUST BE HERE...
LOOK! THERE HE IS! HE'S IN THE MIDDLE OF THAT EXCAVATION SITE.
"THESE ARE THE RUINS OF AN ANCIENT TEMPLE OF THE AZTEC CAPITAL, I THINK. IT WAS HERE UNTIL THE CONQUISTADORS... WELL, YOU KNOW THE HISTORY. THEY ARRIVED, THEY MASSACRED ALL THOSE THEY COULD, AND THEY TOOK POSSESSION OF THE AREA."
IT IS JUST ME OR HAS HE GROWN INCREDIBLY TALL ALL OF A SUDDEN?
HE'S GAINING POWER!
THE VIOLENCE AND THE BLOOD SHED BY HIS RIOTERS NOURISHES HIM. IF WE DON'T VANQUISH HIM QUICKLY, HE WILL SOON BE INVINCIBLE.
THIS IS ROUGH!

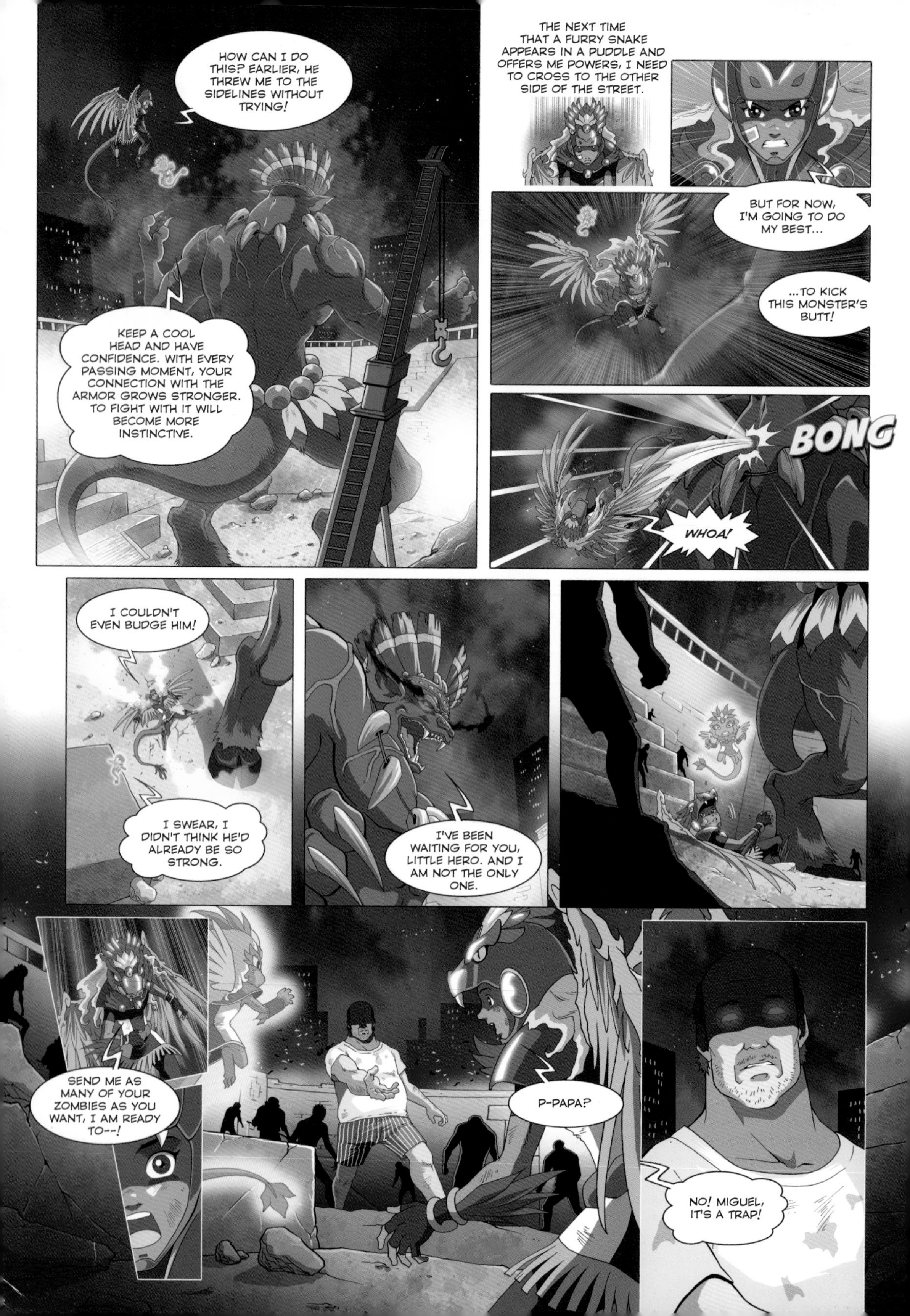
HOW CAN I DO THIS? EARLIER, HE THREW ME TO THE SIDELINES WITHOUT TRYING!
KEEP A COOL HEAD AND HAVE CONFIDENCE. WITH EVERY PASSING MOMENT, YOUR CONNECTION WITH THE ARMOR GROWS STRONGER. TO FIGHT WITH IT WILL BECOME MORE INSTINCTIVE.
THE NEXT TIME THAT A FURRY SNAKE APPEARS IN A PUDDLE AND OFFERS ME POWERS, I NEED TO CROSS TO THE OTHER SIDE OF THE STREET.
BUT FOR NOW, I'M GOING TO DO MY BEST...
...TO KICK THIS MONSTER'S BUTT!
BONG
WHOA!
I COULDN'T EVEN BUDGE HIM!
I SWEAR, I DIDN'T THINK HE'D ALREADY BE SO STRONG.
I'VE BEEN WAITING FOR YOU, LITTLE HERO. AND I AM NOT THE ONLY ONE.
SEND ME AS MANY OF YOUR ZOMBIES AS YOU WANT, I AM READY TO--!
P-PAPA?
NO! MIGUEL, IT'S A TRAP!

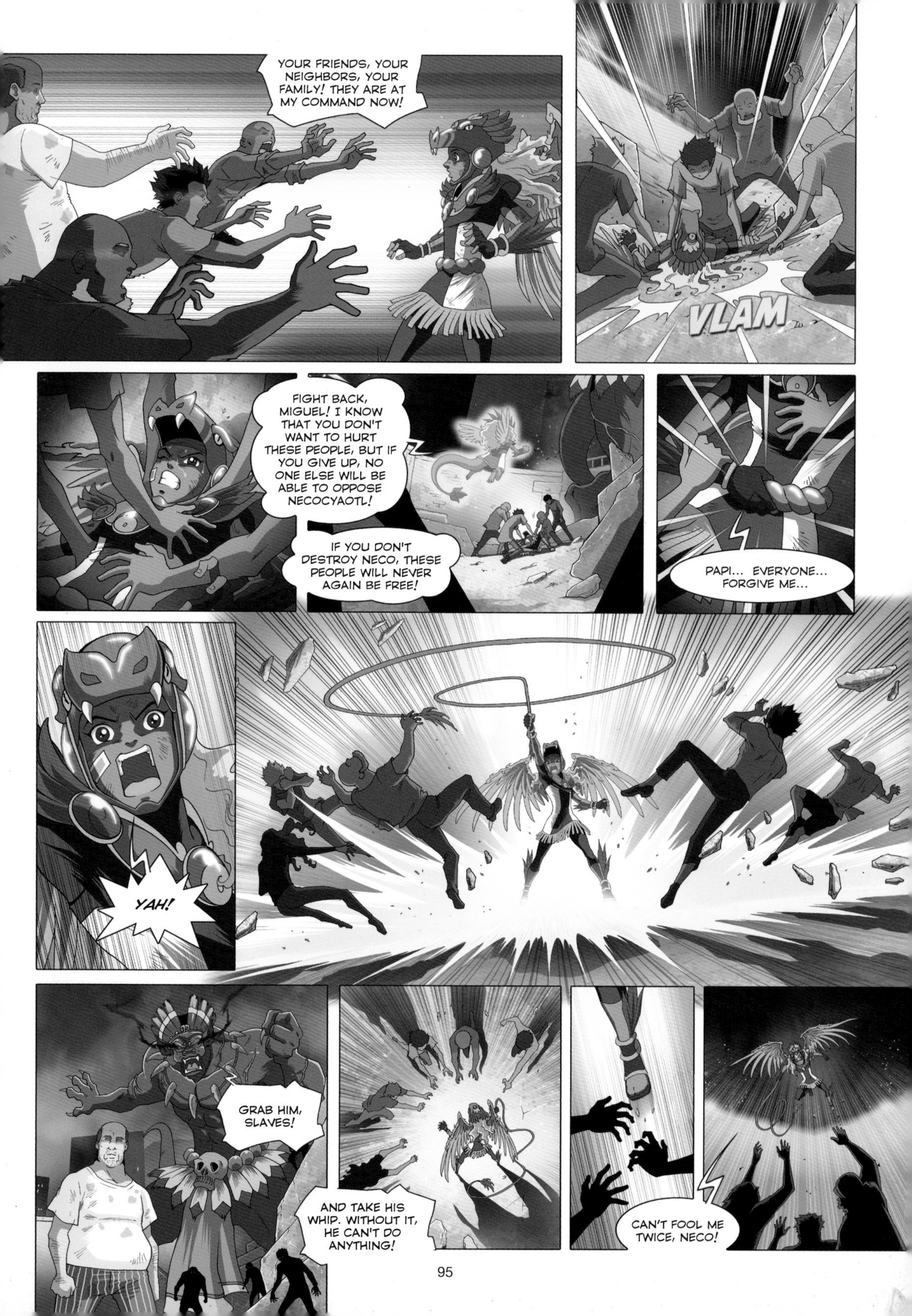
YOUR FRIENDS, YOUR NEIGHBORS, YOUR FAMILY! THEY ARE AT MY COMMAND NOW!
VLAM
FIGHT BACK, MIGUEL! I KNOW THAT YOU DON'T WANT TO HURT THESE PEOPLE, BUT IF YOU GIVE UP, NO ONE ELSE WILL BE ABLE TO OPPOSE NECOCYAOTL!
IF YOU DON'T DESTROY NECO, THESE PEOPLE WILL NEVER AGAIN BE FREE!
PAPI... EVERYONE... FORGIVE ME...
YAH!
GRAB HIM, SLAVES!
AND TAKE HIS WHIP. WITHOUT IT, HE CAN'T DO ANYTHING!
CAN'T FOOL ME TWICE, NECO!

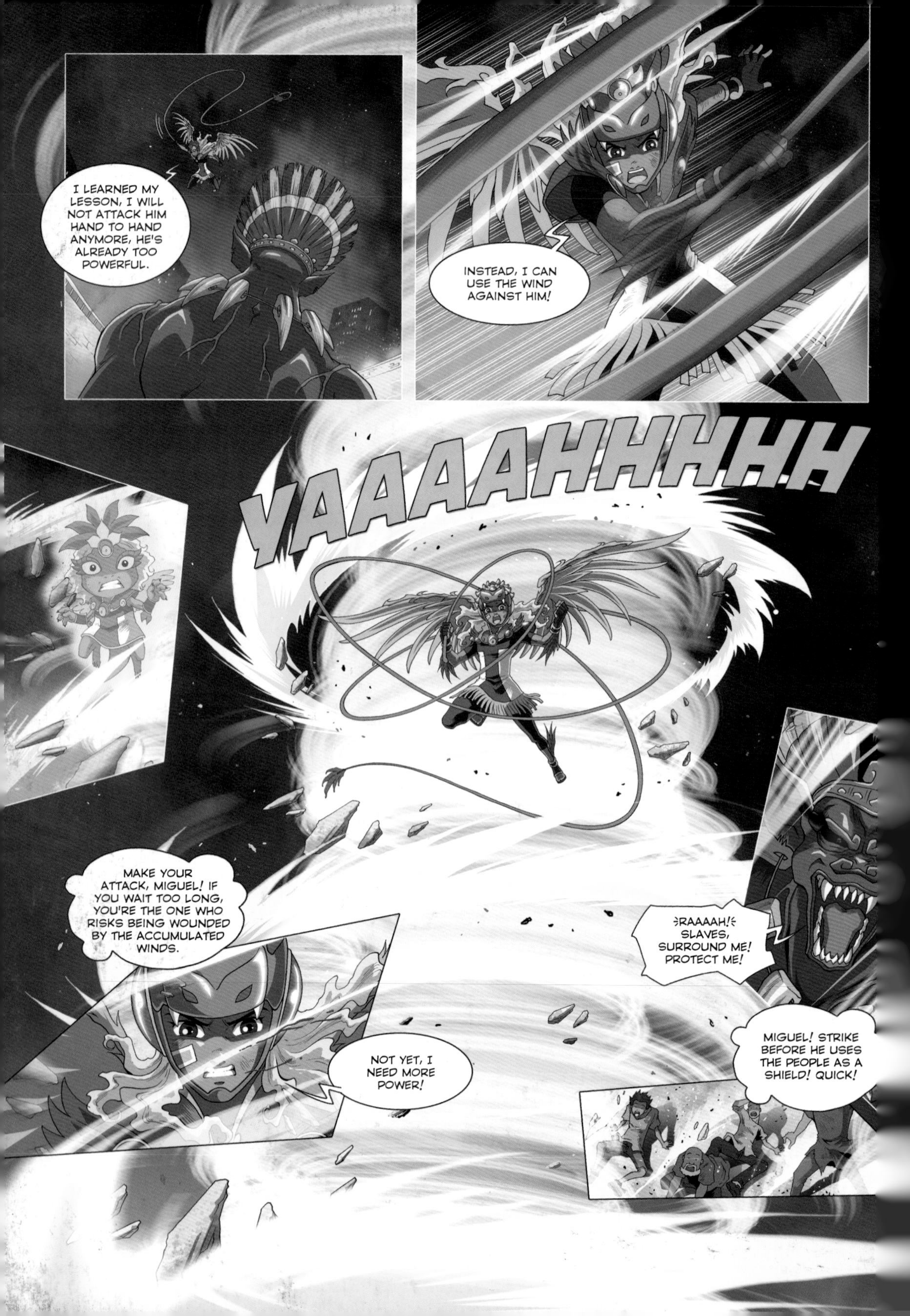
I LEARNED MY LESSON, I WILL NOT ATTACK HIM HAND TO HAND ANYMORE, HE'S ALREADY TOO POWERFUL.
INSTEAD, I CAN USE THE WIND AGAINST HIM!
YAAAAHHHHHH
MAKE YOUR ATTACK, MIGUEL! IF YOU WAIT TOO LONG, YOU'RE THE ONE WHO RISKS BEING WOUNDED BY THE ACCUMULATED WINDS.
¡RAAAAH! SLAVES, SURROUND ME! PROTECT ME!
NOT YET, I NEED MORE POWER!
MIGUEL! STRIKE BEFORE HE USES THE PEOPLE AS A SHIELD! QUICK!

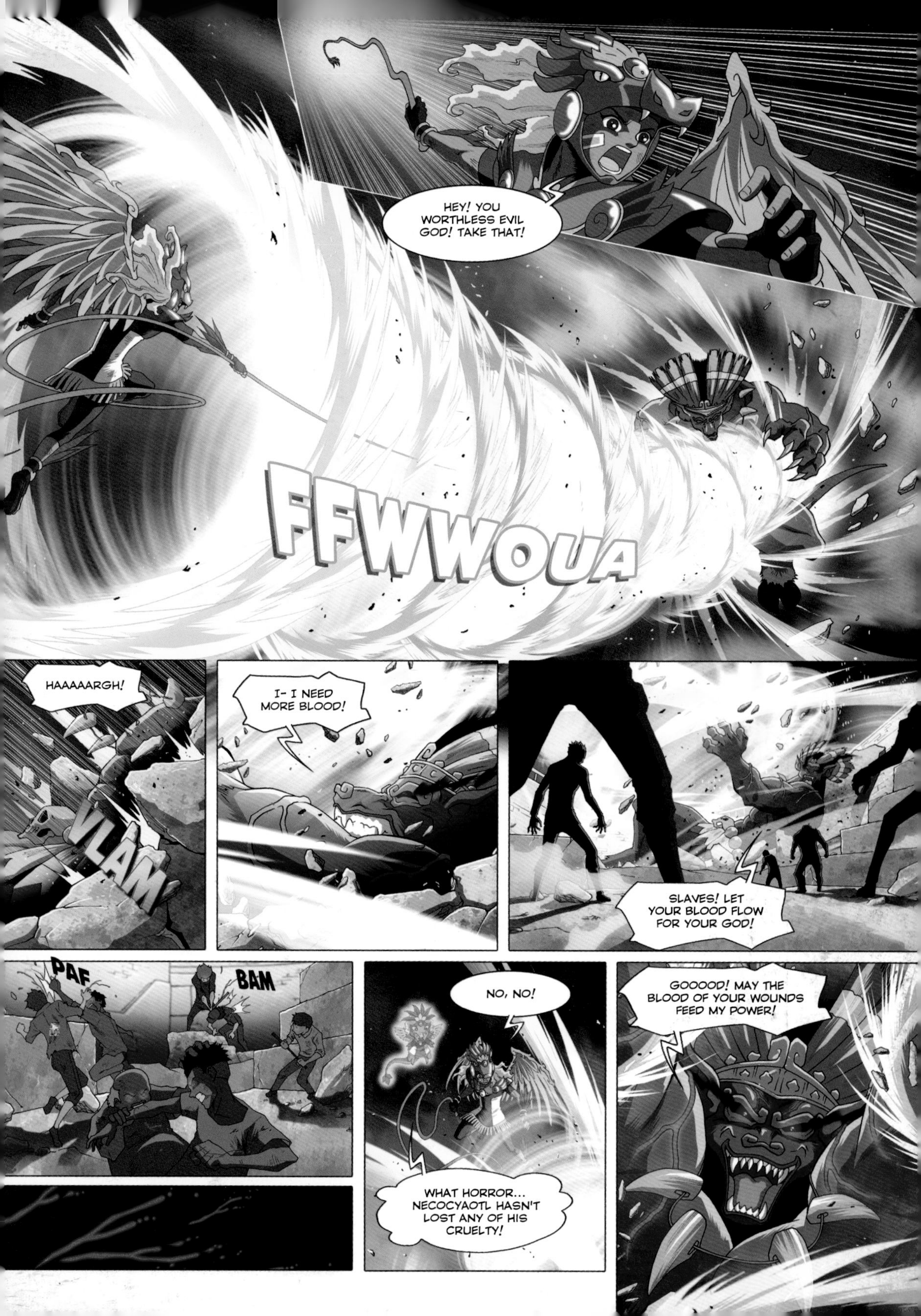
HEY! YOU WORTHLESS EVIL GOD! TAKE THAT!
FFWWOUA
HAAAAARGH!
VLAM
I- I NEED MORE BLOOD!
SLAVES! LET YOUR BLOOD FLOW FOR YOUR GOD!
PAF
BAM
NO, NO!
WHAT HORROR... NECOCYAOTL HASN'T LOST ANY OF HIS CRUELTY!
GOOOOD! MAY THE BLOOD OF YOUR WOUNDS FEED MY POWER!

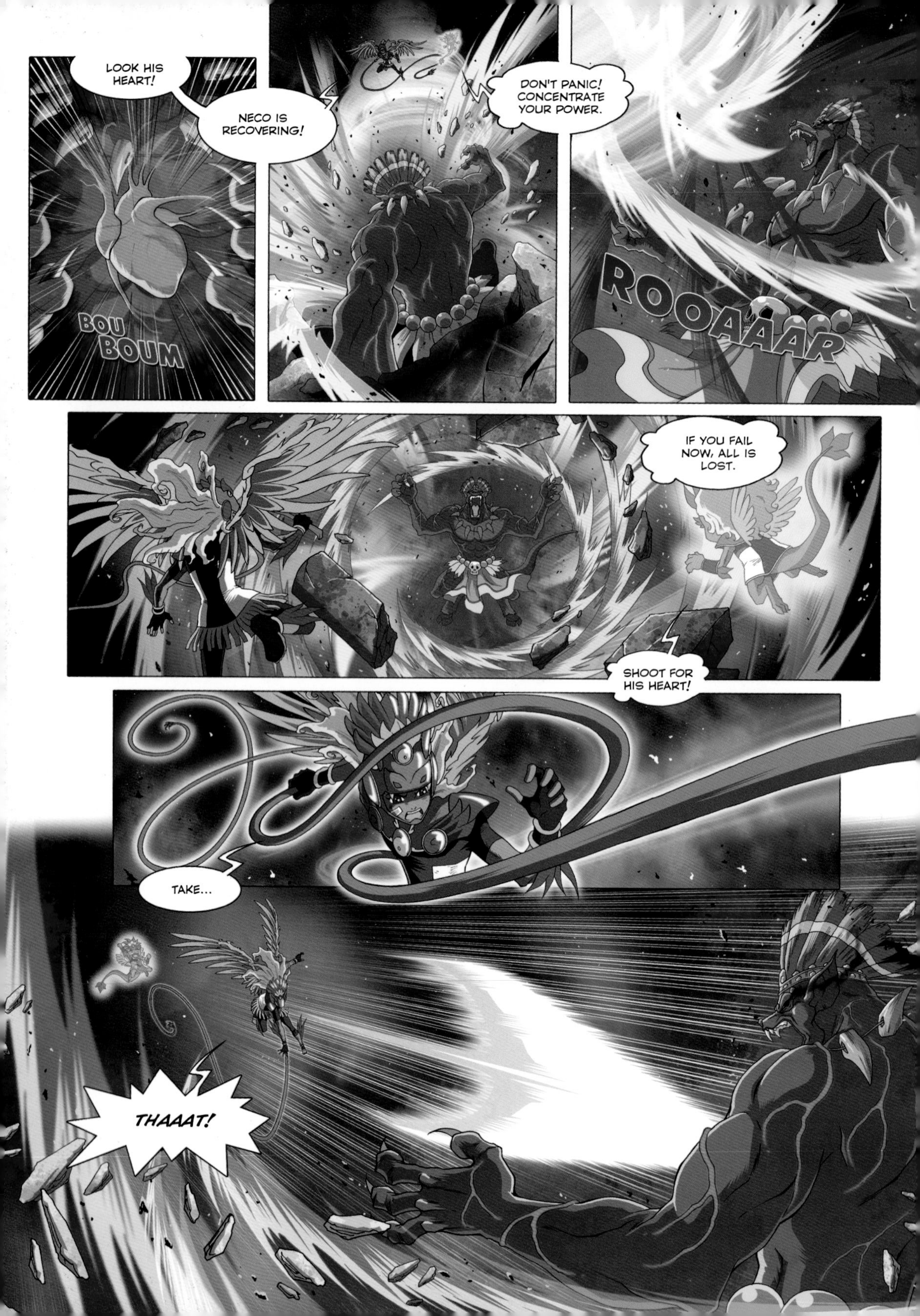
LOOK HIS HEART!
BOU BOUM
NECO IS RECOVERING!
DON'T PANIC! CONCENTRATE YOUR POWER.
ROOAAAAR
IF YOU FAIL NOW, ALL IS LOST.
SHOOT FOR HIS HEART!
TAKE...
THAAAT!

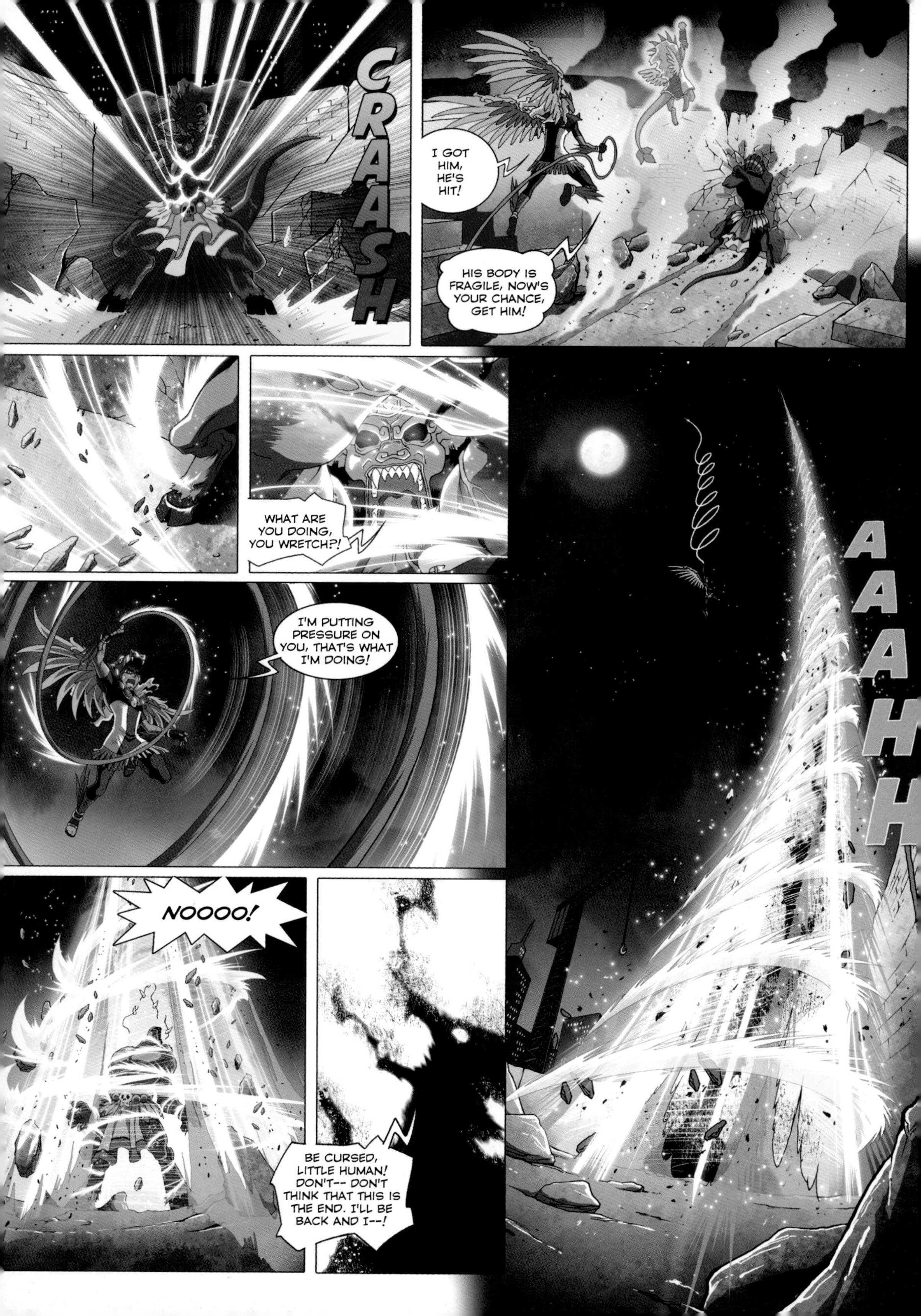
CRAASH
I GOT HIM, HE'S HIT!
HIS BODY IS FRAGILE, NOW'S YOUR CHANCE, GET HIM!
WHAT ARE YOU DOING, YOU WRETCH?!
I'M PUTTING PRESSURE ON YOU, THAT'S WHAT I'M DOING!
NOOOO!
BE CURSED, LITTLE HUMAN! DON'T-- DON'T THINK THAT THIS IS THE END. I'LL BE BACK AND I--!
AAAAHHH

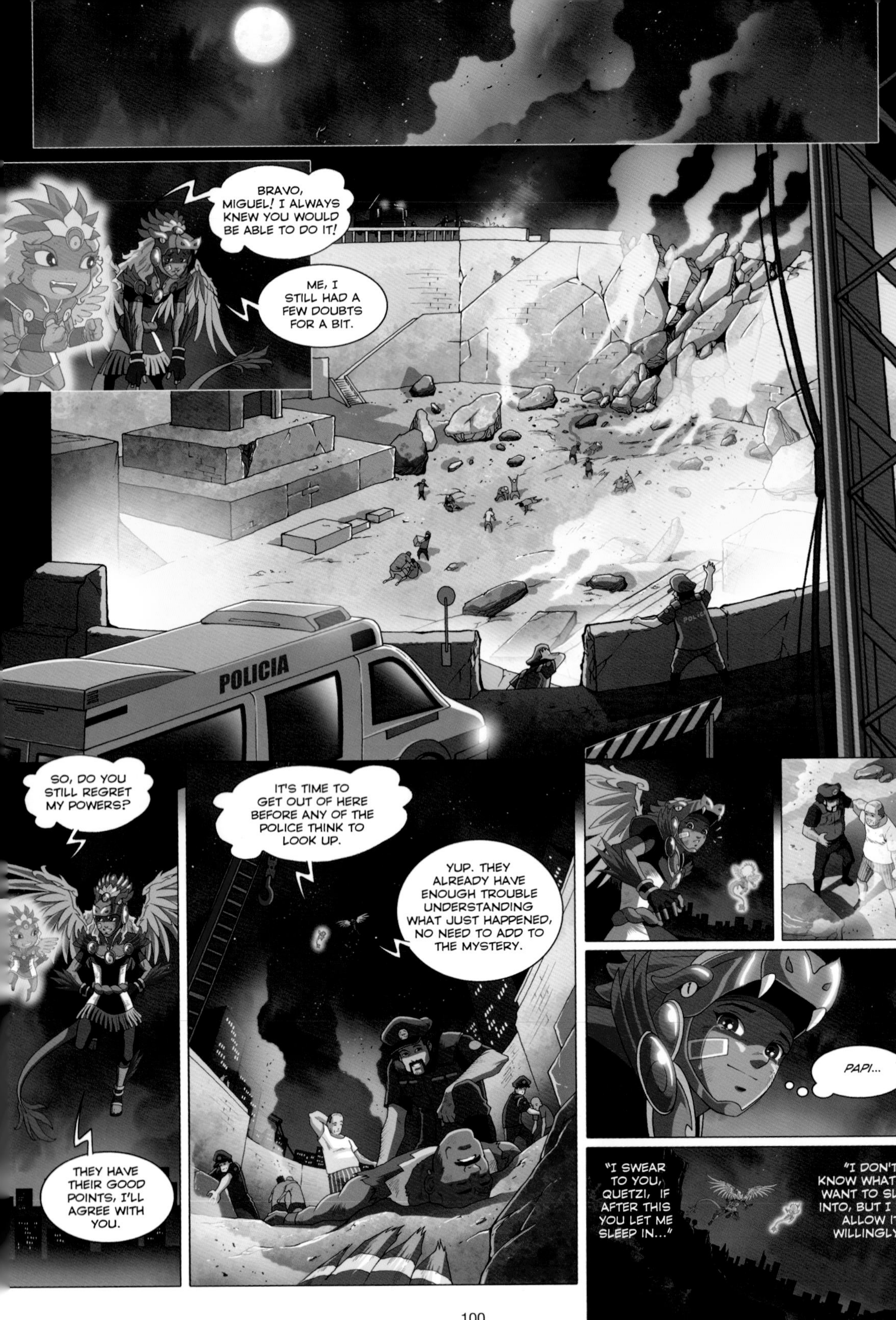
BRAVO, MIGUEL! I ALWAYS KNEW YOU WOULD BE ABLE TO DO IT!
ME, I STILL HAD A FEW DOUBTS FOR A BIT.
POLICIA
SO, DO YOU STILL REGRET MY POWERS?
THEY HAVE THEIR GOOD POINTS, I'LL AGREE WITH YOU.
IT'S TIME TO GET OUT OF HERE BEFORE ANY OF THE POLICE THINK TO LOOK UP.
YUP. THEY ALREADY HAVE ENOUGH TROUBLE UNDERSTANDING WHAT JUST HAPPENED, NO NEED TO ADD TO THE MYSTERY.
PAPI...
"I SWEAR TO YOU, QUETZI, IF AFTER THIS YOU LET ME SLEEP IN..."
"I DON'T KNOW WHAT YOU WANT TO SLEEP INTO, BUT I WILL ALLOW IT WILLINGLY."

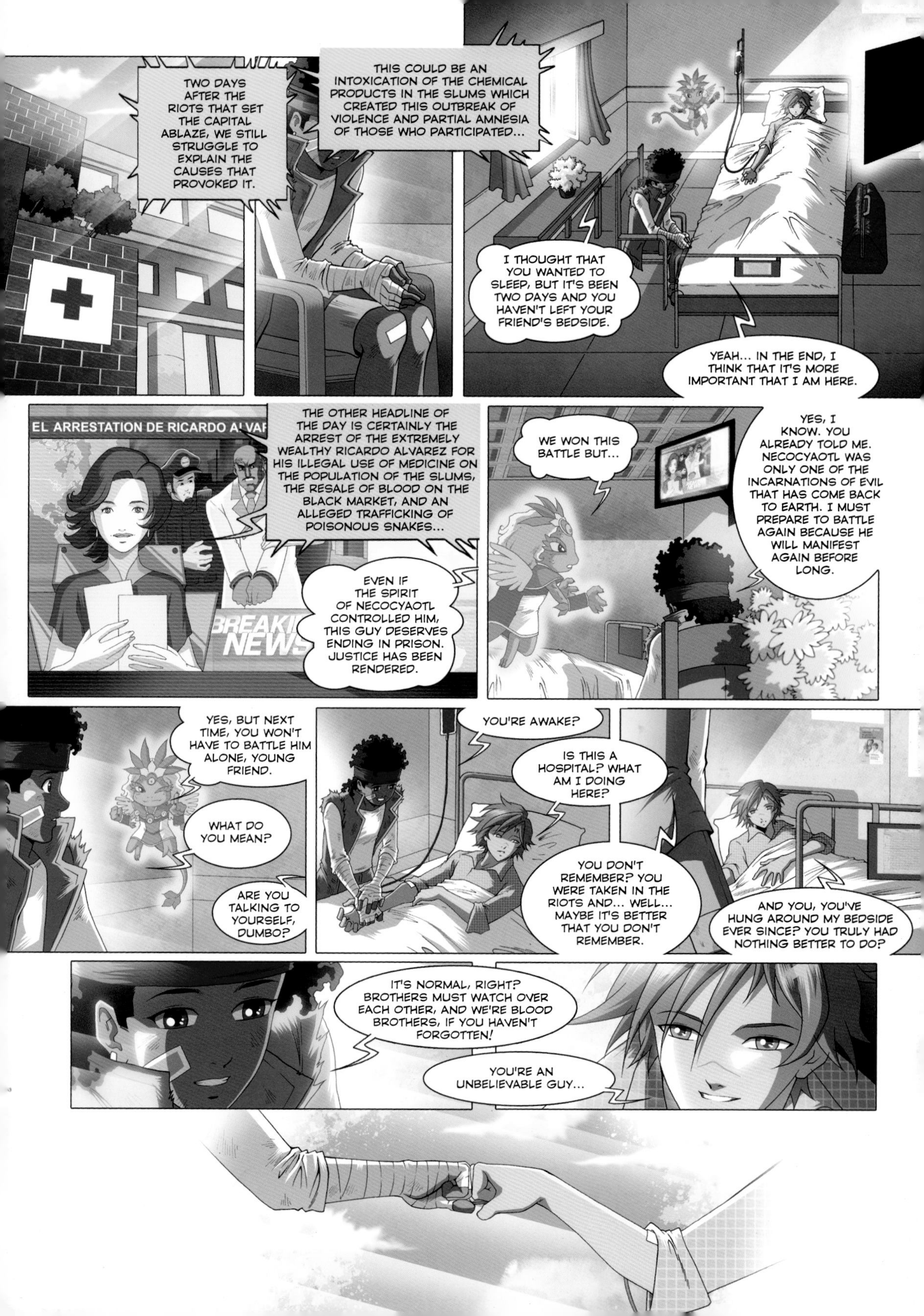
TWO DAYS AFTER THE RIOTS THAT SET THE CAPITAL ABLAZE, WE STILL STRUGGLE TO EXPLAIN THE CAUSES THAT PROVOKED IT.
THIS COULD BE AN INTOXICATION OF THE CHEMICAL PRODUCTS IN THE SLUMS WHICH CREATED THIS OUTBREAK OF VIOLENCE AND PARTIAL AMNESIA OF THOSE WHO PARTICIPATED...
I THOUGHT THAT YOU WANTED TO SLEEP, BUT IT'S BEEN TWO DAYS AND YOU HAVEN'T LEFT YOUR FRIEND'S BEDSIDE.
YEAH... IN THE END, I THINK THAT IT'S MORE IMPORTANT THAT I AM HERE.
EL ARRESTATION DE RICARDO ALVAR
THE OTHER HEADLINE OF THE DAY IS CERTAINLY THE ARREST OF THE EXTREMELY WEALTHY RICARDO ALVAREZ FOR HIS ILLEGAL USE OF MEDICINE ON THE POPULATION OF THE SLUMS, THE RESALE OF BLOOD ON THE BLACK MARKET, AND AN ALLEGED TRAFFICKING OF POISONOUS SNAKES...
BREAKI
NEWS
EVEN IF THE SPIRIT OF NECOCYAOTL CONTROLLED HIM, THIS GUY DESERVES ENDING IN PRISON. JUSTICE HAS BEEN RENDERED.
WE WON THIS BATTLE BUT...
YES, I KNOW. YOU ALREADY TOLD ME. NECOCYAOTL WAS ONLY ONE OF THE INCARNATIONS OF EVIL THAT HAS COME BACK TO EARTH. I MUST PREPARE TO BATTLE AGAIN BECAUSE HE WILL MANIFEST AGAIN BEFORE LONG.
YES, BUT NEXT TIME, YOU WON'T HAVE TO BATTLE HIM ALONE, YOUNG FRIEND.
WHAT DO YOU MEAN?
ARE YOU TALKING TO YOURSELF, DUMBO?
YOU'RE AWAKE?
IS THIS A HOSPITAL? WHAT AM I DOING HERE?
YOU DON'T REMEMBER? YOU WERE TAKEN IN THE RIOTS AND... WELL... MAYBE IT'S BETTER THAT YOU DON'T REMEMBER.
AND YOU, YOU'VE HUNG AROUND MY BEDSIDE EVER SINCE? YOU TRULY HAD NOTHING BETTER TO DO?
IT'S NORMAL, RIGHT? BROTHERS MUST WATCH OVER EACH OTHER, AND WE'RE BLOOD BROTHERS, IF YOU HAVEN'T FORGOTTEN!
YOU'RE AN UNBELIEVABLE GUY...

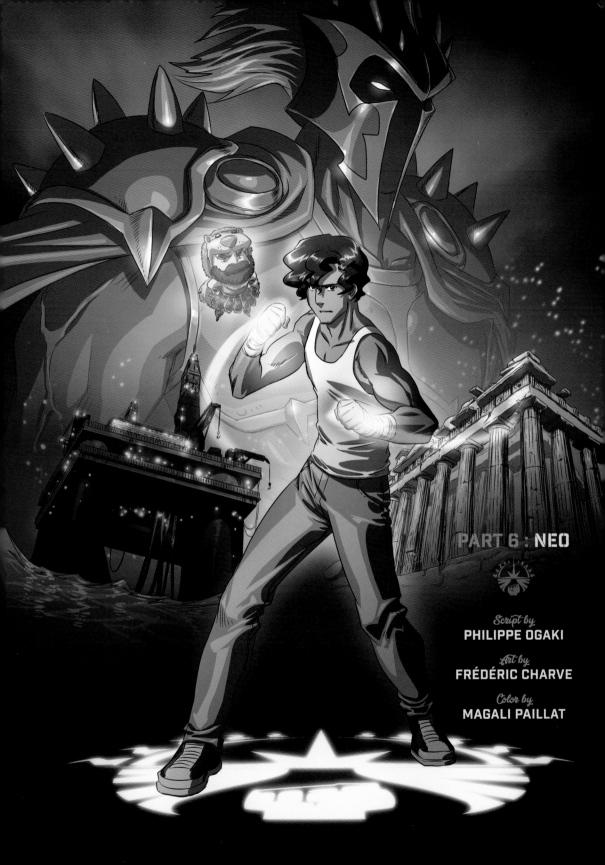

PART 6 : NEO

Script by
PHILIPPE OGAKI

Art by
FRÉDÉRIC CHARVE

Color by
MAGALI PAILLAT

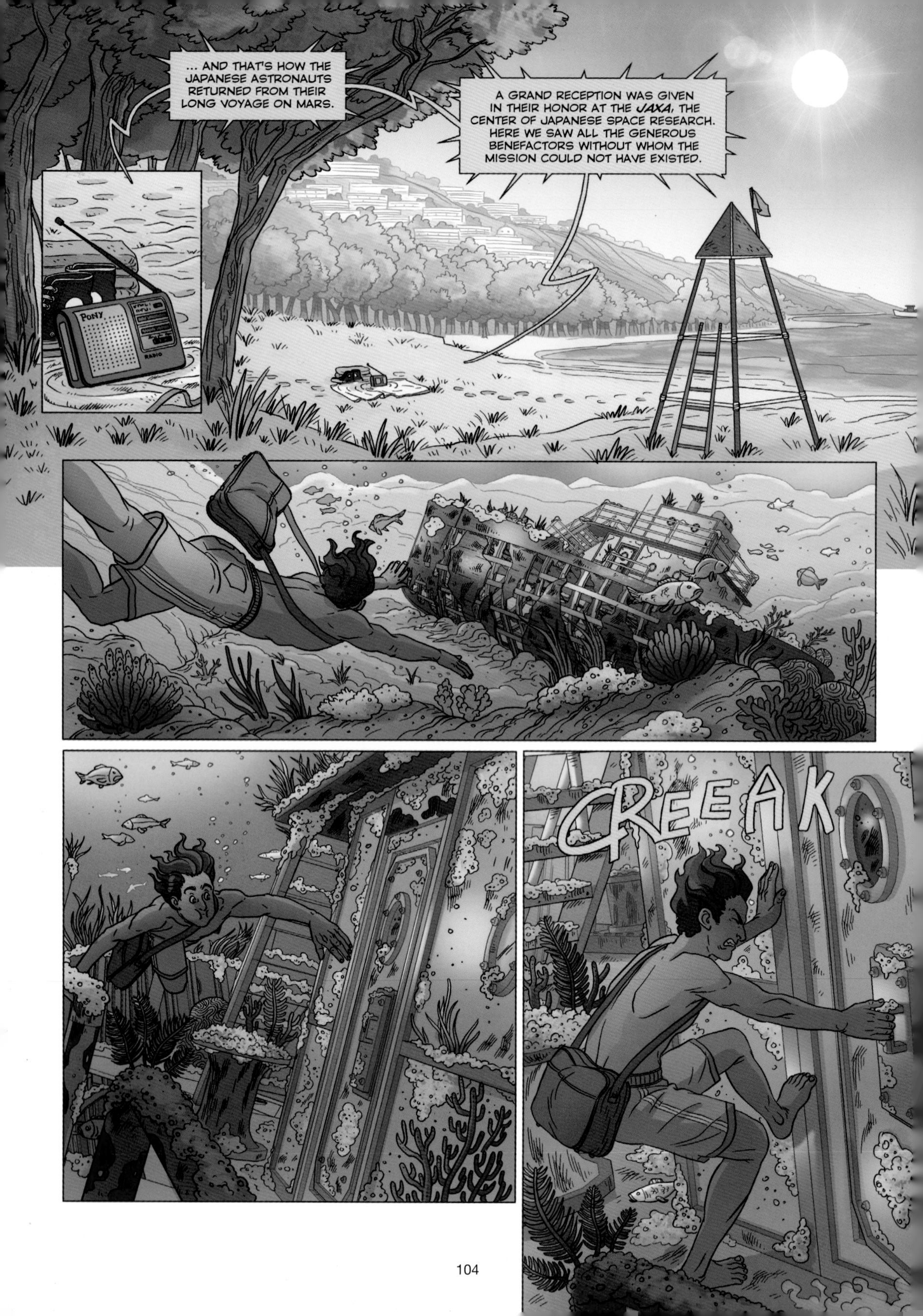
... AND THAT'S HOW THE JAPANESE ASTRONAUTS RETURNED FROM THEIR LONG VOYAGE ON MARS.
A GRAND RECEPTION WAS GIVEN IN THEIR HONOR AT THE JAXA, THE CENTER OF JAPANESE SPACE RESEARCH. HERE WE SAW ALL THE GENEROUS BENEFACTORS WITHOUT WHOM THE MISSION COULD NOT HAVE EXISTED.
PONY
RADIO
CREEAK

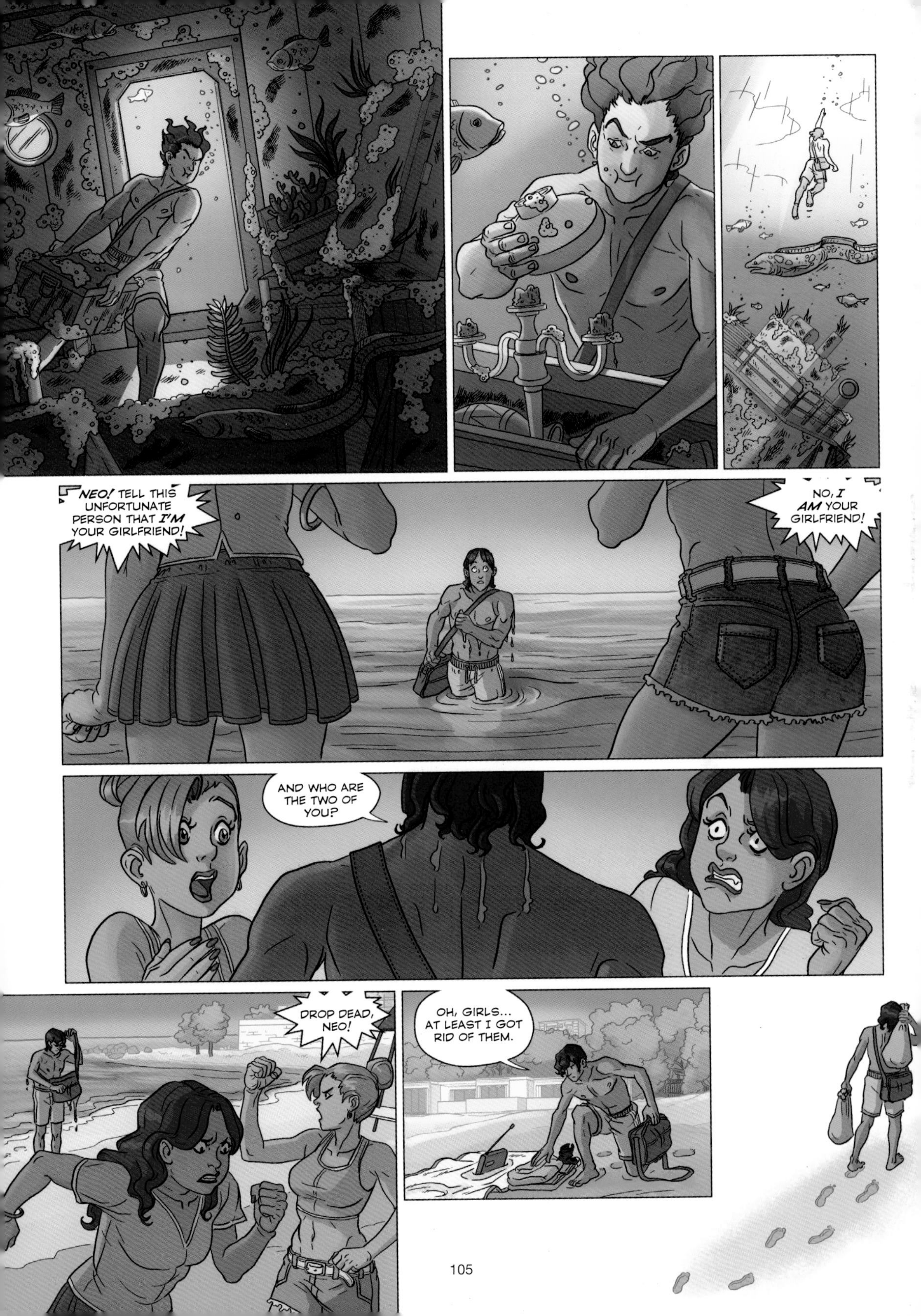

NEO! TELL THIS UNFORTUNATE PERSON THAT I'M YOUR GIRLFRIEND!
NO, I AM YOUR GIRLFRIEND!
AND WHO ARE THE TWO OF YOU?
DROP DEAD, NEO!
OH, GIRLS... AT LEAST I GOT RID OF THEM.

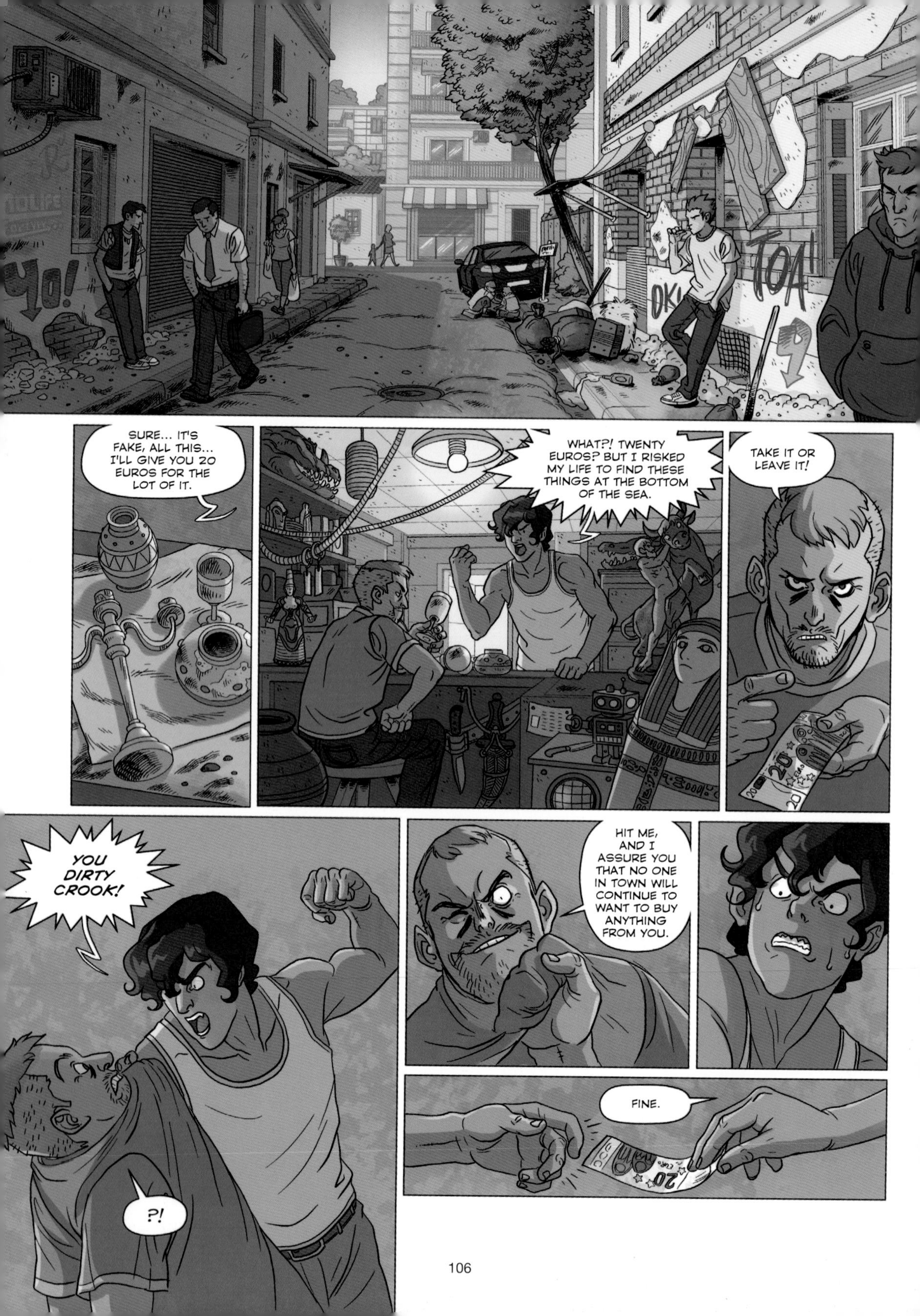
YO!
OK!
TOA!
SURE... IT'S FAKE, ALL THIS... I'LL GIVE YOU 20 EUROS FOR THE LOT OF IT.
WHAT?! TWENTY EUROS? BUT I RISKED MY LIFE TO FIND THESE THINGS AT THE BOTTOM OF THE SEA.
TAKE IT OR LEAVE IT!
YOU DIRTY CROOK!
?!
HIT ME, AND I ASSURE YOU THAT NO ONE IN TOWN WILL CONTINUE TO WANT TO BUY ANYTHING FROM YOU.
FINE.

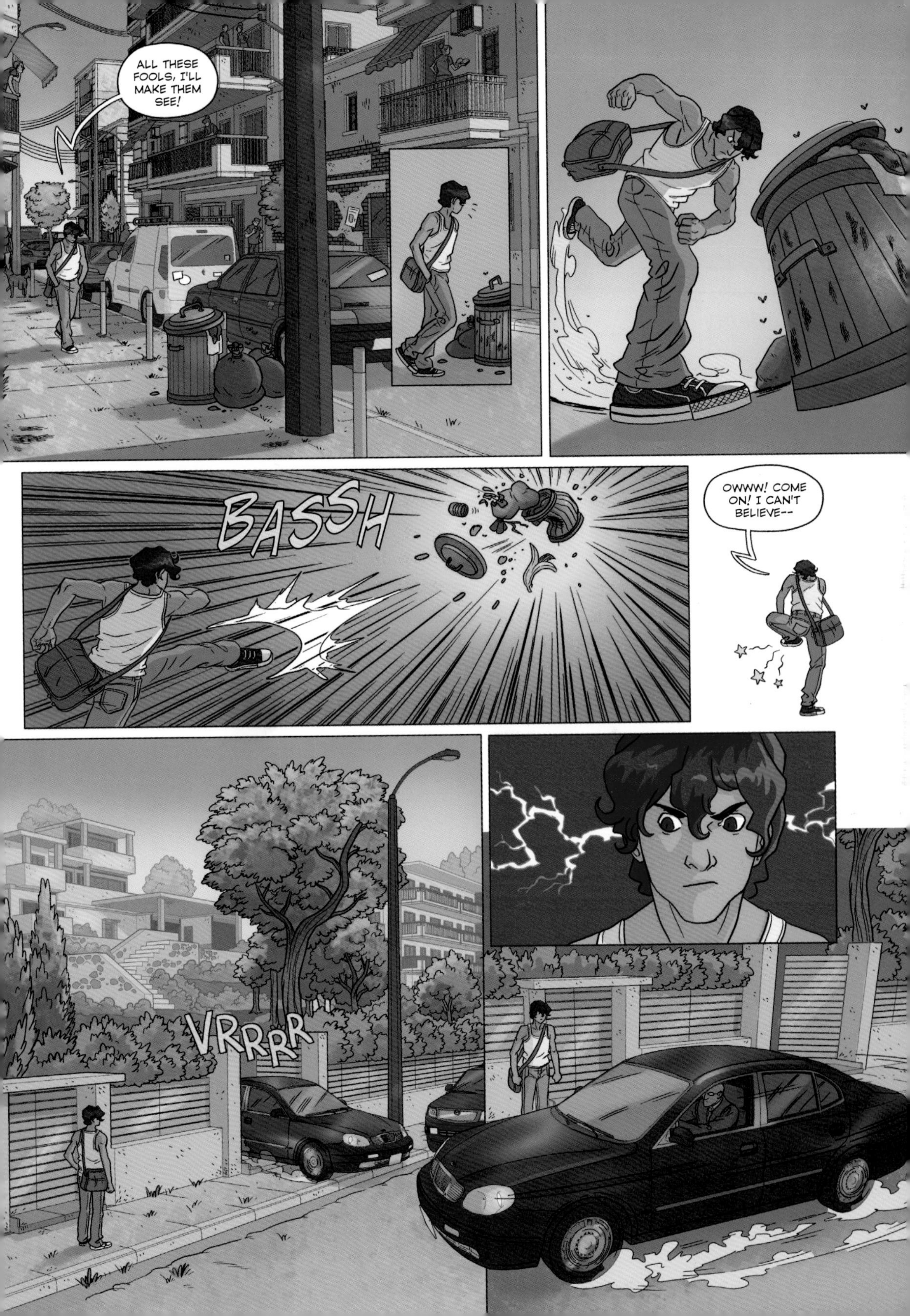
ALL THESE FOOLS, I'LL MAKE THEM SEE!
BASSH
OWWW! COME ON! I CAN'T BELIEVE--
VRRRR

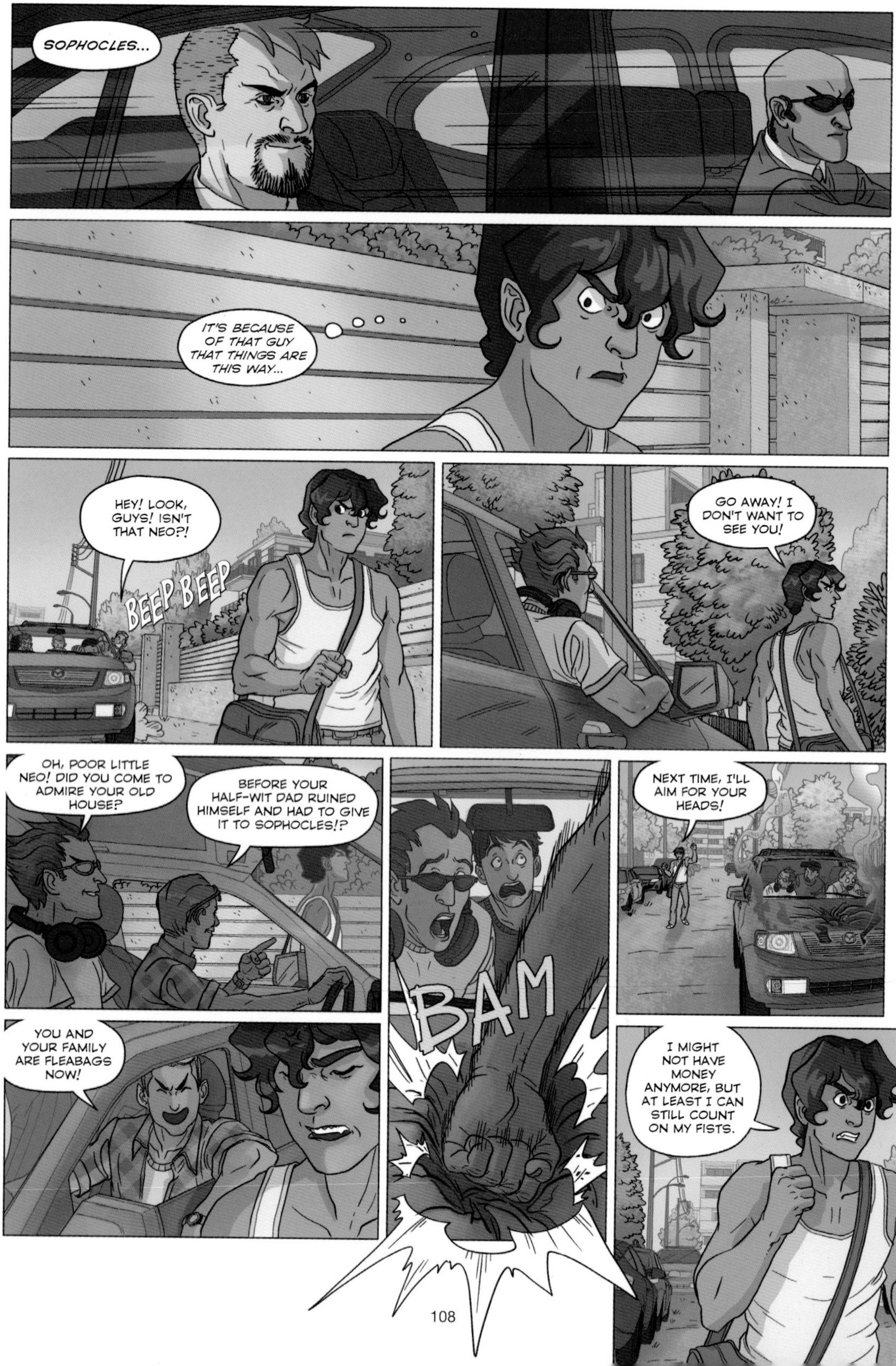
SOPHOCLES...
IT'S BECAUSE OF THAT GUY THAT THINGS ARE THIS WAY...
HEY! LOOK, GUYS! ISN'T THAT NEO?!
BEEP BEEP
GO AWAY! I DON'T WANT TO SEE YOU!
OH, POOR LITTLE NEO! DID YOU COME TO ADMIRE YOUR OLD HOUSE?
BEFORE YOUR HALF-WIT DAD RUINED HIMSELF AND HAD TO GIVE IT TO SOPHOCLES!?
YOU AND YOUR FAMILY ARE FLEABAGS NOW!
BAM
NEXT TIME, I'LL AIM FOR YOUR HEADS!
I MIGHT NOT HAVE MONEY ANYMORE, BUT AT LEAST I CAN STILL COUNT ON MY FISTS.

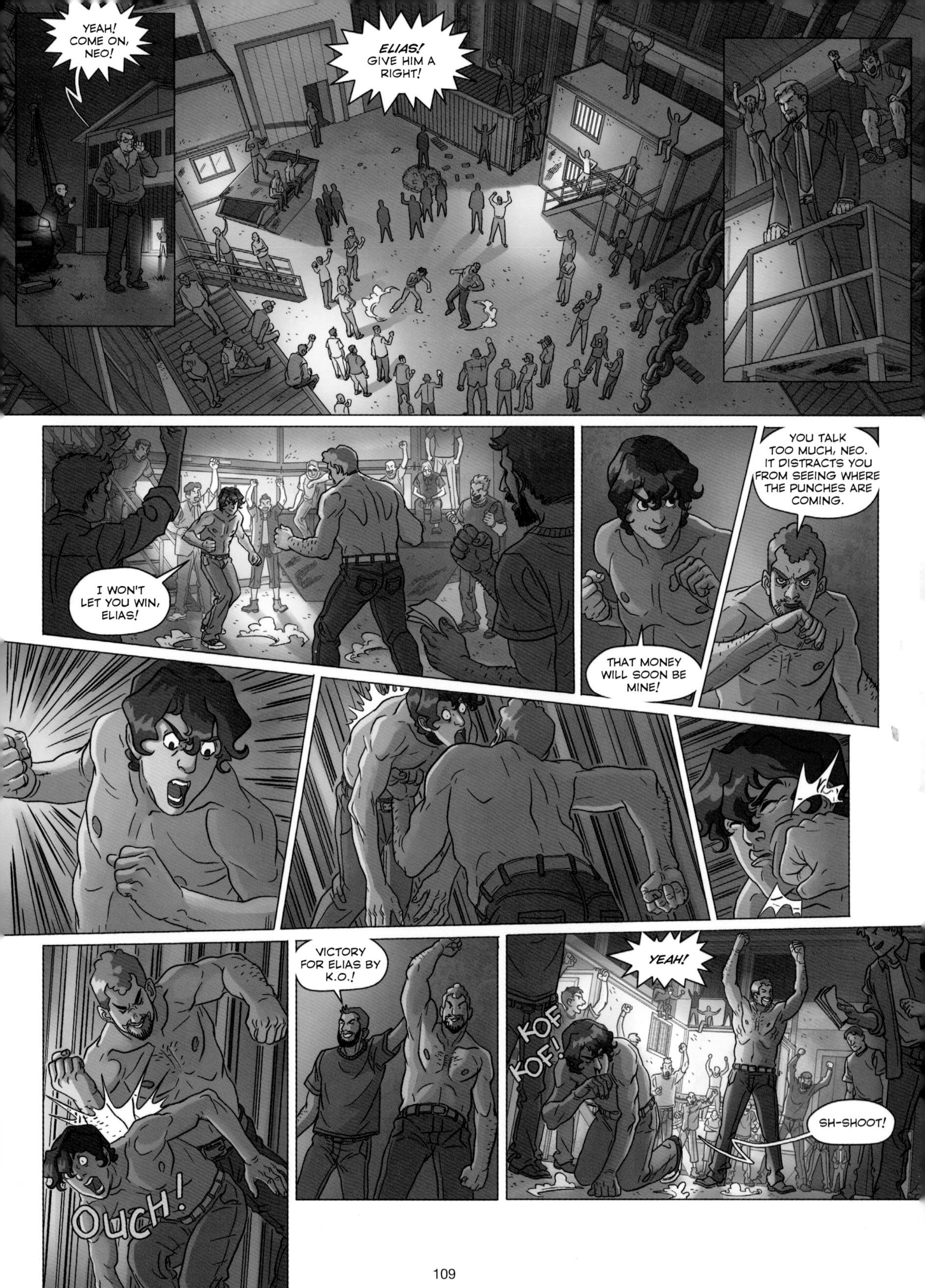
YEAH! COME ON, NEO!
ELIAS! GIVE HIM A RIGHT!
I WON'T LET YOU WIN, ELIAS!
YOU TALK TOO MUCH, NEO. IT DISTRACTS YOU FROM SEEING WHERE THE PUNCHES ARE COMING.
THAT MONEY WILL SOON BE MINE!
OUCH!
VICTORY FOR ELIAS BY K.O.!
YEAH!
KOF KOF!
SH-SHOOT!

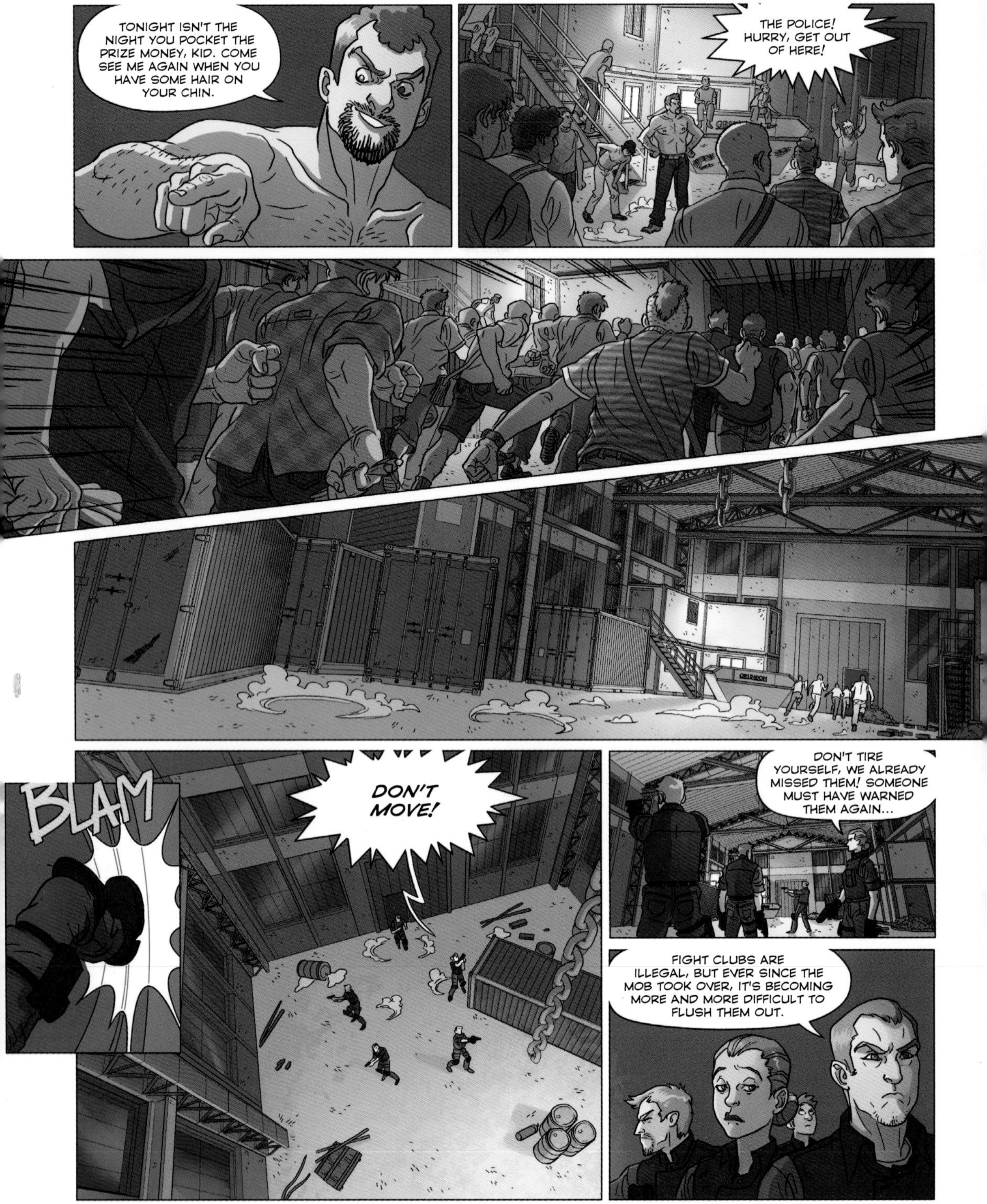
TONIGHT ISN'T THE NIGHT YOU POCKET THE PRIZE MONEY, KID. COME SEE ME AGAIN WHEN YOU HAVE SOME HAIR ON YOUR CHIN.
THE POLICE! HURRY, GET OUT OF HERE!
BLAM
DON'T MOVE!
DON'T TIRE YOURSELF, WE ALREADY MISSED THEM! SOMEONE MUST HAVE WARNED THEM AGAIN...
FIGHT CLUBS ARE ILLEGAL, BUT EVER SINCE THE MOB TOOK OVER, IT'S BECOMING MORE AND MORE DIFFICULT TO FLUSH THEM OUT.

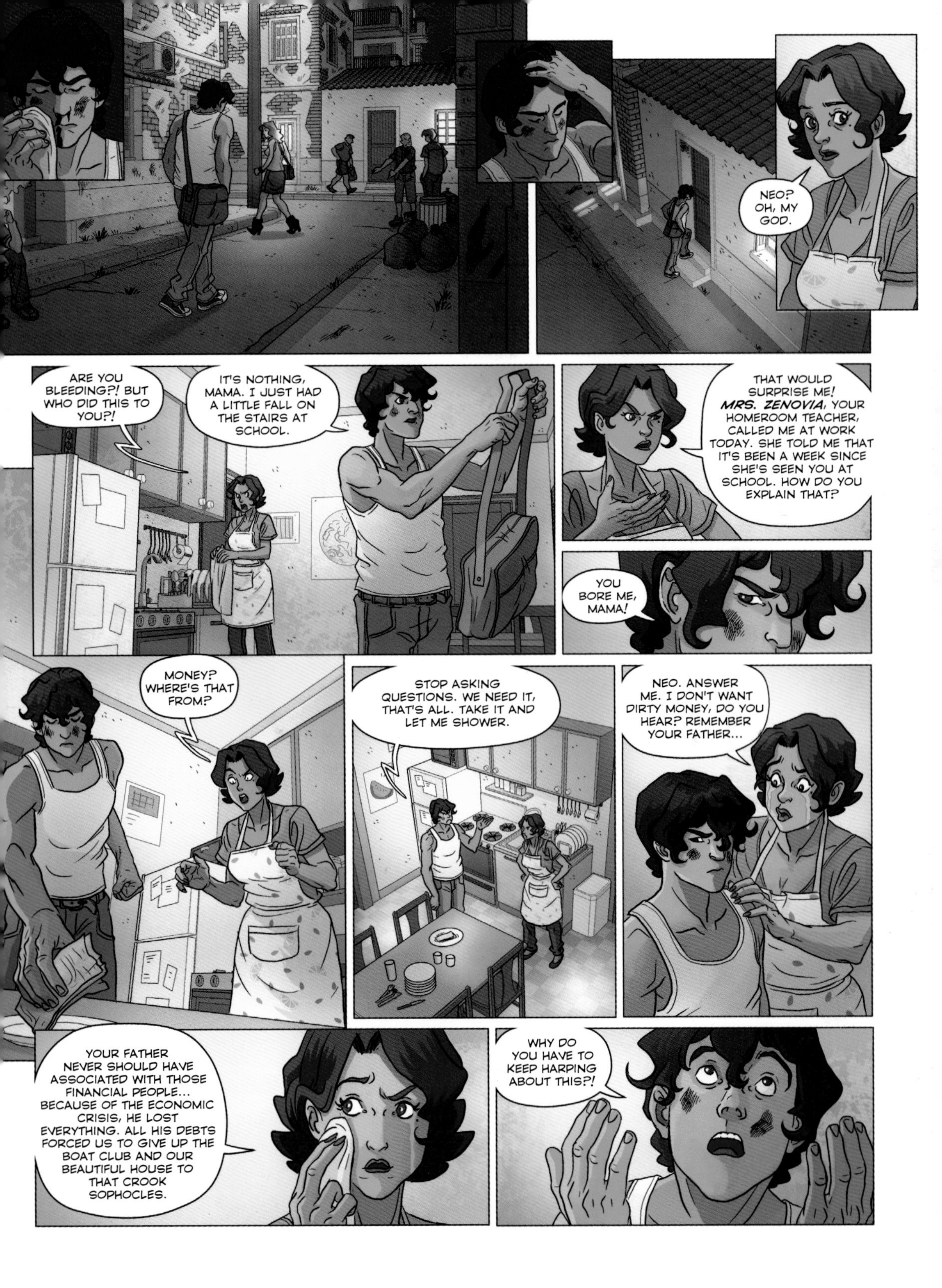

NEO? OH, MY GOD.
ARE YOU BLEEDING?! BUT WHO DID THIS TO YOU?!
IT'S NOTHING, MAMA. I JUST HAD A LITTLE FALL ON THE STAIRS AT SCHOOL.
THAT WOULD SURPRISE ME! MRS. ZENOVIA, YOUR HOMEROOM TEACHER, CALLED ME AT WORK TODAY. SHE TOLD ME THAT IT'S BEEN A WEEK SINCE SHE'S SEEN YOU AT SCHOOL. HOW DO YOU EXPLAIN THAT?
YOU BORE ME, MAMA!
MONEY? WHERE'S THAT FROM?
STOP ASKING QUESTIONS. WE NEED IT, THAT'S ALL. TAKE IT AND LET ME SHOWER.
NEO. ANSWER ME. I DON'T WANT DIRTY MONEY, DO YOU HEAR? REMEMBER YOUR FATHER...
YOUR FATHER NEVER SHOULD HAVE ASSOCIATED WITH THOSE FINANCIAL PEOPLE... BECAUSE OF THE ECONOMIC CRISIS, HE LOST EVERYTHING. ALL HIS DEBTS FORCED US TO GIVE UP THE BOAT CLUB AND OUR BEAUTIFUL HOUSE TO THAT CROOK SOPHOCLES.
WHY DO YOU HAVE TO KEEP HARPING ABOUT THIS?!

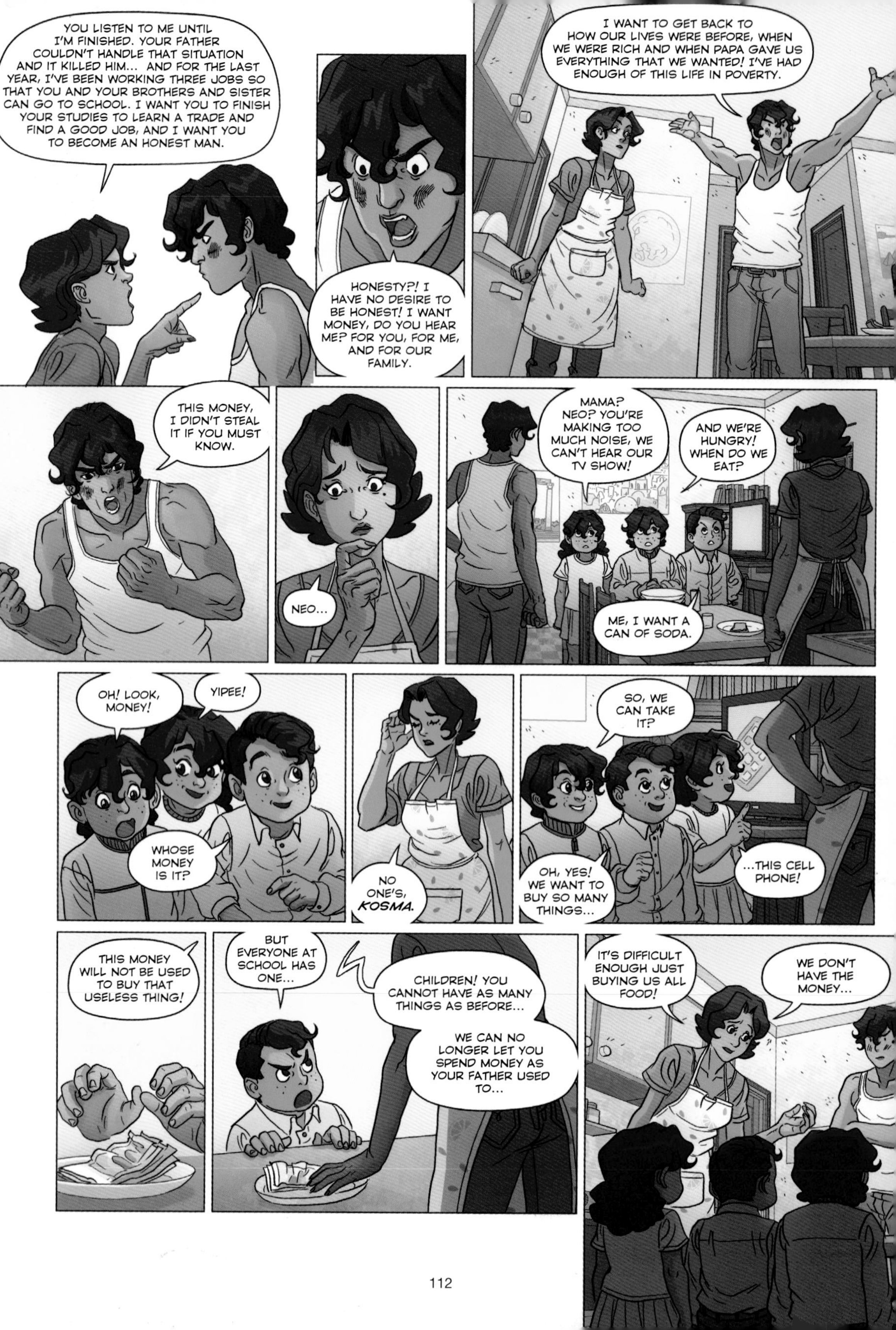
YOU LISTEN TO ME UNTIL I'M FINISHED. YOUR FATHER COULDN'T HANDLE THAT SITUATION AND IT KILLED HIM... AND FOR THE LAST YEAR, I'VE BEEN WORKING THREE JOBS SO THAT YOU AND YOUR BROTHERS AND SISTER CAN GO TO SCHOOL. I WANT YOU TO FINISH YOUR STUDIES TO LEARN A TRADE AND FIND A GOOD JOB, AND I WANT YOU TO BECOME AN HONEST MAN.
HONESTY?! I HAVE NO DESIRE TO BE HONEST! I WANT MONEY, DO YOU HEAR ME? FOR YOU, FOR ME, AND FOR OUR FAMILY.
I WANT TO GET BACK TO HOW OUR LIVES WERE BEFORE, WHEN WE WERE RICH AND WHEN PAPA GAVE US EVERYTHING THAT WE WANTED! I'VE HAD ENOUGH OF THIS LIFE IN POVERTY.
THIS MONEY, I DIDN'T STEAL IT IF YOU MUST KNOW.
NEO...
MAMA? NEO? YOU'RE MAKING TOO MUCH NOISE, WE CAN'T HEAR OUR TV SHOW!
AND WE'RE HUNGRY! WHEN DO WE EAT?
ME, I WANT A CAN OF SODA.
OH! LOOK, MONEY!
YIPEE!
WHOSE MONEY IS IT?
NO ONE'S, KOSMA.
SO, WE CAN TAKE IT?
OH, YES! WE WANT TO BUY SO MANY THINGS...
...THIS CELL PHONE!
THIS MONEY WILL NOT BE USED TO BUY THAT USELESS THING!
BUT EVERYONE AT SCHOOL HAS ONE...
CHILDREN! YOU CANNOT HAVE AS MANY THINGS AS BEFORE...
WE CAN NO LONGER LET YOU SPEND MONEY AS YOUR FATHER USED TO...
IT'S DIFFICULT ENOUGH JUST BUYING US ALL FOOD!
WE DON'T HAVE THE MONEY...

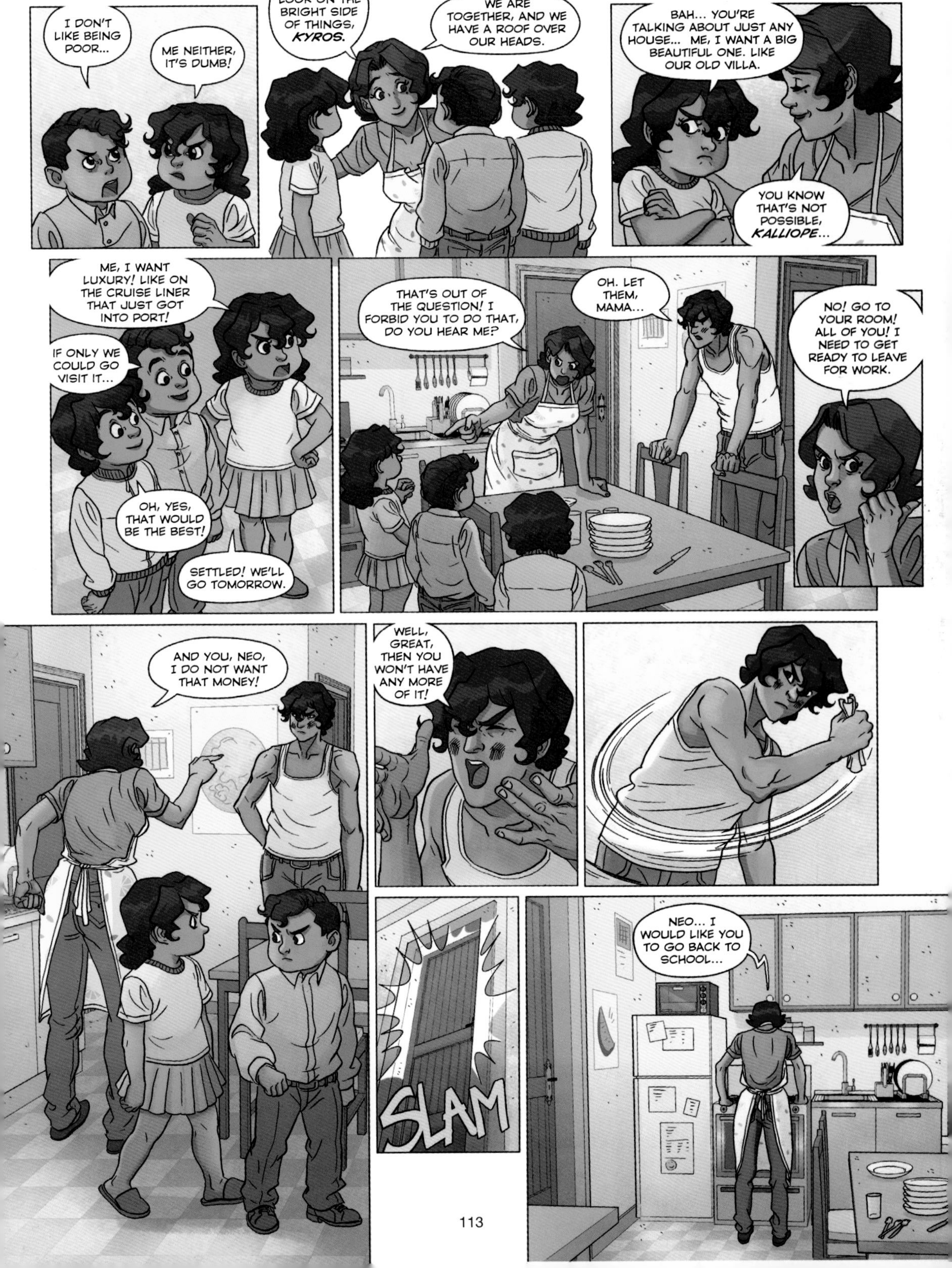
I DON'T LIKE BEING POOR...
ME NEITHER, IT'S DUMB!
WE MUST LOOK ON THE BRIGHT SIDE OF THINGS, KYROS.
WE ARE TOGETHER, AND WE HAVE A ROOF OVER OUR HEADS.
BAH... YOU'RE TALKING ABOUT JUST ANY HOUSE... ME, I WANT A BIG BEAUTIFUL ONE. LIKE OUR OLD VILLA.
YOU KNOW THAT'S NOT POSSIBLE, KALLIOPE...
ME, I WANT LUXURY! LIKE ON THE CRUISE LINER THAT JUST GOT INTO PORT!
IF ONLY WE COULD GO VISIT IT...
OH, YES, THAT WOULD BE THE BEST!
SETTLED! WE'LL GO TOMORROW.
THAT'S OUT OF THE QUESTION! I FORBID YOU TO DO THAT, DO YOU HEAR ME?
OH. LET THEM, MAMA...
NO! GO TO YOUR ROOM! ALL OF YOU! I NEED TO GET READY TO LEAVE FOR WORK.
AND YOU, NEO, I DO NOT WANT THAT MONEY!
WELL, GREAT, THEN YOU WON'T HAVE ANY MORE OF IT!
SLAM
NEO... I WOULD LIKE YOU TO GO BACK TO SCHOOL...

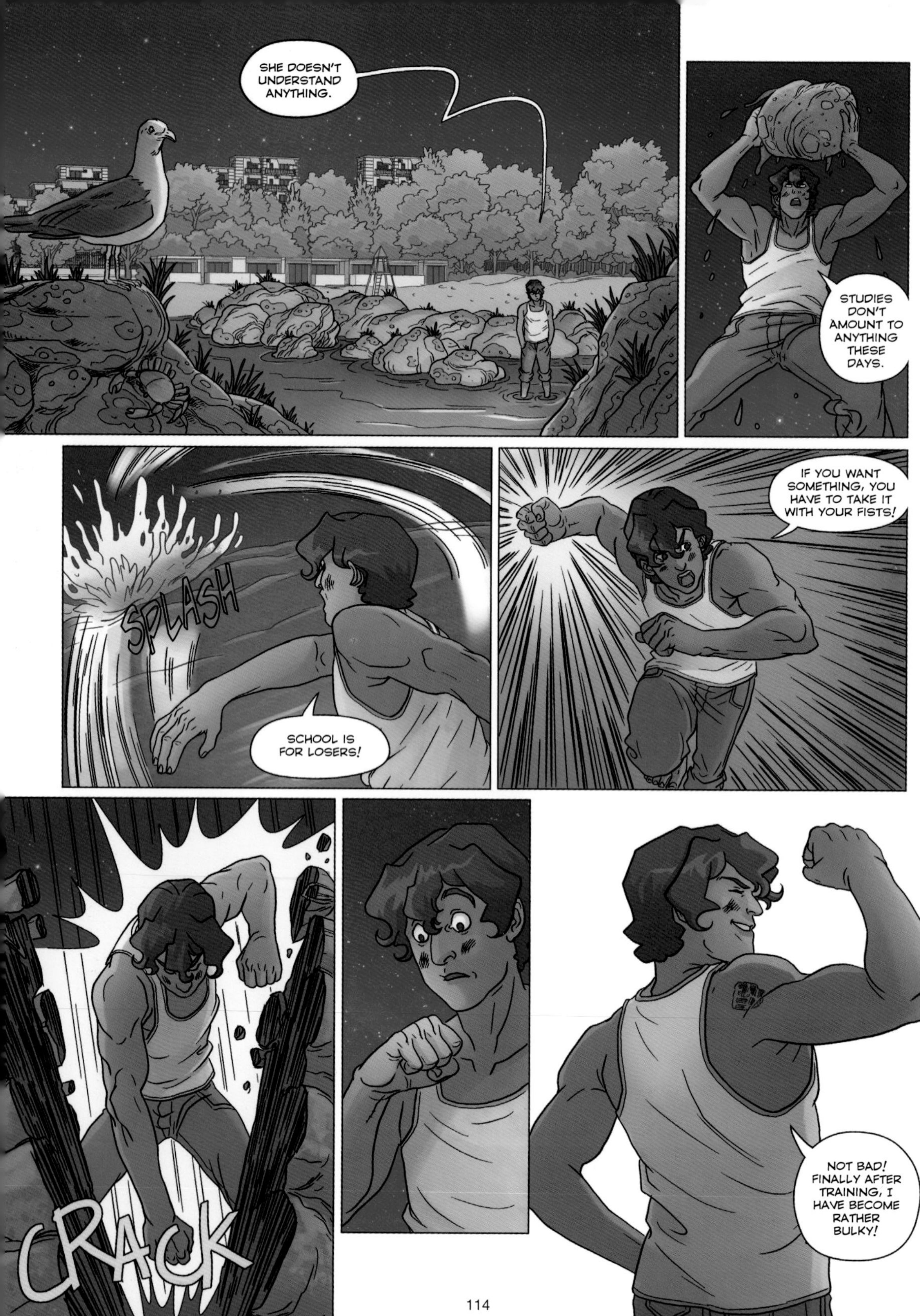
SHE DOESN'T UNDERSTAND ANYTHING.
STUDIES DON'T AMOUNT TO ANYTHING THESE DAYS.
SPLASH
SCHOOL IS FOR LOSERS!
IF YOU WANT SOMETHING, YOU HAVE TO TAKE IT WITH YOUR FISTS!
CRACK
NOT BAD! FINALLY AFTER TRAINING, I HAVE BECOME RATHER BULKY!

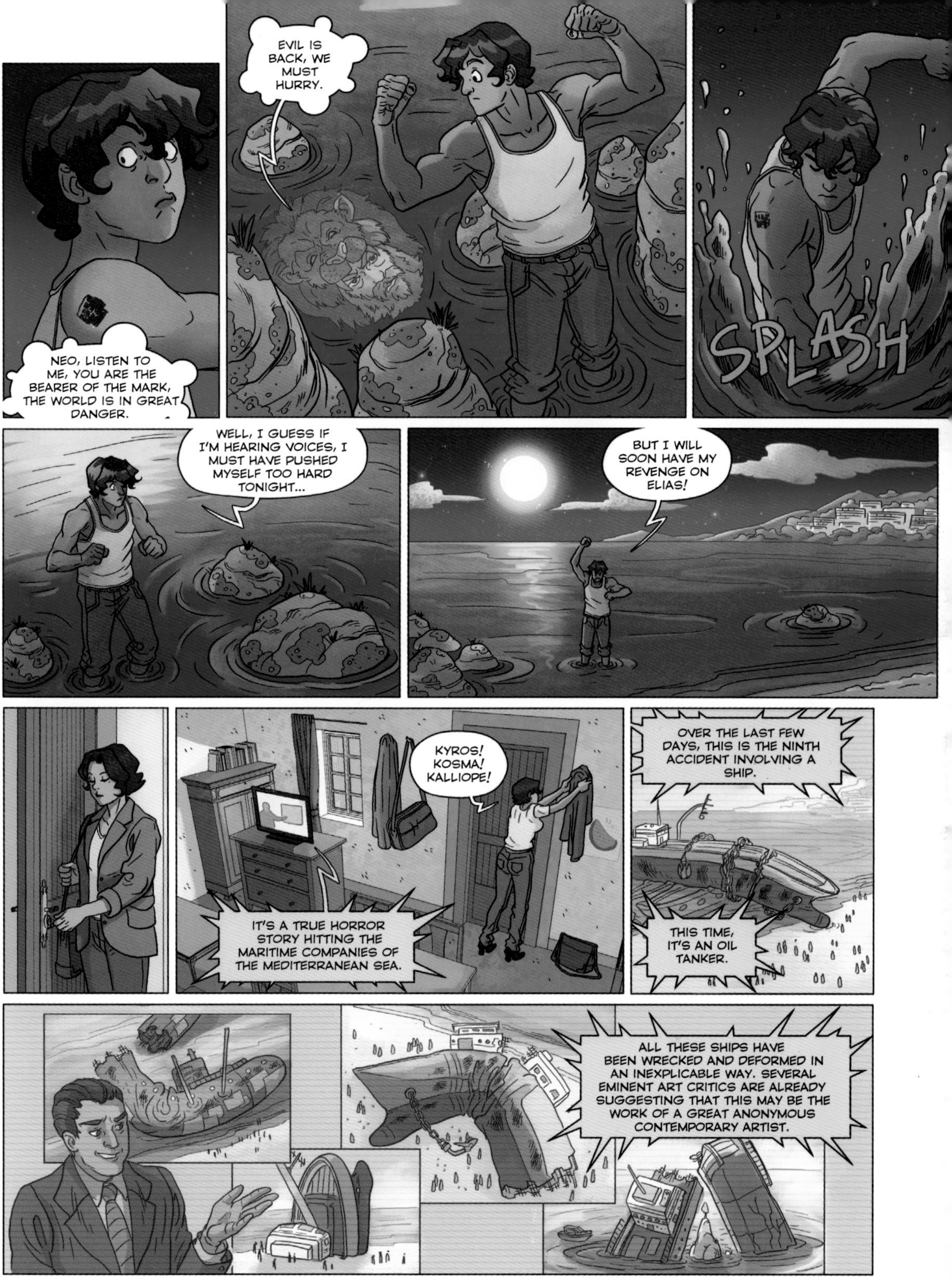
NEO, LISTEN TO ME, YOU ARE THE BEARER OF THE MARK, THE WORLD IS IN GREAT DANGER.
EVIL IS BACK, WE MUST HURRY.
SPLASH
WELL, I GUESS IF I'M HEARING VOICES, I MUST HAVE PUSHED MYSELF TOO HARD TONIGHT...
BUT I WILL SOON HAVE MY REVENGE ON ELIAS!
KYROS! KOSMA! KALLIOPE!
IT'S A TRUE HORROR STORY HITTING THE MARITIME COMPANIES OF THE MEDITERRANEAN SEA.
OVER THE LAST FEW DAYS, THIS IS THE NINTH ACCIDENT INVOLVING A SHIP.
THIS TIME, IT'S AN OIL TANKER.
ALL THESE SHIPS HAVE BEEN WRECKED AND DEFORMED IN AN INEXPLICABLE WAY. SEVERAL EMINENT ART CRITICS ARE ALREADY SUGGESTING THAT THIS MAY BE THE WORK OF A GREAT ANONYMOUS CONTEMPORARY ARTIST.

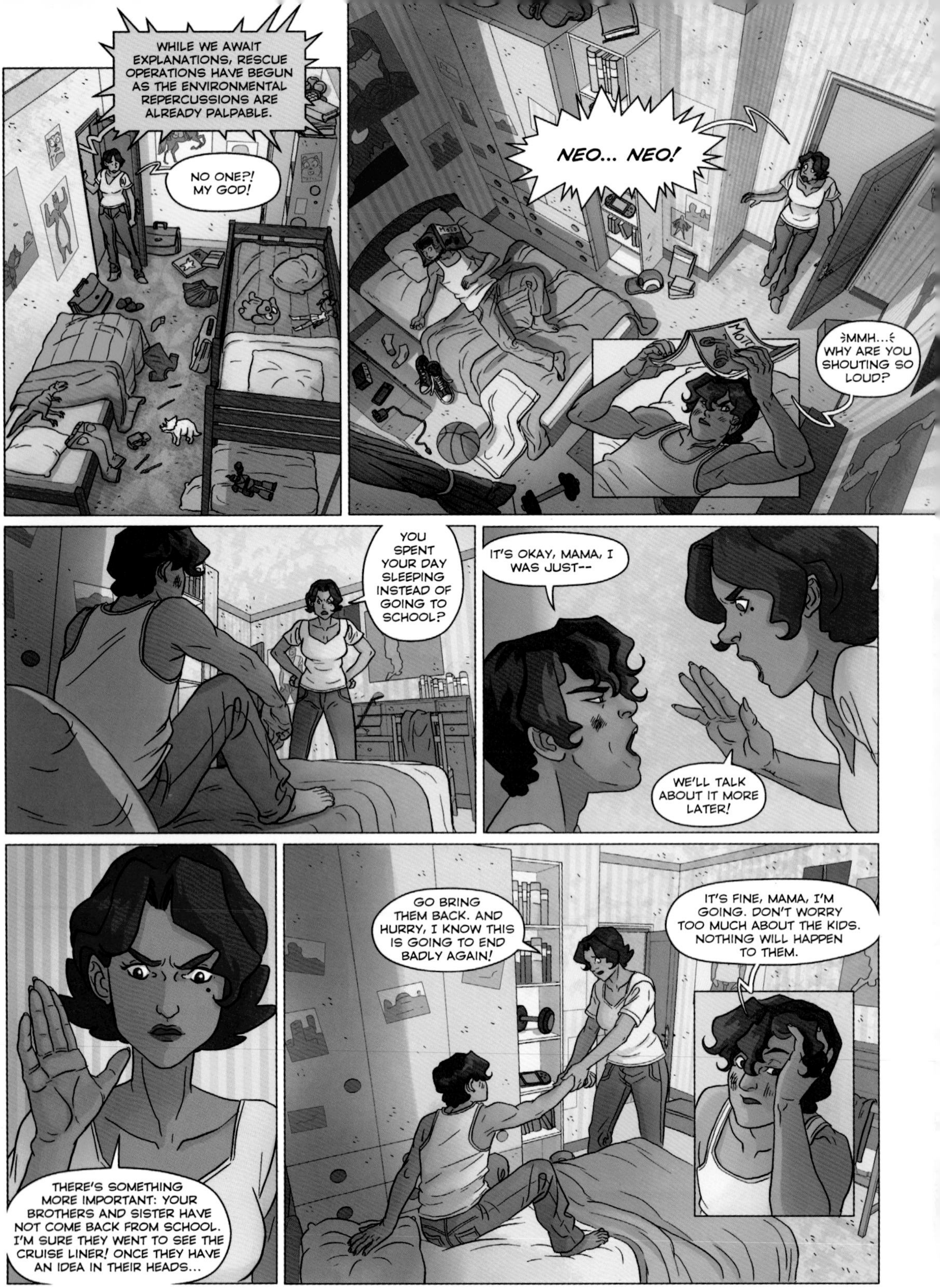
WHILE WE AWAIT EXPLANATIONS, RESCUE OPERATIONS HAVE BEGUN AS THE ENVIRONMENTAL REPERCUSSIONS ARE ALREADY PALPABLE.
NO ONE?! MY GOD!
NEO... NEO!
MMH... WHY ARE YOU SHOUTING SO LOUD?
YOU SPENT YOUR DAY SLEEPING INSTEAD OF GOING TO SCHOOL?
IT'S OKAY, MAMA, I WAS JUST--
WE'LL TALK ABOUT IT MORE LATER!
THERE'S SOMETHING MORE IMPORTANT: YOUR BROTHERS AND SISTER HAVE NOT COME BACK FROM SCHOOL. I'M SURE THEY WENT TO SEE THE CRUISE LINER! ONCE THEY HAVE AN IDEA IN THEIR HEADS...
GO BRING THEM BACK. AND HURRY, I KNOW THIS IS GOING TO END BADLY AGAIN!
IT'S FINE, MAMA, I'M GOING. DON'T WORRY TOO MUCH ABOUT THE KIDS. NOTHING WILL HAPPEN TO THEM.

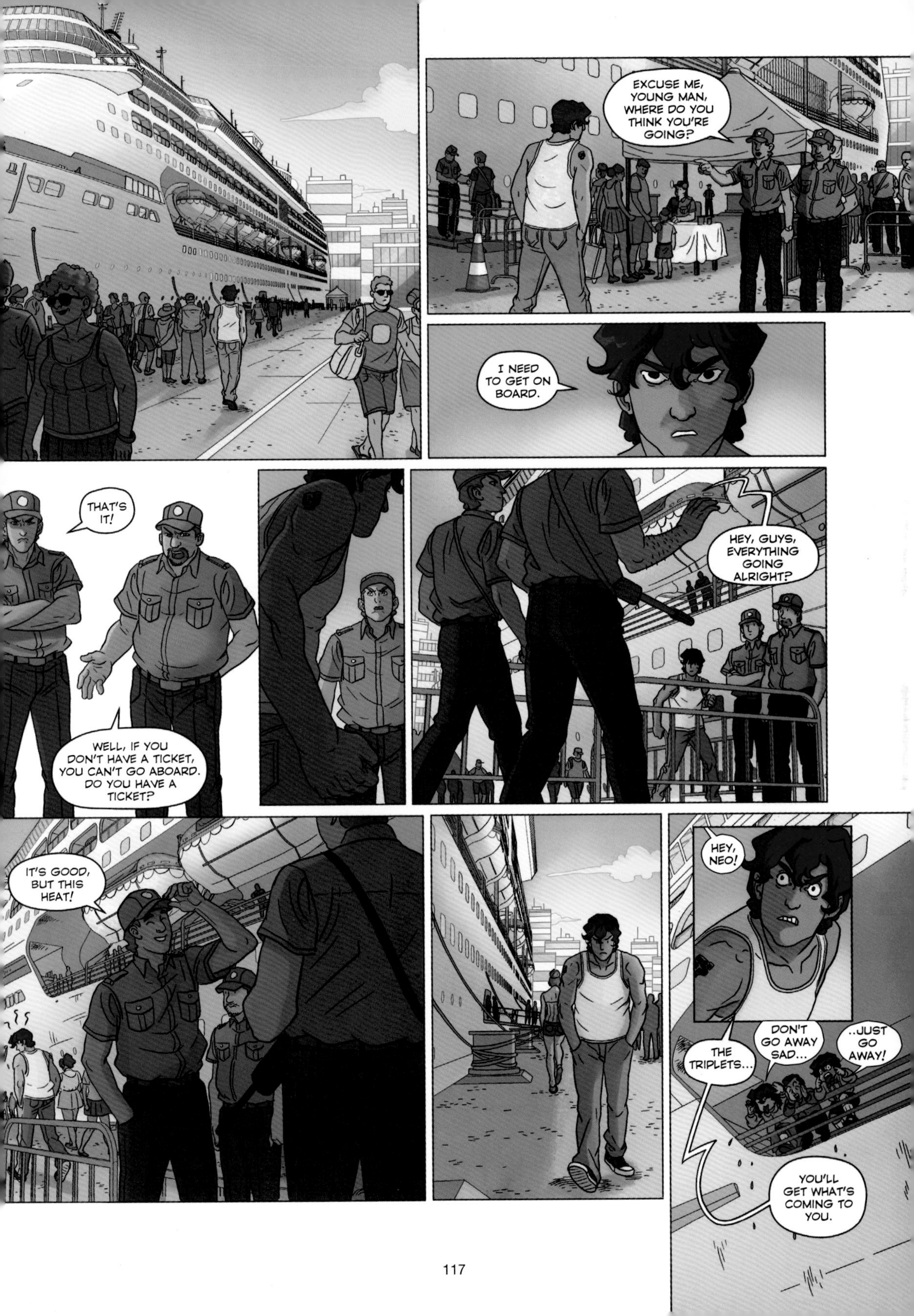
EXCUSE ME, YOUNG MAN, WHERE DO YOU THINK YOU'RE GOING?
I NEED TO GET ON BOARD.
THAT'S IT!
WELL, IF YOU DON'T HAVE A TICKET, YOU CAN'T GO ABOARD. DO YOU HAVE A TICKET?
HEY, GUYS, EVERYTHING GOING ALRIGHT?
IT'S GOOD, BUT THIS HEAT!
HEY, NEO!
THE TRIPLETS...
DON'T GO AWAY SAD...
..JUST GO AWAY!
YOU'LL GET WHAT'S COMING TO YOU.

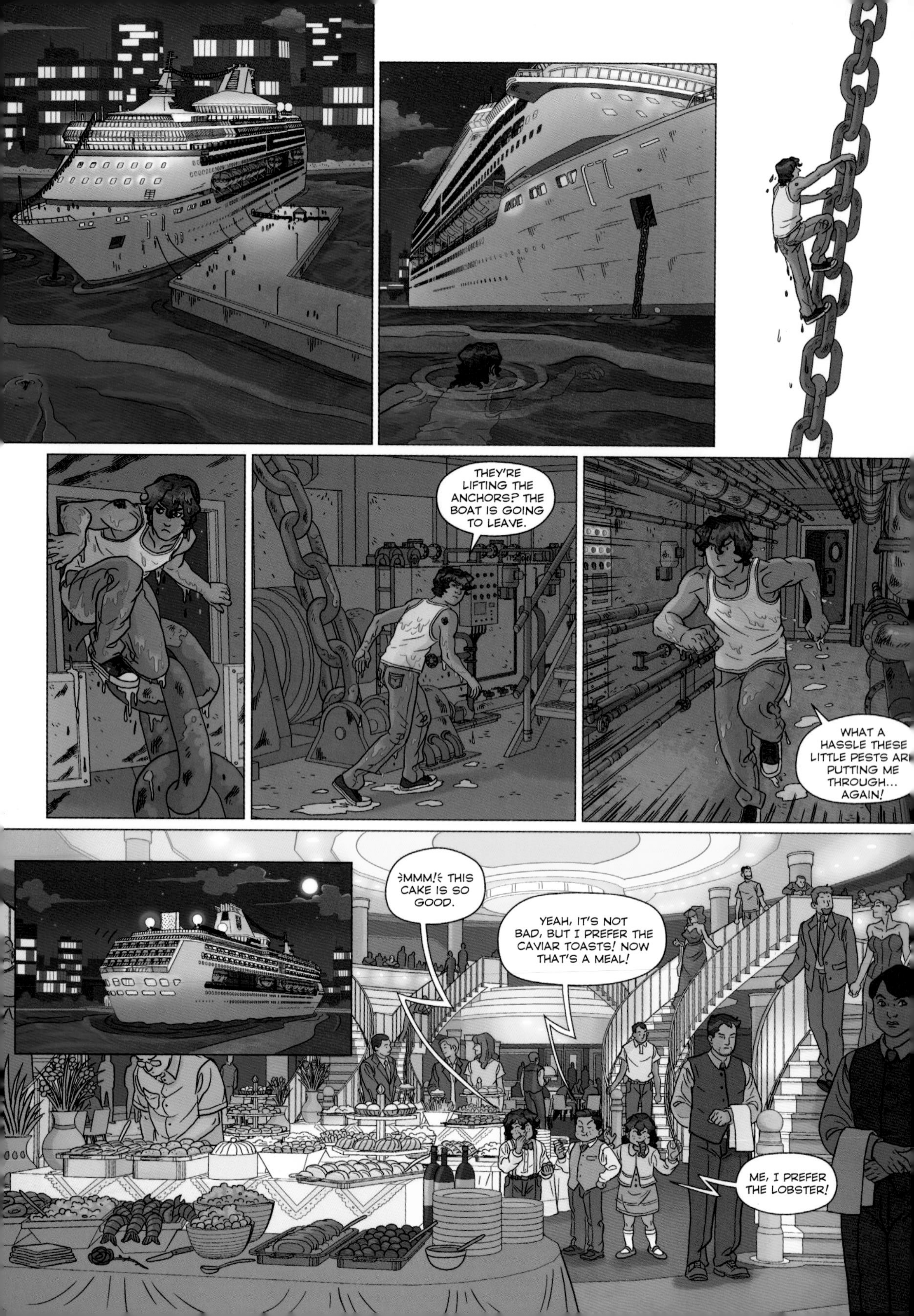
THEY'RE LIFTING THE ANCHORS? THE BOAT IS GOING TO LEAVE.
WHAT A HASSLE THESE LITTLE PESTS AR PUTTING ME THROUGH... AGAIN!
MMM! THIS CAKE IS SO GOOD.
YEAH, IT'S NOT BAD, BUT I PREFER THE CAVIAR TOASTS! NOW THAT'S A MEAL!
ME, I PREFER THE LOBSTER!

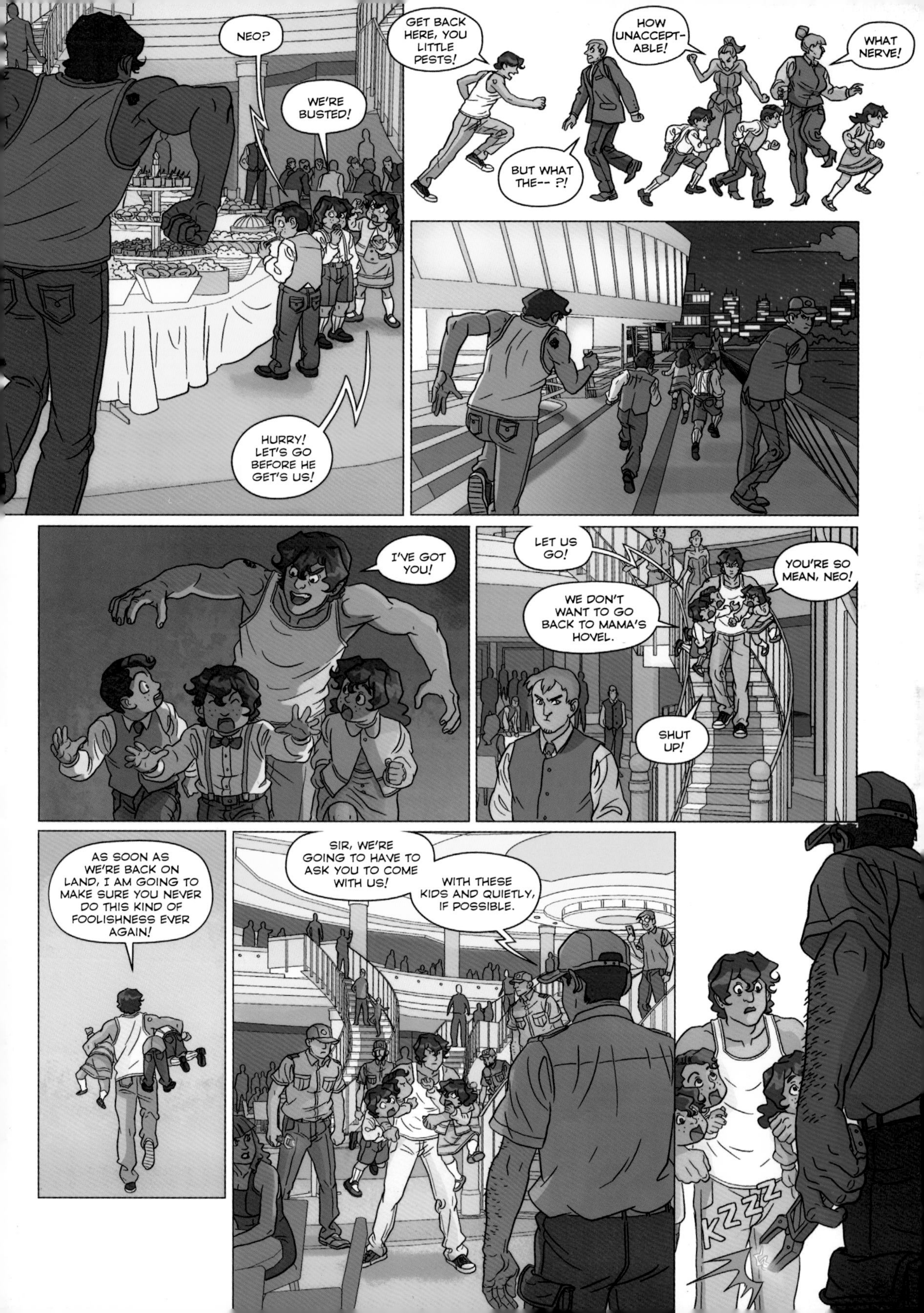
NEO?
WE'RE BUSTED!
HURRY! LET'S GO BEFORE HE GET'S US!
GET BACK HERE, YOU LITTLE PESTS!
HOW UNACCEPT-ABLE!
WHAT NERVE!
BUT WHAT THE-- ?!
I'VE GOT YOU!
LET US GO!
WE DON'T WANT TO GO BACK TO MAMA'S HOVEL.
YOU'RE SO MEAN, NEO!
SHUT UP!
AS SOON AS WE'RE BACK ON LAND, I AM GOING TO MAKE SURE YOU NEVER DO THIS KIND OF FOOLISHNESS EVER AGAIN!
SIR, WE'RE GOING TO HAVE TO ASK YOU TO COME WITH US!
WITH THESE KIDS AND QUIETLY, IF POSSIBLE.
KZZZ

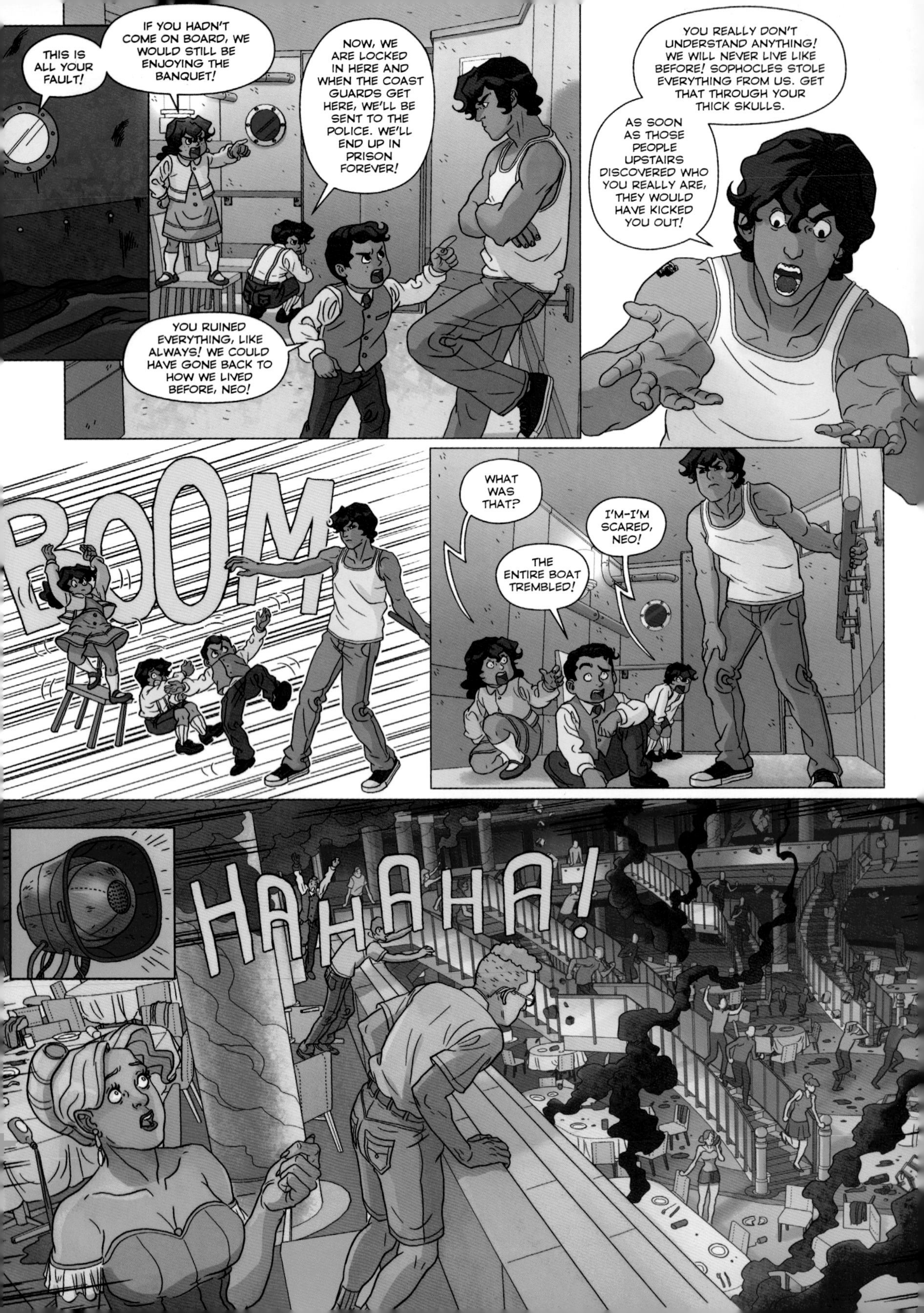
THIS IS ALL YOUR FAULT!
IF YOU HADN'T COME ON BOARD, WE WOULD STILL BE ENJOYING THE BANQUET!
NOW, WE ARE LOCKED IN HERE AND WHEN THE COAST GUARDS GET HERE, WE'LL BE SENT TO THE POLICE. WE'LL END UP IN PRISON FOREVER!
YOU RUINED EVERYTHING, LIKE ALWAYS! WE COULD HAVE GONE BACK TO HOW WE LIVED BEFORE, NEO!
YOU REALLY DON'T UNDERSTAND ANYTHING! WE WILL NEVER LIVE LIKE BEFORE! SOPHOCLES STOLE EVERYTHING FROM US. GET THAT THROUGH YOUR THICK SKULLS.
AS SOON AS THOSE PEOPLE UPSTAIRS DISCOVERED WHO YOU REALLY ARE, THEY WOULD HAVE KICKED YOU OUT!
BOOM
WHAT WAS THAT?
THE ENTIRE BOAT TREMBLED!
I'M-I'M SCARED, NEO!
HAHAHA!

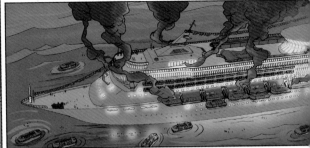

HEY! IS ANYONE THERE?! HELP US! WE'RE LOCKED IN, COME LET US OUT!

IT'S NO GOOD! NO ONE CAN HEAR US!

NEO! *NEO!* THERE'S WATER AT OUR FEET!

THE WATER'S RISING!

WE'RE GOING TO DROWN! HELP!

OH, REALLY?
I THOUGHT THAT I WOULDN'T BE ABLE TO MAKE CONTACT EVER AGAIN. YOU DON'T HAVE MIRRORS AT YOUR HOUSE? ANYWAY, LET'S MOVE ON TO THE SPECIFICS.
I AM *HERCULES.*
SPLASH
THAT'S POINTLESS... OKAY, LET ME EXPLAIN TWO OR THREE THINGS TO YOU... FIRST, I AM NOT REALLY HERE.
I'M IN THE SPIRIT WORLD. SO, PUNCHING THE WATER DOES NOTHING EXCEPT TO GET YOU EVEN MORE SOAKED.
SECOND, YOU ARE THE ONLY ONE WITH THE POWER TO SEE ME, SO IT'S USELESS TO SPEAK ALOUD.
AND THIRDLY, IF I'M HERE IT'S BECAUSE YOU ARE THE NEW HERO CHARGED TO FIGHT EVIL, AND WE DON'T HAVE MUCH TIME LEFT.
I DON'T KNOW WHO YOU ARE, GRAMPS, BUT HERE AND NOW, I'M JUST TRYING NOT TO DROWN WITH THE LITTLE ONES.
MY BAD! IF YOU DIE, YOU CAN'T FIGHT EVIL. SO, LET'S FIX THIS AS QUICKLY AS WE CAN. OKAY, DO WHAT I TELL YOU: OPEN THIS DOOR AND LEAVE!
ARE YOU STUPID?! YOU REALLY THINK THAT IF I WAS CAPABLE OF OPENING THIS DOOR, THAT I WOULD STAY HERE SPLASHING AROUND?
SIGH.
YOU'VE INHERITED MY STRENGTH. SO, YOU CAN TAKE THAT DOOR, PULL IT OFF ITS HINGES, AND LEAVE WITH YOUR FAMILY! DO YOU UNDERSTAND WHAT I'M TELLING YOU?

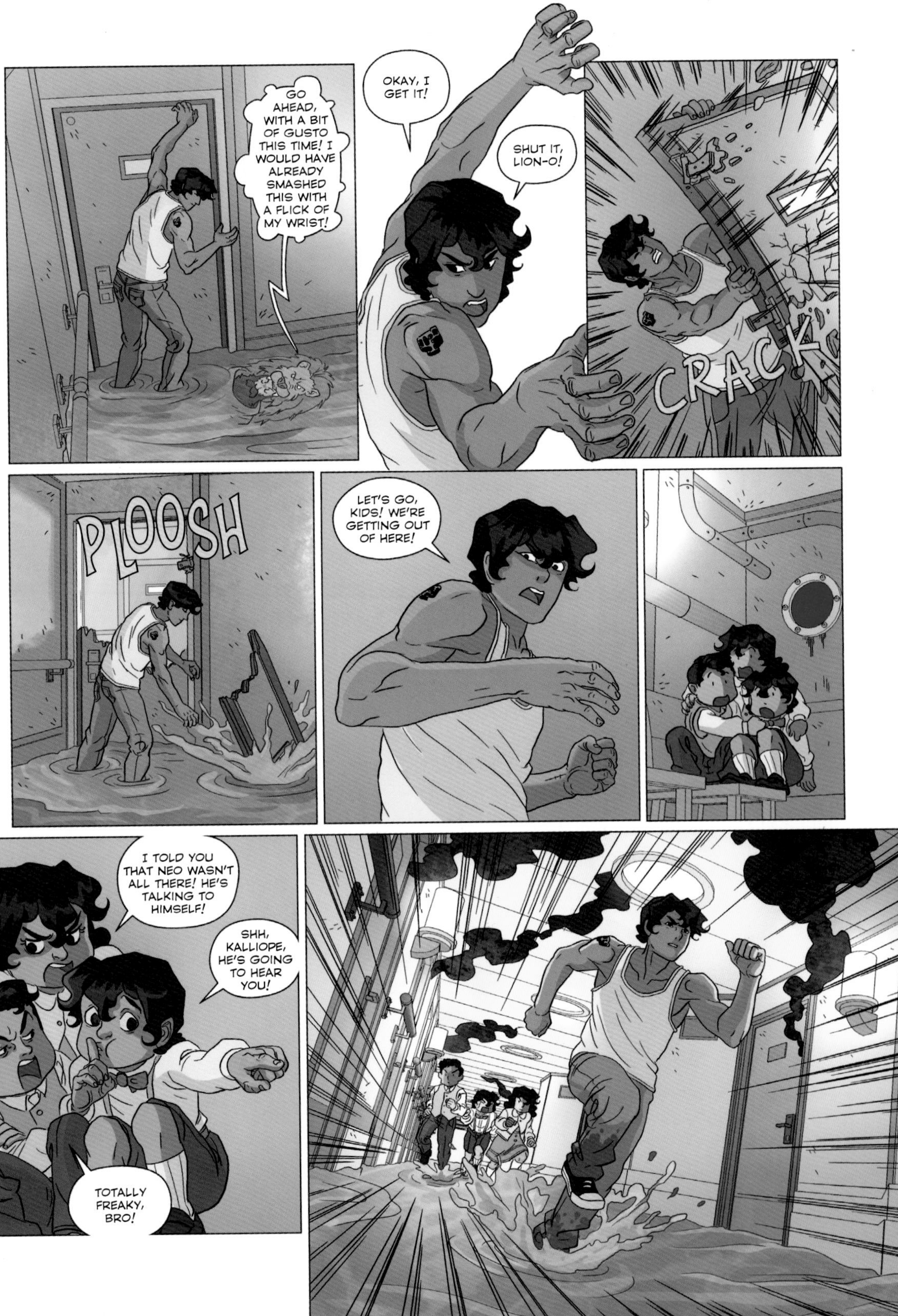
GO AHEAD, WITH A BIT OF GUSTO THIS TIME! I WOULD HAVE ALREADY SMASHED THIS WITH A FLICK OF MY WRIST!
OKAY, I GET IT!
SHUT IT, LION-O!
CRACK
PLOOSH
LET'S GO, KIDS! WE'RE GETTING OUT OF HERE!
I TOLD YOU THAT NEO WASN'T ALL THERE! HE'S TALKING TO HIMSELF!
SHH, KALLIOPE, HE'S GOING TO HEAR YOU!
TOTALLY FREAKY, BRO!

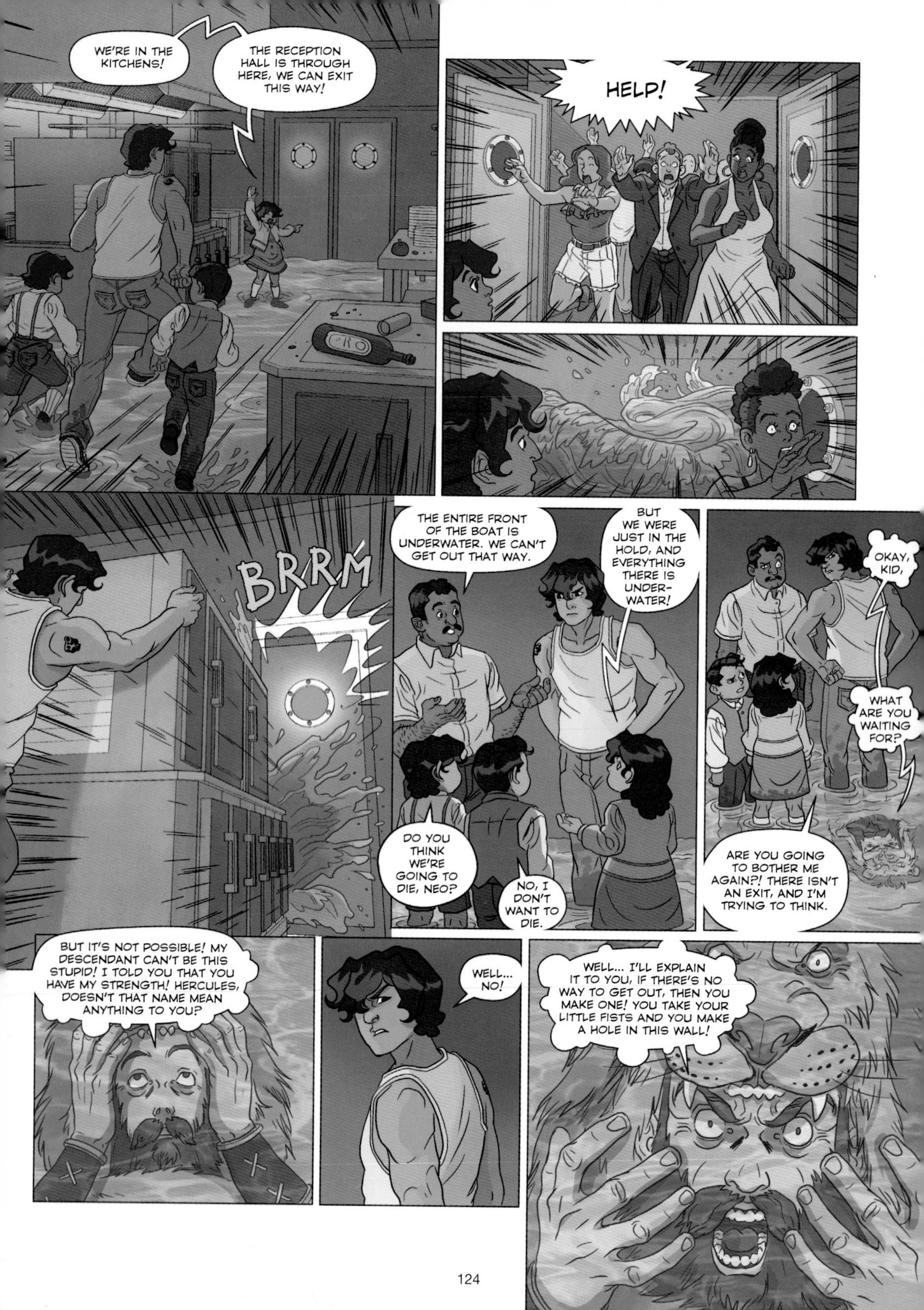
WE'RE IN THE KITCHENS!
THE RECEPTION HALL IS THROUGH HERE, WE CAN EXIT THIS WAY!
HELP!
BRRM
THE ENTIRE FRONT OF THE BOAT IS UNDERWATER. WE CAN'T GET OUT THAT WAY.
BUT WE WERE JUST IN THE HOLD, AND EVERYTHING THERE IS UNDER-WATER!
DO YOU THINK WE'RE GOING TO DIE, NEO?
NO, I DON'T WANT TO DIE.
OKAY, KID,
WHAT ARE YOU WAITING FOR?
ARE YOU GOING TO BOTHER ME AGAIN?! THERE ISN'T AN EXIT, AND I'M TRYING TO THINK.
BUT IT'S NOT POSSIBLE! MY DESCENDANT CAN'T BE THIS STUPID! I TOLD YOU THAT YOU HAVE MY STRENGTH! HERCULES, DOESN'T THAT NAME MEAN ANYTHING TO YOU?
WELL... NO!
WELL... I'LL EXPLAIN IT TO YOU, IF THERE'S NO WAY TO GET OUT, THEN YOU MAKE ONE! YOU TAKE YOUR LITTLE FISTS AND YOU MAKE A HOLE IN THIS WALL!

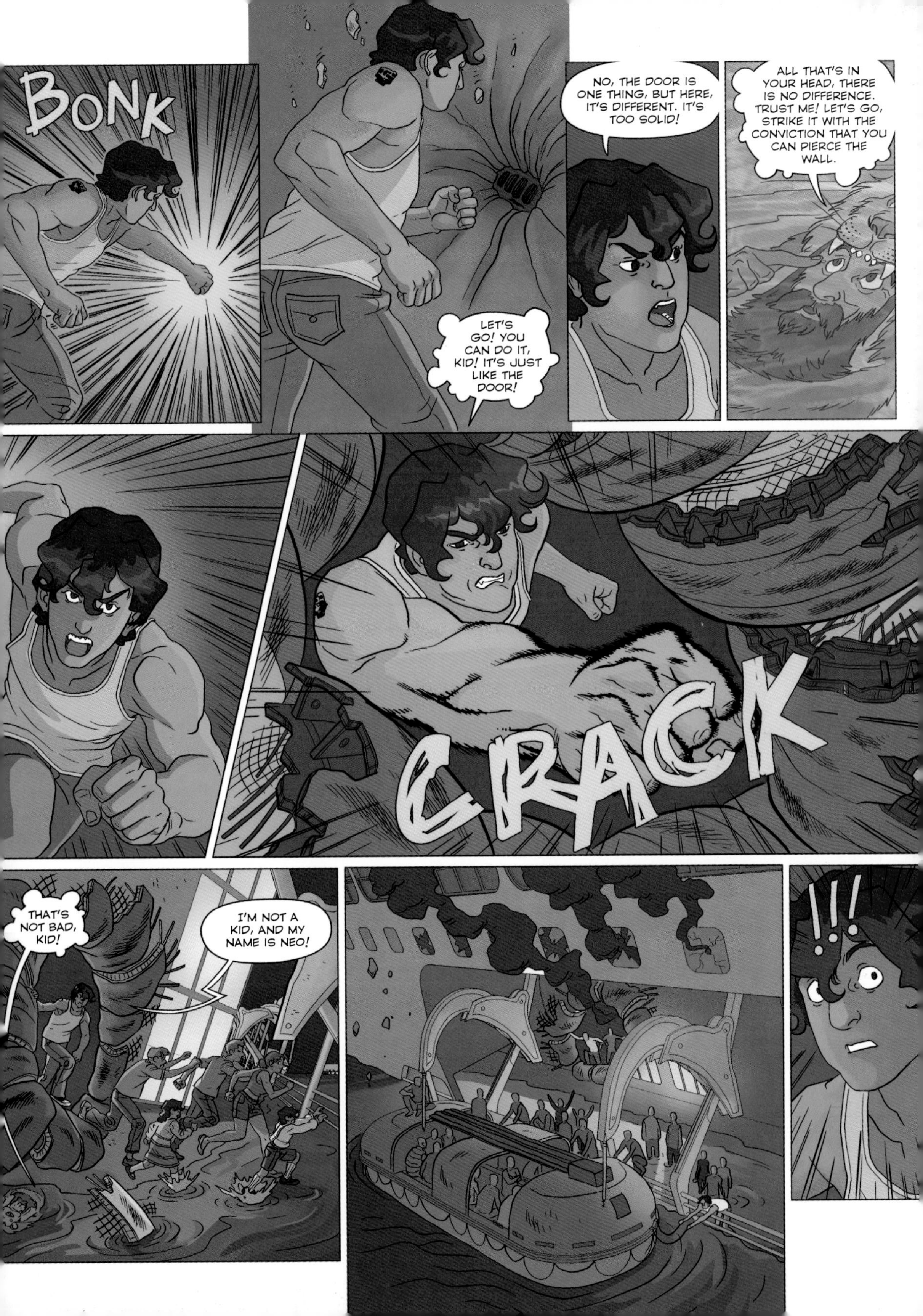
BONK
LET'S GO! YOU CAN DO IT, KID! IT'S JUST LIKE THE DOOR!
NO, THE DOOR IS ONE THING, BUT HERE, IT'S DIFFERENT. IT'S TOO SOLID!
ALL THAT'S IN YOUR HEAD, THERE IS NO DIFFERENCE. TRUST ME! LET'S GO, STRIKE IT WITH THE CONVICTION THAT YOU CAN PIERCE THE WALL.
CRACK
THAT'S NOT BAD, KID!
I'M NOT A KID, AND MY NAME IS NEO!
!!!

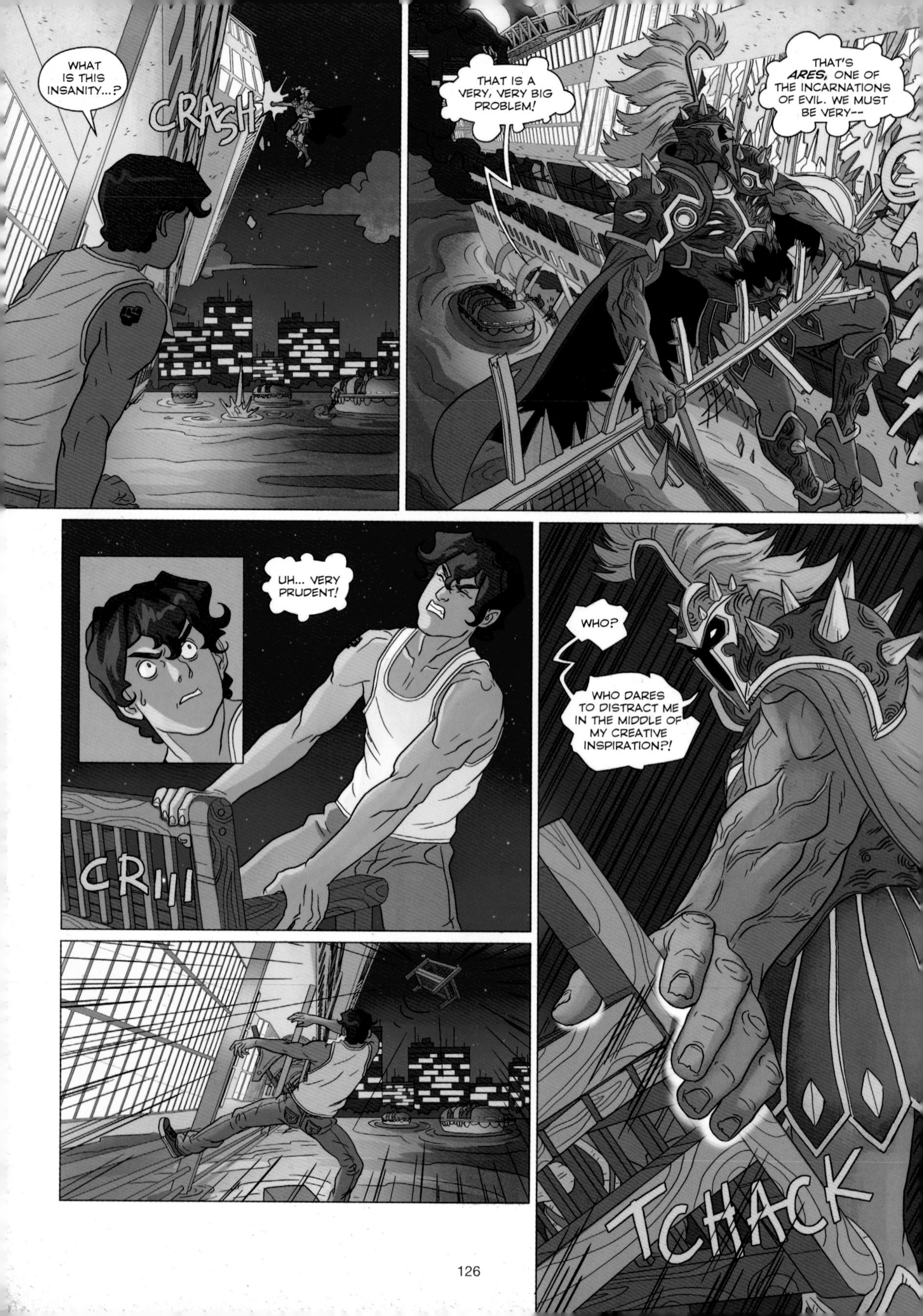
WHAT IS THIS INSANITY...?
CRASH
THAT IS A VERY, VERY BIG PROBLEM!
THAT'S ARES, ONE OF THE INCARNATIONS OF EVIL. WE MUST BE VERY--
UH... VERY PRUDENT!
CRIII
WHO?
WHO DARES TO DISTRACT ME IN THE MIDDLE OF MY CREATIVE INSPIRATION?!
TCHACK

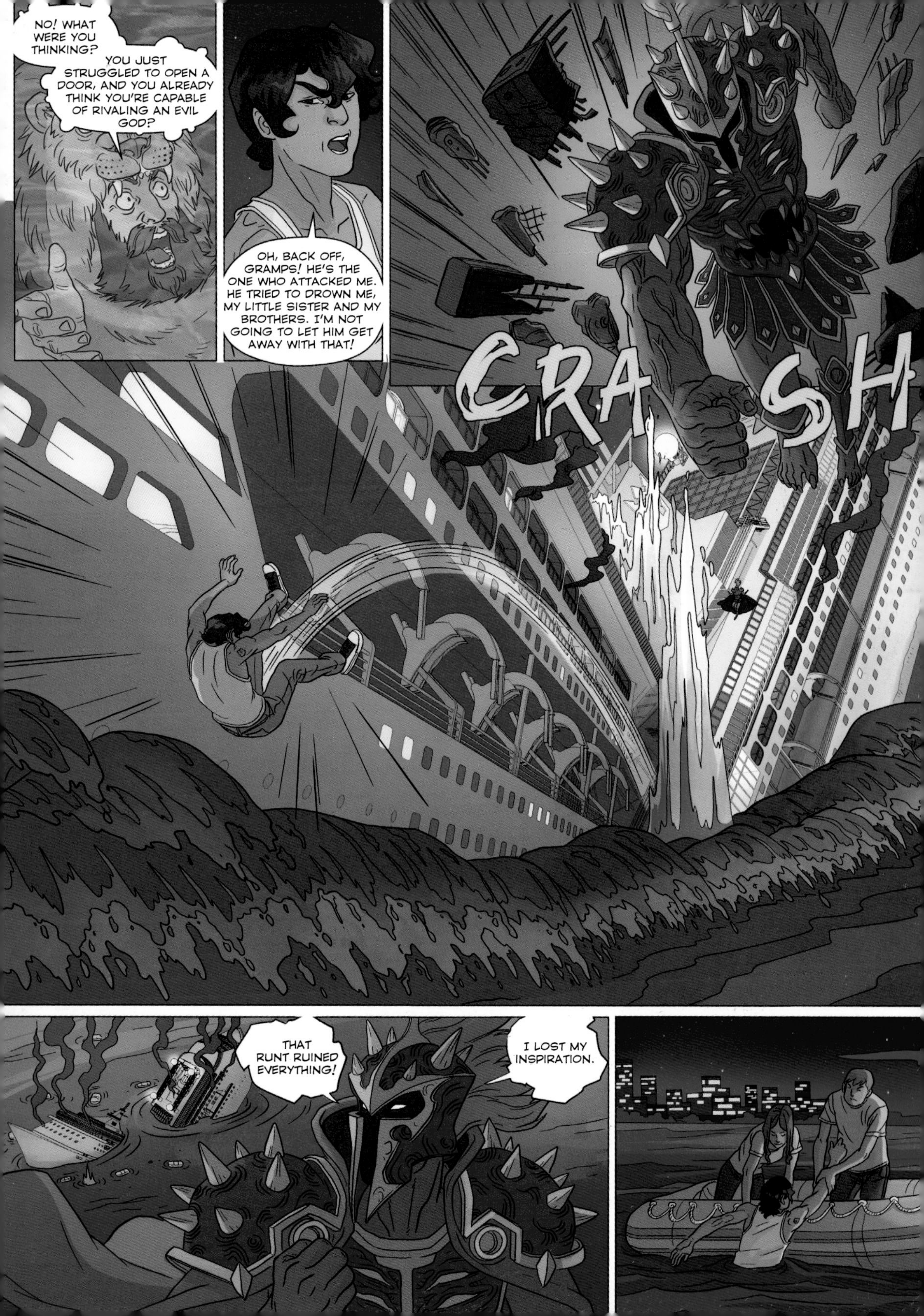
NO! WHAT WERE YOU THINKING?
YOU JUST STRUGGLED TO OPEN A DOOR, AND YOU ALREADY THINK YOU'RE CAPABLE OF RIVALING AN EVIL GOD?
OH, BACK OFF, GRAMPS! HE'S THE ONE WHO ATTACKED ME. HE TRIED TO DROWN ME, MY LITTLE SISTER AND MY BROTHERS. I'M NOT GOING TO LET HIM GET AWAY WITH THAT!
CRASH
THAT RUNT RUINED EVERYTHING!
I LOST MY INSPIRATION.

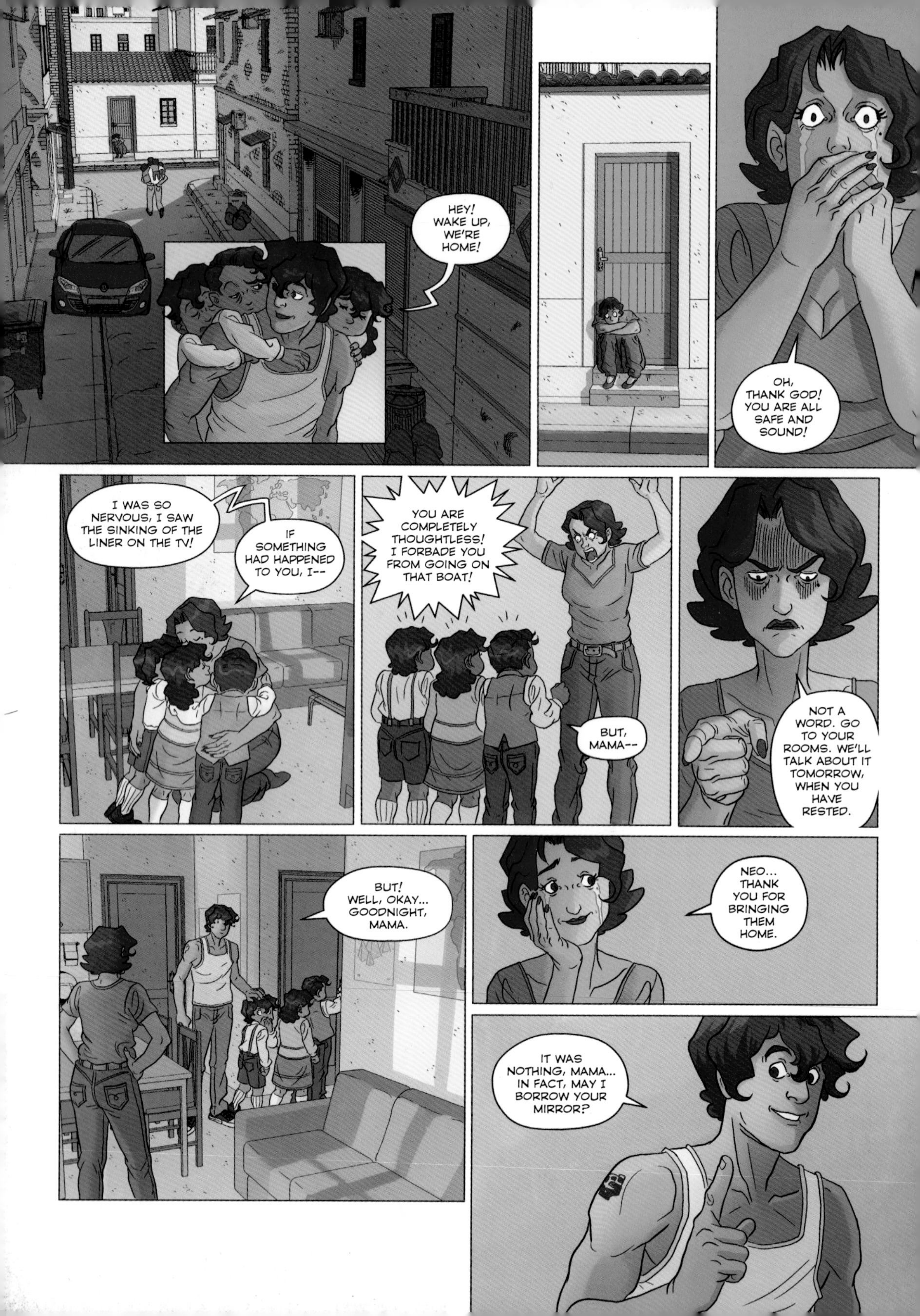

HEY! WAKE UP, WE'RE HOME!
OH, THANK GOD! YOU ARE ALL SAFE AND SOUND!
I WAS SO NERVOUS, I SAW THE SINKING OF THE LINER ON THE TV!
IF SOMETHING HAD HAPPENED TO YOU, I--
YOU ARE COMPLETELY THOUGHTLESS! I FORBADE YOU FROM GOING ON THAT BOAT!
BUT, MAMA--
NOT A WORD. GO TO YOUR ROOMS. WE'LL TALK ABOUT IT TOMORROW, WHEN YOU HAVE RESTED.
BUT! WELL, OKAY... GOODNIGHT, MAMA.
NEO... THANK YOU FOR BRINGING THEM HOME.
IT WAS NOTHING, MAMA... IN FACT, MAY I BORROW YOUR MIRROR?

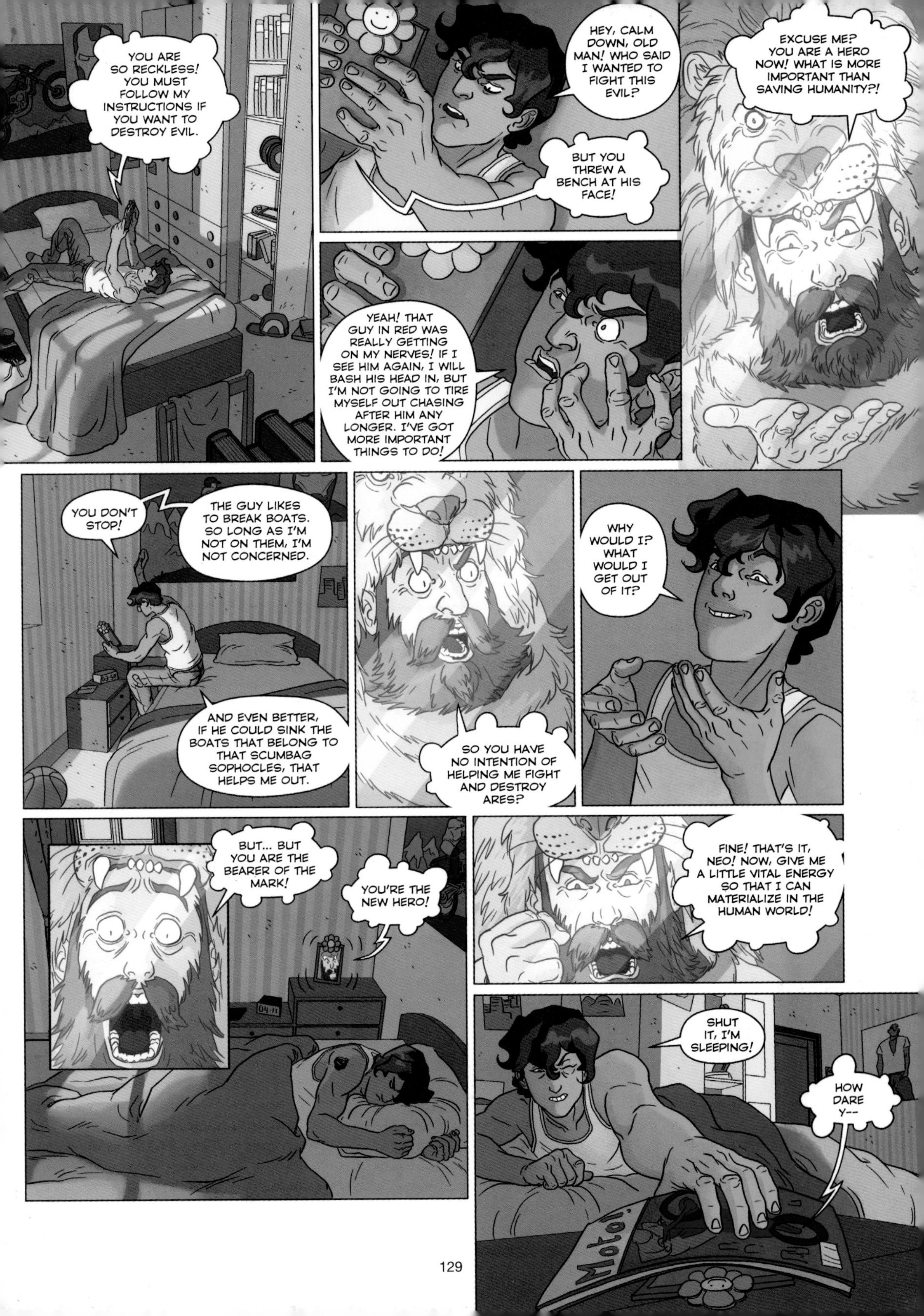
YOU ARE SO RECKLESS! YOU MUST FOLLOW MY INSTRUCTIONS IF YOU WANT TO DESTROY EVIL.
HEY, CALM DOWN, OLD MAN! WHO SAID I WANTED TO FIGHT THIS EVIL?
BUT YOU THREW A BENCH AT HIS FACE!
YEAH! THAT GUY IN RED WAS REALLY GETTING ON MY NERVES! IF I SEE HIM AGAIN, I WILL BASH HIS HEAD IN, BUT I'M NOT GOING TO TIRE MYSELF OUT CHASING AFTER HIM ANY LONGER. I'VE GOT MORE IMPORTANT THINGS TO DO!
EXCUSE ME? YOU ARE A HERO NOW! WHAT IS MORE IMPORTANT THAN SAVING HUMANITY?!
YOU DON'T STOP!
THE GUY LIKES TO BREAK BOATS. SO LONG AS I'M NOT ON THEM, I'M NOT CONCERNED.
AND EVEN BETTER, IF HE COULD SINK THE BOATS THAT BELONG TO THAT SCUMBAG SOPHOCLES, THAT HELPS ME OUT.
SO YOU HAVE NO INTENTION OF HELPING ME FIGHT AND DESTROY ARES?
WHY WOULD I? WHAT WOULD I GET OUT OF IT?
BUT... BUT YOU ARE THE BEARER OF THE MARK!
YOU'RE THE NEW HERO!
FINE! THAT'S IT, NEO! NOW, GIVE ME A LITTLE VITAL ENERGY SO THAT I CAN MATERIALIZE IN THE HUMAN WORLD!
SHUT IT, I'M SLEEPING!
HOW DARE Y--
Moto!

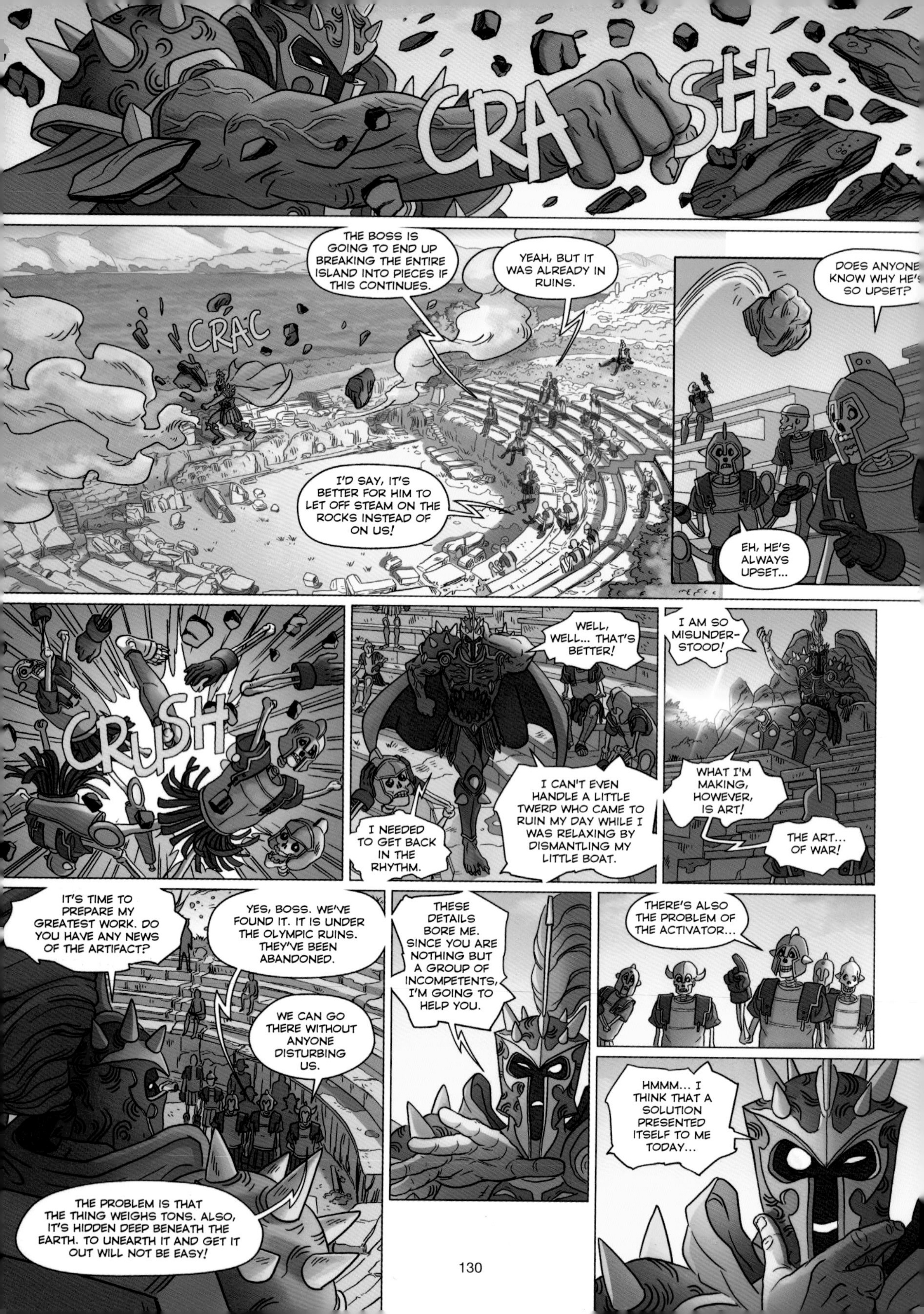
CRASH
CRAC
THE BOSS IS GOING TO END UP BREAKING THE ENTIRE ISLAND INTO PIECES IF THIS CONTINUES.
YEAH, BUT IT WAS ALREADY IN RUINS.
I'D SAY, IT'S BETTER FOR HIM TO LET OFF STEAM ON THE ROCKS INSTEAD OF ON US!
DOES ANYONE KNOW WHY HE'S SO UPSET?
EH, HE'S ALWAYS UPSET...
CRUSH
WELL, WELL... THAT'S BETTER!
I NEEDED TO GET BACK IN THE RHYTHM.
I CAN'T EVEN HANDLE A LITTLE TWERP WHO CAME TO RUIN MY DAY WHILE I WAS RELAXING BY DISMANTLING MY LITTLE BOAT.
I AM SO MISUNDER-STOOD!
WHAT I'M MAKING, HOWEVER, IS ART!
THE ART... OF WAR!
IT'S TIME TO PREPARE MY GREATEST WORK. DO YOU HAVE ANY NEWS OF THE ARTIFACT?
YES, BOSS. WE'VE FOUND IT. IT IS UNDER THE OLYMPIC RUINS. THEY'VE BEEN ABANDONED.
WE CAN GO THERE WITHOUT ANYONE DISTURBING US.
THE PROBLEM IS THAT THE THING WEIGHS TONS. ALSO, IT'S HIDDEN DEEP BENEATH THE EARTH. TO UNEARTH IT AND GET IT OUT WILL NOT BE EASY!
THESE DETAILS BORE ME. SINCE YOU ARE NOTHING BUT A GROUP OF INCOMPETENTS, I'M GOING TO HELP YOU.
THERE'S ALSO THE PROBLEM OF THE ACTIVATOR...
HMMM... I THINK THAT A SOLUTION PRESENTED ITSELF TO ME TODAY...

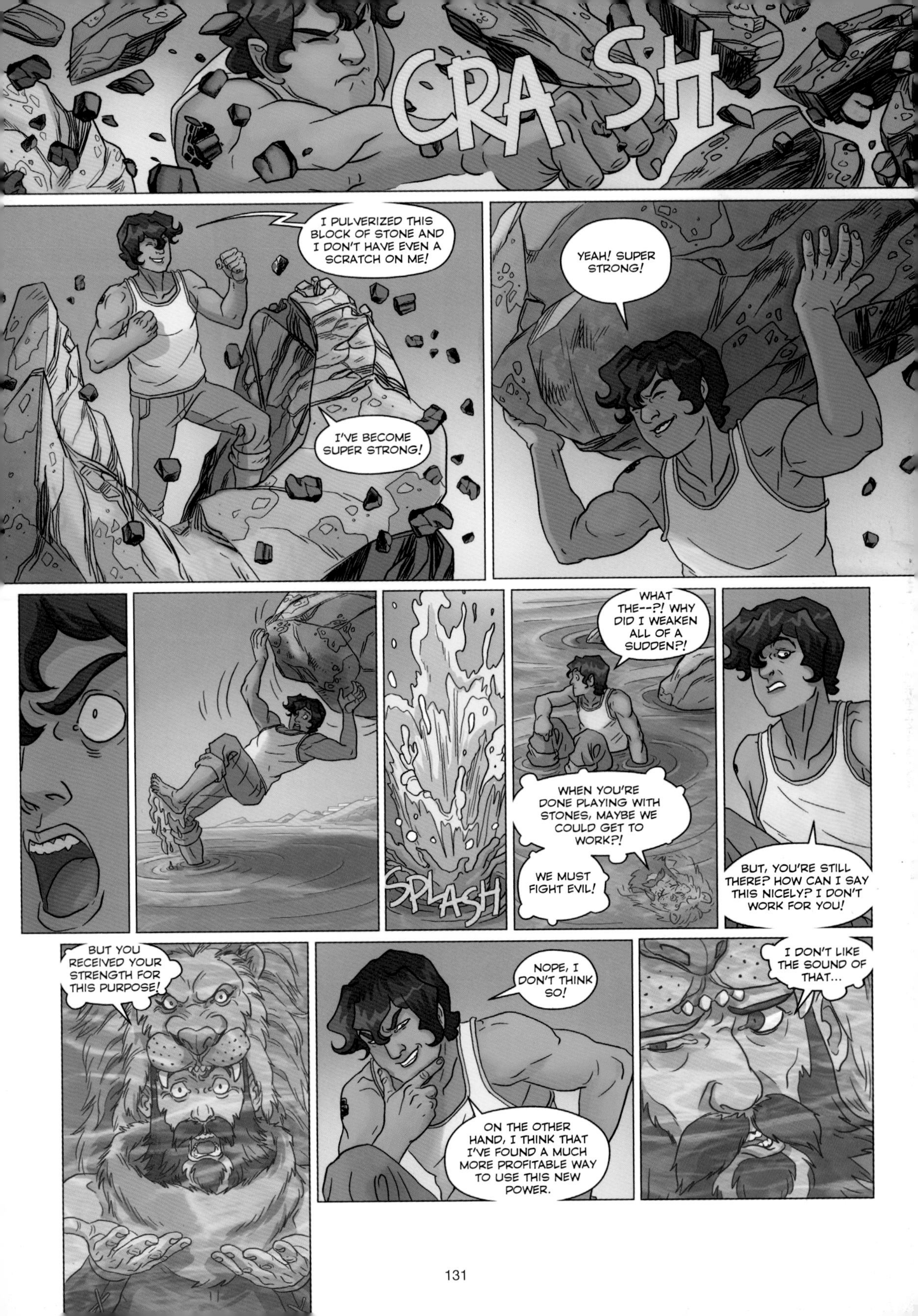
CRASH
I PULVERIZED THIS BLOCK OF STONE AND I DON'T HAVE EVEN A SCRATCH ON ME!
I'VE BECOME SUPER STRONG!
YEAH! SUPER STRONG!
SPLASH
WHAT THE--?! WHY DID I WEAKEN ALL OF A SUDDEN?!
WHEN YOU'RE DONE PLAYING WITH STONES, MAYBE WE COULD GET TO WORK?!
WE MUST FIGHT EVIL!
BUT, YOU'RE STILL THERE? HOW CAN I SAY THIS NICELY? I DON'T WORK FOR YOU!
BUT YOU RECEIVED YOUR STRENGTH FOR THIS PURPOSE!
NOPE, I DON'T THINK SO!
ON THE OTHER HAND, I THINK THAT I'VE FOUND A MUCH MORE PROFITABLE WAY TO USE THIS NEW POWER.
I DON'T LIKE THE SOUND OF THAT...

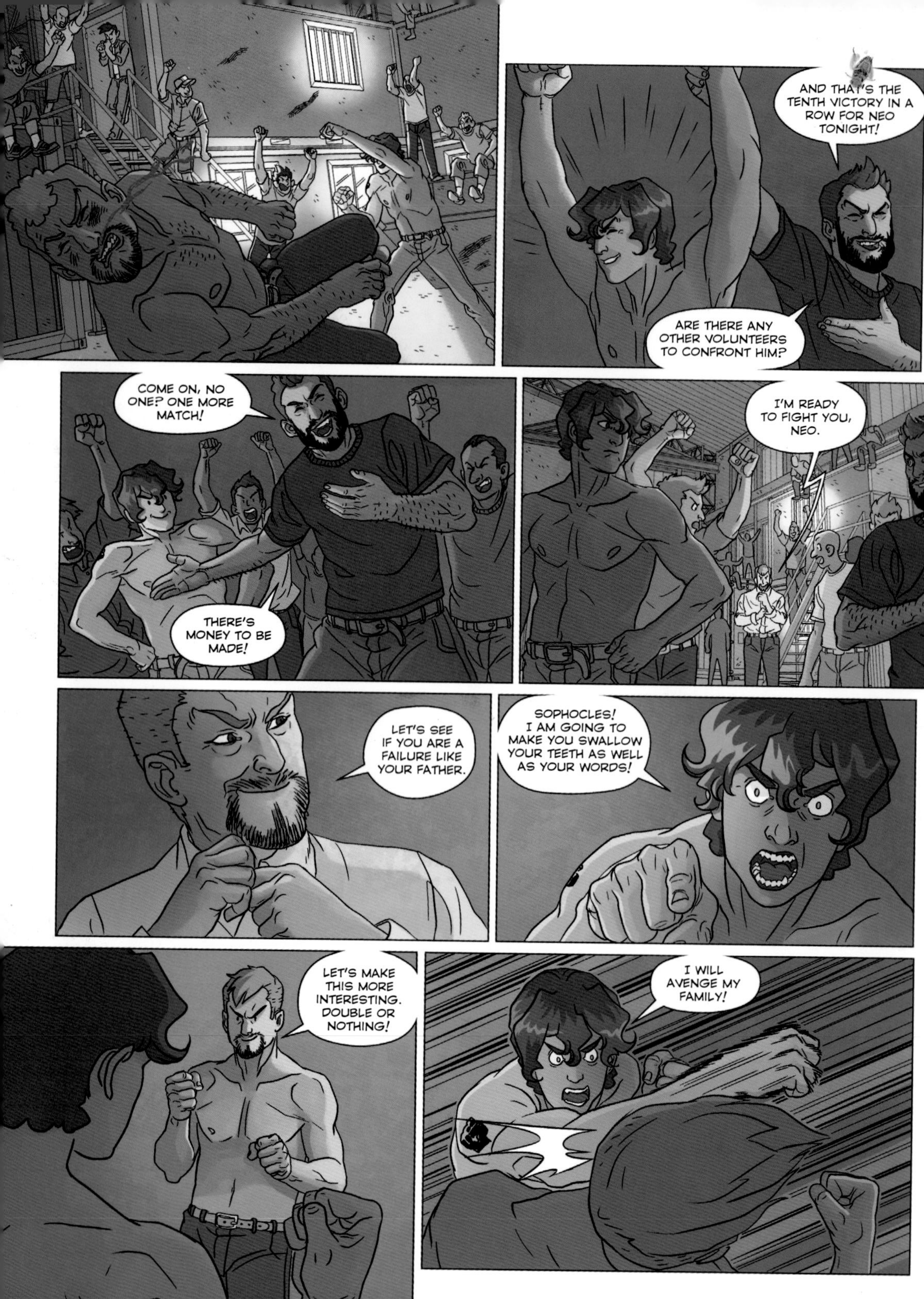
AND THAT'S THE TENTH VICTORY IN A ROW FOR NEO TONIGHT!
ARE THERE ANY OTHER VOLUNTEERS TO CONFRONT HIM?
COME ON, NO ONE? ONE MORE MATCH!
THERE'S MONEY TO BE MADE!
I'M READY TO FIGHT YOU, NEO.
LET'S SEE IF YOU ARE A FAILURE LIKE YOUR FATHER.
SOPHOCLES! I AM GOING TO MAKE YOU SWALLOW YOUR TEETH AS WELL AS YOUR WORDS!
LET'S MAKE THIS MORE INTERESTING. DOUBLE OR NOTHING!
I WILL AVENGE MY FAMILY!

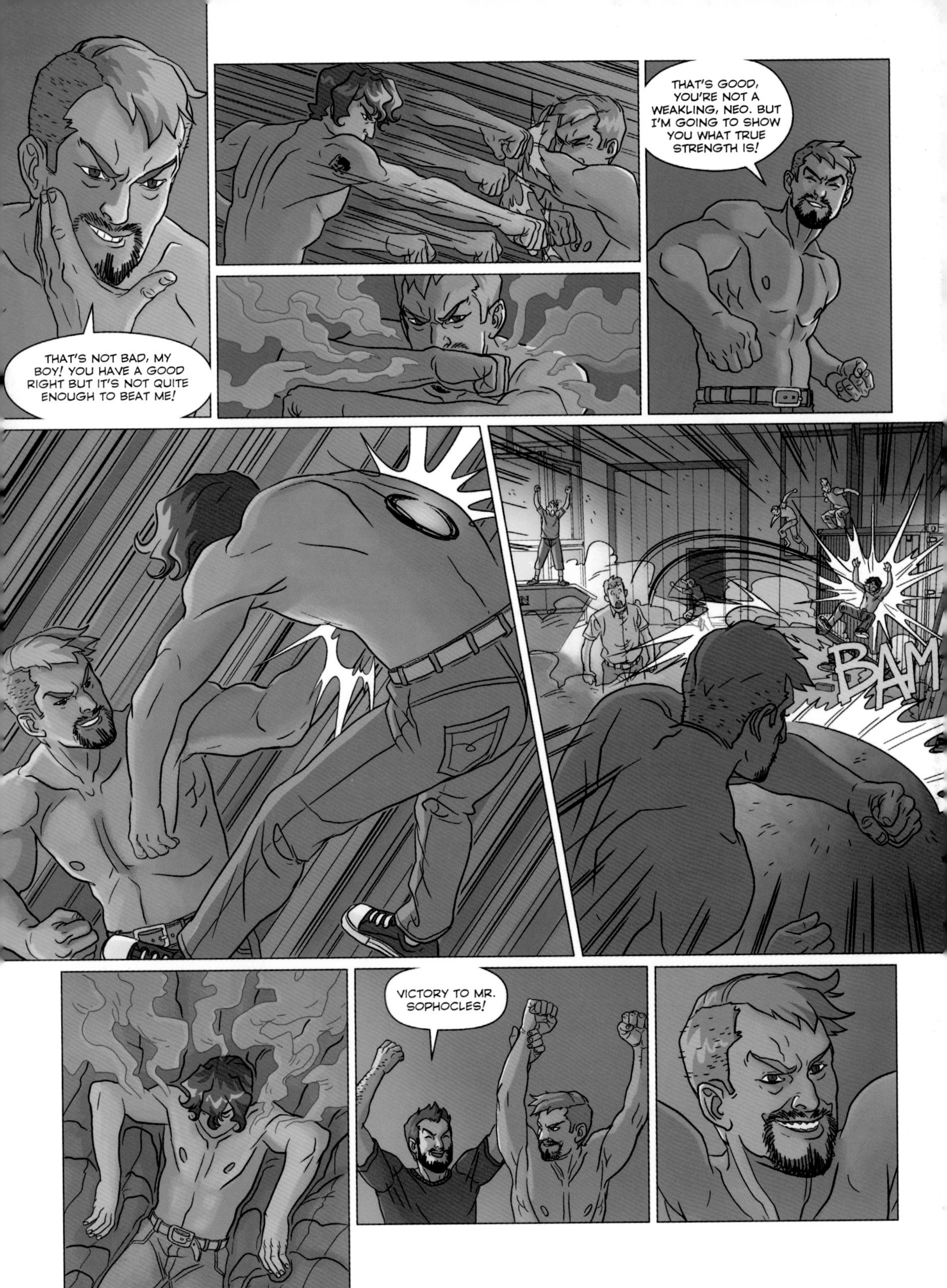

THAT'S NOT BAD, MY BOY! YOU HAVE A GOOD RIGHT BUT IT'S NOT QUITE ENOUGH TO BEAT ME!
THAT'S GOOD, YOU'RE NOT A WEAKLING, NEO. BUT I'M GOING TO SHOW YOU WHAT TRUE STRENGTH IS!
BAM
VICTORY TO MR. SOPHOCLES!

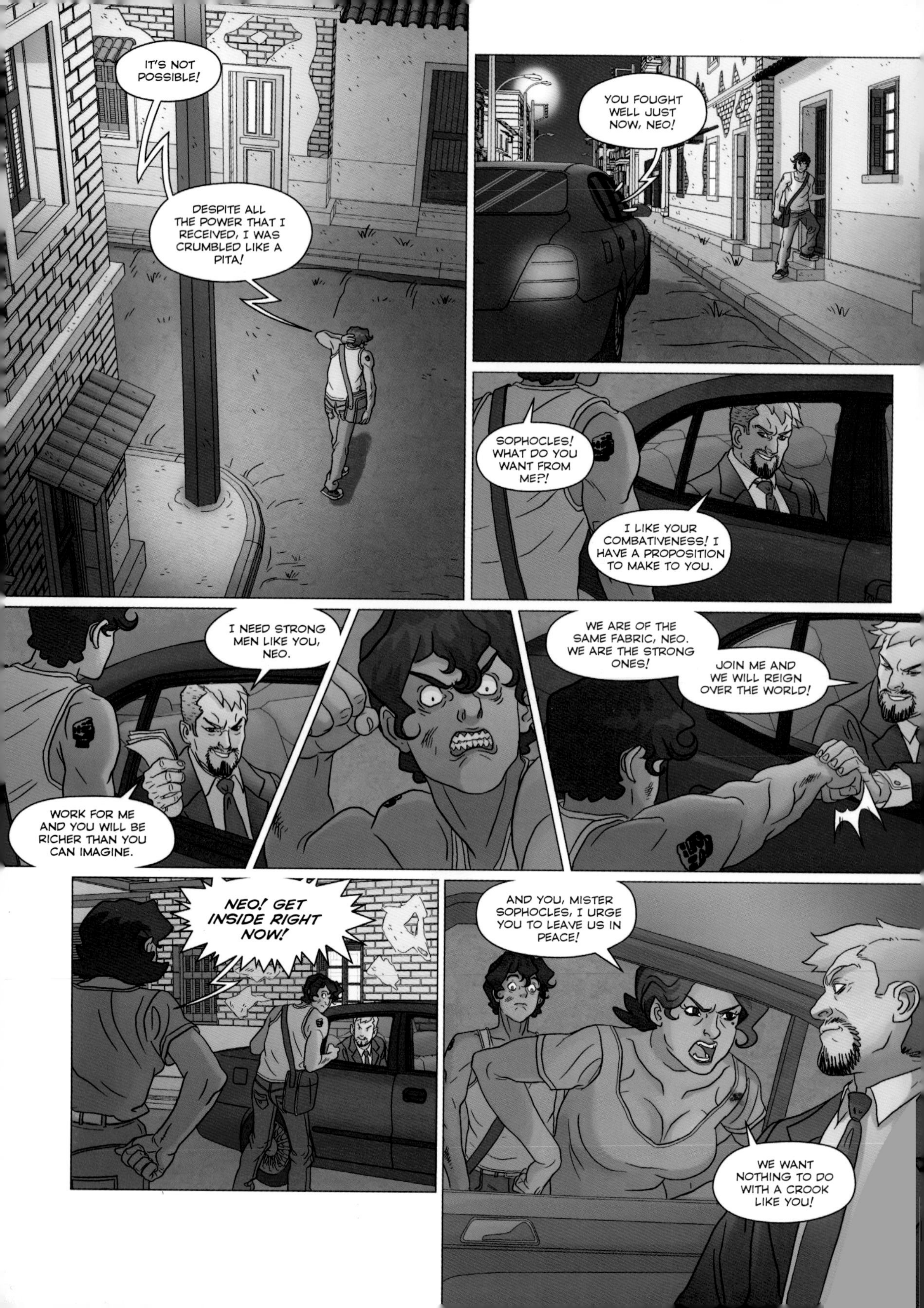
IT'S NOT POSSIBLE!
DESPITE ALL THE POWER THAT I RECEIVED, I WAS CRUMBLED LIKE A PITA!
YOU FOUGHT WELL JUST NOW, NEO!
SOPHOCLES! WHAT DO YOU WANT FROM ME?!
I LIKE YOUR COMBATIVENESS! I HAVE A PROPOSITION TO MAKE TO YOU.
I NEED STRONG MEN LIKE YOU, NEO.
WORK FOR ME AND YOU WILL BE RICHER THAN YOU CAN IMAGINE.
WE ARE OF THE SAME FABRIC, NEO. WE ARE THE STRONG ONES!
JOIN ME AND WE WILL REIGN OVER THE WORLD!
NEO! GET INSIDE RIGHT NOW!
AND YOU, MISTER SOPHOCLES, I URGE YOU TO LEAVE US IN PEACE!
WE WANT NOTHING TO DO WITH A CROOK LIKE YOU!

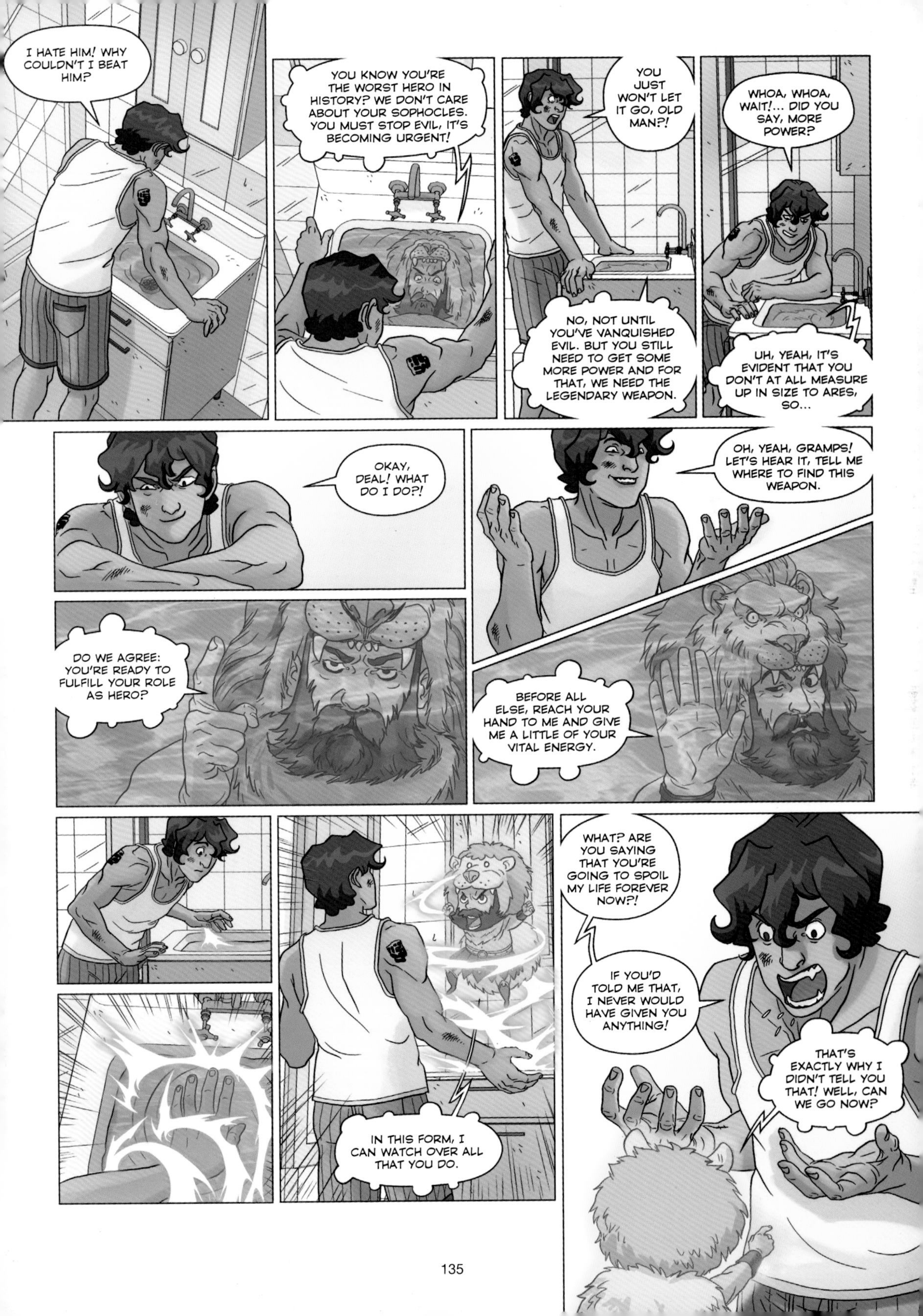
I HATE HIM! WHY COULDN'T I BEAT HIM?
YOU KNOW YOU'RE THE WORST HERO IN HISTORY? WE DON'T CARE ABOUT YOUR SOPHOCLES. YOU MUST STOP EVIL, IT'S BECOMING URGENT!
YOU JUST WON'T LET IT GO, OLD MAN?!
NO, NOT UNTIL YOU'VE VANQUISHED EVIL. BUT YOU STILL NEED TO GET SOME MORE POWER AND FOR THAT, WE NEED THE LEGENDARY WEAPON.
WHOA, WHOA, WAIT!... DID YOU SAY, MORE POWER?
UH, YEAH, IT'S EVIDENT THAT YOU DON'T AT ALL MEASURE UP IN SIZE TO ARES, SO...
OKAY, DEAL! WHAT DO I DO?!
OH, YEAH, GRAMPS! LET'S HEAR IT, TELL ME WHERE TO FIND THIS WEAPON.
DO WE AGREE: YOU'RE READY TO FULFILL YOUR ROLE AS HERO?
BEFORE ALL ELSE, REACH YOUR HAND TO ME AND GIVE ME A LITTLE OF YOUR VITAL ENERGY.
IN THIS FORM, I CAN WATCH OVER ALL THAT YOU DO.
WHAT? ARE YOU SAYING THAT YOU'RE GOING TO SPOIL MY LIFE FOREVER NOW?!
IF YOU'D TOLD ME THAT, I NEVER WOULD HAVE GIVEN YOU ANYTHING!
THAT'S EXACTLY WHY I DIDN'T TELL YOU THAT! WELL, CAN WE GO NOW?

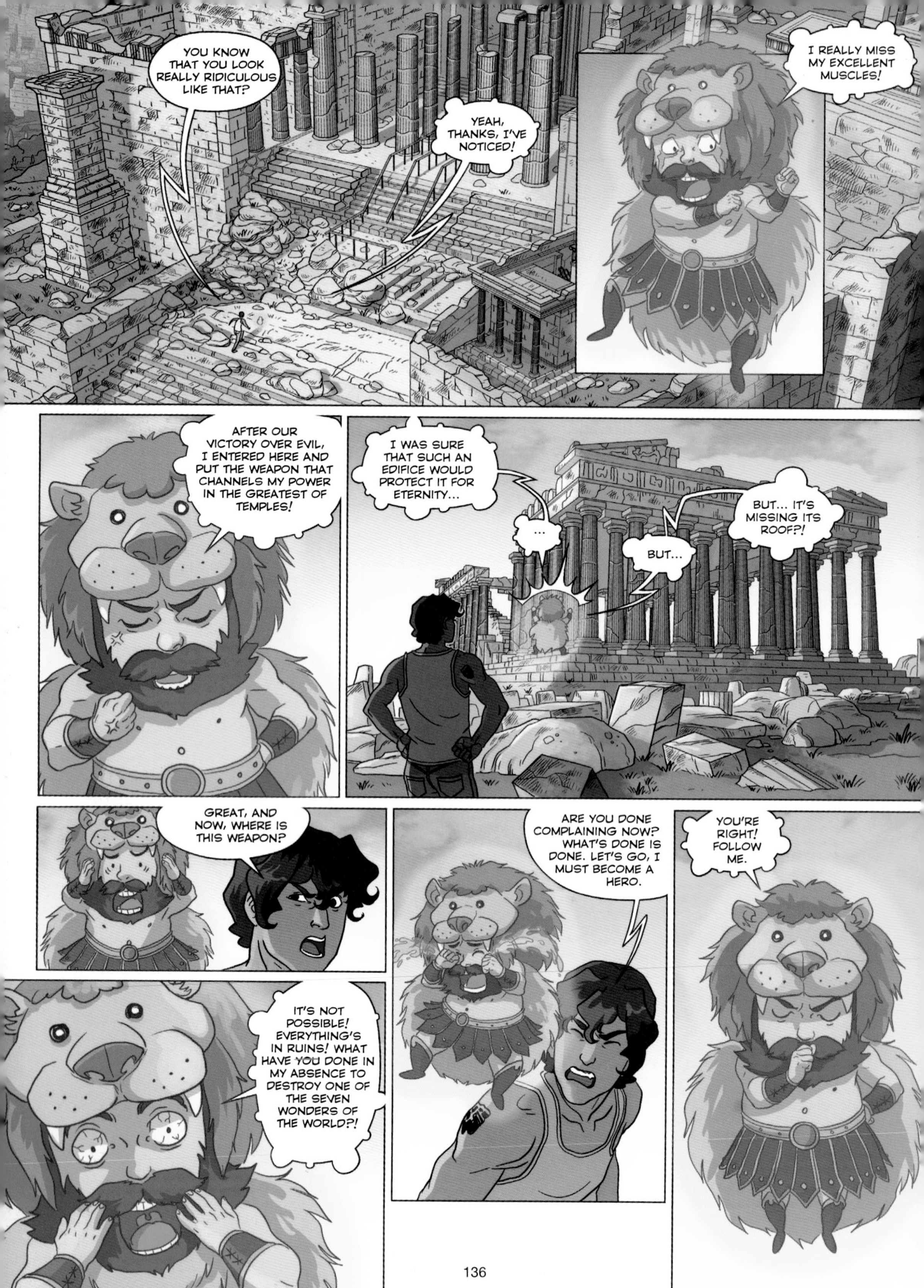
YOU KNOW THAT YOU LOOK REALLY RIDICULOUS LIKE THAT?
YEAH, THANKS, I'VE NOTICED!
I REALLY MISS MY EXCELLENT MUSCLES!
AFTER OUR VICTORY OVER EVIL, I ENTERED HERE AND PUT THE WEAPON THAT CHANNELS MY POWER IN THE GREATEST OF TEMPLES!
I WAS SURE THAT SUCH AN EDIFICE WOULD PROTECT IT FOR ETERNITY...
...
BUT...
BUT... IT'S MISSING ITS ROOF?!
GREAT, AND NOW, WHERE IS THIS WEAPON?
IT'S NOT POSSIBLE! EVERYTHING'S IN RUINS! WHAT HAVE YOU DONE IN MY ABSENCE TO DESTROY ONE OF THE SEVEN WONDERS OF THE WORLD?!
ARE YOU DONE COMPLAINING NOW? WHAT'S DONE IS DONE. LET'S GO, I MUST BECOME A HERO.
YOU'RE RIGHT! FOLLOW ME.

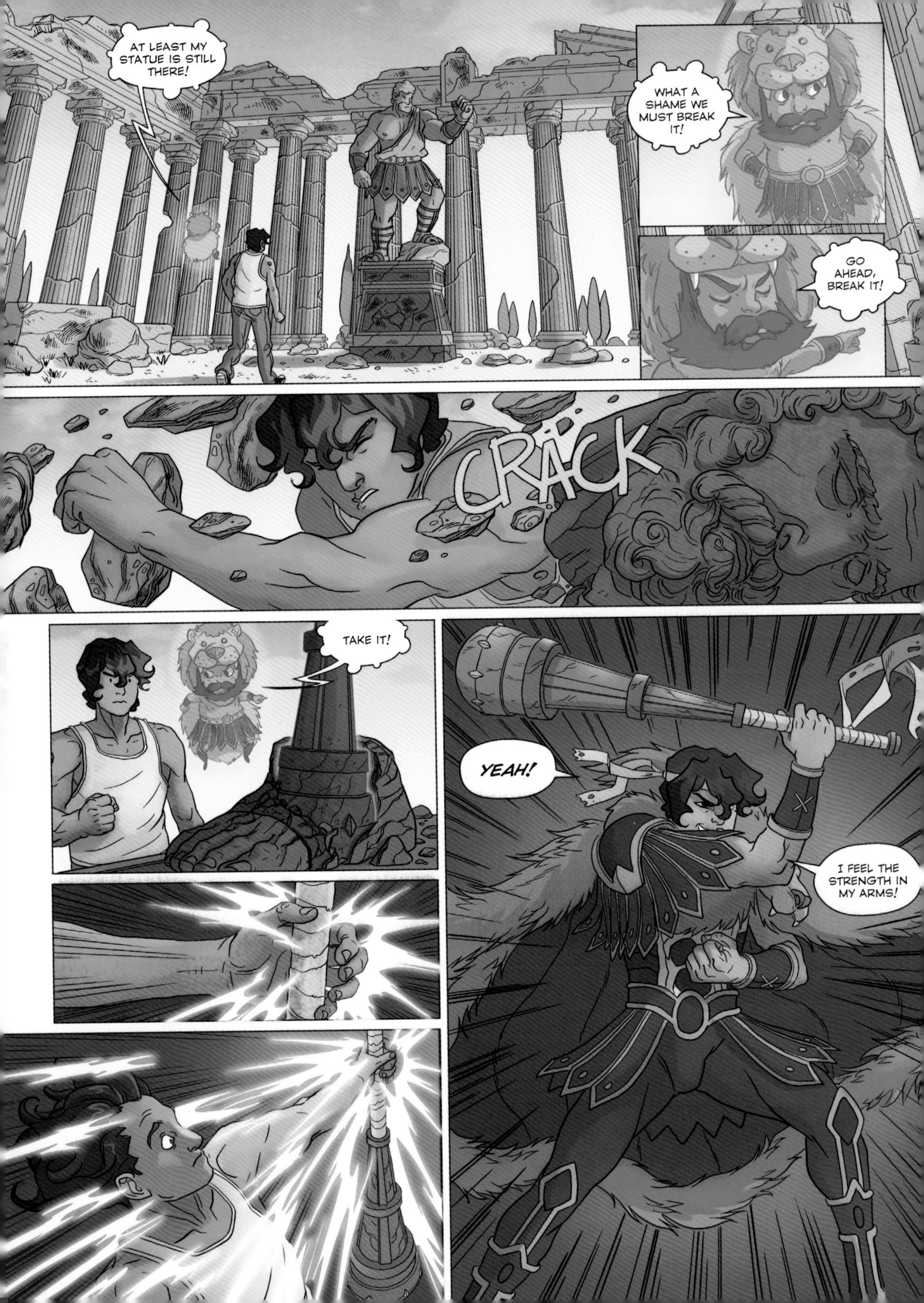
AT LEAST MY STATUE IS STILL THERE!
WHAT A SHAME WE MUST BREAK IT!
GO AHEAD, BREAK IT!
CRACK
TAKE IT!
YEAH!
I FEEL THE STRENGTH IN MY ARMS!

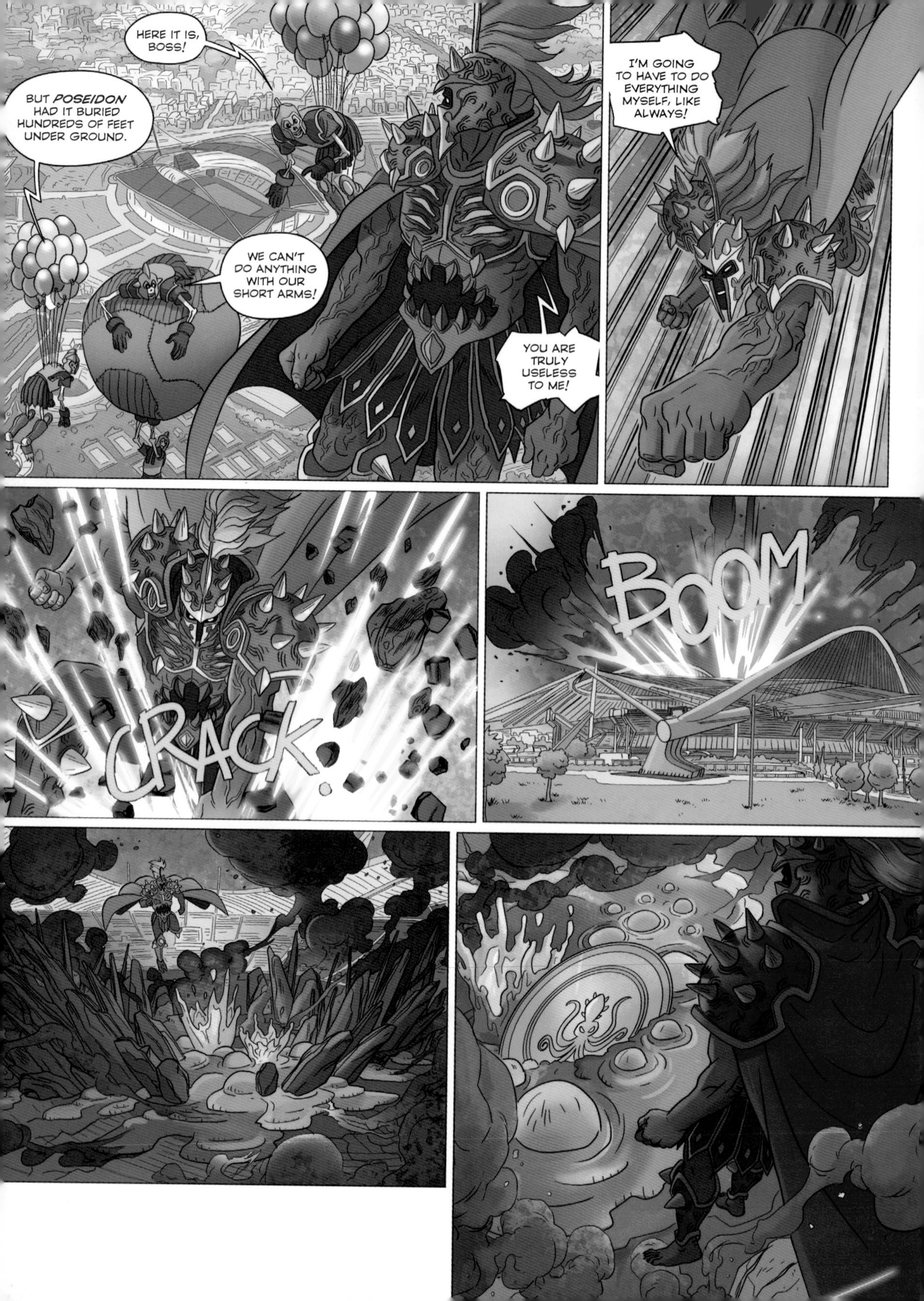
HERE IT IS, BOSS!
BUT *POSEIDON* HAD IT BURIED HUNDREDS OF FEET UNDER GROUND.
WE CAN'T DO ANYTHING WITH OUR SHORT ARMS!
YOU ARE TRULY USELESS TO ME!
I'M GOING TO HAVE TO DO EVERYTHING MYSELF, LIKE ALWAYS!
CRACK
BOOM

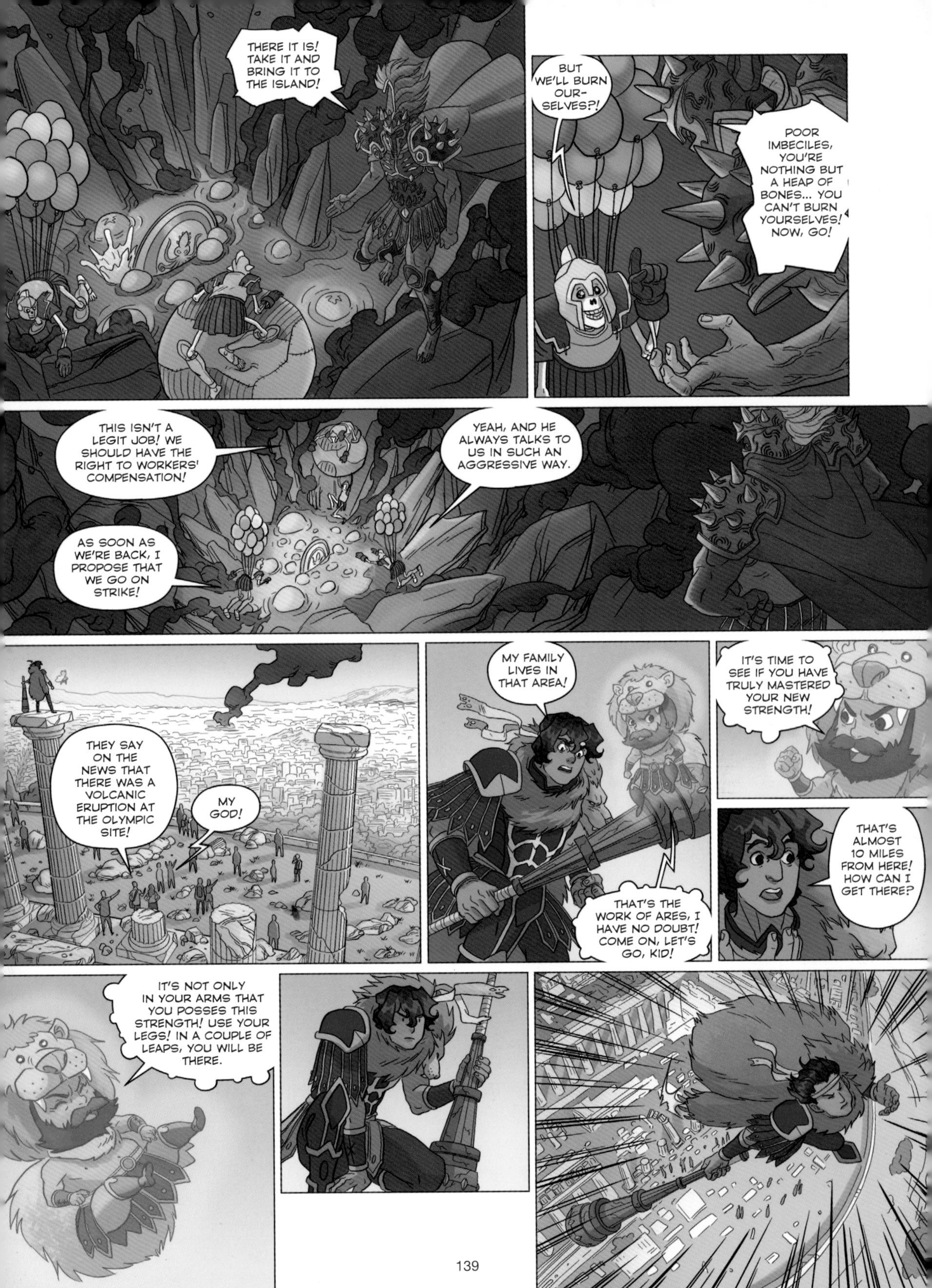

THERE IT IS! TAKE IT AND BRING IT TO THE ISLAND!
BUT WE'LL BURN OUR-SELVES?!
POOR IMBECILES, YOU'RE NOTHING BUT A HEAP OF BONES... YOU CAN'T BURN YOURSELVES! NOW, GO!
THIS ISN'T A LEGIT JOB! WE SHOULD HAVE THE RIGHT TO WORKERS' COMPENSATION!
AS SOON AS WE'RE BACK, I PROPOSE THAT WE GO ON STRIKE!
YEAH, AND HE ALWAYS TALKS TO US IN SUCH AN AGGRESSIVE WAY.
THEY SAY ON THE NEWS THAT THERE WAS A VOLCANIC ERUPTION AT THE OLYMPIC SITE!
MY GOD!
MY FAMILY LIVES IN THAT AREA!
THAT'S THE WORK OF ARES, I HAVE NO DOUBT! COME ON, LET'S GO, KID!
IT'S TIME TO SEE IF YOU HAVE TRULY MASTERED YOUR NEW STRENGTH!
THAT'S ALMOST 10 MILES FROM HERE! HOW CAN I GET THERE?
IT'S NOT ONLY IN YOUR ARMS THAT YOU POSSES THIS STRENGTH! USE YOUR LEGS! IN A COUPLE OF LEAPS, YOU WILL BE THERE.

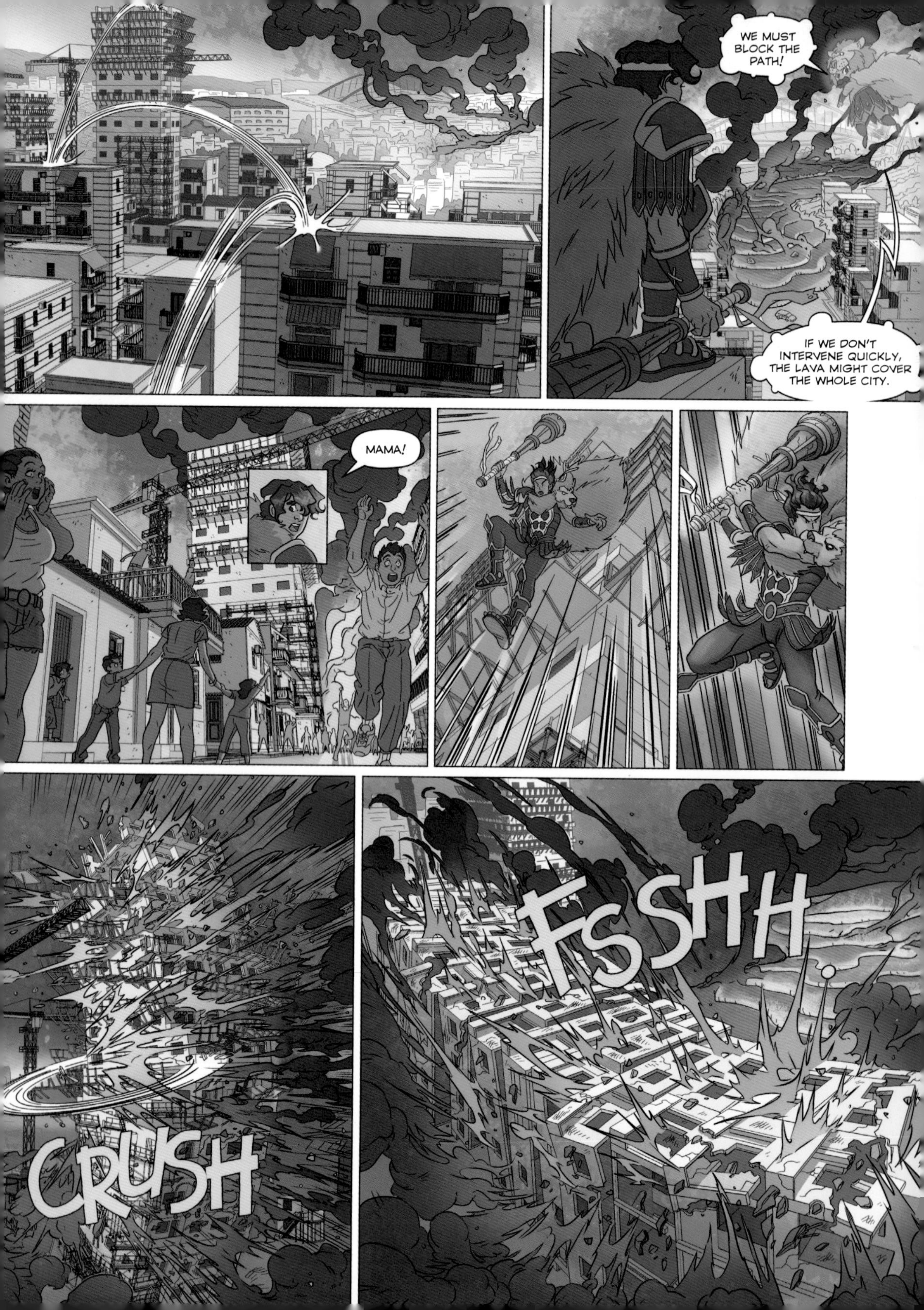
WE MUST BLOCK THE PATH!
IF WE DON'T INTERVENE QUICKLY, THE LAVA MIGHT COVER THE WHOLE CITY.
MAMA!
CRUSH
FSSHH

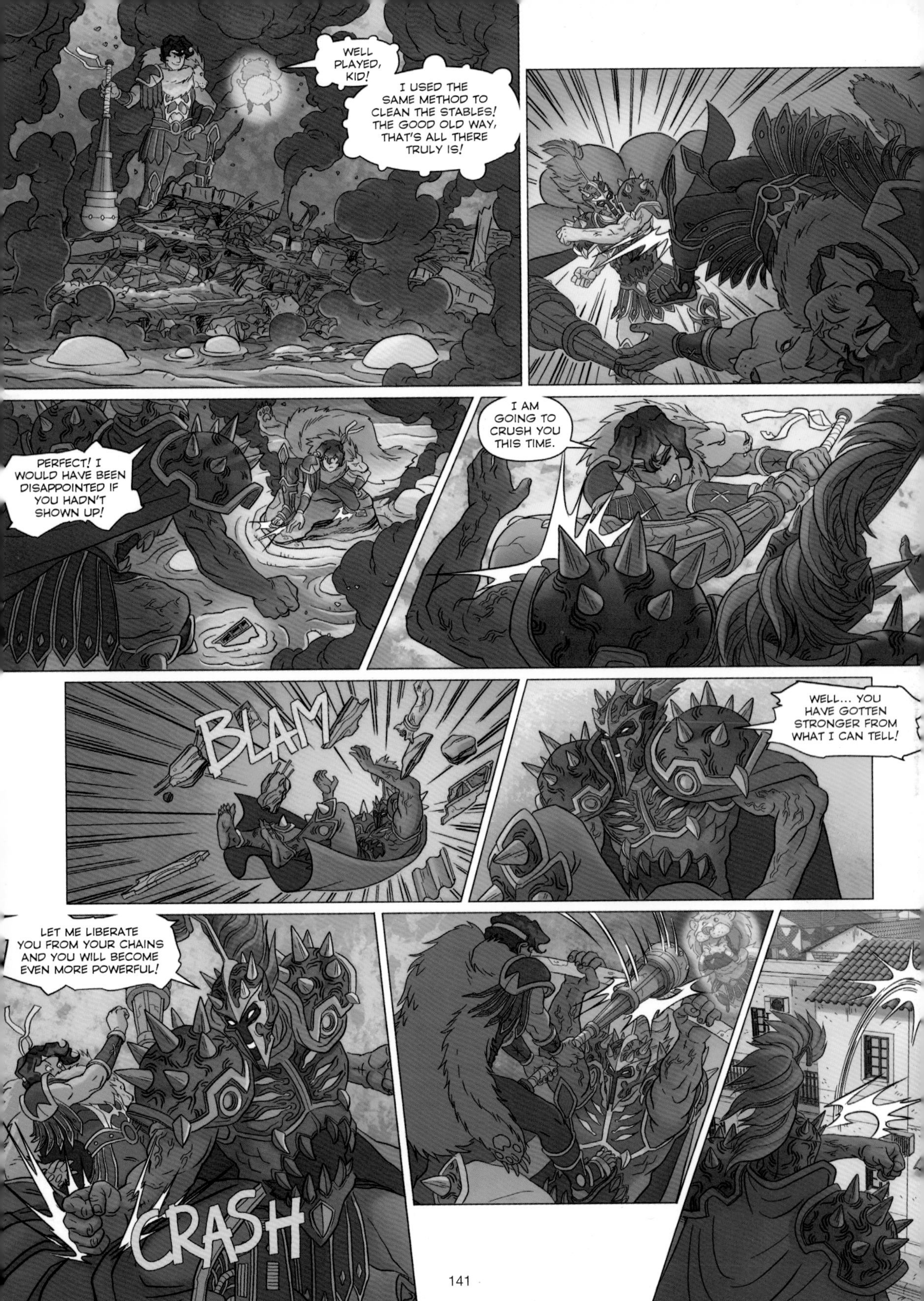

WELL PLAYED, KID!
I USED THE SAME METHOD TO CLEAN THE STABLES! THE GOOD OLD WAY, THAT'S ALL THERE TRULY IS!
PERFECT! I WOULD HAVE BEEN DISAPPOINTED IF YOU HADN'T SHOWN UP!
I AM GOING TO CRUSH YOU THIS TIME.
BLAM
WELL... YOU HAVE GOTTEN STRONGER FROM WHAT I CAN TELL!
LET ME LIBERATE YOU FROM YOUR CHAINS AND YOU WILL BECOME EVEN MORE POWERFUL!
CRASH

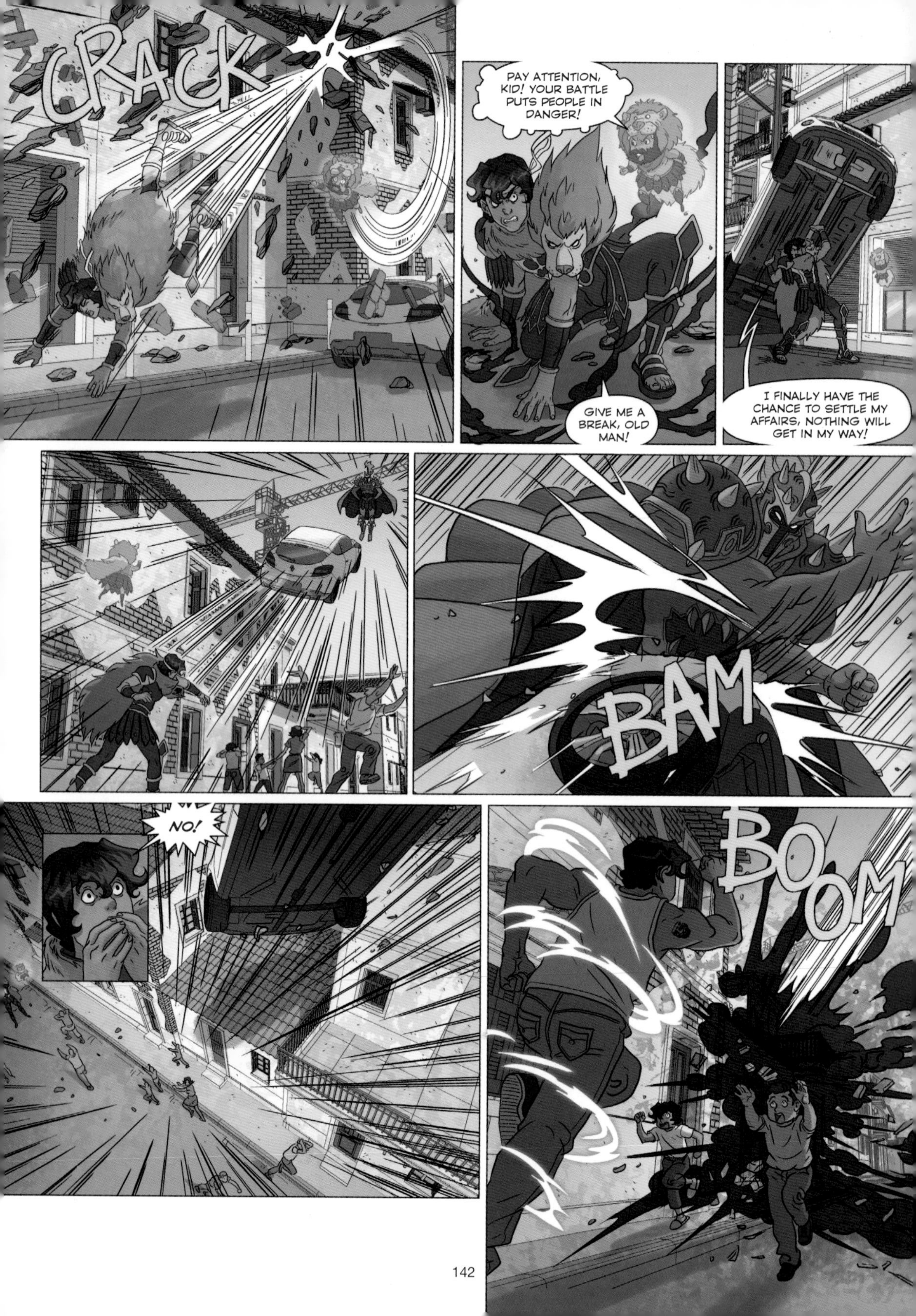
CRACK
PAY ATTENTION, KID! YOUR BATTLE PUTS PEOPLE IN DANGER!
GIVE ME A BREAK, OLD MAN!
I FINALLY HAVE THE CHANCE TO SETTLE MY AFFAIRS, NOTHING WILL GET IN MY WAY!
BAM
NO!
BOOOM

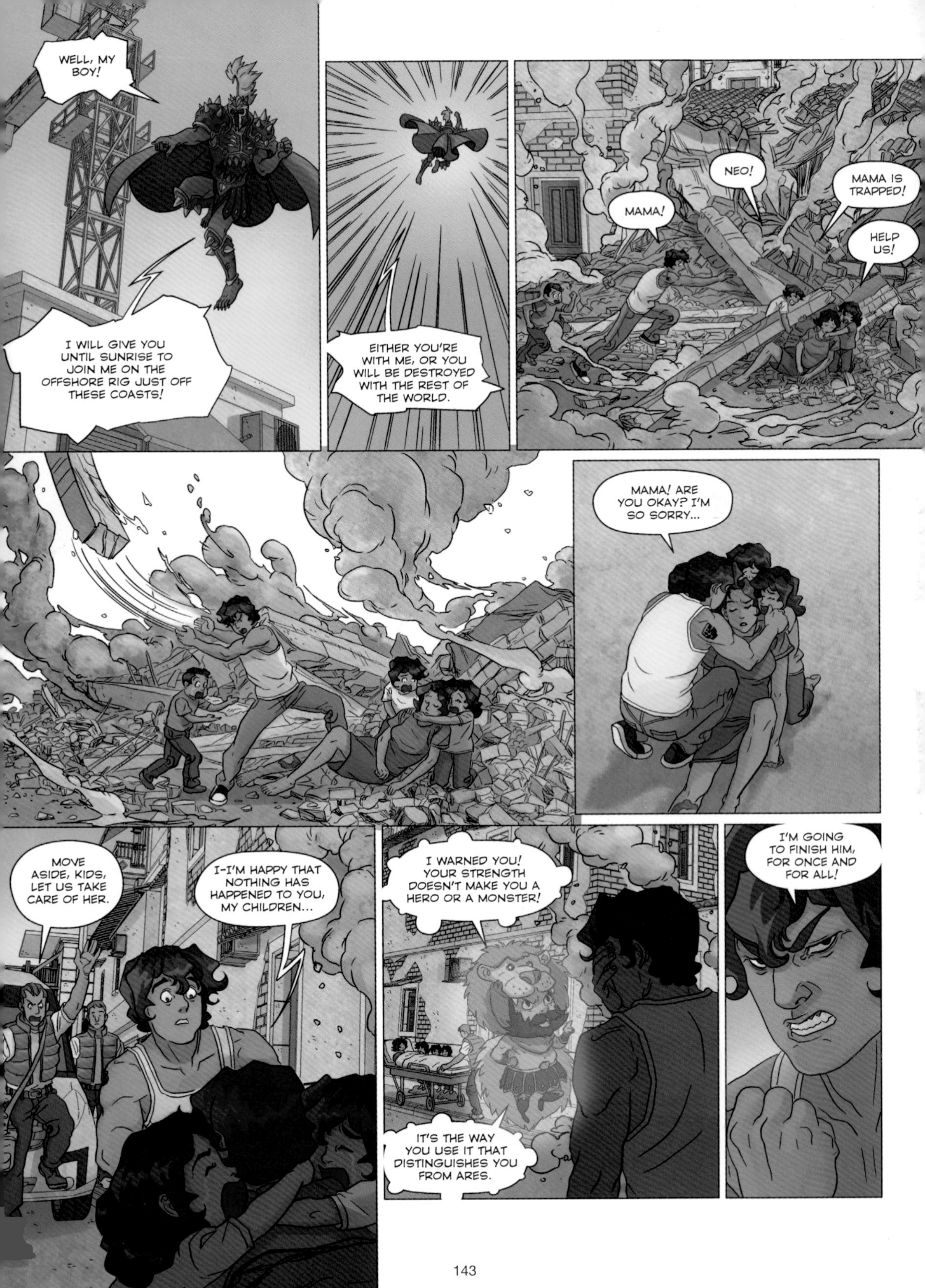
WELL, MY BOY!
I WILL GIVE YOU UNTIL SUNRISE TO JOIN ME ON THE OFFSHORE RIG JUST OFF THESE COASTS!
EITHER YOU'RE WITH ME, OR YOU WILL BE DESTROYED WITH THE REST OF THE WORLD.
MAMA!
NEO!
MAMA IS TRAPPED!
HELP US!
MAMA! ARE YOU OKAY? I'M SO SORRY...
MOVE ASIDE, KIDS, LET US TAKE CARE OF HER.
I-I'M HAPPY THAT NOTHING HAS HAPPENED TO YOU, MY CHILDREN...
I WARNED YOU! YOUR STRENGTH DOESN'T MAKE YOU A HERO OR A MONSTER!
IT'S THE WAY YOU USE IT THAT DISTINGUISHES YOU FROM ARES.
I'M GOING TO FINISH HIM, FOR ONCE AND FOR ALL!

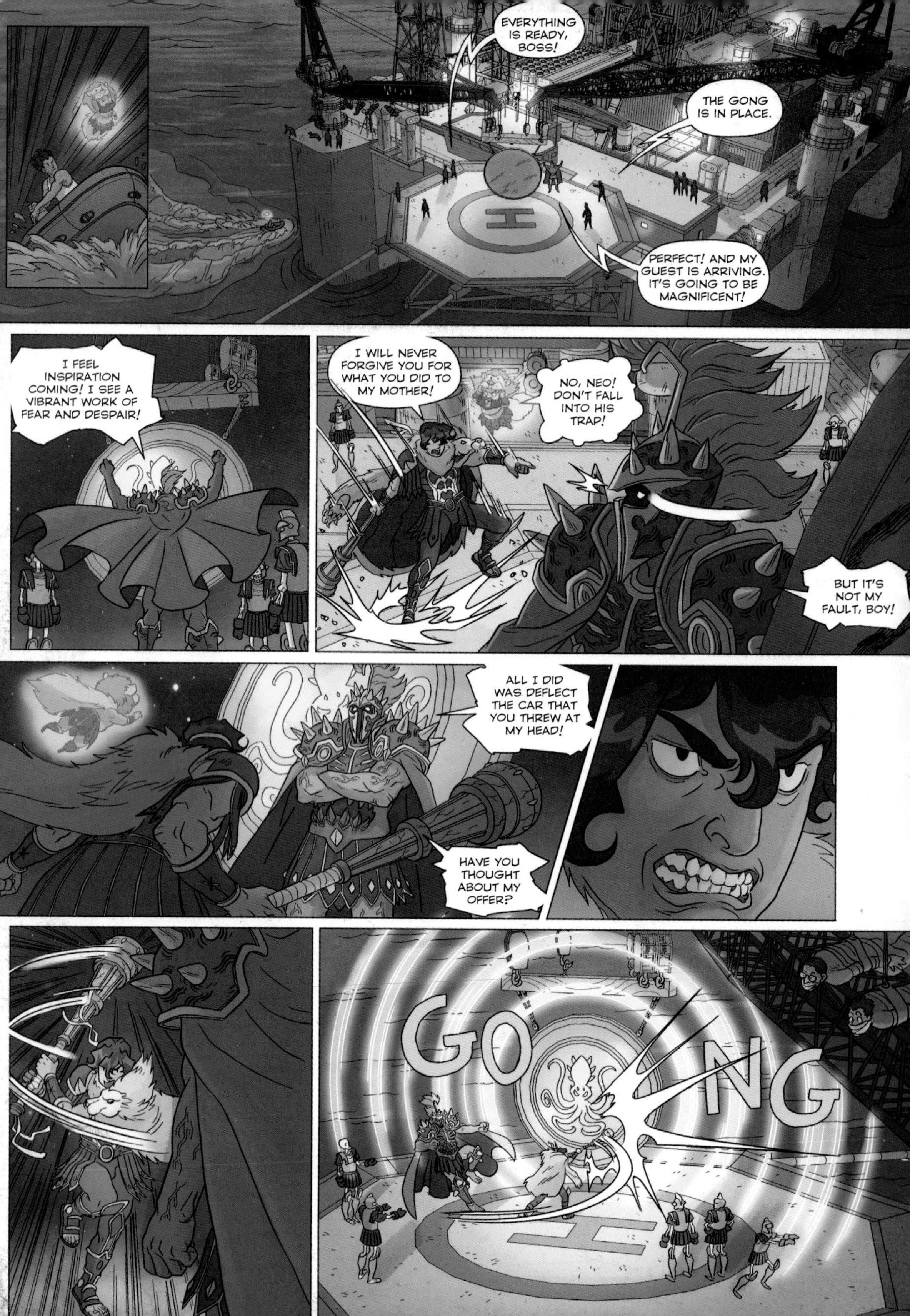
EVERYTHING IS READY, BOSS!
THE GONG IS IN PLACE.
PERFECT! AND MY GUEST IS ARRIVING. IT'S GOING TO BE MAGNIFICENT!
I FEEL INSPIRATION COMING! I SEE A VIBRANT WORK OF FEAR AND DESPAIR!
I WILL NEVER FORGIVE YOU FOR WHAT YOU DID TO MY MOTHER!
NO, NEO! DON'T FALL INTO HIS TRAP!
BUT IT'S NOT MY FAULT, BOY!
ALL I DID WAS DEFLECT THE CAR THAT YOU THREW AT MY HEAD!
HAVE YOU THOUGHT ABOUT MY OFFER?
GONG

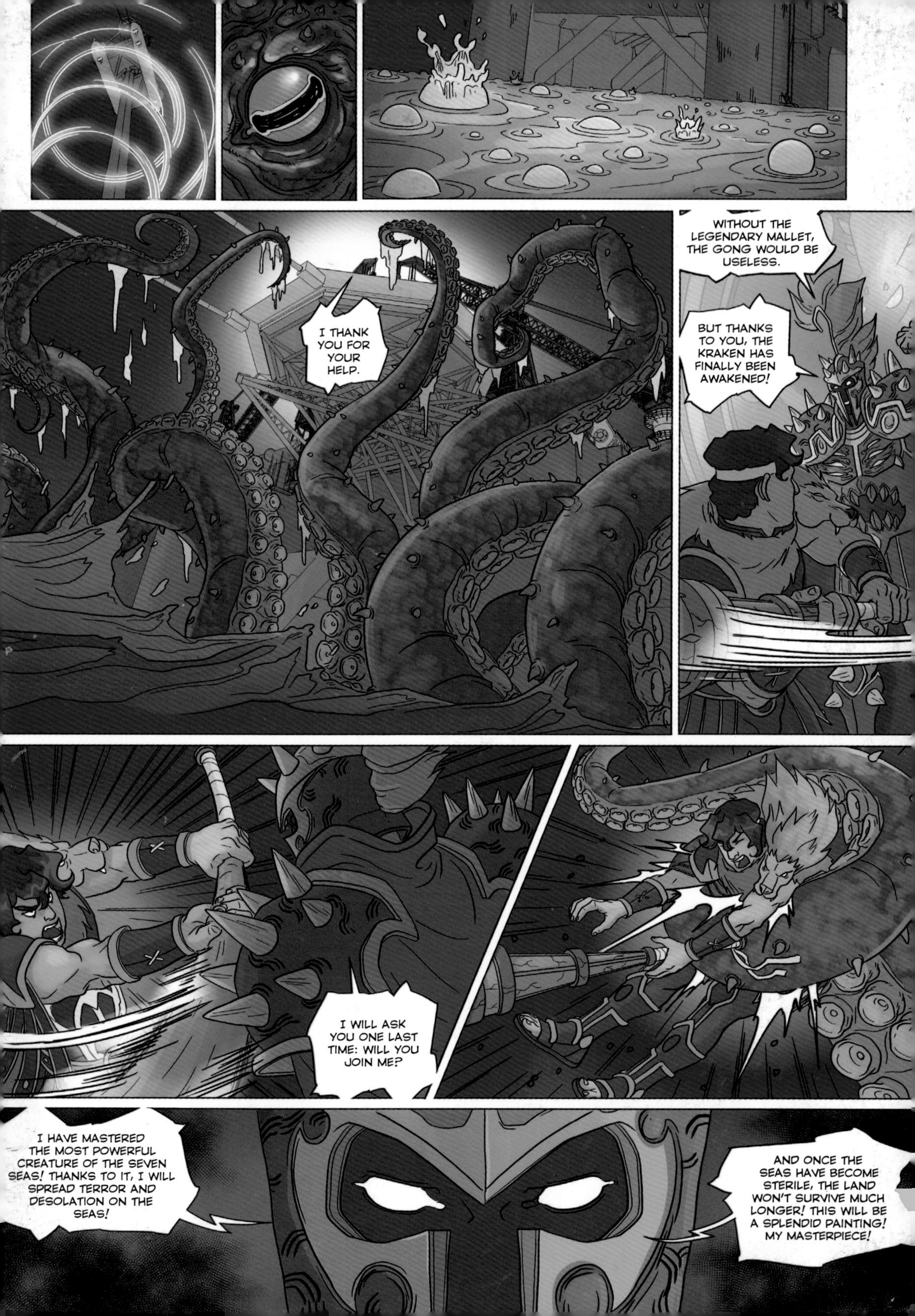
I THANK YOU FOR YOUR HELP.
WITHOUT THE LEGENDARY MALLET, THE GONG WOULD BE USELESS.
BUT THANKS TO YOU, THE KRAKEN HAS FINALLY BEEN AWAKENED!
I WILL ASK YOU ONE LAST TIME: WILL YOU JOIN ME?
I HAVE MASTERED THE MOST POWERFUL CREATURE OF THE SEVEN SEAS! THANKS TO IT, I WILL SPREAD TERROR AND DESOLATION ON THE SEAS!
AND ONCE THE SEAS HAVE BECOME STERILE, THE LAND WON'T SURVIVE MUCH LONGER! THIS WILL BE A SPLENDID PAINTING! MY MASTERPIECE!

I'M GOING TO MAKE A PASTA DISH OUT OF YOUR CALAMARI!

CRACK

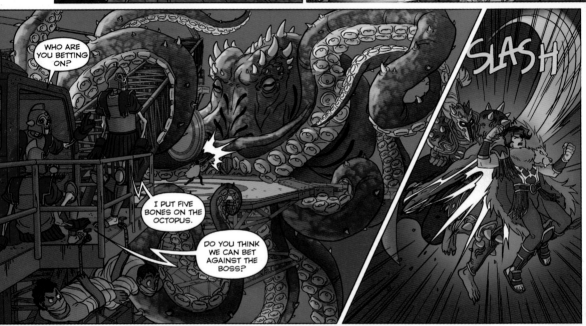

WHO ARE YOU BETTING ON?

I PUT FIVE BONES ON THE OCTOPUS.

DO YOU THINK WE CAN BET AGAINST THE BOSS?

SLASH

AND HERE I THOUGHT YOU WOULD JOIN ME...

BUT YOU DON'T KNOW HOW TO SEIZE OPPORTUNITIES, IN THE END YOU'RE NOTHING BUT A WEAKLING...

LIKE YOUR FATHER, NEO!

WHAT?...

YOU... YOU ARE SOPHOCLES?!

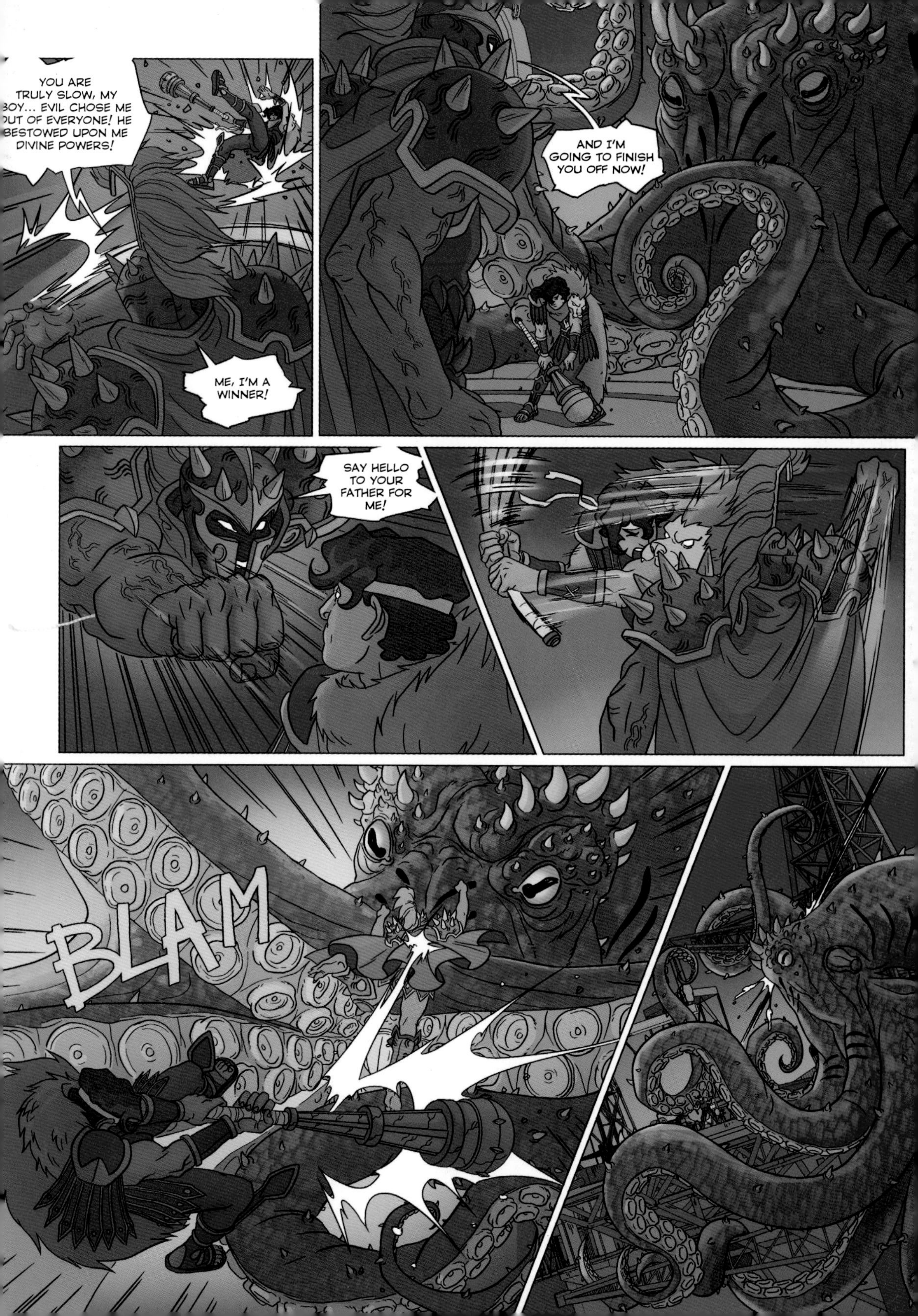
YOU ARE TRULY SLOW, MY BOY... EVIL CHOSE ME OUT OF EVERYONE! HE BESTOWED UPON ME DIVINE POWERS!
ME, I'M A WINNER!
AND I'M GOING TO FINISH YOU OFF NOW!
SAY HELLO TO YOUR FATHER FOR ME!
BLAM

SPLASH

THERE, THAT'S HOW I SEIZE OPPORTUNITIES!

CONGRATULATIONS, KID! YOU'RE A HERO AFTER ALL!

BUT YOU SHOULD FISH HIM OUT AND TAKE CARE OF THE PRISONERS AND THINK OF GETTING RID OF THAT GONG.

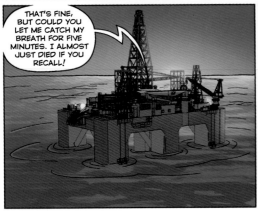

THAT'S FINE, BUT COULD YOU LET ME CATCH MY BREATH FOR FIVE MINUTES. I ALMOST JUST DIED IF YOU RECALL!

HEY! I TOLD YOU IT WAS A TRAP!

YOU'RE ALWAYS RIGHT, HUH?

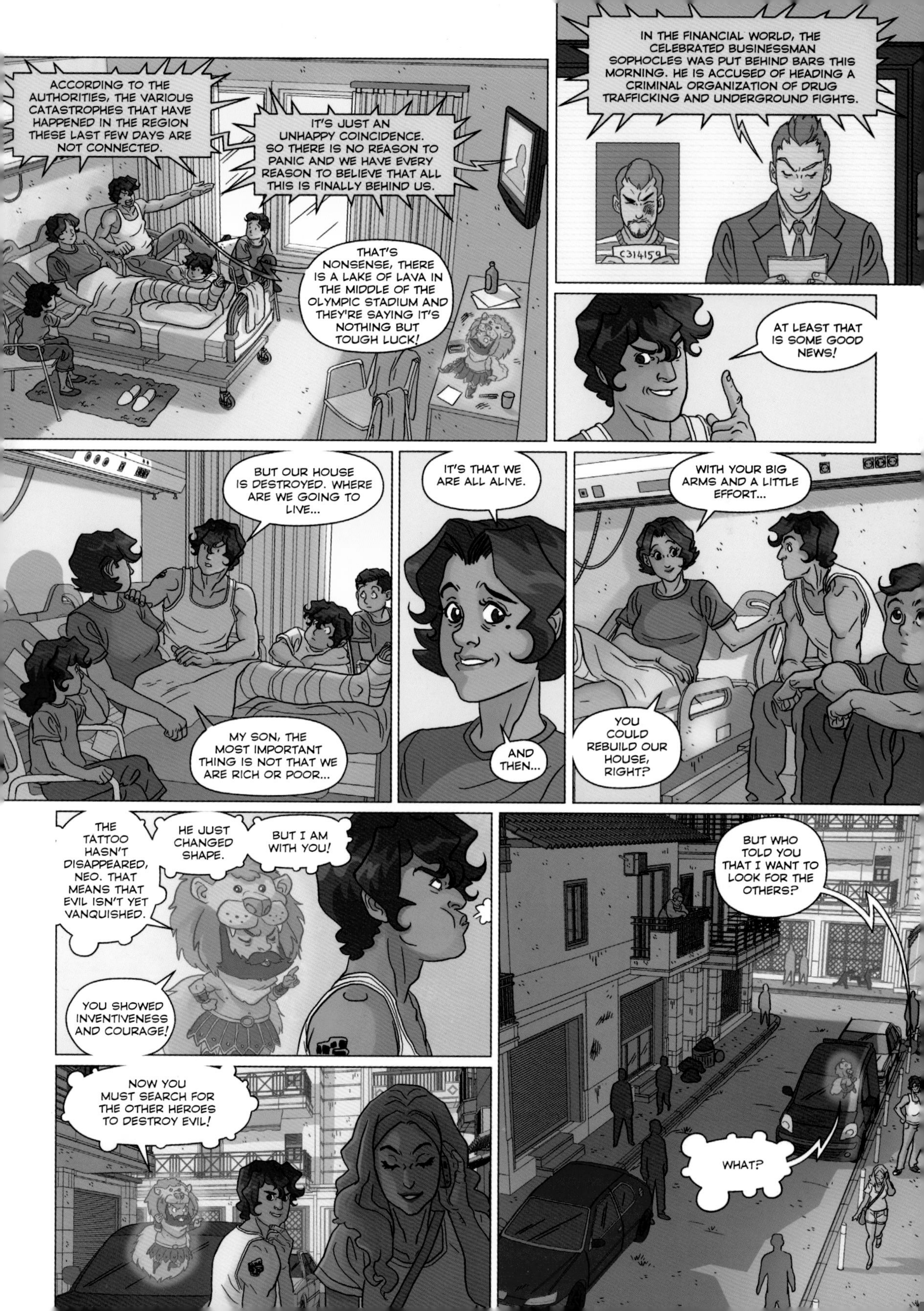
ACCORDING TO THE AUTHORITIES, THE VARIOUS CATASTROPHES THAT HAVE HAPPENED IN THE REGION THESE LAST FEW DAYS ARE NOT CONNECTED.
IT'S JUST AN UNHAPPY COINCIDENCE. SO THERE IS NO REASON TO PANIC AND WE HAVE EVERY REASON TO BELIEVE THAT ALL THIS IS FINALLY BEHIND US.
THAT'S NONSENSE, THERE IS A LAKE OF LAVA IN THE MIDDLE OF THE OLYMPIC STADIUM AND THEY'RE SAYING IT'S NOTHING BUT TOUGH LUCK!
IN THE FINANCIAL WORLD, THE CELEBRATED BUSINESSMAN SOPHOCLES WAS PUT BEHIND BARS THIS MORNING. HE IS ACCUSED OF HEADING A CRIMINAL ORGANIZATION OF DRUG TRAFFICKING AND UNDERGROUND FIGHTS.
C314159
AT LEAST THAT IS SOME GOOD NEWS!
BUT OUR HOUSE IS DESTROYED. WHERE ARE WE GOING TO LIVE...
MY SON, THE MOST IMPORTANT THING IS NOT THAT WE ARE RICH OR POOR...
IT'S THAT WE ARE ALL ALIVE.
AND THEN...
WITH YOUR BIG ARMS AND A LITTLE EFFORT...
YOU COULD REBUILD OUR HOUSE, RIGHT?
THE TATTOO HASN'T DISAPPEARED, NEO. THAT MEANS THAT EVIL ISN'T YET VANQUISHED.
HE JUST CHANGED SHAPE.
BUT I AM WITH YOU!
YOU SHOWED INVENTIVENESS AND COURAGE!
NOW YOU MUST SEARCH FOR THE OTHER HEROES TO DESTROY EVIL!
BUT WHO TOLD YOU THAT I WANT TO LOOK FOR THE OTHERS?
WHAT?

WATCH OUT FOR PAPERCUTZ

Welcome to the surprising sophomore edition of THE MYTHICS, "Teenage Gods," by Patrick Sobral, Patricia Lyfoung, Philippe Ogaki, Alice Picard, Jérôme Alquié, and Frédéric Charve, from Papercutz—those mere mortals dedicated to publishing great graphic novels for all ages. I'm Jim Salicrup, the Editor-in-Chief and God of Typos, here to tell you about other Papercutz graphic novels you might enjoy if you loved THE MYTHICS…

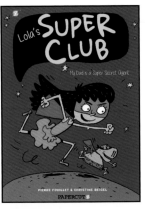

Unlike Yuko, Amir, Abigail (you remember them from THE MYTHICS #1, right?), Parvati, Miguel, and Neo, most of us can only dream about being granted great powers and having incredible adventures. But some of our dreams may be more vivid and exciting than others. For example, there's Lola, the star of the new Papercutz graphic novel series LOLA'S SUPER CLUB, and she imagines truly amazing adventures featuring her toys and cat, Hot Dog. In LOLA'S SUPER CLUB #1 "My Dad is a Super Secret Agent," Lola imagines her dad is James Blond, the famous super-spy, and that Max Imus and his double-O agents (Zero + Zero) are after him. It's up to Super-Lola, in her tutu, along with Super-James, in his undies, Hot Dog, and a whole bunch of super-friends to save her dad. In the very same graphic novel, Super-Lola and her Super Club must also save her mom, who is somehow trapped in time by Max Imus. Her time-travels are especially fun for Papercutz fans, as she visits 50 BC, the time the ASTERIX graphic novel series is set in, and she even meets a somewhat sillier version of Quetzalcoatl back in 1492. He's not exactly like the Quetzalcoatl that Miguel met in this graphic novel, but you know how those feathered serpent gods can be, right?

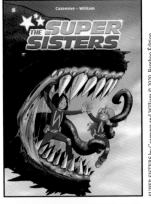

If you enjoy Lola's imaginary adventures that she dreams up, you may also enjoy THE SISTERS by Cazenove and William, the Papercutz graphic novel series about sisters Wendy and Maureen, who lead fairly ordinary lives driving each other crazy, but then they also imagine themselves as the Super Sisters, and have awesome real-life inspired adventures. These mini-adventures are so popular within their already super popular series, that an entire graphic novel has been created by Cazenove and William devoted exclusively to their super-hero fantasies, Naturally it's called THE SUPER SISTERS, and it's a lot of fun, even if at times they seem to be fighting more with each other than their actual villains.

There's another new Papercutz graphic novel series that's just about the opposite of LOLA'S SUPER CLUB and THE SUPER SISTERS, it's about a girl named Tara Smith who for years was living a life that she believed was real, but it was totally false. She believed her parents were her parents, but they weren't. And she thought she was just a regular human girl. She's not. To find out the shocking reality of Tara's life, check out SCHOOL FOR EXTRATERRESTRIAL GIRLS #1 "Girl on Fire," by Jeremy Whitley and Jamie Noguchi, available at booksellers everywhere. There's also a special preview on page 153.

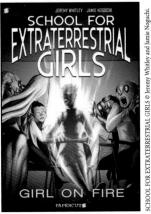

But back to THE MYTHICS. Now that you've met the six chosen ones, the big question is what's next? Or as Hercules said: WHAT?! The answer is that Evil isn't defeated yet, so our heroes still have a lot of work to do. So, we're finally going to start seeing our young heroes meet each other in THE MYTHICS #3 "Apocalypse Ahead,"* coming soon. You don't want to miss it!

Thanks, Jim

Lola's SUPER CLUB
My Dad is a Super Secret Agent
PIERRE FOUILLET & CHRISTINE BEIGEL
PAPERCUTZ

Cazenove • William
THE SUPER SISTERS

JEREMY WHITLEY JAMIE NOGUCHI
SCHOOL FOR EXTRATERRESTRIAL GIRLS
GIRL ON FIRE
PAPERCUTZ

STAY IN TOUCH!

EMAIL:	salicrup@papercutz.com
WEB:	www.papercutz.com
TWITTER:	@papercutzgn
FACEBOOK:	PAPERCUTZGRAPHICNOVELS
REGULAR MAIL:	Papercutz, 160 Broadway, Suite 700, East Wing, New York, NY 10038

*If that title sounds a bit familiar it's because I mistakenly said in THE MYTHICS #1 that it was the title for this volume. Oopsie.

Special preview of SCHOOL FOR EXTRATERRESTRIAL GIRLS #1 "Girl on Fire"...

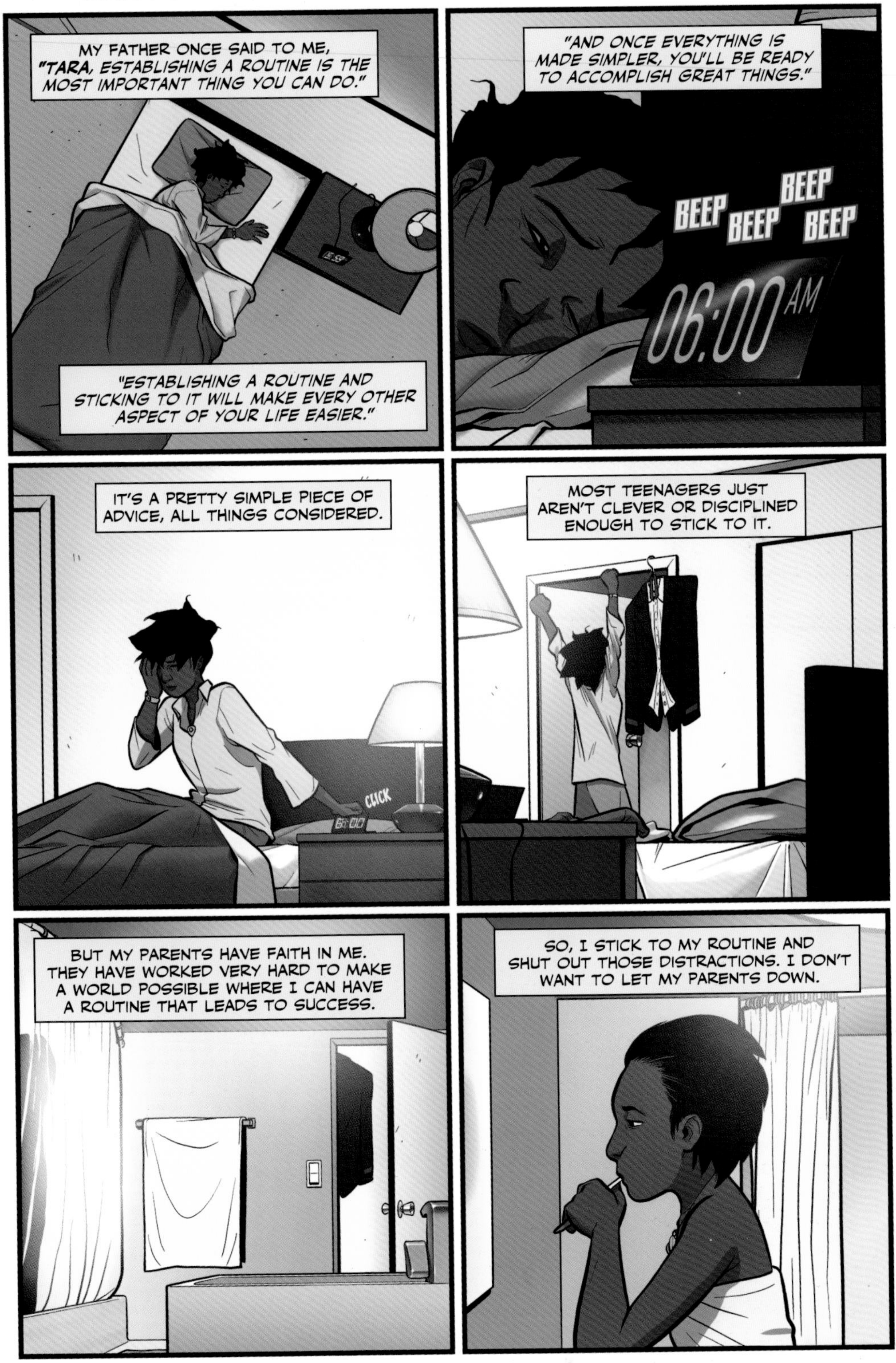
MY FATHER ONCE SAID TO ME, "TARA, ESTABLISHING A ROUTINE IS THE MOST IMPORTANT THING YOU CAN DO."
"ESTABLISHING A ROUTINE AND STICKING TO IT WILL MAKE EVERY OTHER ASPECT OF YOUR LIFE EASIER."
"AND ONCE EVERYTHING IS MADE SIMPLER, YOU'LL BE READY TO ACCOMPLISH GREAT THINGS."
BEEP BEEP BEEP BEEP
06:00 AM
IT'S A PRETTY SIMPLE PIECE OF ADVICE, ALL THINGS CONSIDERED.
CLICK
MOST TEENAGERS JUST AREN'T CLEVER OR DISCIPLINED ENOUGH TO STICK TO IT.
BUT MY PARENTS HAVE FAITH IN ME. THEY HAVE WORKED VERY HARD TO MAKE A WORLD POSSIBLE WHERE I CAN HAVE A ROUTINE THAT LEADS TO SUCCESS.
SO, I STICK TO MY ROUTINE AND SHUT OUT THOSE DISTRACTIONS. I DON'T WANT TO LET MY PARENTS DOWN.

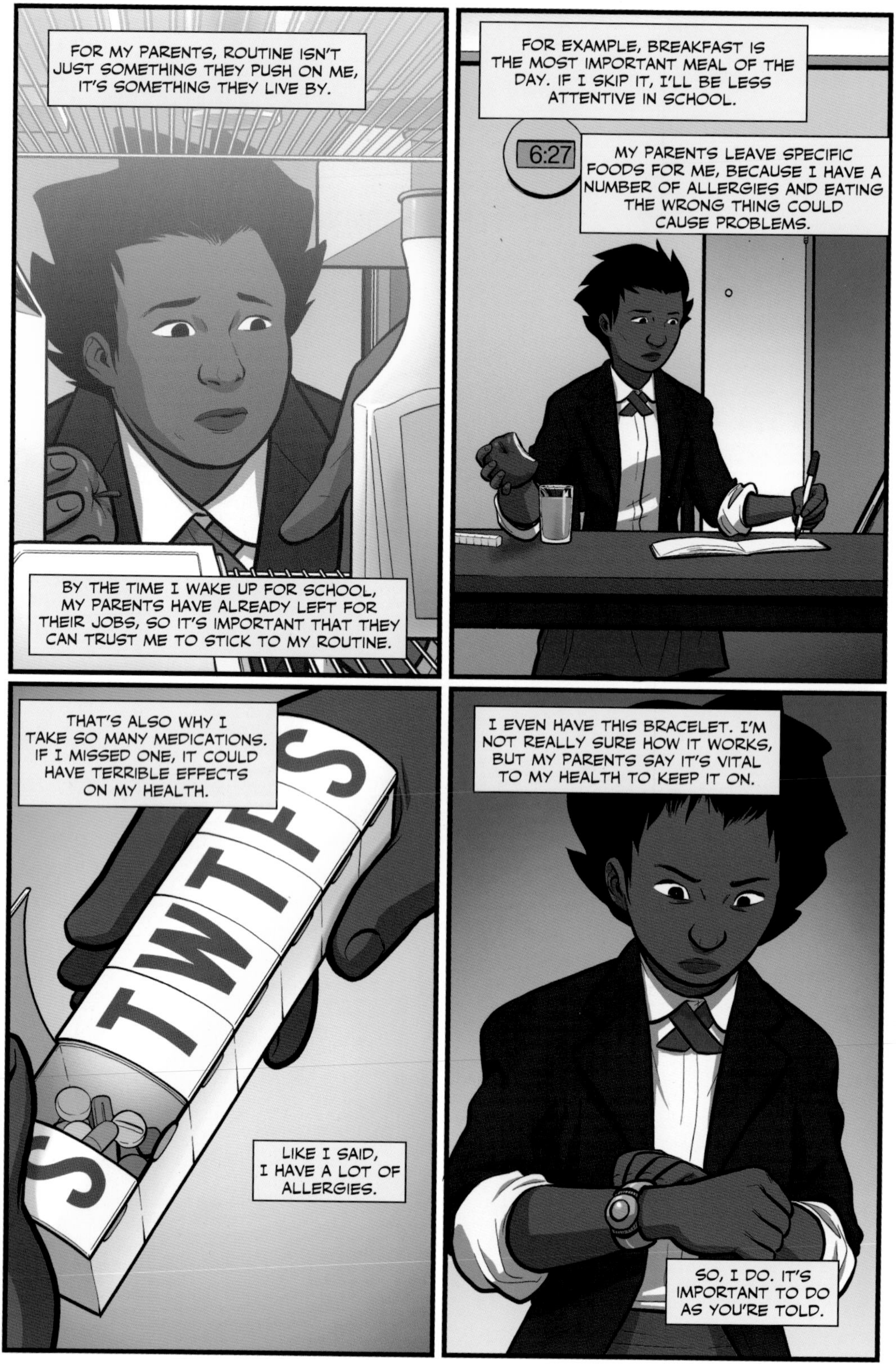
FOR MY PARENTS, ROUTINE ISN'T JUST SOMETHING THEY PUSH ON ME, IT'S SOMETHING THEY LIVE BY.
BY THE TIME I WAKE UP FOR SCHOOL, MY PARENTS HAVE ALREADY LEFT FOR THEIR JOBS, SO IT'S IMPORTANT THAT THEY CAN TRUST ME TO STICK TO MY ROUTINE.
FOR EXAMPLE, BREAKFAST IS THE MOST IMPORTANT MEAL OF THE DAY. IF I SKIP IT, I'LL BE LESS ATTENTIVE IN SCHOOL.
6:27
MY PARENTS LEAVE SPECIFIC FOODS FOR ME, BECAUSE I HAVE A NUMBER OF ALLERGIES AND EATING THE WRONG THING COULD CAUSE PROBLEMS.
THAT'S ALSO WHY I TAKE SO MANY MEDICATIONS. IF I MISSED ONE, IT COULD HAVE TERRIBLE EFFECTS ON MY HEALTH.
S T W T F S
LIKE I SAID, I HAVE A LOT OF ALLERGIES.
I EVEN HAVE THIS BRACELET. I'M NOT REALLY SURE HOW IT WORKS, BUT MY PARENTS SAY IT'S VITAL TO MY HEALTH TO KEEP IT ON.
SO, I DO. IT'S IMPORTANT TO DO AS YOU'RE TOLD.

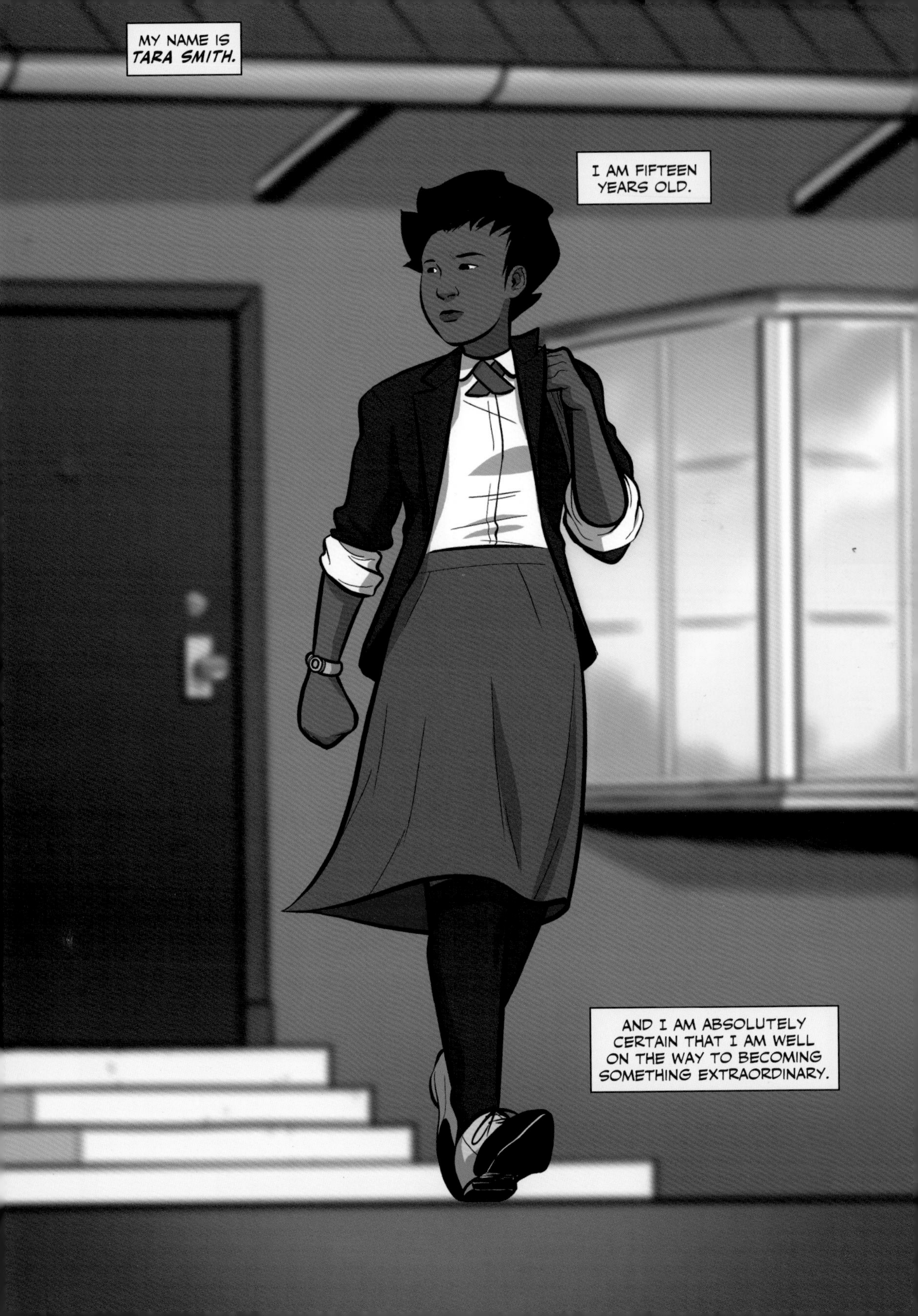
MY NAME IS TARA SMITH.
I AM FIFTEEN YEARS OLD.
AND I AM ABSOLUTELY CERTAIN THAT I AM WELL ON THE WAY TO BECOMING SOMETHING EXTRAORDINARY.

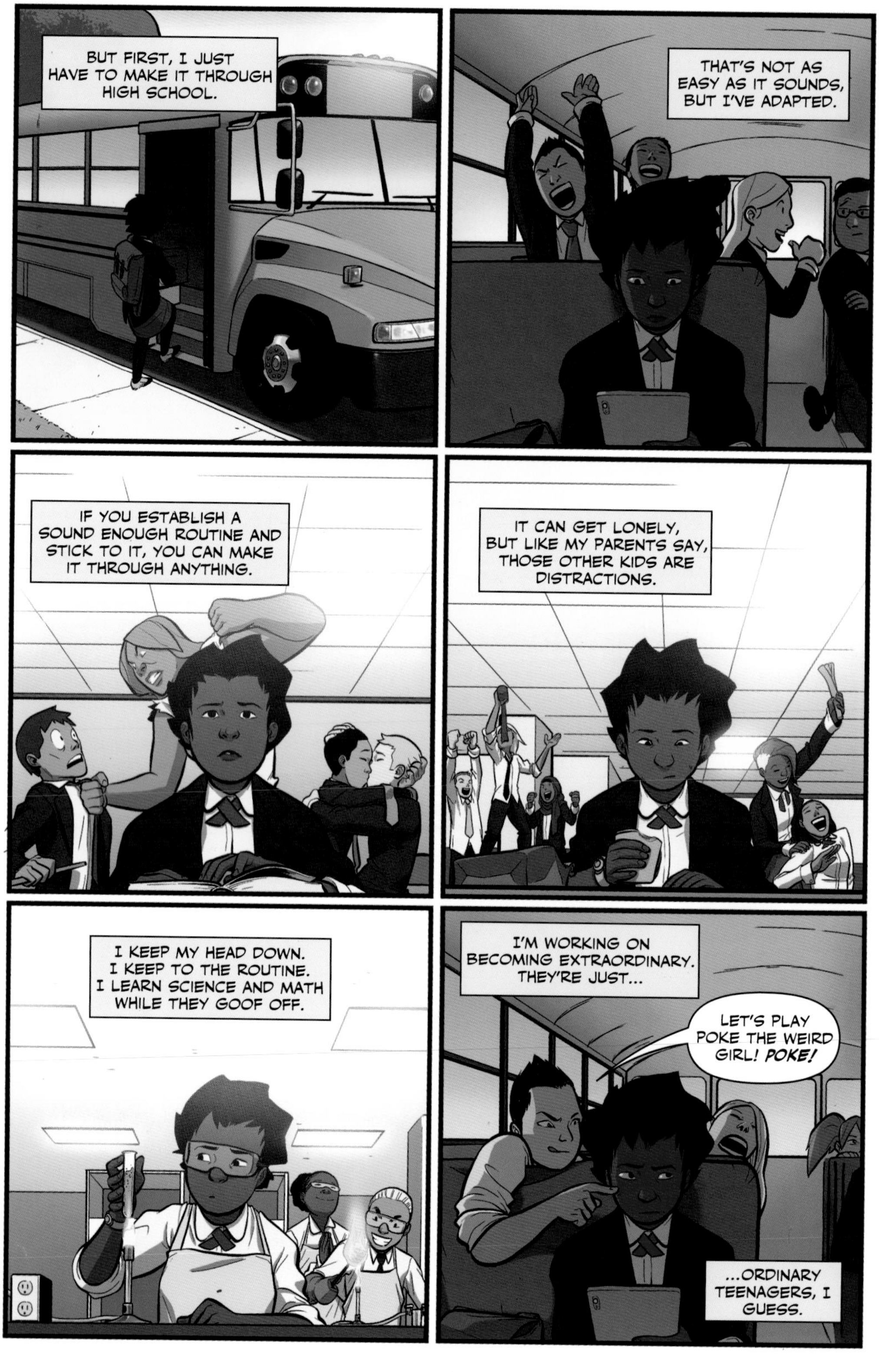
BUT FIRST, I JUST HAVE TO MAKE IT THROUGH HIGH SCHOOL.
THAT'S NOT AS EASY AS IT SOUNDS, BUT I'VE ADAPTED.
IF YOU ESTABLISH A SOUND ENOUGH ROUTINE AND STICK TO IT, YOU CAN MAKE IT THROUGH ANYTHING.
IT CAN GET LONELY, BUT LIKE MY PARENTS SAY, THOSE OTHER KIDS ARE DISTRACTIONS.
I KEEP MY HEAD DOWN. I KEEP TO THE ROUTINE. I LEARN SCIENCE AND MATH WHILE THEY GOOF OFF.
I'M WORKING ON BECOMING EXTRAORDINARY. THEY'RE JUST...
LET'S PLAY POKE THE WEIRD GIRL! *POKE!*
...ORDINARY TEENAGERS, I GUESS.

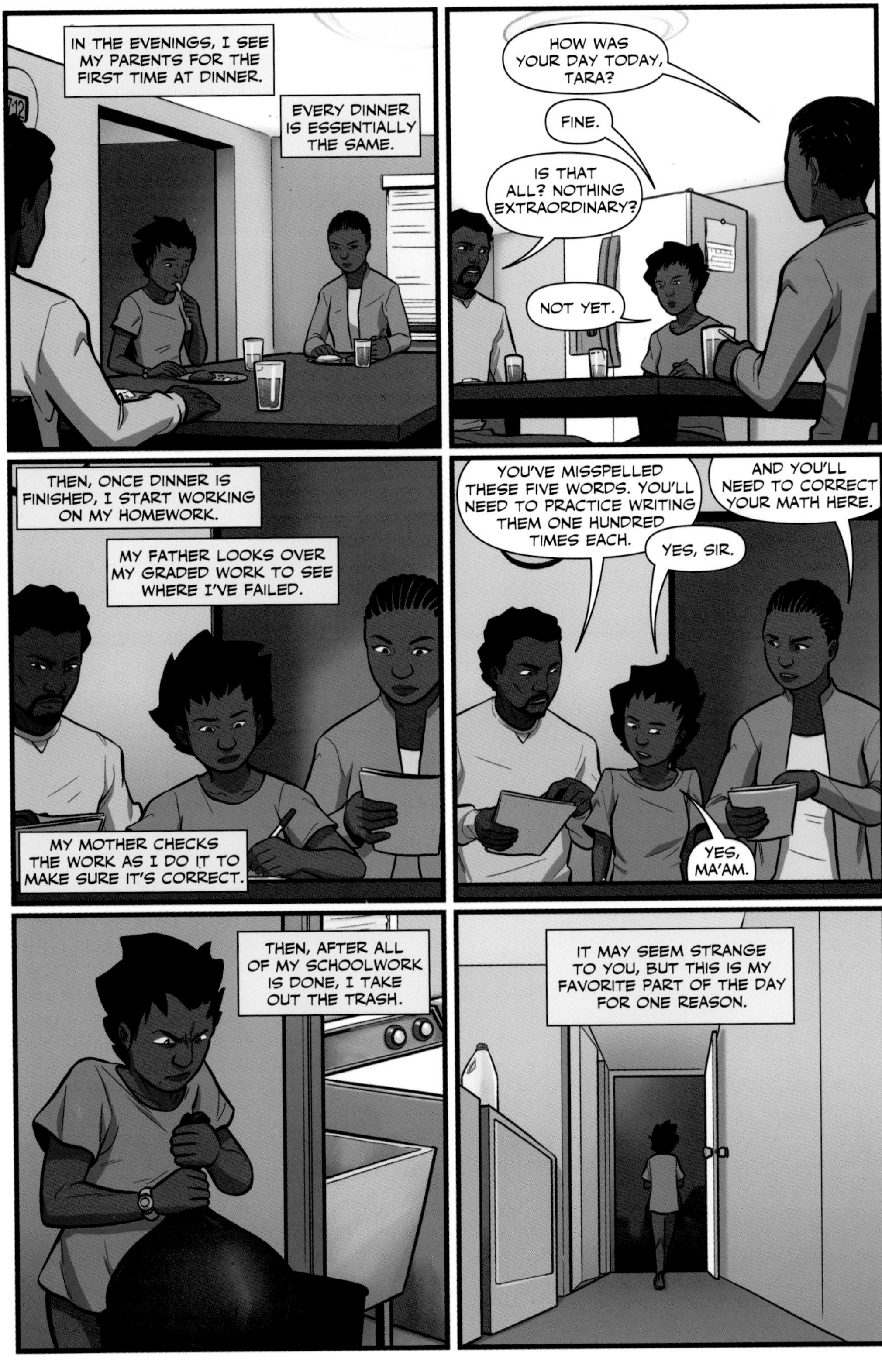
IN THE EVENINGS, I SEE MY PARENTS FOR THE FIRST TIME AT DINNER.
EVERY DINNER IS ESSENTIALLY THE SAME.
HOW WAS YOUR DAY TODAY, TARA?
FINE.
IS THAT ALL? NOTHING EXTRAORDINARY?
NOT YET.
THEN, ONCE DINNER IS FINISHED, I START WORKING ON MY HOMEWORK.
MY FATHER LOOKS OVER MY GRADED WORK TO SEE WHERE I'VE FAILED.
MY MOTHER CHECKS THE WORK AS I DO IT TO MAKE SURE IT'S CORRECT.
YOU'VE MISSPELLED THESE FIVE WORDS. YOU'LL NEED TO PRACTICE WRITING THEM ONE HUNDRED TIMES EACH.
YES, SIR.
AND YOU'LL NEED TO CORRECT YOUR MATH HERE.
YES, MA'AM.
THEN, AFTER ALL OF MY SCHOOLWORK IS DONE, I TAKE OUT THE TRASH.
IT MAY SEEM STRANGE TO YOU, BUT THIS IS MY FAVORITE PART OF THE DAY FOR ONE REASON.

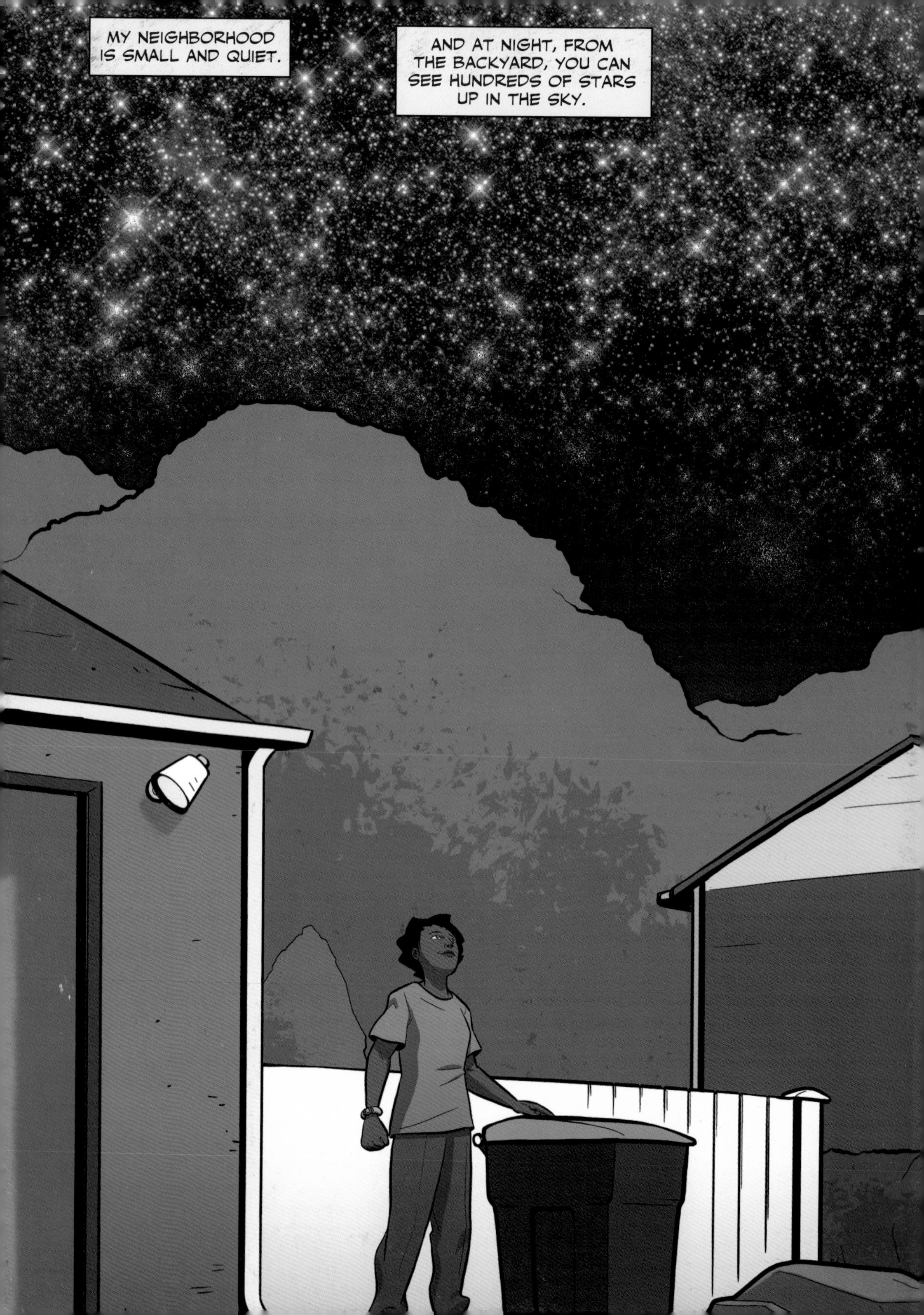
MY NEIGHBORHOOD IS SMALL AND QUIET.
AND AT NIGHT, FROM THE BACKYARD, YOU CAN SEE HUNDREDS OF STARS UP IN THE SKY.

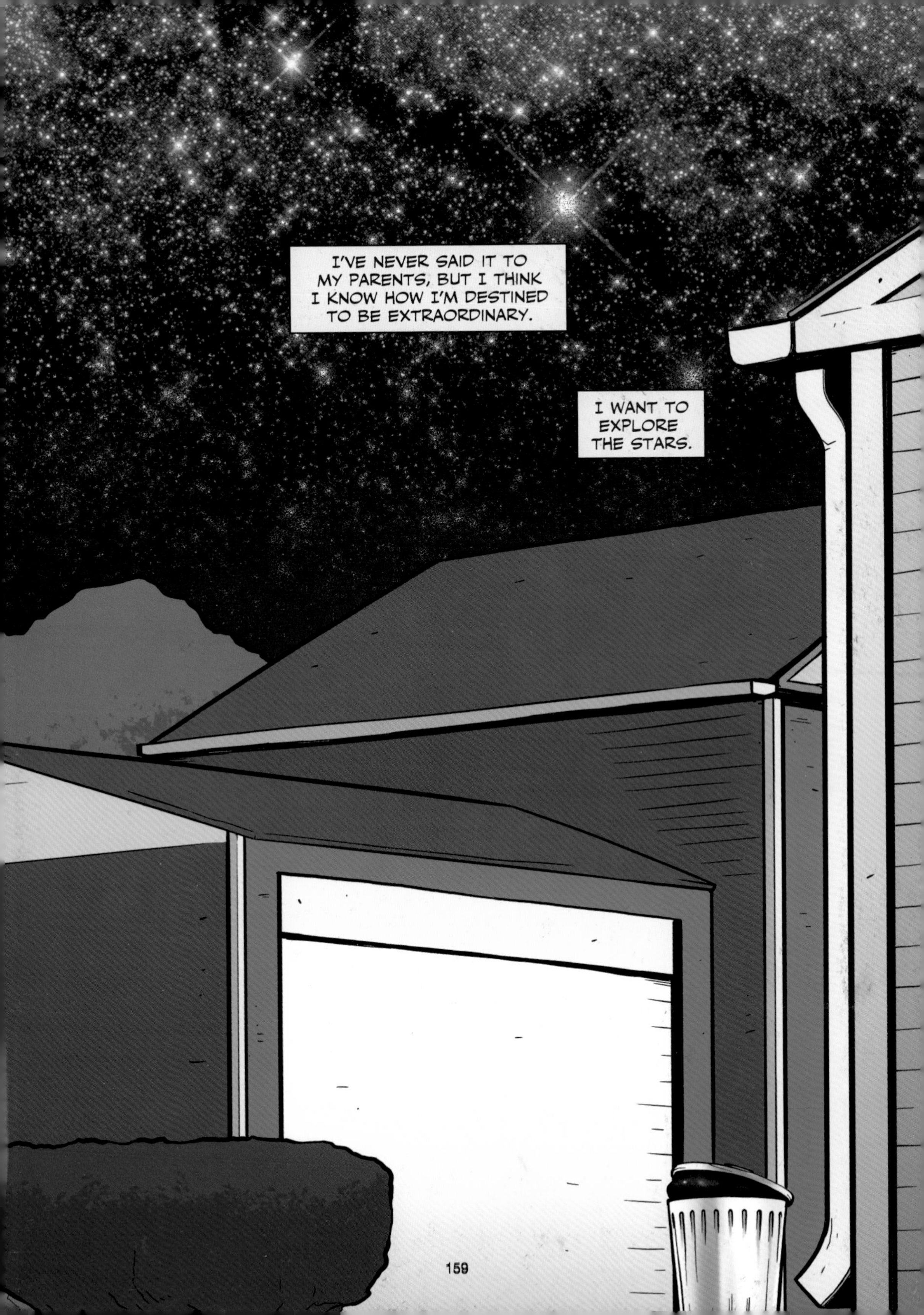
I'VE NEVER SAID IT TO MY PARENTS, BUT I THINK I KNOW HOW I'M DESTINED TO BE EXTRAORDINARY.
I WANT TO EXPLORE THE STARS.

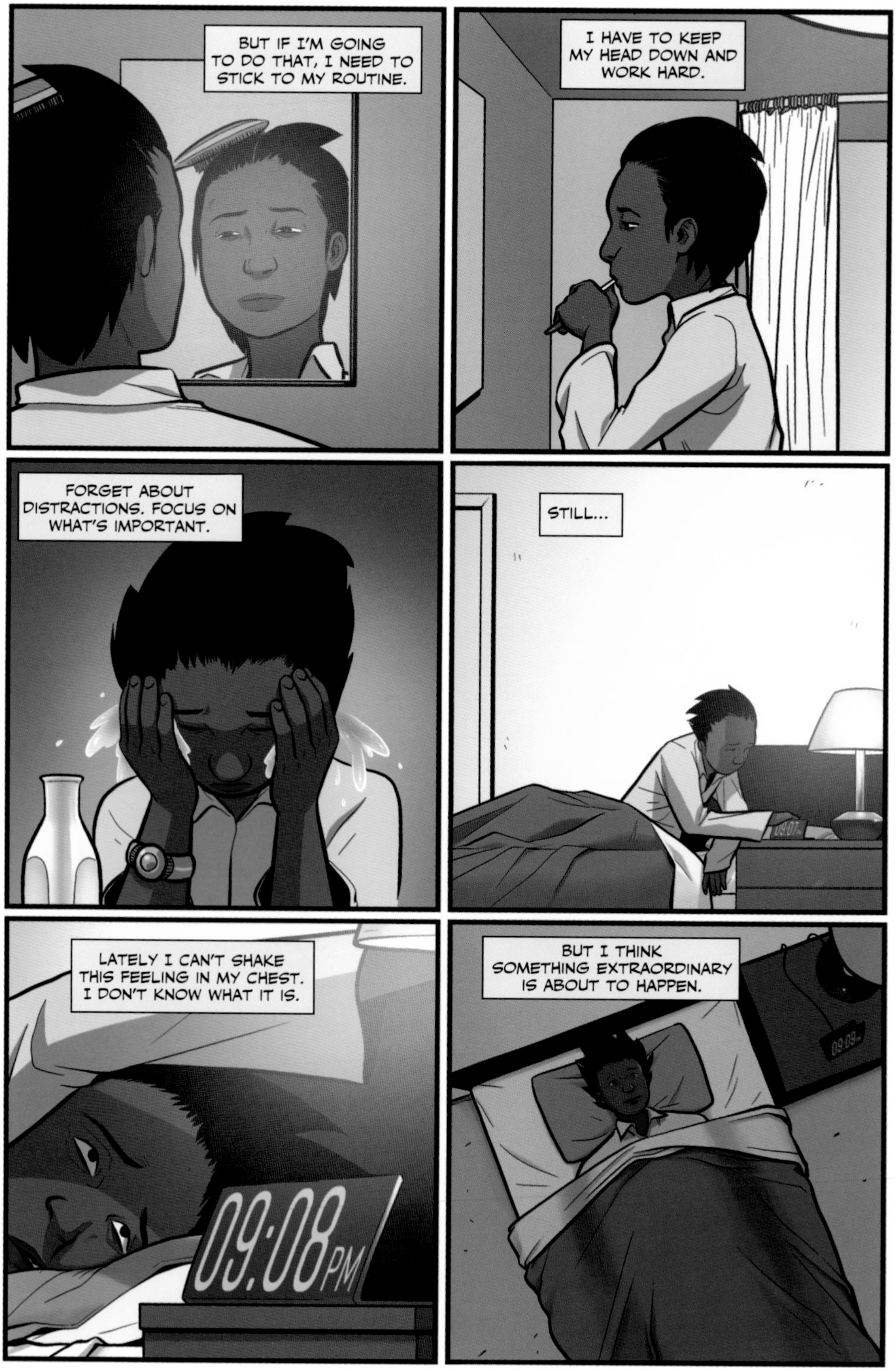
BUT IF I'M GOING TO DO THAT, I NEED TO STICK TO MY ROUTINE.
I HAVE TO KEEP MY HEAD DOWN AND WORK HARD.
FORGET ABOUT DISTRACTIONS. FOCUS ON WHAT'S IMPORTANT.
STILL...
LATELY I CAN'T SHAKE THIS FEELING IN MY CHEST. I DON'T KNOW WHAT IT IS.
09:08PM
BUT I THINK SOMETHING EXTRAORDINARY IS ABOUT TO HAPPEN.

Don't miss the rest of SCHOOL FOR EXTRATERRESTRIAL GIRLS available now at booksellers and libraries everywhere.

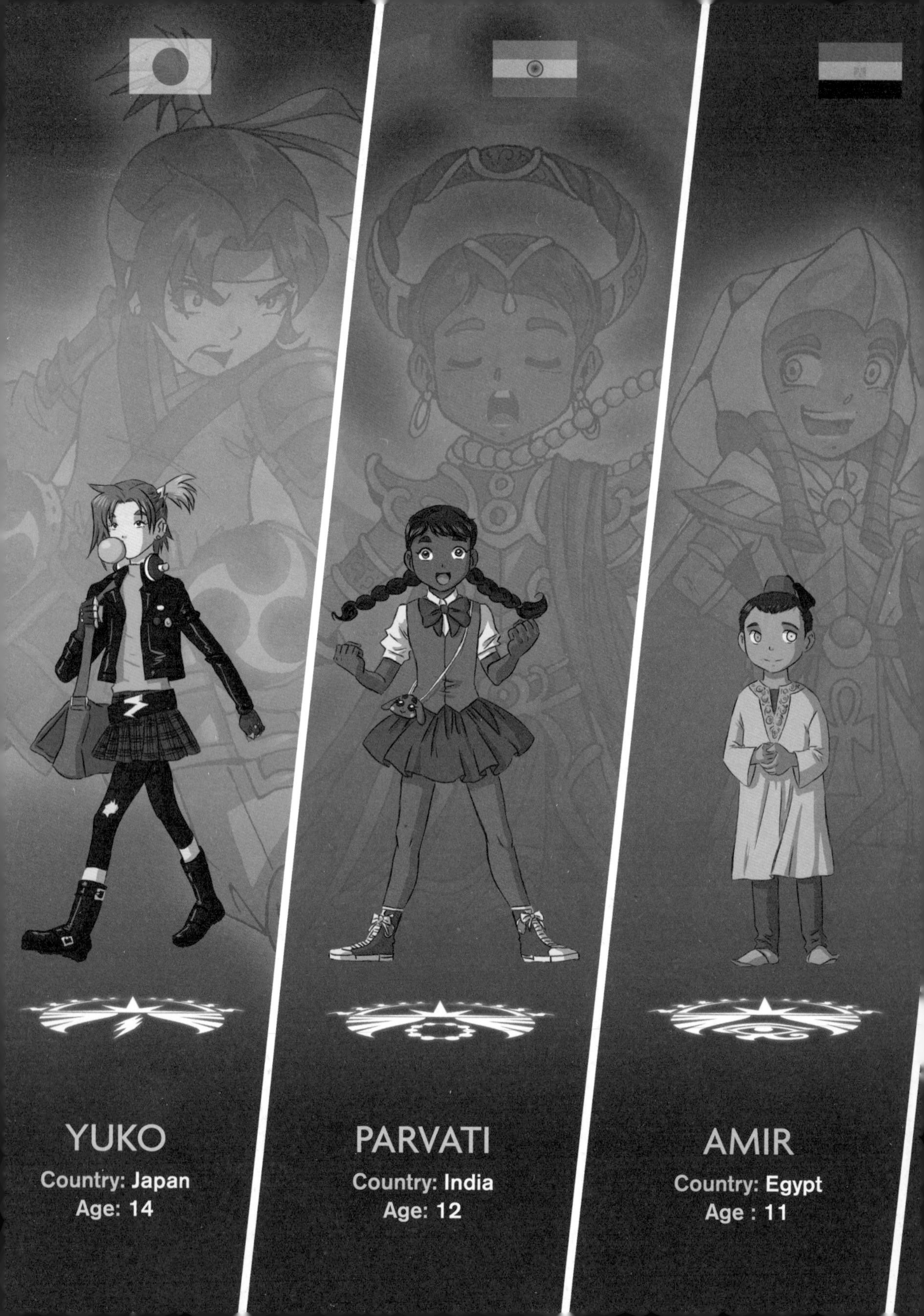
YUKO
Country: Japan
Age: 14
PARVATI
Country: India
Age: 12
AMIR
Country: Egypt
Age : 11